LEAVING WINTER

LEAVING WINTER

A Novel

Shannon Cowan

For Wayne,
Many thanks
; best wishes.
Shannon Cowan

OOLICHAN BOOKS
LANTZVILLE, BRITISH COLUMBIA, CANADA
2000

Canadian Cataloguing in Publication Data

Cowan, Shannon, 1973-
      Leaving winter

ISBN 0-88982-186-0

I. Title.
PS8555.0858L42 2000   C813'.6   C00-910358-9
PR9199.3.C6672L42 2000

We gratefully acknowledge the support of the Canada Council for the Arts for our publishing program.

The Canada Council | Le Conseil des Arts
for the Arts | du Canada

Grateful acknowledgement is also made to the BC Ministry of Tourism, Small Business and Culture for their financial support.

BRITISH
COLUMBIA
ARTS COUNCIL

We acknowledge the financial support of the Government of Canada through the Book Publishing Industry Development Program for our publishing activities.

Canadä

Cover image by Stephanie Hill

Published by
Oolichan Books
P.O. Box 10, Lantzville
British Columbia, Canada
V0R 2H0

Printed in Canada by
Morriss Printing Company,
Victoria, British Columbia

For Mary Cowan,
who remembers,
and for my parents

Acknowledgements

I am happily indebted to the following people for their talent and support: editors Ursula Vaira, Ron Smith, and Hiro McIlwraith; writers Fred Stenson, Susan Kernohan, William Lynch and the WC Club; the staff at the North Shore Museum and Archives, and the Heart and Stroke Foundation. I would also like to thank the following people for their encouragement and advice: Janice Kulyk-Keefer, Catherine Manansala, Paul Quarrington, Nancy Ginzer, Rachel Wyatt, and John Gould.

Details of Horseshoe Bay dances and North Vancouver during the 1920s are courtesy of Mary Cowan; the notion of a cat who waits at a bus stop is from May Cowan; the term "silly cone tits" is courtesy of Kate Richmond. The following sources were also extremely helpful: *The Age of Motoring Adventure*, edited by T. R. Nicholson; *The Men Who Marched Away: Canada's Infantry in World War I*, by James R. Steel; *The Right Instrument for Your Child* by Atorah Ben Tovim and Douglas Boyd; *The Laughing Bridge* by Eleanore Dempster; the *Indexed Guide Map of the City of Vancouver and Suburbs, 1914*, The Vancouver Map and Blueprint Company Ltd; selected readings from the personal diaries of Sgt. Walker MacKay Draycot, 1914-1930, presently archived at the North Vancouver Museum and Archives; and the Eaton's Catalogue, 1918. Special thanks to my parents, who are not in this book, and to Patrick, whose calming influence and gentle prodding has made everything possible.

ITCH

1

ELSIE

Elsie left winter behind. She climbed on a train and turned her back on its frozen lakes, its salty streets and scraped-thin air, and got off at the other end of the country where it existed only at high altitudes. She did this despite the fact that she liked hoarfrost and hot chocolate, despite the reality that winter was her favourite season, affording her so much sleep.

She left behind winter so that she could leave behind other things – a basement apartment in London, Ontario, her job as a piano teacher at the Royal Conservatory, a man – but if asked what she was leaving back in the fall of 1995, just as the last of autumn was swept into the streets, Elsie would have denied she was leaving anything at all.

"I need to sort out a few things for my grandmother," she would have said dismissively, tilting her head and looking at her hands. "I won't even be gone a week."

Of course, Elsie would have been in denial. She knew

she would be gone much longer than that. The lawyer told her so when he phoned from British Columbia.

Denial was something Elsie could define: *The refusal to acknowledge something as real.* She had learned this as a teenager while sitting on the padded chairs of the high-school guidance department, flipping through manuals and charts with her feet on a stool. It was here that she read about complexes, about youth-at-risk, about grief. She learned more from the waiting room than she did from the counsellors, but recognizing denial didn't help her find the way out. Maybe there wasn't a way out.

She told herself she was coming to North Vancouver to take care of her grandmother, a woman she hadn't spoken to in sixteen-and-a-half years and who had just been admitted to a nursing home. Taking care of Violet meant signing papers on her behalf; it meant selling the house on Chesterfield Avenue where Elsie's father had spent his boyhood, and settling the affairs of an old woman who had lost her mind to a stroke. It also meant putting some distance between Elsie and her lover, a man whom she had apparently just left. The sooner her grandmother's affairs were in order, the sooner Elsie could straighten out her own life, something she had been putting off for years.

She arrived in North Vancouver in October. Clouds truncated her view of the mountains. Instead of vistas she saw fog, a thick mass hugging the ocean and sky like a mirror's clouded reflection. She stood at the entrance to Cates Park and listened to seagulls, finding the landscape familiar although she had never set foot in British Columbia. Even with the drizzle the park was crowded.

Children played on swing-sets. A man and a woman cuddled on a bench at the end of the jetty. Elsie followed the shoreline with her back to the couple until she was out of earshot, remembering she was alone for the first time in seven years. Alone and unemployed. Her one consolation was that she still had the key to Daniel's apartment, formerly her apartment, a place with small windows and a warm bed. Things hadn't been so final that she couldn't go back. At the time this idea had been her biggest comfort.

Three months later she looks at the view from her grandmother's house. Outside, snow buries the streets in what has been deemed by radio broadcasters as "The Storm of the Century." Instead of sorting things out, Elsie huddles under a wool blanket and clenches her fists. Things aren't going as planned.

The first problem is the house on Chesterfield Avenue, emptied of life and singing with memories. Pictures of Violet's family line the walls: some of people Elsie has never seen, others of her father, of herself, back when everyone was on speaking terms; back when everyone was alive. She agreed to help Violet because she was raised to assist, but she didn't anticipate the sting that would be induced by staying in the family home.

The second problem is Elsie, her own apprehension. She thought coming to North Vancouver would be easy. Easy because her back would be turned solidly to the east, blocking off the view of her past, her childhood. Instead she finds a place she has been told about, a place she almost remembers, where her family history is written all over the landscape. She foolishly believed she would be able to ignore these events because they happened before she was born.

She should know by now that life doesn't start with birth, not even with conception, but with the development of your mother into a new human being. From the time that Elsie's mother was fully formed in *her* mother's womb, her own womb contained the makings of Elsie, the genetic make-up that would go on to form half of her body and soul whenever she chose to procreate. When Elsie was born, half of her chromosomes had already been walking around for twenty-four years inside her mother's uterus, soaking in the mountains, the toothpick conifers, drinking up the smells of guilt, desire, and the metal-tinted ocean. She existed in this landscape because families go back as far as their oldest relative, as far back as the sky, and even though her own flesh was not present, parts of her were here, at various times in history, strung out like the bulbs of electric lights that she has seen on downtown streets at Christmas.

This explains the memories.

This also explains why, in an attempt to leave her past behind by coming to North Vancouver, Elsie has somehow dug up a harsher, older past inextricably linked to her own. This past involves her grandmother who is in the Avondale Rest Home; it includes despotic arguments between her mother and Violet, visions, lust, the ability to do the Charleston, and a significant garnishing of red hair.

To get on with things Elsie must buckle down. She must take heed and be brave, because this kind of nostalgia is exactly what she'd hoped to avoid. She is not prepared for the sharp edges, the cutting tongues; she is not strong or bold enough to face the onslaught of ancestral failures culminating in the misery of her own. If she wants to get on with her life, the one she intended to try out in her grandmother's house (minus her grandmother) she must proceed with caution and keep her eyes wide open. She has had experience with this kind of messaging, these cagey prophecies, and she is not at all sure if she wants to see them again.

They cause her so much stress.

2

The man's voice is rough, as if he has been at sea long hours without sleep. Elsie listens to him talk, cradling the phone beneath her chin. Something about his way of speaking reminds her of her father, naturally, but the association still unnerves her.

"I tell you she's not herself Elsie," he says. "The stroke affected her. You can see it in her face. She is almost ninety for Christ's sake, but just so you know. When I went in to see her she roared at me."

"Roared?" says Elsie, shifting the receiver on her shoulder. The man on the phone is her Uncle Lawrence, her father's brother whom she has not seen since 1973. She imagines him the way he was then, twenty-three years ago: brown polyester pants hitched up with a wide belt. Sideburns creeping down his cheeks and into his ears. Long distance from Prince George, he sounds smaller than she remembers.

"Snarled. You know, like an animal. She was upset. Maybe by me, maybe by the nurses, I don't know. I just know she surprised me. She was always so composed."

"She's probably disoriented," says Elsie.

"Or senile," says Uncle Lawrence. His tone changes and he sounds younger, farther away. "But since you're the one in charge of things now, I thought I should let you know."

Silence fills the line and Elsie winces. She didn't ask to be in charge. She doesn't like the fact that Violet overlooked her own sons when doling out responsibility, but according to the lawyer, she can't do anything about it. Violet made these decisions herself, years ago. "Thanks Uncle Lawrence," she says, appreciative. "You've been a big help. I'll do my best to get things rolling."

And she will, of course, if only she knew where exactly to begin. She hangs up the phone and returns to the piano, sliding onto the bench, which is still warm. Instead of playing, she strokes the keys: lean, icy, removed. She's glad to have bought the piano before the storm, before snowdrifts bewildered the city into shutting down all the freeways, the entrances to the bridge. The feeling of ivory against her fingers is a sensual one, one that used to make her experience slight pangs of guilt. When she was younger she couldn't help associate pleasure with shame, tagged on like an extra set of buttons in their unforgettable satchel. Somewhere in the world children starved while Elsie practiced her *Musette*. Did she know that? She was a very lucky girl.

The man who sold her the piano said his daughter *grew up*. He spoke as though this was a kind of abnormality on her part—that she should now prefer late-night flicks with rubbery popcorn, or the sweat of high-school dances, to her walnut brown piano. He said she'd been gifted, his daughter, and had *thrown it all away*. *Boys*, probably, thinks Elsie, although teenagers are beyond anything she can now imagine.

The piano fits into her grandmother's house like an overwhelming umbrella stand; there is no hallway, no intermediary pause between front door inset with bubble glass and the green loopy wall-to-wall of the living room. Luckily her grandmother avoided the clutter that many elderly people adopt when they are pressed into smaller and smaller living quarters, forcing each heirloom armoire, tea tray, and wood-paneled television set into a room the size of a broom closet. This was because her grandmother had lived in the same house for so many years; she never had to face that compaction of time-honoured possessions. The basement is another story.

Elsie's placement of the piano allows enough space to pass into the kitchen and bedrooms via the lean beige hallway furnished with translucent plastic runners. Each of these runners is outfitted with a series of sharp spikes that anchor the plastic to the carpet beneath. In the bathroom there are also peach-coloured tub ornaments in the shapes of seahorses cut from sand-textured vinyl, which prevent Elsie from slipping when she takes a bath; slippage is something she is becoming acutely aware of while living in her grandmother's house.

Beneath the piano Elsie has marooned two plush coasters with aluminum rims to protect the carpet from the imprints of the piano's wheels. She has opened the bowels of the instrument to aerate its strings, and placed jam jars of water along the soundboard to guard against cracking. The first time Elsie realized she could open up a piano from a latch beneath the keyboard she was six years old; she wanted to crawl inside with the spider webs and wood dust and curled-up hardened millipedes, and hide.

"What do you think you're doing?" Her mother had said. "Come out of there right now." Marian grabbed her by the collar with a jerk that suggested Elsie better have a good explanation, *or else*.

"Dusting," said Elsie, searching her mother's face for approval.

"Well stay above ground from now on. You're not old enough to deal with that much filth. You'll get contaminated."

Her mother had a phobia of germs, the kind that wriggled prehistorically on the surfaces of everything in the house, advancing their foul dictatorship onto the bristles of toothbrushes, the unsuspecting tines of forks. It didn't matter if a dish had been used or not. Marian would go through the entire house scouring banisters, tiles, soap dishes, spreading her smells of disinfectant and chalky, abrasive cleansers. She vacuumed light fixtures; she set plaid washcloths and dishrags into a sink full of bleach to soak and kill the germs. "I want them stone dead," she would say. *Stone*: a cold, finalized sort of death from which there was no return; a different kind altogether from the one Marian herself now occupies.

Although she always dreamed of playing a silky grand piano with bulbous Corinthian feet, Elsie bought an overstrung upright model to conserve space and, let's face it, money. She doesn't yet know what assets her grandmother has (she will meet with the lawyer next Thursday) beyond this house which will need repairs: a new fence, a back staircase to replace the present sagging one, possibly eaves, a roof, shingles. The piano is an investment, a replacement for the one she left with Daniel. (What will he do with it, pluck its abandoned keys, stack beer cans on the lid?) She needs it for work.

The first thing she should have done when she arrived in North Vancouver was visit her grandmother. Back in October that item had been foremost in her mind. She picked up the keys to her grandmother's house from the lawyer, and signed papers proclaiming her responsible for her grandmother's property. Fifteen years ago Violet had named her co-owner of her house and had given her the power of attorney over what was left of her estate. Elsie had been too young at the time to have a legal signature, so a witness had attested to the validity of the agreement. This had all been done when Elsie's father was still alive.

Three months have gone by since her arrival and Elsie has yet to set foot in the Avondale rest home. Shame. If it weren't for her grandmother, Elsie would not have a roof over her head; a leaky one, but still a roof. She might still be with Daniel, eating Zoodles out of his aluminum camping pots, watching another rerun of *Star Trek*. If it weren't for her grandmother, Elsie would never have been born.

She was not avoiding the reunion, there was just so much to be done. She needed some kind of income; finding a piano, students, that took time. Then there was the squirrel living in the chimney, the raccoons in the

backyard compost heap. But now that things are more
or less in order, she has no excuse. Tomorrow, or the
next day, when the snow melts, she will go.

Her grandmother will be older: eighty-six. What does
eighty-six look like? The last image Elsie has of her
grandmother is of her face, flushed red with anger and
frustration, the words, "Dammit Clifford, your wife's a
bitch!" flying from her mouth.

Elsie had been twelve at the time, and didn't believe
that grandmothers could use the word *bitch*. The word
seemed to belong to another generation entirely than
one that produced grandmothers. Violet had stood in the
hallway of the house in Brimstock with her lips pressed
tightly together, talking to Elsie's father.

"Why don't you teach her some manners?"

"Mother, calm down."

"I am calm for God's sake. Calm enough to know that
you are being walked all over by an unfeeling zealot.
She's sick Clifford. She'll turn Elsie into a freakchild. Have
a little backbone for a change. Lord knows it's about time."

"Mother—"

"I've had enough. Just don't expect to hear from me
again. That woman is an insult to God's green earth."

Then her grandmother's back moving down the walkway, arms pumping furiously towards the street.

Her father looked at himself in the hallway mirror
after that. Pink smudges for cheeks; eyes and mouth
pinched into a scowl of defeat.

Since then Elsie's grandmother had more or less kept
her word. Elsie had spoken with her on the telephone
four or five times. She wrote letters in response to the

presents that arrived at Christmas and on her birthday, wrapped in anonymous butcher paper and wound around with string.

> *Dear Grandma,*
> *Thank you very much for thinking of me this year. I liked the purse very much and am using it to keep my pennies in.*
> *From Elsie*

She did this out of a childish desire to hold things together. As if sending her words two thousand miles west, lovingly sealed in pastoral envelopes, textured and scented with her grandmother's favourite perfume— *Chantilly Lace*—could reel her back to the bosom of Elsie's family. Her family's bosom was already so astonishingly flat.

On her mother's side there was no one. Just a list as long as your arm of dead people who may or may not have been blood relatives—Marian was adopted, so anything was possible. On her father's side two uncles graced the family tree, one married with a single older child who taught English-as-a-second-language to the children of wealthy businessmen, the other already gone to the dogs. Or to the devil, as Marian would have it. He died before Elsie could score a picture of his face into her memory. All she has left is the unreliable image painted by her mother.

"His hair was red, and that's enough."

These kinds of comments inevitably led back to Elsie's grandmother, Violet. Violet, the red-haired woman of abandon. Dancing in her two-inch patent heels across ballroom floors made pliant by rows of rubber tires. *Ain't she sweet, see her coming down the street* . . . . Sweat on her upper lip. Streaks of fire where her shoes heat up the floor. The Charleston Queen of North Vancouver who right this moment sits hunched over in the Avondale rest home attempting to feed pabulum to a doll. Or at least, that's what Elsie imagines. Considering.

The only positive thing about her grandmother's present condition is that she will not notice how long it has taken Elsie to visit. Although Elsie doesn't believe in grudges, she supposes she must have one against Violet—a counsellor told her so after she leaked the story of her grandmother's departure from the family. She doesn't believe in grudges, but she believes even less in abandonment. Forgiving Violet has been difficult despite Elsie's years of training.

From the scant pictures she sees of Violet in the house, and from her languishing memories, Elsie has a hard time believing that the two of them are actually related. True, she has inherited the placid wave that used to beset her grandmother's bobbed hairdo, but Violet is a relatively small woman with a voice the size of an ambulance siren. Elsie on the other hand, is tall, and more or less reserved. Even as a child she was large enough to reach the pedals from her spot on the piano bench. *Big boned,* her grandmother said. Realistically she was gangly, with a proportionately large head of auburn hair. Her hands and feet were oversized and dangled from her body like an unused set of mittens. Her father told her she would grow out of it, this gigantism, but she only got larger, more exaggerated. She tried to pare herself down by dressing first in loose, billowy jumpers sewed from bright

[21]

patterned cotton, and then in tighter spartan blue jeans—
to hide herself by concealment or furious squeezing—
but neither worked. She ended up looking like a fruity
pillowcase; either that or a giant oriental kite.

The merits of being large were few: Elsie could reach
the top shelf of the bookcase and read the daily entries
of her mother's work journal, in addition to the scrib-
bled intentions that she planned on submitting to the
parish prayer box; she could toss a skipping rope over
her head with relative ease and watch it sail through the
delft blue sky on its journey toward her feet. Being large
also meant people usually mistook her for someone older
than she really was, and said with mild surprise when
they discovered the truth, *my you are a big girl for your
age.* Members of her church often told her she acted like
a little adult, and wouldn't God be pleased when he saw
how hard she was trying? She was setting such a good
example for the other children. Now that she is almost
thirty, and has thankfully stopped growing, the same
kinds of people tell her she doesn't seem like someone
who has ever been a child. She resists the impulse to
respond with, *I never was.*

Lucky for her she is big all over, and big women are
coming back into fashion. She sees them on posters
downtown, sticking out their voluminous chests, forcing their horses' mouths full of shiny, newly-capped
teeth open for all to see: *Do you hate me because I'm
beautiful?* they ask. Elsie doesn't hate them at all, which
shows just how far she has come.

One of the pedals on the piano—the damper—refuses
to soften notes the way it should when Elsie presses her
foot to the floor. This will have to be repaired. She opens

the red and white cover of her grade one Royal Conservatory songbook and eyes the yellowing stickers, one for each song she was able to memorize when she was a student: pink spring tulips and lop-eared grey bunnies; a grinning jack-o-lantern with a waifish black cat; a Christmas tree festooned with birds and sparkling candles. To her own students Elsie gives teddy bears, dinosaurs, and plump cartoon penguins reclining in flannelette pajamas. She doesn't have to lick the backs of the stickers the way her own teacher did, flattening her tongue like a pork sausage and dabbing the edges of her mouth with a tissue. She simply peels them off a glossy adhesive paper, and smoothes them onto the page. They are slick, first-rate stickers sold at stationery stores, guaranteed not to discolour or flake off like an old scab. They are permanent evidence of what a student does, or does not do, and there is no way to get them off save tearing out the page.

If it weren't for the storm, Elsie would be teaching her first lesson in North Vancouver today. There is so much snow on the streets that some of her pupils couldn't find their cars.

"I would bring Avery for her session, but I don't know which one is mine," one of the mothers said. "We spent a whole hour digging out the wheels of somebody else's Jeep!" Elsie looks out the parlour window at white lumps rising from the roadway: gigantic melted marshmallows, or rounded, intermittent molehills iced in egg white. The streets are covered with about sixty centimetres; a lot even by Elsie's standards. People are out sliding into ditches. They stand coolly at the sides of the roads, dragging on cigarettes, staring at their cars balancing dangerously on the edge of the ravine. Outside the window two women with their umbrellas blown inside out worm along the sidewalk in their running shoes, magazines in front of their faces to block the wind.

Elsie pulls herself up from the bench and moves into the bedroom in search of her metronome, eyeing the single unmade twin and its dislocated sheets strewn across the floor. If she doesn't watch herself, she'll become a slob. Picking up after Daniel kept her alert; she knew where to find old plates encrusted with egg yolk, how to sniff out his sour cast-off work shirts fermenting in a heap. Living alone demands greater concentration: she will have to motivate herself.

In the closet she rummages through her unpacked boxes. How did so many useless items follow her to North Vancouver: the remains of her chipped faux glass candle holders, a bent iron lamp wrestled from garage sale hounds? And where were the practical things? The carrot peeler, the set of porcelain bread bowls, the rolling pin? She must have left them with Daniel, although the prospect of what he might do with such things is beyond her. She did remember the metronome, *thank goodness*, and yanks it from its dark hiding place with a grunt. She isn't totally out to lunch. A colleague from the Royal Conservatory even went so far as to tell Elsie, before she left, that she was finally getting it together; *it* being her life. *After seven years, well, you know what they say about that* (Elsie hadn't known), *you have guts.* Guts, thinks Elsie, refers to the gooey, elastic innards of road kill, smeared into an arch along the pavement. *If that's what I have, why did it take me seven years to find out?*

[24]

3

Elsie doesn't have anything against her hometown, Brimstock, Ontario, she just never wants to go back. But certain things keep her from forgetting the place entirely. She dreams about its parks, the bleak cenotaphs overlooking the Credit River where autumn leaves fighting their way to Lake Ontario are snagged by tin cans. And in the daytime, when she's shopping or riding the bus, she sees the insistent faces of Brimstock people—school teachers, town clerks—in the ruddy cheeks of strangers. They live on the sly in her subconscious, eating away at her from the inside out.

The last time she went to Brimstock, Elsie had a sick feeling. She was visiting a friend who insisted on taking her for a tour of the changes that had occurred since she'd been away at university. See that subdivision with its cookie-cutter houses? *Wildwood Estates*, they're called. And the restaurant that used to be the old train station? They loaded it piece by piece onto a truck and carted it up Broadway. Now it's a café run by a draft dodger. Elsie noticed that people in Brimstock thought they had come a long way, that they were making progress, because of the proliferation of big box chain stores—*We now have two McDonald's, four Tim Horton's, an A&W, and a Blockbuster Video.* The latest addition had been a Wal-Mart, surrounded on all sides by vast expanses of pavement, divided into parking spaces by little yellow lines. This could be anywhere, Elsie thought as they drove through town, any flat green valley in Canada with a muddy creek running through its centre.

Coming to North Vancouver had been a switch. She had to get used to the noise of delivery trucks backing up into shipping-receiving tunnels, and to police cars wailing through the streets at two in the morning. Living at her grandmother's house also meant she was in charge of something, a piece of property, a house. She was a landlord of sorts and had to think about things like replacing light bulbs and keeping the grout between the shower tiles free from encroaching mildew. She had to be responsible.

Now she is not so sure that her decision to come was the right one. For instance, what does she know about taking care of a house, especially a house in a snowstorm? Outside the weather continues to rear its inclement head, burying lawns and trees and automobiles, piling up on power lines like thick vanilla fingers. Elsie swaddles herself in silk scarves dredged from her grandmother's bureau and opens the back door. Even though she has only been on the coast a short time, she has already developed a sensitivity to cold. Her fingers demand fleece-lined leather gloves; her lips chap at ten degrees. It must be the moisture, she thinks. Or the proximity to the sea. Shivering, she realizes she should have kept her goose down jacket before coming west. Everyone told her she was migrating to lotus land. How was she to know?

On the porch a green plastic bag contains the wettest of last week's trash. The dry items, things like cardboard containers and the paper flyers that come in the mail *(You too can have perfect fingernails!!)*, Elsie has saved for the fireplace. She picks up the bag and makes her way through the backyard snow, waddling more than she knows is dignified. Even though there is little chance that the sanitation department is working – the buses have already stopped running – she feels better knowing the garbage is safe in its aluminum can. One slip in her normal routine might mean letting everything go to pot. She does not want to take any chances and lapse into dementia, replacing the present with events long past, muddling her days with the imaginary voices of dead relatives. Things like that run in families. She has done some reading to prepare herself, so she knows what to expect.

She locates the trash can in the alley running behind her grandmother's house. The snow is almost level with the lid, but after some digging she deposits the bag and twists the handle. As she works a man clad entirely in red spandex passes her on cross-country skis.

"Beautiful day," he says, huffing and glissading down the road.

"Yes," says Elsie hoarsely, her voice sounding rough and ill-used. In the space of three months she has not carried on any extensive conversations, save a few with her students' overeager parents who have been calling to register for classes. Her main companion is an orange tomcat that she feeds outside the kitchen door. The cat turned up on the landing three nights in a row at exactly five o'clock, mewing anxiously as if he had made an appointment. When Elsie tried to shoo him away, he rubbed up against her legs and clawed his way into her lap.

Since the snowfall Elsie has been worried about the cat. How can he move around in all this snow? On CBC the weatherman said to expect a melt on Thursday, but that is still days away. She flattens a path from the back door to the alley. On her feet she wears Violet's galoshes, two sizes too small. Impermeable in mud puddles, but cold as steel in below zero temperatures. "Who said it never snows in North Vancouver?" she says out loud. She is talking to herself again.

The first week at her grandmother's house was marked by conversations like this, conversations with herself; there had been no one else there to listen. She wandered around the living room, down the stairs to the basement, into the bathroom, saying aloud: *Where would you hide a screwdriver if you were eighty-six*, and *If I were a light bulb where would I be?* These kinds of role playing scenarios rarely worked, but Elsie had a large repertoire stashed away in case of emergencies. Various counsellors, in high school and again in university, had used them on her like lines in a bar. They wanted to solve her, crack her open like a pesky safe that resists decoding. She confounded them by being unsolvable.

Having the cat around means Elsie has someone to talk to. She doesn't let him in the house yet – she can't take a chance on adopting a pet when she doesn't even know if she can take care of herself – but she likes his company. He isn't demanding. When she sits on the back porch reading *The North Shore News*, he curls up in her lap and vibrates softly like a small, insulated motor. Last week he even followed her to the bus stop, waiting with her beneath the Plexiglas shelter until the bus arrived. Elsie realizes the cat is the only one who cares about how she spends her time. The thought does not depress her as much as it would have last year.

She knows she should try and get out, meet people. She's single isn't she? She has her youth. Some of her older colleagues told her, before she left the conservatory, that she was at an age to be envied. *When I was thirty I had the world at my feet*, they said. *There was nothing I couldn't do*. There is nothing I want to do, thinks Elsie, which is awful and she knows it. She should join a political party, go to rallies. Initiate lunch dates with clever men in laid-back shirts who congregate in Yaletown eating Bali wraps and drinking freshly squeezed juices; they carry laptops. She sees them on their bicycles shouting into cellular telephones, wearing Gore-Tex rain pants with Velcro at the ankles. These are the marks of her generation: portable, breathable, cholesterol free.

She attributes most of her apathy to Daniel, her ex-lover. *Loverboy*, thinks Elsie, *ugh*. She used to be in charge of things, she used to be ambitious. She used to rise early and set the table with the yellow and green eggcups shaped like chicks, inserting the soft-boiled eggs into their heads. *Peep*, she imagined them saying, as the yolk oozed down the sides of their cheeks, adhering them to the place mats by their porcelain feet. She never associated the chicks with what she was eating; they were too innocent, too cheerfully unreal. Their demure fuzziness went along with Easter. Nobody referred to them as meat.

Daniel would rise moaning, his mouth cavernous and child-like when he yawned. His mouth had been part of the problem, screaming (quietly, timidly) *Help me, I need you, get me in order.* How could Elsie resist that mouth, bunching tightly in the centre of his face with all its delicate folds, its look of helplessness? Elsie felt that mouth on her navel, the lips fluttering across her heart like relentless butterflies. Forget it, she tells herself, this time without conviction.

Instead she stays inside or walks up Fourteenth Street to Lonsdale where there are enough people moving around – popping in and out of banks, standing in front of the Asian food market squeezing lichee nuts – to preserve her anonymity. This is something she cherishes after spending her childhood in Brimstock.

On Chesterfield Avenue, her grandmother's street, there is less chance of going unnoticed. Santa Fe style condominiums emerge at intervals along the sidewalk, tri-level buildings with terra cotta shingles and tiled ceramic courtyards. Their exteriors are done in pink stucco, the kind of pink that reminds Elsie of laxatives; spiky agave plants explode in postage-stamp front yards like oversized sea urchins.

Farther down the street some of the original houses still exist: Edwardian and Victorian styles with real backyards and picket fences. Their numbers are shrinking because of the land values; within walking distance to Lonsdale it is more worthwhile for developers to tear down single-family dwellings and replace them with duplexes or townhouses, than to rebuild a single lot-hogging house. A waste of space. Elsie saw the same thing happen in Brimstock, although on a smaller scale. People no longer need the hassle of lawns, the mowing, the thatched-up sod; they can walk to the park, if there is one nearby. If not, they can take the bus.

Violet's house is one of the originals, with a peaked roof. On the outside the cedar shingles have been painted yellow, with white trim around the windows. A white staircase leads up to the front door from a cement walkway and to the back from a dirt path. In the front yard a towering cedar tree at least thirty or forty feet tall shades the only window on the street side of the house; its drooping branches cast a gloomy haze into the living room. Luckily the kitchen is bright, with windows on two sides.

Elsie goes back into the house to make herself a cup of tea. Violet's cupboards are still well-stocked: Irish breakfast, jasmine spice. There is also a selection of pre-sealed tea bags with the centres cut out for improved flow and steepage, in addition to the loose-leaf variety that Elsie always has trouble measuring correctly. She selects a circular bag from the jar labelled *orange pekoe* and pops it into her mug. While the kettle builds up to a stable hiss, she flips through a book of glossy photographs that Violet has perched on the window ledge *Mountain Ranges of the West Coast* and chews on a piece of toast.

She remembers the pictures in this book; Violet brought it on one of her visits to Brimstock, the first one, before the fight. The two of them sat down together on the living-room sofa and Violet pointed out the peaks. *The Lions, Golden Ears,* and to the north, *Grouse.* Elsie remembers the full-colour eight-by-ten of Mount Baker looming across the border, volcanic and snow-covered, a gleaming white crescent in a desert of green.

"That one belongs to the Yanks," Violet had said, "but it's nice to look at just the same."

"What's a Yank?" Elsie had wanted to know.

"An American," said Violet. "From the U.S.A. They're not good for much, but they did invent the Charleston. I'll give them that. What would life be without dancing?"

"I can't dance," said Elsie, studying her hands. "I'm not allowed."

"Of course you can," said Violet. "Your mother and Clifford just haven't taught you because they don't know themselves. I'm not surprised, they're stiffer than an old man in long johns. It's easy, I'll show you."

To Elsie's horror Violet turned on the radio and adjusted the dial to a station that was playing music. The music was twangy, with a quick rhythm of swing and brass that Violet soon captured in her leaping feet. "Come on Elsie," she said. "This is how it goes. The song isn't perfect, but it will do." She kicked her legs out to the sides and waved her right hand in the air, her index finger pointing up towards the ceiling as it twitched to the beat. "I won a lot of competitions doing this Elsie. You might not believe it by looking at me now, but I set a record in 1926 for the quickest feet on the north shore."

Elsie smiled and started to relent, but by the time she reached her grandmother, the song had ended.

"Don't worry," said Violet puffing. "There will be another."

"No there won't," said Marian, who had materialized in the entryway. She removed her boots and crossed the olive carpet to the radio. In a minute the silence was permanent.

Elsie pours the hot water into her cup and settles into a kitchen chair. Holed up in Violet's house she feels like a hermit. She doesn't go out except to buy groceries, and she doesn't want to interact with strangers, especially ones that might mistake her for someone who cares. People like that have a way of making her feel guilty. She takes gentle sips from the tea to avoid singeing her taste buds, and thinks about what to do next. Vacuuming would be practical. Or swabbing the bathroom porcelain and its chrome fixtures (the last two times she took a bath, she noticed a build-up of soap scum and calcium carbonate on the taps), but there is so much to choose from. Instead she stands up and looks out the window: someone is in the backyard coming towards the house. She can hear the clatter of footsteps on the staircase.

"Hello!" a voice says through the door.

Elsie recognizes the woman. She is the same one who stood in the alley in a blue-flowered dress the day Elsie arrived from Ontario, eyeing her with a look of mistrust.

"I'm a relative," Elsie had said at the time. "I'm getting things in order for Mrs. Leggett."

Today the woman shuffles her feet and stares past Elsie into the living room. She wears a pair of leather boots that come just above her ankles. Already the rims are full of snow. "Mrs. Leggett not back?" she asks, "Mrs. Leggett had heart attack."

"A stroke," says Elsie, taken aback. How many people know her grandmother? The thought never occurred to her. Of course she would have friends; she lived on the same street for most of her life. And this woman is obviously a neighbour.

"She called, *My leg my leg.* " The woman moans softly, imitating a cry for help. Her small mouth forms itself into a quivering circle. "I hear her on my way to the garbage can. I hear her and rap on the door. She lying on kitchen floor. They take her away."

"Yes, to the Avondale Rest Home."

This offends the woman. She herself is elderly, although Elsie can't tell how old. She says indignantly, "She no crazy. She fine."

"Yes," says Elsie again, not believing. She has seen her grandmother's basement. She has found her gold watch in the refrigerator.

"You get her out," the woman say accusingly, pointing her wiry finger in Elsie's direction.

Elsie feels the guilt return. It has been a while but the taste is still familiar: tart, like fermented apple juice. This is the guilt from her childhood, from her adolescence; the guilt that her counsellors advised her, at various points in her life, would disappear if only she gave it some room to breathe. How much room does it need? thinks Elsie, who figures three thousand kilometres should be ample. Almost a whole country.

Obviously not. She is already responsible for doing something bad, something indecent, and she hasn't even begun to pick up the pieces.

4

When Elsie was fourteen and Marian died, Violet did not come back to Brimstock for the funeral. Clifford sent the announcement from the paper after the fact in an otherwise empty envelope:

> **Leggett**—*Marian, died at Brimstock District Hospital, into the presence of her Lord on April 17, 1978, age 38 years. Survived by her husband Clifford and daughter Elsie. Mass of Christian burial will be held at Our Lady of the Immaculate Conception Parish Church, 128 Church St., on Wednesday, April 20 at 1:30 p.m. In lieu of flowers donations may be made to the Our Lady Mission Fund.*

One week later Elsie received a sympathy card postmarked in North Vancouver: white calla lilies draped solemnly over a lace tablecloth, *To bear your sorrow.* She didn't feel the way she should have—the way people from church expected her to feel—motherless at four-teen: abandoned, devastated. Women who Elsie had never seen talking to her mother came to the service in black veiled hats and leather gloves; they patted her shoulders, offered her limp smiles of condolence. *You angel,* they said, *your mother was a saint,* dabbing at their eyes with wads of Kleenex. To each other they said, *She was a strange one,* and *the Lord works in mysterious ways.* Elsie considered these statements: true, her mother had suffered the way saints are supposed to suffer. She had been an orphan, and had lived in various foster homes; she was born to an unwed mother and admitted to an orphanage at age two. But she hadn't performed any miracles, she hadn't healed any blind people or cured any lepers. That was Elsie's job, what Marian was preparing her to be: saintly. *You'll learn to suffer,* she told her many times, *it's God's will.*

Instead Elsie stood at the double doors of the church hall nodding at the small line-up of people that came for the visitation; she felt dried up, like a hardened piece of fruit left too long in the cupboard, a raisin, a banana chip. A lump of coal. She could feel the dark weight swelling inside her, testing the limits of her organs to see if they would burst. She knew something that none of the mourners did, something not even her father could know—although maybe he suspected. He could be perceptive if he paid attention. She was responsible for Marian's death. She was just not prepared to think about it.

Clifford stood beside her, staring out into the parking lot. He had on his best suit, the one he had been married in. Elsie remembers thinking how lucky men were to have styles that remained relatively consistent throughout time; less hassle, less energy expended in bothersome choices. She never saw her father standing in front of the mirror grimacing, wrestling with his hair, his eyebrows, demanding *What should I wear?* at his innocent, yet somehow derelict reflection. Come to think of it, she never saw Marian doing that either. Despite her prayers, Marian was wholly unlike other girls' mothers.

Both of them stood silently at the entrance to the church, Elsie and Clifford—motherless daughter, wifeless husband—their expressionless faces misinterpreted by visitors as shock, raw grief. Neither of them had much to say, which was acceptable considering the circumstances.

Whatever Violet had against Elsie's mother, it did not end with Marian's death. She did not rematerialize, as Elsie had hoped she would, waltzing through the front door with her suitcases, her travelling vanity pack and hanging plastic clothes-keepers. She did not come back at all.

She wrote letters addressed *To Elsie Leggett,* short one-page notes about the weather and her trips to lodges in places with exotic sounding names: Squamish, Kamloops, Osoyoos; she sent photos with inscriptions on the back: *Violet on the Sunshine Coast, Violet at the Horseshoe Bay Ferry Dock waiting for ice cream!*

In one of the photos she was posing next to a wooden sculpture of a woman whose arms were extended straight into the air. The woman was naked except for a patterned loincloth, a headband, armband, and bracelets. On her feet she wore what looked like running shoes. Violet stood next to the sculpture with her own arms in the air, smiling out at an invisible photographer. Elsie thought this was in bad taste.

Elsie stopped answering her grandmother in her third year of high school; Violet's letters arrived, shortened now to postcards or a few paragraphs on the front sides of flowered stationery, and Elsie placed them in her bedroom desk and closed the drawer. She accumulated quite a stack of them before they stopped coming. Elsie doesn't know if Clifford saw the letters. She usually beat him home and checked the floor in front of the letter slot and under the hallway rug as soon as she came in the door. She wanted to protect him from the bad feelings that must exist between himself and Violet, because why else would two people stop talking to each other? She became annoyed at her grandmother for tormenting her this way. What did she want with a woman who rejected her father? What did this woman want from her?

By Wednesday the snow is three feet deep. Elsie hears the warnings on the radio: Houses are sliding into the water in Deep Cove, at the end of Indian Arm, peeling away from the shoreline; boats at the North Vancouver Yacht Club are sinking under the snow's weight. Already two people have slipped from their ridge poles and given themselves concussions while trying to clean off their roofs. *Be careful out there. The worst storm in history.* Greenhouse effect, thinks Elsie, David Suzuki was right.

In the back yard snow slumps down in heavy rolls over Elsie's pathway. Washing machines left out for the garbage truck are unrecognizable mounds. How old are those shingles, Elsie wonders looking up at her grandmother's house: thirty, forty years? Despite admonitions from the CBC weatherman, Elsie decides to take the risk and clean off Violet's roof. *If I were a snow shovel...* She searches the basement because where else would a snow shovel be in a house this size? Already she has begun moving things around in a half-hearted attempt to organize whatever it was her grandmother had going on down there, a museum, a junk collection? On the surface the debris could be trash, part of a cheap display in a thrift-store window crafted to draw bargain hunters and seedy second-hand antique dealers, except that things are too arbitrary, too trivial. What would Violet do with a wooden-handled drill labelled *McCardle and Sons?* There's no evidence that she was ever into woodworking. Or a collection of bent spoons? There's a whole box of them, pounded flat on one end and curled around like bracelets. Perhaps she didn't like to throw anything out; perhaps she was saving up for the afterlife like the Egyptians; the same thing Daniel said he was doing with all those record albums. *It's no use,* Elsie thinks, sighing. In all likelihood, Violet never owned a snow shovel, and if she did, let's face it, she's eighty-six years old. Victim of a stroke. She probably can't even bend over.

Elsie settles for a garden rake that she finds in a dark corner behind the freezer. The rake is old, pre-war industrial, with a screw-in handle and a set of metal teeth that remind her of the reptilian jaw casts she has seen in museums.

Beneath the back porch is a ladder, the telescoping aluminum kind that shrieks as Elsie slides it into position. She braces it against the chimney, slips it into the snow, and ascends it until she is above the eaves trough. "If Daniel could see me now," she huffs. Daniel had always liked to think of himself as the handy type, capable of fixing things. When Elsie broke something, or needed something worked on, she took it to him first; he found that kind of brain work soothing. In the end they always called a professional, but at least he took a shot. Those were his words, *let me take a shot at that.*

[39]

Her improvised snow shovel would impress him. It is the kind of thing he would create using the broken parts of other projects: a coat hanger, an elastic band. The only difference is that hers is working, and this time there is no hope of calling in a professional. All the professionals are stuck in the snow.

She begins clearing in long awkward strokes, tossing the rake into the air as if fly fishing, then wedging down and drawing back towards her body. Her progress is laughable: narrow tracks in a thick expanse, but she continues with determination, making small dents. At the end of each stroke, a clump of snow hits the ground with a satisfying thud.

As she works, she ascends the ladder, the rake wobbling at the neck. She doesn't stand on the roof—she is not that coordinated—but she does manage to get a view of the neighbourhood. Across the alley a woman in snowshoes attempts to navigate the maze of branches deposited in her backyard by the storm. On the opposite side of Chesterfield, two people struggle with a hockey net, dragging it behind them as a kind of steel-and-mesh snowplow. An illuminated set of plastic Christmas carollers leftover from the holidays flickers, then goes out.

"Oh no," Elsie says.

She descends the ladder and returns to the house. The lights are off. The radiator is making a spitting sound. On top of the fridge Violet's clock radio has gone black, stripped of its slender red numbers and familiar mechanical hum.

"Well," says Elsie. "At least there's the fireplace." Which is little consolation without wood. She locates a meagre stack in a green box two feet from the hearth.

Dry as a bone. On top of the stack is a 1986 copy of the *Vancouver Sun. Welcome to Expo,* reads the headline.

"Obviously Violet is not that fond of fires," says Elsie. "Either that or the power only goes out once every ten years." She hopes the phones are as reliable. She is expecting a phone call from her cousin, Tia, whose parents are Uncle Lawrence and Aunt Alexandra. (*Call me Alex,* she said to Elsie the one time that they met.) The fact that Tia has come this far in life with two living parents is something that doesn't go unnoticed by Elsie. *Sheer luck,* her father would say, patting her on the shoulder; *God's will,* Marian would intone; *Lucky Duck,* Violet would say lightly, the only one of the three still alive; which reminds Elsie of how much she has to lose if she doesn't visit Violet soon.

Elsie has never met Tia in person. She met her parents when Aunt Alex was pregnant, so technically Tia was there in the form of a sixteen-week fetus. Her head would have been as big as a kiwi fruit, her facial features and organs would have been formed. Alex's belly was just starting to swell, and she was experiencing something she called *quickening*: the first movements of the fetus. Signs of life. Up until that point, she explained to Elsie, there had been nothing except vomiting and constipation. She said these words flippantly, as if they were ordinary things that people talked about. "Put your hand on my stomach," She said to Elsie. "You just might feel something." Elsie could see Marian watching her with a glint in her eye; a familiar look of damnation. She knew she would probably never see Aunt Alex again.

She spoke to Tia briefly last week and they arranged to have lunch; her voice was high-pitched, like her mother's. When she calls to confirm, Elsie is trying to light a fire in the fireplace.

"Elsie. How's twelve-thirty on Friday? The buses should be running by then."

"Great. You name the place. I haven't eaten out yet."

"In three months? Elsie, I'll have to show you around. How about L'Orange, on Burrard? You can take the 210 and get off at Burrard Station."

"Fine," says Elsie. "I have a map."

When she hangs up, Elsie has just ignited a rectangular flap of cardboard torn from the lid of a cereal box. The words *All Bran* disappear in yellow and green flames. Among other things, Violet must have suffered from irregularity. *Please God, don't let me get old,* Elsie thinks, but she knows better than to pray for things like that.

Instead of rising neatly up the chimney, the smoke from Elsie's fire billows into the living room. She has forgotten about the flue. How many times has she done this? Elsie feels her way around the dark chimney with her already coal-black fingers, until she grasps the handle. One pull forces the damper open, and simultaneously sends a wad of cloth and plastic into the fire where it lands and starts to hiss. Elsie grabs at the bundle and burns her hand. "Dammit," she says to no one in particular; to her own stupidity. As she unwraps the layers of cloth, an inner layer of plastic bags and newspaper, then more cloth, Elsie finds a bundle of money—hundred-dollar bills, sombre brown, with the face of Sir Robert Borden looking stern behind a walrus mustache. She counts them: seven thousand dollars. Then she remembers Violet, hair cropped, eyebrows raised, telling her on one of her visits: *Never trust banks my dear, banks get robbed.*

[42]

5

VIOLET

At the Avondale Rest Home they serve you boiled dinners and continental breakfasts. Violet knows why they call them *continental:* the toast is cooked and buttered in Toronto, flown out on a jet to Richmond, transported by truck to the Avondale kitchen, then reheated and put on her plate. She heard from one of the nurses that all the rest homes get their toast from the east now; it's just plain faster not to have to make it yourself.

Thinking about the words *rest home* makes her cringe; rest from what? As far as she can tell the Avondale provides two kinds of rest. They either bring you here to give your adult children a rest from your incontinence and involuntary belching, or they bring you here to rest the public eye from watching you struggle into the drug store with gravy stains on your chin. Either way, it's your final rest. The only time anyone leaves Avondale is to go underground.

No thank you, thinks Violet, as if she had a choice.

[43]

Violet's right side was damaged by the stroke, so she gets around most of the time in a wheelchair. Part of her face was paralyzed—from the edge of her nostril all the way to her earlobe—so until she can sound like a normal person she refrains from speaking out loud, except to herself in the bathroom. That is where she practises on the sly, perched on the sink, gazing into the mirror, enunciating words like *huckleberry* and *fifty-fifty* that the speech language pathologist told her would help improve control of her face. She makes sounds with her lips, raspberries, tongue-galloping, to strengthen the muscles and whip them into shape. She is afraid she will lose the ability to make noise, even if it does only come out a demented growl, but she is also afraid of looking like a fool. There are enough of those in here already. Violet was almost capsized once by Mr. Donovan from Wing D; he is not one of the ones that kicks and screams and pulls out hair, but he is the kind that sends his fork soaring into the air with the flat of his palm at dinnertime.

If she had a daughter, Violet wouldn't be here right now.

She hasn't spoken to Clifford in over fifteen years, since her last visit to Ontario. Now, of course, she will never speak to him again. When she was younger, she used to wonder how her own mother could go so long without seeing her family, who were still in England as far as she could remember; but then travelling was more difficult, more expensive. You saved your whole life for a boat trip or a train ride. Now there are so many ways to communicate—except that Violet is lousy on the telephone, impossible now that she can only snarl. She could have written him a letter, she supposes, that wouldn't have been hard, but she kept expecting him to materialize, to come to his senses; to choose her side. Her love was not about battles, about winning, but somehow she botched things up. *Tough love,* they call it now. What was meant to teach him a lesson ended up hurting her as well.

In the mornings after breakfast Violet sits at her favourite spot by the window. The nurse with the blonde hair wheels her down the hall to a reasonably quiet corner, behind a potted tropical fern, where she can see out onto the grounds of the Avondale, which are paltry as far as she's concerned, but who asked her? At least there are people down there, sometimes children or teenagers, doing active things like kicking a soccer ball or chasing each other. Living a normal life. She feels sorry for the nurses, especially the blonde-haired one who goes by the name of Nyome (what were her parents thinking?) stuck inside all day with a bunch of old farts who giggle and hiss and break dishes over their heads. If she wasn't so sure of her own sentience she would swear this place was a funny farm.

Violet was a healthy woman—didn't the doctor tell her so?—with all her own teeth. She hadn't been in the hospital since she was a child and had her tonsils removed, wrenched from her throat like two underdone pork chops. She had avoided all the childhood sicknesses, the plagues that raged through North Vancouver, killing her mother, her girlfriends: the Spanish Influenza, TB, polio; she never even got colds.

So the stroke was unexpected. She had been up early

making herself a piece of toast, awakened by another one of those dreams where all the men in her life congregated in the lobby of the Capilano Hotel. Her father Jack was there, and so was her husband, but instead of black hair he had red; he also insisted on walking around the elegant Chippendale furniture with his head tucked neatly beneath his underarm.

"Hobert," Violet said. "Put that thing back on. You look a mess. Do you want your sons to see you that way?" She was mad, but also anxious. Russell, Clifford, and Lawrence had been by her side just a minute ago. Now they were gone. "Where are the boys?" she asked Hobert, bending down to peer into his face. "I just saw them."

Hobert didn't answer right away, but considered the question with intensity. "Gone," he said finally, his mouth brushing against his shirt sleeves. "Gone, gone."

When Violet woke up she was clawing at the pillow case with her fingernails. Thank goodness for percale, there was hardly a mark. She also had a throbbing headache, and a hole in the centre of her body that demanded peanut butter on whole grain toast. She hauled herself out of her sagging bed and into the kitchen, muttering under her breath that she ought to put a stop to the midnight snacks of crackers and pimentos—she no longer had the stamina for nightmares—then opened the back door to let out the cat. The air was cold that day, Violet remembers that much. A sub-Arctic front had moved over the north shore and was stripping the ornamental maples of their leaves. Piles of them collected along the fence. There was also a mouse on the back porch, flattened and subdued-looking, dead as a doornail with his licorice whip tail dragging out behind him like a pull-cord. Her neighbour was in the alley fumbling with the garbage can, and Violet gave her a friendly wave before closing the door and digging out the A.S.A. On her way to the sink she stubbed her toe on one of the kitchen chairs, and although furious at her own neglect, she started to cry. Angry as the fires of hell, and yet here she was crying. That was when she knew something was wrong.

Her next memory is of the green linoleum: outdated and faithfully sanitized, pushing against her cheek. Pressing against her jawbone and the dim sensation of pain that was falling away from parts of her body that used to be attached, but which now seemed painfully, unrecognizably numb. She also recalls a rising anxiety over the linoleum: what happened to the hardwood floors? Did her mother replace them? What was she thinking, that woman? Jack was going to be furious. Or would be, she added to her thoughts with panic, if he was still alive.

She needed to know what year it was, what place. She needed to know why she was lying with her face against the floor when the rest of her body was bent around the chair. Someone was making a noise; was that her? Even though her mouth felt as if it were full of food, and parts of her lips were frozen as if she'd just seen the dentist, she was making a sound. The noise was not words; at least, it didn't sound like any words she knew. It sounded, Violet thinks to herself in retrospect, like a chortled vacuum cleaner.

A woman peered in the square of glass inset into the kitchen door, and saw her lying on the linoleum. Within seconds she was inside.

"Mrs. Leggett—" she said, anxiously, scolding as she entered. "Mrs. Leggett—"

Violet could only nod her head and attempt to wave her arm with its fingers clamped shut. Her good one was pinned beneath her shoulder. *Help me,* she tried to say, *help.* But she couldn't speak; her lips weren't responding.

The woman bent over Violet's contorted body, biting her lower lip. She tried to hold Violet still, to protect her head from the kitchen cupboards. Her hands smelled sweet. Violet knew the smell: licorice root, port wine. The woman was Mrs. Wang, one of her neighbours.

Violet stopped moving her arm and kept her body still; she looked into Mrs. Wang's eyes with a concentrated look of seriousness and terror. She flapped her hand softly, periodically, in an attempt to communicate.

"Call ambulance," Mrs. Wang said aloud as she shuffled to the phone and dialled zero. "Hospital," she said loudly, shouting into the receiver. "Ambulance."

Violet searched the room for something she recognized. Teapots, whitewashed kitchen cupboards. Nothing seemed familiar, not really. Her mind was humming, as if there were a storm in her brain.

"What?" said Mrs. Wang. "Oh, she live on one-eighteen Chesterfield."

Chesterfield, Violet thought, *Chesterfield.* The name of her street. *Her* street. This was *her* house, *her* kitchen floor. An orange cat brushed by Violet's arm and curled up at her elbow. She knew him, he was her cat. He purred into her ear.

After Mrs. Wang hung up the phone, she knelt down beside Violet and took her hand. "Gonna be okay," she said smiling. "You gonna be fine." Her face had a crooked grin and Violet noticed there were gaps in her mouth, as if someone had applied theatrical black-out to her teeth. Still, she was reassuring.

Violet nodded, her head lopsided on her neck. *Damn straight,* she said to herself as she tried to slow down her breathing. But her eyes were wet.

After the attack in the kitchen, Violet lay in a hospital bed terrified, unable to move one side of her body. She alternated between crying and raging, snivelling at the nurses who shot her glances of pity or ignored her all together. After forty-two hours she remembered how to move her lips, to form words; the trouble remained that half of her face was paralyzed, inhibiting her ability to use her tongue. Be calm, the doctor told her. It's still too early to tell. To tell what? Violet wanted to know. If any of these scars are permanent. After seventy-two hours she made a breakthrough: she moved her thumb, the right one, flinching it back an inch so that her whole body shivered with pleasure. And pain. She did not remember ever working so hard for such a small result.

A speech pathologist visited her in the hospital and gave her a mirror framed by twelve illustrations of facial exercises she could practice on her own by looking into the glass. By then Violet had recovered most of the feeling in the right half of her body, but the side still felt weak, spastic. She was put on a waiting list for physical rehabilitation, and moved to the Avondale where she saw another speech pathologist less frequently. *I will get well,* she told herself, because believing was half the battle.

Now after three months, she is still trying to convince herself.

"You try learning to walk when you're seventy-nine years old. That's what I said to her, and boy, that shut her up."

Violet nods to the woman who sits next to her in a wheelchair much like her own. As the woman speaks she fiddles with a paper napkin placed neatly next to a white porcelain bowl. The table is set for lunch, with identical sets of cutlery—forks and spoons (but no knives)—laid out across a mint green polyester tablecloth. Violet envies the woman's ability to move her hands like that, both of them simultaneously, picking at the napkin with her fingernail and tapping the tabletop with her palm. She wishes she would take her own good advice and be quiet.

"She told me I was being difficult, but I don't care. They should try switching places with us if they think it's so easy."

You're just a chicken, Violet thinks, referring not to the woman's lack of courage, but to her age. *A spring chicken. I've got seven years on you and they won't even let me try to walk.*

Violet has been demanding physiotherapy on the steno pad given to her by the nurse. She has had to learn to write all over again with her left hand—short cryptic messages like *I walk again,* or *lift my arm.* Her penmanship is dreadful but what should she expect? Someone should come in and help her hold a pencil, properly, with her right hand; help her make a fist. Doesn't the health care system pay for things like that? So far they have been putting her off, pleading with her to rest, telling her she is on the list. Instead she practices in bed, tensing up her legs, her arms, lifting them up and down under the ghost-white sheets until her back hurts; she won't tell them about the pain—nothing broke when she fell, a miracle really, although her father always said she had good bones—because she knows what they will say. *All the more reason to take it easy.* She will not take it easy. *Not bloody likely.*

Writing with her left hand is frustrating, but it will have to do until she has enough coordination to return to the right. And she is almost there: she can now hold her own fork. Outside the lunch-room window snow piles up. Violet doesn't remember ever seeing a storm like this, but she figures it will melt, it always does. The nice thing about the unpredictable weather in North Vancouver is that sooner or later it always does something predictable. She hopes the cat will find a warm place to sleep.

"Oh no!" The woman next to Violet lets out a small, contemptuous cry. She glares at the waitress who hands them both a bowl of soup. "Not cream of cauliflower again. I swear they are trying to poison us with too much salt. Knock us all down dead of heart attacks. They've reduced my blood thinners, you know. Just two pills in the morning now, and such low doses."

Violet smiles graciously and reaches for the salt shaker with her good hand. The woman scoffs and turns away, sulking. *Shunned,* thinks Violet, *bravo.*

If only she could be so vocal. Perhaps when she learns to talk again, she will be as annoying as this woman, shrieking at every opportunity, nattering on to anyone who will listen. She will get herself a collection of outrageous hats and talk to strangers on the bus. She used to feel sorry for the listeners, the poor dupes who sat politely trapped in the window seat while some old biddy yacked their ear off; but now she sides with the biddies, the eccentric ladies with gumption enough to corner and pin down. She understands their compulsion, their inability to hold back: *I must tell you about my job as a nurse in World War Two*, they say, looking their victims straight in the eye, staring them down. Maybe they too were silenced once.

It's not that she is a spiteful person, although some may care to argue. She sips at her soup, pursing her lips to take the heat. At least the Avondale knows how to make a hot bowl of soup, although it's probably cooked in Winnipeg.

The chatty woman has moved on to the man across the table now; they are talking about laxatives. To make her point, that every one of them turns her colon to lead unless she drinks gallons, the woman taps her fingers on the edge of her bowl, and stomps her feet abruptly. Tap, stomp. For the love of Pete, thinks Violet. If someone had told her, when she was younger, that one day women would discuss bowel movements with men, she would have laughed in her face. *Never*. There are a lot of things about the present she can't believe.

For instance:

Violet gets on the bus, an eighty-six-year-old woman, to find the courtesy seats occupied by young men in ripped-up blue jeans. On their chins are the swatches of a weeks' worth of hair, shaven into unruly diamonds or arrows or moons; on the backs of their heads, where a ledge of freshly dyed pink or green gives way to stubble, the names of rock stars are carved down to the skin using an electric shaver: *Anthrax*, or *Brother D*. Sometimes the messages are worse: *Go home whiteboy. Put bitches on their backs. Kill the cop.* Violet stands in the aisle, holding on to the leather strap above her head, intending not to stare. The young men look at the ground or out the window and bop to the inaudible rhythm fed to their brains by sponge-covered earphones inserted into their ears. She imagines the music they listen to is the sort she has seen on television: riotous, violent songs delivered by long-haired or shorn adolescents who writhe and twist and wriggle their heads on their necks like broken jack-in-the-boxes, thrusting their hips side to side, baring their sweaty chests. They have teeth like sharpened garden stakes, coffee-stained, smoky; they spit at their audiences, smash up their electric guitars and drum kits. Where's the appeal?

When Violet was younger there were real instruments: pianos, trombones, saxophones, whole brass sections of song; she went to the Horseshoe Bay dance hall every Saturday night to do the Charleston, the Flea Hop, to listen to the band swing into high gear. There were steps to memorize then, rhythms to harness; there were dance partners, and handsome men with bear grease in their hair. But no more. The world is a different place, she has been told many times.

Still, she wants to get out of the Avondale; she must. Her plants will shrivel up in their green plastic pots, the ivies, the philodendrons, and of course, the African violets, her namesake; they are only drought tolerant to a point. The cat will give up on her, assume betrayal. Carpenter ants will infiltrate. Aphids will destroy the rosebushes, moths will eat holes in her camisoles. Even worse than that, someone might break in to her house, the same thief as last time or someone new (does it matter? They always go for the same things—jewellery, appliances, money, although they left the TV, it being so cumbersome), despite the bars on the basement windows. And this time they might think to look in the chimney.

Go home. Violet writes on her steno pad, not for the first time. *My house.* She shows the message to the supervisor who walks through the lunch room on her midday rounds. The woman is tall, her long legs clothed respectably in seamless panty-hose.

Home, she moans.

The supervisor bends down cheerfully. "Why Mrs. Leggett, you needn't worry yourself. Haven't you been told that someone is looking after your house?"

Violet shakes her head silently, because, no, she has not been told.

6

Lawrence came to visit almost twelve weeks ago. He walked in the door of her private room—*apartment* in Avondale terminology (who do they think they're fooling?)—with a bouquet of white Easter lilies and placed them awkwardly on Violet's lap. A peace offering. Violet winced, seeing the lilies first, then Lawrence; lilies reminded her of funerals.

"Mother," he said, looking hopeful. It was a declaration, a statement of intent; it meant, *I will not feel guilty for living my own life.* He followed with: "Looks like you're all settled."

She stared at him coldly and shook her head no; she had not yet mastered the steno pad enough to use it in public. *Settled* was a word for dirt, for sediment once bobbing improbably on the surface of stormy waters, now sunk to the bottom in a gesture of submission; it implied permanence, contentment. She was far from being settled. She was on her way back up.

"Well now," he said, changing his tactic. "The nurse

said you're doing fine. That you're eager to walk again. I think that's great, as long as you don't overdo it too soon. Make sure you take it easy."

Those words again. Violet wanted to tell him that nothing in her life had been easy, why start now?

He continued. This was hard for him, she could tell. She supposed she should give a little and try to understand his position. "I'll be coming down periodically to visit Tia. I'll check in on you. So if there's anything you need, well, let me know and I can bring it, when I'm in the area."

Violet gave a half-hearted smile. Where to begin?

"I went by the house, to make sure everything was in order. I thought you might want to, you know, sell it, so I contacted your lawyer."

The gall. Violet's eyes widened to glassy pools flecked with veins. Sell it! She had no such intention. She slammed her claw hand against the arm of her chair, rocked her body against the seat. How primitive and dubious, this display, but how else could she communicate? Sign language was not an option. She was so furious, she could feel her heart seethe, and she let him see. How much she's learned since then.

"Okay, okay," Lawrence drew back," Calm down. The lawyer told me that you had plans. He didn't go into much detail, except to say that the power of attorney was in someone else's hands."

Uncomfortable silence.

"I thought, naturally, though wrongfully I see now, that being your son I would be that person."

Violet quieted. He was hurt, even though he had never cared about such things in the past; his lower lip hung a

[56]

little, the way it used to when he was a boy and he had been denied his dessert. He was the baby of the family, always riding on his father's shoulders, used to being taken care of, but not very responsible. A little heavy on the drink. Violet thought she could smell gin on his breath. Poor Lawrence. His fragile cheeks, his hair disappointingly brown. If he'd had the option, would he have chosen to be the last faithful son? Not likely. He avoided those kind of allegiances like the plague.

"But I'm sure you know what you are doing."

Would he leave it at that? Violet looked at the lilies, sagging now in their coloured paper, dripping off the edges of her wheelchair like silk replications, like melting vanilla ice cream. He was a good boy—a man, after all.

Lawrence shifted uncomfortably in his chair, toying with his keys. Was he in a hurry? He leaned forward, as if to reveal something, a confidence, a secret. His hair had thinned on top to a few hardy strands. "Are you okay Mother?"

It occurred to Violet then what he wanted out of the visit: to be let off the hook. Someone was responsible for putting her here, in the Avondale, for signing some papers, giving the go-ahead over the phone; someone had made the decision, to transfer her not home, but to the Avondale from the hospital, where she was lying helpless, translucent tubes in her arms, catheter jammed up her urethra. She did not do that herself. No. She was not given the option. Lawrence did, all the way from Prince George, grudgingly perhaps, at the insistence of the doctors, or even worse, gleefully, because he would no longer have to worry, to care about his mother. How many times had he said to her over the last thirty years, *I worry about you alone in that house?* I'll take my chances, she always replied.

But more than that, Lawrence wanted to be exonerated, for not doing enough, being enough; for not being *the one.* Violet could see it then, their failure—hers, as well as his—their inability to measure up as mother and son. Suddenly the world was a harsher place, harsher even than that morning when she had woken up sobbing, dredged from a dream she couldn't remember. She sat up in bed and looked around her room, her *apartment,* her heart sinking. Why did everyone have to fail each other?

But forgiving him at that moment would mean accepting everything, including this place: the group craft sessions where she was goaded into making clothespin ballerinas from scraps of cloth, the forced mealtimes where food was scorched or served still bleeding; the group trips to the toilet, in the morning, when half the woman still had curlers in their rigid, milky hair, and everyone shared in the symphony of each other's digestive systems releasing a cacophony of noise—low, bassoon-like intonations, or high staccatoed streams of gas—from their depths. She could not forgive this place, she was not capable. She didn't know then what she knows now: to play it cool. *Make like a cucumber.*

Instead she opened her mouth and let out a guttural wail, bemoaning anything and everything they'd ever done to one another, on purpose or inadvertently, as only those who love one another enough to cause scarring can do; the sound was ferocious anger, despair, meant to invoke pity, empathy, and resolution; meant to sound

[58]

like *get me out of here Lawrence, you know I don't belong here.* But she frightened him away.

"Jesus Murphy Mother—" He looked at his hands, defeated, thinking no doubt, *She's really gone off the deep end.* Couldn't she have just let him off the hook? He thought she was being malicious. He put the lilies on her bedside table, arranging them next to her alarm clock, and gathered up his coat. He said, "I'll be seeing you," and walked out the door.

7

When Violet gave Elsie the power of attorney to her estate she had a plan. If she dropped dead, the girl would not have to wait until the will went to probate before accessing her account and paying off her bills, although Violet made an effort not to have credit cards and to avoid all forms of plastic money. She learned these simple tricks when her own husband died of a heart attack thirty-two years ago, and she was left with the unsightly bill for their unpaid refrigerator.

She was mad at Clifford when she drew up her will. Extra mad, because Clifford had sided with Marian over an issue where she was plainly in the wrong. Could he not see what psychological harm that woman was doing to his daughter? Obviously not.

Elsie had been twelve years old, a neat, though somewhat inhibited young lady; she needed a little freedom to help her spread her wings, a little bolstering and support. Violet would show her that she believed in her by trusting her, giving her a chance. She was, after all, the only family member who ever listened.

She never told Clifford about the arrangement, how could she? She hasn't spoken to him since, unless she counts the anonymous phone calls made to him in the evenings when she would sit quietly and listen to his voice, breathing there on the end of the line, a faint heartbeat in all that wiry crackling. He was always patient, asking cautiously, "Who is this? Hello? Is anyone there?" never suspecting it could be his own mother. Violet Leggett: *Crank caller.* Clifford was a kind man, like his father Hobert, only too kind. Perhaps if he ever got mad he could have told off that wife of his, sent her packing. Even as a boy he was always trying to please, never knowing quite how; the middle child in every way.

How did he end up with a woman like Marian? Violet has nothing against religion, providing it stays where it belongs, which is in a church, or better yet, back in the Sumerian desert where it crawled out of the sand in the first place, skittering across the foreheads of unsuspecting shepherds. She just wishes people under its influence had a little self-control; that they stopped parading their divine ecstasy up and down the streets, in the papers, and now, on television, outfitted in the purple-and-cream robes of parrots and crowned with golden chalices on their heads. There is something to be said for humility.

Marian must have seduced him, although Lord knows how when she was so dead-set against anything remotely associated with the body. They came back engaged from Vancouver Island, the place where Clifford built logging roads for H.R. MacMillan. Today people would throw rocks at him for that, not just young punks bent on hellfire, but business presidents in three-piece suits, children, grandparents; *Degradation,* they would holler, pummelling his Lincoln with chewed-up sticks and salal berries. *Stop the clear-cut.* In those days taking down trees was more acceptable. Necessary, even. Marian had worked at one of the logging camps, the only woman for miles.

After lunch Violet decides to watch the news. She does not have her own television set, so she begins the long trek down the hallway to the social lounge where a communal big-screen version has been jacked up on an imitation oak sideboard. Because she still lacks control of her right hand, she is unable to grip the wheels of her chair properly and is soon lurching along the speckled hallway tile in a crooked line. One of the nurses sees her struggling and grabs the handles at the back of her chair.

"Here Mrs. Leggett, I'll give you a hand."

Once she is tucked in, propped up, and thoroughly prodded in all possible places, Violet settles down to watch the latest coverage of the snow storm. A large crowd of other spectators has also been arranged around the television set like a collection of poorly dressed, ill-attended dolls. Some of them wear flowered plastic bibs stained with oozing strands of drool; others have neglected hairdos, with exploding nests of curls or too-tight perms that make them look like the near-sighted hedgehogs Violet has seen in children's books. Many of them stare past the television set altogether, with looks of intoxicated gladness, or is it remorse, passing through their vacancy like thinning clouds.

On the news the anchorman wears too much blush, while the newswoman's waxed-apple mouth deflects studio lighting back at the camera. *In days of yore,* thinks

Violet fondly, *Clara Bow was all the rage.* Pictures flash on the screen: people in goose-down jackets and snowmobile suits shovelling their driveways with anything that will hold snow—blue plastic buckets, hubcaps, bicycle helmets, cardboard boxes, extra-large Rubbermaid garbage cans with handles; buses stopped on Mountain Highway, unable to make the grade, line-ups of snow-dotted cars backing down behind them, their drivers' anxious heads out windows, arms braced. For one instant Violet is glad not to be home alone, stranded without electricity, her savings up the flue; condemned to eat cold spaghetti from a can day after day, meal after meal, rationing her last spotted banana.

But then the thought occurs to her: If someone is taking care of my house, who is it? Not Mrs. Wang, with her own husband to feed, and her litter of stray, yowling cats? And certainly not Lawrence. If Lawrence is right, and the lawyer is going by her latest will, then wouldn't Elsie have been notified by now? Wouldn't she have been contacted and filled in on Violet's legal plans? Indeed, thinks Violet, she would have. Then where is she?

SOFT AND LOUD

8

The first time Elsie met Violet, she was six years old. It was early spring, when the slush of March had just begun to transform into the mud of April, and Brimstock was fortunate enough to have a dry spell. Everywhere people dug into the thawing earth to plant new bulbs and to repair fences. On the calendar Easter was looming. Lent had begun and Elsie collected pennies from the sidewalk to add to the container for poor children overseas that her mother kept on the kitchen counter. Elsie remembers the time all right: she had just begun to meet her demons.

She lived with her parents in a two-bedroom house. The house had a front gable with a triangular window that was inset with wavy bubbled glass, and hardwood floors which her mother planned to cover in something more sensible called Congoleum. Elsie believed from an early age that houses were always in this state of flux, their shoddy elements being replaced by newer, more practical materials as humans had the sense to invent them. At some point in her house's history someone had seen fit to remove the cut-glass doorknobs and replace them with metal ones, the kinds that never needed oiling; the walls had been repapered with successively fancier patterns, the final attempt being an expensive paisley design made from raised velvet, which, Clifford said, looked like a bordello. (Marian forbade Elsie to repeat the word.) Even the exterior was not immune to this inexorable remodelling. Before Elsie was born the red brick had been entirely covered in small, grey pebbles, embedded against the clay in layers of carefully applied cement. If Elsie was feeling bold, she might pick away at the pebbles with her fingernails to see if she could make any of them come loose; there was perverse joy in this dismantling, this low-grade vandalism; the act infused her with a delicious fleeting power. But there was also a curiosity behind her sabotage: Elsie's house, like most of the early houses in Brimstock, was a commemorative onion; she could peel away the layers if she wanted—if Marian would let her—work her way down to a core of plaster dust and horse hair to the beginning of history.

That spring her father worked for the municipal department of highways, overseeing the creation of new thoroughfares, administering road surveys and dispatching snow plows. Part of his job involved deciding whose potholes would be filled and whose would be left for another year. Elsie's own street, Magnolia Avenue, was always terrifically smooth.

Marian worked at home or in the community; *charity work*, she called it. Although she didn't get paid like Elsie's father, her work was somehow more important, crucial to the existence and eventual salvation of Elsie's family. *Essential*, in fact, *for the survival of the soul.*

Neither Elsie nor her father questioned this statement. It had been a fact as long as they could remember.

Her work involved going to nursing homes, to hospitals, paying heed to the less desirable sides of life. She gave Elsie the details when she came home to prepare her for her future as a servant of the church. The dirtier the task the better: swishing out chamber pots, changing soiled underwear, wiping bums for the invalid, calling in the priest for the last rites. Anything involving grime, bodily functions, smells; anything involving suffering.

Suffering was good, Elsie knew that; it was called for, necessary. When Marian cleaned the shit from someone else's bedpan she was wiping away dirt, and by association, sin. Elsie quickly learned that all things coming from the body—secretions, smells, absent-minded farts, the awful lumps that climbed the throat and turned into burps and belches—all these things were undesirable. She determined that the entire inside of the body was infested, a bloody, unclean soup needing to be scoured white by diligence and careful prayer. She also learned that she must never, never ever, mention those kinds of things out loud. *Diarrhea. Menstruation.* The words reeked of ill-repute.

It followed then, that everything that went on in the bathroom was shameful. Her mother would check up on her, to make sure she took her lessons seriously. "Did you flush the toilet," she would say, lifting the lid. If by chance Elsie forgot, Marian would smack her across the head. "That's disgusting." Sometimes this would be followed by the cellar.

On the first Saturday of every month, Elsie went with

Marian on her rounds. In the morning they worked at the mission, and in the afternoon at the hospital. Her role at their first stop was fairly straightforward: Elsie stood behind the serving table in an apron and put buns on people's plates as they passed. The buns were white and so were the people, but the people were worn looking, with dried-up faces and shabby coats. At the hospital Elsie was less sure of herself. Her tasks varied depending on the day. Sometimes she was instructed by her mother to read aloud particular verses of the Bible to patients in a coma; other times she carried trays of dirty dishes up and down the hallways until she found a doorway that led into the kitchen. Her favourite task was distributing bouquets of flowers that had been donated by the funeral parlour, bundles of daffodils and sugar-tipped carnations replete with ferns that she would leave by the bedsides of the elderly, remembering to first remove the tags that read *In Memoriam*, or *Rest in Peace*.

If she happened to come upon someone in the act of dying, Elsie was supposed to throw salt on their feet as a way of warding off the devil. Both she and Marian carried mother-of-pearl salt shakers in their pockets in case of such an emergency, but so far, no one had died with Elsie in the room. Could she throw salt on the devil if he came after her? she wanted to know. Only if she was dying, said Marian, in which case she would probably be too busy to remember where she put her shaker— she did have a habit of losing things. Because of this warning Elsie kept her shaker safely within reach at all times, rubbing its surface like a talisman with the tips of her fingers.

Where was her father during these episodes? Elsie wonders. Although Marian was definitely disturbed, she has to admit now with a hint of malice *(Grief, grief!* her counsellors would scream, *go with those feelings!),* her father was more or less stable, with very few fixations. Where was he indeed. Most likely in front of the television, *Mary Tyler Moore* blaring from its metal-grid speakers; or reading the newspaper, his head tucked artfully behind the sports pages. Staying out of things. If Elsie had to equate Clifford with an animal, she would pick a Cocker Spaniel—hopeful, eager to please—or a basset hound with its look of drab contentment. She loved him, but the harsh truth is that he preferred to be out of trouble, comfortably seated in his overstuffed easy chair, asleep in front of the heat vent. Good-natured. Elsie is beginning to see this as a vice.

When he did speak out he used his jovial voice, the one riddled with light-heartedness. Marian would come home from her rounds and go right to the sink to scrub her hands, her face, her neck, with castile soap; she would scrub and scrub until the skin around her eyelids was red and puffy like a burn. Sometimes as she scrubbed she emitted a sound like growling dogs or irate bumblebees.

"If it displeases you so much, why go?" Clifford might say.

To this Marian would scoff, as if no one but her husband could ask such a question. "You know very well I have no choice. It's my lot in life, my terms."

Elsie learned about her own lot in life at a young age; she was luckier than her mother, she would not have to stoop to the same depths to demonstrate her faith. "You will be pure till the day you die," her mother told her many times, her mouth twitching with seriousness.

Marian's lot in life was a form of punishment; self-administered, true enough, but by necessity. It had something to do with her life before Elsie, before her marriage to Clifford: *her past*. "I had no way out," she told Elsie. "I had to make do. But you have options. We'll make sure you keep them."

This punishment was related to Elsie's father, who sat hunched over in the easy chair during these conversations like a lamentable piece of furniture, a garish lamp shade with too many frills bought on impulse, a crooked plant stand. He was a fellow conspirator, a partner in crime; but more than that, he had spurred her mother on, caused her to commit a felony in the eyes of God. What they had done together was a vague, repulsive sort of act that was somehow a prerequisite for Marian's deliverance from her former situation. She had been the cook in a logging camp, way out in the bush. When Marian said *the bush* Elsie imagined row upon row of bark-hardened trees, their branches exploding into impenetrable tufts of needles.

"I signed on at the logging camp after running away from my foster home," Marian told Elsie. "I had to." Elsie knew why; her mother told her the story regularly to ensure that she understood the presence of evil in the world. The home was the last in a long succession of moth-eaten shacks with sullen-mouthed women and sinful men who made Marian sit in their laps. Sometimes these men wore sweaty undershirts with soup-stains on the front, or launched into coughing fits when they tried to laugh. Most of them had devices to keep Marian in line: broken bottles, cigarettes. One even had a horse-whip.

Marian snuck out as soon as she turned sixteen, into the wilds of the Northern B.C. bush, and the rest, she told Elsie, is history. "If I thought the foster homes were bad, the camp was ten times worse," she would say. "I had to lock myself in the tool shed, or the kitchen cellar when the men were back. I had to make sure never to go into the pantry alone."

"Why not?" Elsie would say.

"They were after me. The men."

The men Marian talked about were burlier versions of Paul Bunyan, with five-day beards and protruding eyebrows and mud-soaked tartan shirts; they wore dungarees with suspenders; they had woollen caps, and steel-toed boots that laced right up to their knees. These loggers formed Elsie's first impression of men: swarthy, raucous, waiting in ambush for women behind sagging, leaky outhouses. They were like wild beasts that had to be fended off; they were relentless.

Elsie knew her father was one of these men. He worked at the camp supervising the construction of roads. He sat down at a long wooden table hewn from logs every single night to eat Marian's dinner with the rest of the rabble.

"There was only one way out," Marian said, suggesting that her entrapment was imminent, that she was a hunted animal who graciously surrendered. Her marriage to Clifford was a surrender. Ever since then she had been repenting.

Elsie's grandmother lived in North Vancouver, a faraway place with trees like towers and water bigger than anything Elsie had ever seen. As far as Elsie could tell, everything about North Vancouver was bigger: the trees, the water, the hills, the buildings. Even the bridges were bigger, spanning bigger rivers, with bigger fish that travelled bigger distances before they washed up on riverbanks, gasping for air. Elsie knew all this because of the pictures, and because her father talked about his home on *the coast*: the place where he grew up and where his mother still lived. Sometimes he spoke so mournfully about *the coast* that Elsie thought he said *the ghost*, but then he told her stories about sawmills and air raids, and she remembered he was far from home.

Elsie gets off from school at three forty-five and heads down Church Street to her parents' house. She doesn't live far from the school or the chapel, which are built on the same lot, out of the same brown brick and white mortar. On the front of one of the buildings are large white letters: *Our Lady of the Immaculate Conception Elementary School.* Yellow blobs the size of silver dollars stain the C and E where someone has thrown eggs at the wall in a public display of malice aimed at the school's principal, Mr. Jarvis. Elsie knows this because the student was suspended this morning for three days, and his story was all over the school yard by lunch time. The second building is taller, more foreboding; it slopes up into the Brimstock skyline—an octagonal vaulted ceiling with a central arch—to a point where an eight-foot-high cross sprouts out of its middle and into the sunset, just like on Calvary Hill. Smaller white letters proclaim *Catholic Church of Our Lady, Welcome for Worship.*

Behind both of these buildings is Elsie's grade two classroom, a beige portable set on blocks to keep its floor from rotting. The number of parents wanting to send their children to Our Lady Elementary is on the rise again. Portions of the school's population have overflowed to the parking lot, having to make do with outdoor classrooms that have no shelving space and an extra long trek to the bathroom. There have been complaints from some of the parents that children will catch cold moving to and from these portables in the wintertime, that they will be vulnerable to strangers with candy bars who loiter in parking lots waiting for opportunities to cart them off, but Mr. Jarvis just shrugs his shoulders and smiles piously, saying in his charitable voice: *We can't deny any deserving child. We'll just have to make provisions.* There are four of these outdoor classrooms now. *Outdoor,* said Marian, *like a flock of outhouses.*

As Elsie rounds the corner of her own street she notices her father's blue Lincoln in the driveway: he is home early today. If she is lucky—although she isn't supposed to believe in luck because everything is God's will—her mother will be out shopping. She speeds up her feet, strapped tightly into plain brown sandals with three sets of buckles bought from the Ladies' department at the Biway. The noise of her legs running inside her leotards is *swish swish swish*, the same sound made by the wings of crows when they fly overhead at low altitudes—*Caw,* thinks Elsie as she soars homeward, *Caw Caw.*

Elsie has good reasons to be glad that her father is home. When she and her mother are alone after school Marian sometimes puts Elsie in the cellar. She says the cellar is punishment for being bad, and that it is the place

[75]

where Elsie should sit by herself and *think about her disobedience*. Because of her mother's plans for her future, Elsie has to learn to be better than other children her age. She is going to be trained at a seminary in Montreal when she is older, in a grey stone school where they teach you how to interpret visions. Elsie's mother has settled on this school because, somewhat repugnantly, she has had to admit that Elsie doesn't have any visions of her own—God picks toddlers and old toothless ladies, many who can't speak a word of English—but lucky for her, there is a need for an educated few, well-versed in the workings of Revelations and the Last Judgement. When visionaries are confused by their messages from God, people like Elsie will step in to offer well-informed guidance. She will be useful after all, says Marian.

Elsie knows something that her mother does not, something she doesn't want to tell: she does have her own visions.

The cellar is a dank room that smells of mud puddles and old socks. All the old houses in Brimstock have cellars for the storing of root vegetables and jars of preserves gleaned from fields along the Credit River, the river that used to run on the edge of town, but now runs through the centre. Some of the fields still exist, at the end of Elsie's street where the road dead-ends and turns into a narrow path; the rest have been chopped up into smaller lots and converted into front lawns with garden gnomes and white wire fencing, or paved into parking lots for the IGA grocery store. Elsie has heard from girls at school that some of the cellars are connected to one another by a labyrinth of low, dimly lit tunnels constructed for bootlegging alcohol. She doesn't know what the word *bootlegging* means, but suspects, like anything carried on under an inadequate lighting source, that it must be shameful.

Her own cellar is plain, with raw plank shelving that her mother sometimes uses in a pinch for storing jars of raspberry jam leftover from the annual Christmas bazaar. A rickety set of stairs painted in flaking yellow enamel leads down from the kitchen to the cellar floor which is made of dirt, unevenly packed to a dull shine and criss-crossed all over by hairline cracks; out of these cracks black ants crawl up and into the musty air carrying unwieldy crumbs or pieces of what Elsie thinks must be turds from the old barnyard. The walls of the cellar are rock, glued haphazardly together with a paste of clay, straw, and cement. Elsie has been told by her father that the rock was hauled by hand to their homesite from the banks of the Credit River *by the sweat of an old man's back.* She has yet to figure out which old man he is referring to.

When she is banished to the cellar for misbehaving, Elsie sits on the top stair with her back to the door and imagines she is in a bright meadow full of wild daisies. She is supposed to be praying for her salvation, and she does try. She even folds her hands together and says to herself: *I'm sorry Lord. I will try harder to be good.* What her mother has in mind is ten Hail Marys and a Glory Be, a good decade of the rosary, but all Elsie can ever remember is the ending, which frightens her a little: *As it was in the beginning, is now, and ever shall be, world without end, Amen.* Perhaps if the lights were on she would have an easier time.

She uses the image of the meadow and the wild dai-

[77]

sies to quiet the noise that comes up from the foot of the cellar stairs in periodic blasts. The sound is the furnace, groaning on and off in its dark corner next to the plank shelves; the sound is also the furnace of hell, stoked by a horde of demons who grin out of skull-like mouths and dance around on long tapering legs that terminate in claws. They are waiting around for the weighing-in of Elsie's soul. Marian has told Elsie that this will happen on Judgement Day, which could be any day at all really, you never know when. On that day, if Elsie's heart is heavy with sin, she will tip the scales and the demons will jump with glee. Then they will pounce. The scene of the Last Judgement is carved out in oak relief on the tympanum above the main doors of the Church of Our Lady. There demons stuff the bodies of the damned head-first into the furnaces of hell; they pierce the necks of cowering sinners who have been stripped of their clothes and fork them over their shoulders into the fire.

Elsie tries hard not to be bad so that she will not have to sit on the cellar stairs and listen to the hissing of the demons; but somehow she misses the cues. If she smiles at the wrong time, when her mother is scolding her, Marian calls her a *cheeky girl*. If she doesn't respond at all, her mother gets mad at her for daydreaming. *You have to learn. You're not like other girls.* Elsie wants to be like other girls, but she doesn't tell her mother so.

Sometimes when Elsie is in the cellar she has visions. She doesn't fall to the ground in ecstasy like the girls from Garabandal in Spain, whose frozen, rapturous smiles she has seen in her mother's books on miracles; she doesn't stiffen up with rigor mortis, or become heavier than lead. Instead she sits candidly on the top

[78]

step of the cellar stairs with her hands folded in her lap, and listens with her heart in her mouth. What she sees is an apparition, a ball of light no bigger than a lawn jockey, with a dense horizontal smudge at its centre in the shape of an upset parenthesis. The ball appears out of thin air, emanating a blue-green light, and descends toward Elsie emitting a sound like a spinning top, but louder. Loud enough to drown out the furnace. The drone of the apparition hurts Elsie's ears; it pokes at her ear-drums like the bristles of an inflexible toothbrush, but she doesn't dare block out the noise. She knows from school that the apparition can only mean one thing: the Virgin Mary has chosen Elsie to be her emissary.

Whenever the Virgin Mary appears on earth, she is looking for someone to pass on a message. Elsie has been told about Bernadette at Lourdes, the poor girl who saw Our Lady eighteen times before digging into the ground and finding a hidden spring of blessed water; and about the three shepherd children at Fatima who were given three secrets of the future. She has also seen the girls of Garabandal, Spain, on television in their trances, walk-ing back and forth over rough-hewn ground without looking at their feet, and images of Our Lady delivering her warnings: *Pray! Pray a great deal and make sacri-fices for sinners, for many souls go to hell from not hav-ing someone to pray and make sacrifices for them!*

In her mother's books visionaries are ordered by the divine word of Mary to reveal what they have seen. They are told, somewhat sternly Elsie thinks, to share the messages they have been given with everyone around them: family, friends and, more importantly, with priests, who will carry forth their communications and spread

them through their sermons to the world. Elsie, however, keeps the messages to herself. She believes that
God would understand, in this particular case, because
the Virgin's words seem to be meant for Elsie alone: *Try
harder,* she says, her voice crackling with static like a
shortwave radio. *You must try harder.*

Elsie thinks the Virgin must be referring to the way
she behaves, or misbehaves, as her mother says, when
she tells her to *try harder.* She is entreating her to do
better, because she knows about all the times Elsie has
been bad—forgetting to wash her hands after digging a
hole in the garden and then putting them in her mouth,
or peeling back the wallpaper in her bedroom to see what
was there before. She would know all these things because the Virgin is full of magic, and can see everything
that happens to her children on earth. This is one of the
reasons Marian tells Elsie never to touch herself, not
even in the bathroom, because for everything she does
there is a holy witness. *Do you want Our Lady to see
you doing that?* she says, curling her upper lip. *You better smarten up!* Elsie wants to try harder like the Virgin
says, and she does, helping out her mother in the kitchen
and around the house, bringing her father his sports
pages, but something always goes wrong; she slips up,
and then she ends up back in the cellar. *Try harder,* the
Virgin says in her quavering voice. *I will,* Elsie replies. *I
will.* She wants to please Our Lady more than anything
else in the world.

But today when Elsie comes home from school, her father is sitting on the front step, two jumps down from
the screen door. In his hand is a glass tumbler with

squares etched diagonally onto its surface. A dark liquid bubbles inside.

"Elsie, there's someone here to see you," he says.

Elsie's head tightens, as if someone is pulling her hair: a man, a bad man—the kind her mother told her would come up from the earth when she misbehaved—a relative of Lucifer and the fallen angels. She drew on the blackboard during lunch hour: pictures of girls from her class holding hands with boys, which wasn't even her idea in the first place, but now she's responsible.

"Hello Elsie," A woman says as she comes out of the front door holding a smaller glass. Her hair is coppery brown with grey wisps; she has it pinned up with tortoiseshell barrettes into loose bundles on the sides of her head. She is wearing a striped vest knitted from earth-toned wool, and a russet-coloured pair of slacks. "I haven't seen a picture of you since you were just this big," she says, making the shape of a watermelon with her arms. "I live in North Vancouver—all the way in B.C." Elsie doesn't remember ever meeting this woman before. She doesn't seem familiar. She certainly doesn't remember ever being in a place called B.C.

Bee Cee. The woman says the words like notes in a song. Elsie can see them on the keyboard: *B* way at the top of the scale next to a black key, and *C*, all the way down at the bottom under the thumb in root position. *Every Good Boy* for the right hand, and *All Cars* for the left. She is just learning to play the piano, but she can already hear the notes in her head.

"Elsie," says Clifford. "This is my mother. Your grandmother. She's going to be staying with us for a while. "

Elsie looks up. "Are you Violet?" she says. The woman

[81]

isn't anything like Elsie imagined. Marian has a list of words for Violet, which she uses periodically when her face is red: long-winded, vulgar, faithless, inconstant, fallen, profane, unsanctified, reprobate, agnostic (one of the harder ones), slack, loose. The last two are the only ones Elsie understands; they have something to do with coming apart at the edges, hanging down. *Loose* particularly refers to Violet's morals, Marian says, and other things Elsie doesn't know anything about. Because of the words, Elsie has always imagined her grandmother to be something like a doll riddled with leaks, her seams breaking open in tender places, trailing sawdust or pinto beans in long lines down the hallway. She imagined her head, deprived of the necessary support to keep it upright by a flaccid neck, lolling forward onto her chest. How would she see where she was going?

But this woman laughs, throwing her head back so that Elsie can see her teeth. They are lined up inside her mouth like newly polished piano keys. She bends down to Elsie's level, grinning, swirling the liquid around in her glass. She doesn't seem to have any trouble moving around. "In the flesh," is what she says.

Elsie wants to know what *in the flesh* means, but she knows better than to ask Marian. With her mother she has a fifty-percent chance of getting in trouble. Flesh can refer to two things, only one of which is any good: sacred, in the case of the sacrament of the Eucharist where children over age six partake in the eating of Jesus' body at Holy Mass—and sinful, as in *sins of the flesh*. Elsie is not clear on the first one, and has some inklings about possible examples of the second. Either way she sees cuts of flesh stacked up in abattoirs and dark basements, or fresh carcasses strung up feet-first on chains in butcher shop windows, their anonymous arms plucked or skinned to a soft melton pink, reaching down towards the floor. *Help me,* they say, their gaping mouths heinously absent. Elsie wants to, but she doesn't know how.

Upstairs Violet has made herself at home: a fold-out cot has been arranged in Elsie's bedroom next to her bedside table with the Virgin Mary night light; she has been given clean white sheets and a chartreuse blanket with silk on the hem. At the head of the bed, on top of the eyelet-lace pillowcase, Violet's nightdress lies folded in a neat brown square ready for bed. In the bathroom a new lineup of creams and vitamin bottles appears on the counter. Elsie picks them up carefully: Nivea Hand Cream, Oil of Olay, Crest toothpaste, a gold watch with an elasticized metal wristband, plastic cases for soap and a toothbrush, Kleenex with an imprint of red lips—

"Elsie—"

She recoils; she was touching someone else's things. She has been told many times not to, but for some reason she forgot. *Naughty girl.*

"It's all right," Violet smiles. "You don't have to be sorry for being curious."

Elsie knows better than this. You must always be sorry. *Penitent,* is her mother's word, but it means the same thing.

"Here," Violet says, opening the blue jar with the words *Nivea Hand Cream* printed boldly on its surface. "Try some." Elsie takes some of the cream on her index finger and dabs it awkwardly onto her nose; it is thick and white like her father's car wax, but smells instead like vanilla beans.

[83]

"You have lovely skin, so smooth," says Violet. "I used to have skin like that once upon a time."

"You don't have red hair."

"What? Oh—" Violet extends her hand to help Elsie rub in the remainder of the cream. "No, you're right, although I'm not grey yet. That's the gift of having red hair when you're young. You turn into a brunette instead of an old lady."

"You're not old."

"Well, thank you for saying so. I don't feel old. But I used to have the most beautiful red curls. My father called me *the red devil*."

A bad name, Elsie thinks, erasing the words from her head as fast as she can. She is not supposed to remember those kinds of things because they might accidentally spill from her mouth and get her into trouble. Maybe Violet's father didn't like her very much.

"Your Uncle Russ had red hair too—but no one else in the family."

Elsie wants to change the subject, because her mother might overhear. From past conversations she has learned that having red hair is not always a good thing. "What is it like in B.C.?"

"Oh well," says Violet. "On the coast where I come from there are beautiful mountains with snow on the top. There is also the ocean where people can swim, and gigantic ships that pass under the bridge and into the inlet. We also have trees," she adds, "that are as tall as office buildings."

"Is it as nice as Brimstock?" says Elsie.

"Well," says Violet thinking. "Just about."

"Brimstock doesn't have any ocean, but we have our

church. I'm making my First Communion soon. Will you come and see me?"

"What will you be doing?"

I forget, thinks Elsie, but Violet should know, she's an adult. Maybe she's just testing. "I get to eat some bread. And from now on, whenever we go to church, I get to eat the bread with my mother. Like everyone else except the babies."

"Well, perhaps I can eat some too."

Then it occurs to Elsie that her grandmother might be a heathen. Her heart sinks. "Are you Catholic?"

"No." Silence.

Then: "What are you?" She has to belong to something. Some of the other ones are almost Catholic.

"I'm Protestant dear."

What is Protestant? Elsie asks Marian after brushing her teeth and before prayers. Her mother is kneeling beside her on the orange shag rug in her bedroom, warming up for a reading from *Every Children's Bible;* tonight it will be Goliath getting a rock between the eyes. The picture that Elsie remembers best shows the fatal stone imbedded into his brow, his giant lips curled into a snarl of defeat. *Did she tell you she was a Protestant?* her mother snorts. *She's nothing of the sort.* This is the only answer she gets, before Marian launches into the Lord's Prayer. Elsie knows better than to ask again.

Marian is telling a story to Violet and Clifford over a dinner of glazed turnips and roast beef: how Elsie broke her arm when she was four years old. She does this periodically, when company is visiting, to make a point

[85]

about taking chances. The four of them are arranged around the table in the dining room which Elsie's mother insisted on using on account of the special occasion—which is Violet's first Sunday dinner in Brimstock—and which Violet said was "a fuss over nothing." In the centre of the table is a bouquet of daisies and sweet peas fresh from the market, flanked by two pewter candlesticks which commemorate one of Clifford and Marian's wedding anniversaries. The dimmer switch on the chandelier has been set on low to show off the candles, making everyone's face appear sinister, as if they were sharing ghost stories around a campfire.

Elsie knows there is supposed to be a moral in the story, but she hasn't yet been able to figure it out. She listens to her mother's voice which goes from airy and light to dark and hard-edged, and watches her left hand which clutches a butter knife. She is wearing one of her blue jacquard dresses with the cinched waists and respectable hemlines that come well past her knees. On her wrists are two copper bracelets, simple bands no more than two centimetres wide. They are medicinal, worn to ward off the pain of tendinitis, and are therefore acceptable forms of decoration.

As Marian speaks, Elsie notices she has missed some important parts of the story, naturally, because Elsie withheld them from her on purpose. If Elsie were to tell the story herself, using the third person like her mother, it would sound something like this:

This is how everything began: the arching Brimstock roadway lined with poplars on the windy side, a strip of grass growing down its middle. Elsie sits on a purple bicycle behind an older girl with pigtails who tells her to hold on to the chrome bar at the back of the banana seat with both hands. They push off the hard-packed dirt—or the girl does because Elsie's feet can't reach ground—and plummet forward as if falling off a mountain. Elsie feels wind move through her hair, sees a green ocean of alfalfa flecked with fireweed surround the bicycle. They swoop like seabirds at the earth: giant silver handle bars, sparkling plastic grips, purple-and-white streamers, the bell with the Canadian flag, ringing, ringing.

"Don't let go!" says the girl over her shoulder. Elsie hears *Don't* (the rushing and tickling of wind in her ears) *let* (plateaus of grass, evening primrose bobbing on dry stalks) *GO!*

Then sand grabs the tires. They sway too far, slow too quickly.

Elsie lets go of the bicycle; she soars upward, heavenward, the sun on her face. Her hands fan out into wings, her feet flutter-kick the air; she rises like a balloon. Her skirt is a parasol, but she doesn't think about anyone seeing her bare thighs. Something is calling her. She feels the warm hands of the sun, its warm heart throbbing in her own. She reaches up: *That's who you are, I know you.*

But the girl with pigtails screams. Elsie hears her and gulps for air. She tries pushing the sound away, but the girl is too loud. Too large. Fear enters her throat; it rages against her tonsils, presses hard on her tongue; it fills her like heavy water, rioting, demanding, until she has no choice but to swallow.

Now that it is in there, there is no way to get it out.

The warmth recedes, pulls away as Elsie falls, fast now,

towards the ground. *No.* She feels the slap of a fence on her shoulder, hears her arm crack.

"She loved that cast," says Marian to Violet and Clifford, wrapping up her own version of the story which Elsie has largely missed. "She coloured it with her crayons and drew bugs on it."

"They were animals," says Elsie, wanting to contribute out loud. "Two of each, for Noah." She remembers clearly the pairs of lions, zebras, dogs, and cats, done in blotched-up crayon across her forearm. The striped arc of colour had been a rainbow for the covenant, that soggy promise of safety from God. She'd needed security then, so she drew up her own bargain in Day-Glo greens and pinks: *Protection from bullies. From being wrong in school. From the girls change room. Please God. Amen.*

"You couldn't possibly remember. You were barely four years old."

How does she remember? The sensation of wind coursing through her hair, the vibrations from the wobbling vinyl seat; both are makeshift, unreliable memories, yet somehow vivid. Clearer, even, than events that came after. But the fear stuck with her like an extra toe or fingernail—unforgettable. It must have been lurking about for some time.

"You weren't allowed to ride bicycles yet. You didn't know how. I should have kept you inside with me."

What had she been doing on that purple bicycle? Had she expected to fly? She had. Otherwise she never would have gotten on. She knew what "no" meant. She had just not been afraid of it.

Marian reaches for the turnips and says matter-offactly, "Naughtiness is always paid for, you learned that in the end."

What Elsie learned was something different: sweats, blinding light, the lump forced down her throat like a spoonful of castor oil. She equated all these sensations with that memorable thing that struck her on the arm and broke her wrist, cleanly, like a china cup. Not the fading brown fence at the end of the road that slapped her in the shoulder and gave her slivers, that was only a disguise for what really caused her injury: fear. She learned about fear. She swallowed fear. Food for the demons.

After a dessert of lemon poppy-seed cake and strong dark tea, Elsie helps her mother clear away the dishes. This is Marian's favourite part of the meal: the putting of everything back in its place. Napkins in the cabinet drawers. Stainless steel pots with the heat-resistant handles in the corroding pull-out compartment under the oven. She cannot sit down and relax in front of the television until each plate has been scrubbed, each glass relieved of its circular lip-marks and fingerprints by the steaming, soapy water that she runs into the sink.

"It is very important," she says to Elsie, "To make sure everything is absolutely spotless. God loves cleanliness. To be clean is to be pure."

Elsie knows about purity; her mother gives her many lessons, checking her fingernails, the insides of her ears. She wants Elsie to glow like polished silverware, and gives her powder-blue face cloths to scrub the dirt from her limbs.

Purity involves other parts of the body as well. Marian speaks furtively about the offending instincts besotting some humans. Lowly feelings infecting their pelvises, dragging their souls through the mud. *Mud. Soiled.* The words suggest to Elsie a staining, an unremovable dirt. Her mother is charged with washing away the unpalatable muck that displeases God, battling single-handedly the onslaught of germs and contagion that might overtake their house.

Elsie knows that God doesn't like dirt, because in most pictures she sees of him, God is just a white light, a globe of brilliant illumination and empty space with a thundering voice; at other times he is a burning bush, or a bearded old man. Still later he is a bearded young man called Jesus who is also God's son. Elsie doesn't understand how God can be God, and God's son at the same time, but she knows better than to ask Marian. She also knows that God can do anything he wants, and that sometimes this includes dying. Every year when Elsie's class acts out the crucifixion at Easter time, the same thing happens. Jesus is nailed to the cross, and everyone around him—the Romans, the soldiers, the Zealots, the Pharisees, one of the thieves, and all the Jews—gloat and spit on him, except for a scant few who weep ferociously. Elsie weeps ferociously, because isn't she responsible for all this? Everyone tells her she is.

Sometimes God is also the Holy Spirit. In this case, when he is three different things at the same time—*the father, the son, and the Holy Spirit*—he is called the Trinity. This is even more complicated, because although God is Jesus' father, Mary was actually made pregnant by the Holy Spirit. When Elsie asked her mother if all babies were *conceived by the power of the Holy Spirit*, her mother said "All the good ones" and told her to wash the floor. The bad people who go to hell conceive babies by rubbing themselves together like two sticks. Elsie knows this from the boys at school; the resulting spark is a baby riddled full of sin. But even babies born from the Holy Spirit are sinful sometimes, *original sinners,* according to Father Thomas at Elsie's church. That is why he performs baptisms: to wash away their sins with holy water and give them a crack at heaven. Elsie knows all the time her mother spends washing their house has something to do with her family's salvation, so she does her best to help. She does not want to end up in purgatory with the politicians.

In the living room Violet and Clifford lounge in front of *The Tommy Hunter Show* drinking gin and tonics from wide frosted glasses. Elsie can hear them laughing out over the twangy guitar and chorus line hymn-sings.

Marian purses her lips at the noise. "There," she says sternly, closing a drawer. "Your father and Violet sound like a couple of hyenas."

Elsie knows her mother's anger has something to do with the gin and tonics. Up until Violet appeared, her father only drank alcohol from a cold metal flask which he kept hidden in the garage under the first layer of his toolbox. Elsie found him digging around in there last summer while she was looking for her inflatable plastic pool. It was a hot day, she wanted to swim. *Don't tell your mother,* he whispered to Elsie, eyes gleaming. Elsie already knew about whispering from school: sweaty confidences rasped out in dank boiler rooms; pleas for secrecy from sad-eyed pigtailed girls with limp baubles hanging from their heads like drawstrings. *Don't tell anyone you saw me down here. I'll give you my butter-scotch pudding.* Whispering meant deception, possibly sin. Elsie is not allowed to whisper.

But since Violet has arrived, Clifford has been drinking out in the open. *Oh, don't mind if I do,* he says tentatively, eyeing Marian when Violet suggests a taste of the gin she bought at the Brimstock liquor store. They have a drink every day now: a gin and tonic, or a glass of port wine, usually at around five o'clock, the time that Violet calls *Happy Hour.* Only today there are different rules because it is Friday. Today they have a second drink after dinner.

Marian has been invited to share in these drinks but she refuses politely with her mouth taut across her face. She only drinks wine which has been blessed by a priest once a year at church, and which is not wine at all, she explains to Elsie, but the real live blood of Jesus. Elsie witnesses the transformation of this simple wine into blood every Sunday at Mass. Doesn't she remember?

"Elsie, you are missing a good story," Violet says popping her head into the kitchen, around the stuccoed wall next to the refrigerator. Her face is flushed from laughing. "Your father is telling me about the time he snuck into a private wedding reception only to see that his ex-girlfriend was the bride!" Violet is wearing an elegant cream-coloured blouse with a drooping bow on the collar. Her face is powdered with a pale, beige-coloured pancake to eliminate the freckles.

"Elsie has not completed her chores," Marian replies acidly, cutting into Violet's enthusiasm.

"Oh. I apologize." She turns to leave.

"And Violet." Marian's words pull Violet back into the kitchen, all the way this time.

"Yes?" Violet's eyebrows are raised: two narrow caterpillars accentuated by an amber eyebrow pencil.

"Don't you think those kinds of stories are inappropriate for Elsie?" Marian's voice is cunning now, offering up a chance for salvation as it so often does to Elsie, if only she knew the right answer, the one her mother wanted to hear.

Violet thinks for a moment, then shrugs her silky shoulders. "No actually, no I don't."

Marian picks up her cloth and resumes wiping the counter. The chance for salvation has passed. "No. I didn't think you would."

Elsie looks at her grandmother who stands framed by the doorway to the living room. Her smile has wilted to a blank stare. Both of them know that was a trick question.

Elsie doesn't think back to her introduction to fear very often; she just can't remember a time without it. There were things to be loved and cherished, as Marian said: mothers and fathers, priests, nuns, Jesus, lambs, anything newborn (except for the baby birds nesting in the mailbox), and the Bible. Some of the things for loving and cherishing, Elsie found questionable: Jesus' blood, because it looked painful but everyone seemed to drink it anyway, and Father Thomas who had sour nut-breath, and a flaking itchy skin disease he called *eczema*. Everything else, Marian said, was to be feared.

School was a pit of fear: the washroom, the change room, the upper grade boys with peach fuzz and swollen pockets full of race cars. They had gigantic, hurling mouths, flared nostrils; they tortured preying mantises by severing their abdomens, and played Bloody Knuckles in the parking lot. On alternate Thursdays the whole school filed into the gymnasium for a general assembly; Elsie's class sat cross-legged in the front row next to pacing red-eyed Mr. Jarvis with the circles of sweat under his arms. He wore pointed leather shoes that clomped on the gymnasium tiles; he used the strap. Elsie had never seen anyone speak like Mr. Jarvis: terse, haunting comments that scared you to your boots without him yelling a word.

In her own classroom she was more at home. Elsie was one of the lucky children who had been in Miss Pollard's split grade one and two classroom for two years in a row. The class was halfway down one of Our Lady's narrow hallways, with a tissue paper reproduction of the dove of peace on the door. Beneath the dove were the words *Let the little children come*—fashioned from carefully bent pipe cleaners.

Miss Pollard didn't dress like Marian; she wore miniskirt jumpers made from denim, ribbed high-necked pullovers that elongated her arms and made them look delicate. Some of her clothes were slapped all over with colourful patches cut from corduroy, while others had cartoon flowers, mountainscapes, or teacups along the bodice which exploded into mellow frills at the wrists and throat. Like most of the teachers, Miss Pollard had shoulder-length hair that she parted in the middle and ironed flat, except that her hair was blonde, with no bangs; she wore a red velvet hair band that scooped into the strands behind her ears, showing a brilliant stripe of crimson just above the crown of her head.

Elsie wanted to be one of the children who sat in her lap during story time; she wanted to hold her hand at recess while she patrolled the playground in her green kerchief and full-length suede coat with the furry collar. But Elsie was too afraid. Fear pushed on her heart, it trapped her. Nap time, wash time, bathroom break, all cause for alarm. Someone might open the door—it had no lock like home—someone might look up her skirt and see her underwear.

In the morning Miss Pollard led Songs and Exercises. Everyone sizzled on the musty orange carpet pretending to be a piece of bacon in a cast-iron frying pan, or rolled over and over like a soccer ball, the girls holding their skirts between their legs. She launched the daily sing-song with complicated finger plays, making her hands into sea turtles, wet spiders, yawning apple blossoms. She could form a perfect "O" with her mouth, saying, "Good MO-rning everyone."

When Miss Pollard prayed she looked like the Virgin Mary, clothed in flouncy blue, her hair a golden halo shining around her face. She bent her head, brought her milky fingers together and clasped them, each between the other, aloft for all to see. She did this silently, joyously, as if in a commercial for dish soap. Elsie had seen her own mother pray, but never like that. Marian prayed on her knees, arching her back so sharply that her head almost touched the floor; she wrung her hands, pounded her chest, and pleaded in a wavering voice, "Thy will be done, my Lord." When Elsie saw Marian praying she knew her mother was being punished for something, just as she herself was often in the throes of punishment. She knew she would have to be extra good, *or else*. Back to the cellar.

Sometimes Elsie pretended Miss Pollard was her

mother. She imagined they had been separated at birth, which could happen easily enough considering the state of the world, and that she—Elsie—had been delivered to Marian and Clifford by accident. At some point in the future the mistake would be fixed and Miss Pollard would whisk her off to live in her apartment above the Tank and Tummy variety store. The only problem that Elsie had yet to iron out was that Miss Pollard had no husband, and God only gave babies to husbands and wives.

Today is the day Elsie has to tell Miss Pollard the name of the godparent who will be standing next to her on the day that she makes her First Communion. Elsie's class has been preparing all year for the ceremony: they will line up at the front of the church to take their vows, then eat the small disks of bread for the first time. First Communion is an important event.

Secretly Elsie hopes Violet will stand in as her godmother. When Elsie was born Marian did not know anyone who could fill the role of moral provider as well as herself, and being an orphan, she had no real family to choose from (Clifford's family did not count because they were all too far away). *Why take chances?* she said to Elsie, *I was dealing with your soul.*

Elsie has always regretted the absence of this kind of figure from her life. She imagines a godparent to be someone with a direct link to heaven, someone with light billowing from his or her body, points of divinity arranged neatly over their forehead like the Statue of Liberty. She has heard other children talk about their own godparents, the presents that they dole out like luminous year-round Santa Clauses: shiny black shoes with single instep straps and golden buckles, crowns of lace with fluttering lavender ribbons, gold earrings in the shapes of miniature crosses, lockets, gloves, pocket Bibles and mother-of-pearl rosaries. Elsie tries not to be envious. Envy is one of the seven deadly sins.

Violet is the only one in Elsie's life that comes close to what she imagines a godparent to be like. Caught in the sunset, her bejewelled hair could almost be a halo. And she does bring presents, although they are mostly little girls' socks tatted around the edges with lace, or hardcover *Nancy Drew* mystery books which Marian confiscates and puts on the top shelf of the bookcase. Violet says that Elsie needs some spice added to her life, as though she were a pot of chili.

Elsie reminds herself to ask Miss Pollard about Violet after she has finished marking the class' morning spelling dictation. She can see her at her desk now, her legs crossed, her shoulders pressed into perfectly rounded corners, writing comments on their papers like "Stupendous Work!" or "What a speller!" in green felt-tipped markers. Sometimes Miss Pollard reminds Elsie of Teresa of Avila.

In the meantime, Elsie has ten minutes to play until the rest of the students are finished eating. She is always the first to finish her lunch and excuse herself from her desk near the blackboard then head for the back of the classroom where the toys are kept on plywood shelves. This is because Elsie has told Miss Pollard she is a fast eater, which is mostly true; she does eat fast when she likes the food—peanut butter banana rolls, granola squares with chocolate chips, even cheddar cheese on crackers—but she never gets these things. Instead Marian packs jam sandwiches and an apple. The apple is always a Granny Smith pounded all over with bruises, and the jam sandwich has always seeped through the bread as though it were a wad of white Kleenex. Elsie opens her lunchbox and nibbles off the crusts, then closes the lid and puts up her hand. If this was Friday, the day of abstinence, she would be even faster: on Friday she doesn't eat anything at all.

"Elsie you *are* a quick eater," says Miss Pollard. "Make sure your desk is neat, okay?" She winks one of her sparkling eyes and Elsie feels a warm liquid bubble up inside her. This is the oldest grade at Our Lady taught by Miss Pollard. How will Elsie survive next year? She thinks about this all the time.

At the back of the room beside the coat hooks marked with name tags, Elsie hauls a Tupperware washing tub from one of the shelves. The tub is mustard yellow, full of cast-off ceramic and porcelain tiles from a local bathroom shop. Elsie likes to arrange them in a flat rectangle on the floor around her knees, stroking the smooth ones with her fingertips. Her favourites are the double-glazed navy ones that she can look into and see her face; they feel like satin, or what Elsie imagines silkworms to be like. She stacks some into cubes, supporting them against each other like cards. One day she will live in a house entirely made from tiles.

After five minutes of stacking, unstacking, sorting, and repiling, Elsie notices that the tiles in her hands have changed from white to blue-green. "That's funny," she thinks, searching the pile. "I chose the white ones on purpose."

Then she hears the humming.

She raises her head and sees the ball of light descending towards her, floating down like a lightning bug in summer darkness. As it falls, the brightness of the light intensifies, cloaking the room in illumination.

Try harder Elsie, the voice says. *You must try harder.*

Elsie is scared. How does the Virgin know her name? She has never used it before, not once, not even when Elsie was caught playing in the garbage. Not only that, but she has never appeared to Elsie in front of other people.

I haven't done anything bad this time, have I? Elsie thinks, looking around. *I'm not even in the cellar.*

Try harder, try harder.

Elsie stares at the ball of light, then at her classroom. The students are still at their desks eating lunch; Miss Pollard is writing something on the blackboard with green chalk. None of them appears to see anything.

Try harder, the voice says again, this time louder, more pronounced. Elsie thinks the voice is getting angry. *You are not listening. If you don't try harder you will surely be punished.*

I am trying, Elsie thinks, frightened, on the verge of tears. *I am trying.* She puts down the tiles and forms her hands into a lock of prayer.

Not hard enough, the voice says. *You must try harder.*

Then the light wanes and the tiles are white again. Elsie lets the air out of her lungs and realizes at the same time that she is wetting her pants. She feels the warm moisture climbing her leotards, staining the back of her overalls with a dark ring—but she can't stop. She has done it. She sits up one inch off the carpet and sees the circular imprint of her own bum stamped into the carpet nap like a gigantic boot. She sits back down.

"Come on Elsie, recess," says a girl in a yellow cardigan.

Elsie doesn't move. She has never done this before, *never*. She doesn't even wet her bed—hasn't since she can remember.

Somewhere in the school yard the outside bell rings, causing everyone to spill from their desks and slap on their coats. Boys run outside without hats, their zippers gaping open to the wind; girls pull on boots, scarves, earmuffs, and run after them, shrieking, their mittens dangling like pendulums. Cold air surges through the classroom door.

"Elsie?" Miss Pollard's voice comes from the corner, approaching. "Elsie, aren't you going out for recess?"

Elsie shakes her head *No. Thank you.*

"Well, why not?"

Nothing.

"Is something wrong?"

Elsie stares at the floor, her face flushed and hot. She can't tell Miss Pollard—too shameful. She has done the unthinkable and can't tell anyone. And she won't lie. She can only be quiet, sit with her shame.

"Elsie you must answer me. I will not ask you again."

Again, nothing. A wet stare.

"Perhaps you'd rather be alone?" Miss Pollard's voice is angry now. "To think about your misbehaviour? I can leave you here until you are ready to apologize while I am outside with the rest of the class."

Elsie makes no reply and braces herself for punishment. Instead Miss Pollard's voice softens. She bends down and puts a hand on her shoulder. "Honestly Elsie, I don't know what to do with you. You are so intense sometimes. So serious. You have to tell me what is wrong so I can help you."

A tear rolls down Elsie's cheek. How can she explain?

"Is there something wrong at home? I know you love your mother Elsie, but sometimes the people we love do strange things. Remember that, Elsie. Your mother is a good woman, but she also has her own problems."

Elsie doesn't know what to say. What kind of problems is Miss Pollard talking about? Marian takes care of Elsie, that is her job. She teaches her how to be good. Elsie is the one with the problems. Silence or words— either one would be betrayal.

"Well," says Miss Pollard rising. "That's your choice then. I'll see you when you're ready."

Elsie watches Miss Pollard slide on her coat and leave by the front door. There are cramps in her legs tracing their circuitous path to her heart; she feels the pain stop as she stretches and wiggles her feet, but her heart is still broken. Marian would have locked her up for that silence, seen it as evidence of lies, of cheekiness. Silence is the way Elsie deals with her mother's badgering. She does not yet know how to blow her stack.

When everyone is gone she moves the washing tub full of tiles onto the wet spot. She puts on her coat, tugs on her boots, and stands outside against the brick wall. So much for asking Miss Pollard about Violet. In ten minutes the seat of her overalls is frozen solid.

9

Elsie's bedroom is at the beginning of the hallway, across from the bathroom. Violet likes the location because she has to get up several times during the night to relieve herself. "I'm not as fit as I used to be," she says. And: "I can hardly hold a cup of tea." For this reason Elsie makes sure to switch on her Virgin Mary night light; in pitch blackness Violet will have a hard time manoeuvring herself around Elsie's pine blanket box filled with her mother's homemade granny-square afghans, not to mention the pressed-wood desk with the world map on its surface. With Mary's head and arms lit up like a glow bug, Violet will be able to see halfway down the hall.

"If you like, you can sleep with my lamb," Elsie offers. Her grandmother has been having trouble falling asleep, and once she is there, she has problems staying asleep until morning. She usually wakes up at about two-thirty and goes downstairs for a mug of warm milk. Perhaps some company will help her along.

"Well thanks Elsie. Maybe I will." Violet takes the

plush lamb from Elsie's outstretched arm and settles back into the blankets and sheets of the fold-out cot. Her hair is rolled tightly into black wire curlers held in place with pink and green bobby pins. Elsie's own hair is done up in rags, twisted first into spirals by her mother, then bound on the ends by the torn up remnants of old stockings. In the morning she will have a head full of ringlets.

"A couple of beauties, that's what we are," says Violet. "If Prince charming walks in here tonight he'll get quite a fright."

In the night Violet gets out of bed and goes out the door. Elsie can hear her soft corned feet padding down the stairs and into the kitchen on their way to the refrigerator. She hates when her grandmother gets up like this, because it means that she is alone again, back in her old bedroom, the one that feels like a black hole. She starts to imagine things: shifting curtains covered in moonlit dust and the fine grey bodies of spiders, patterns of darkness cast onto the floor by her sedate bedroom furniture. Someone has left the louvered closet doors open again, their infinite rectangles gaping like a hungry set of jaws, like a portal to the underworld, a direct connection to the cellar.

Elsie wants to get up too, but a strange force keeps her pinned to her bed, ties her to the headboard with lengths of invisible cordage. She feels the demons lurching around her room now that her grandmother is not there to protect her. Released from their place in the cellar by the open closet doors, they dance belligerently on her windowsill, and on top of her world map desk. She also sees their fangs. The only safe place is in the glow of the Virgin's illuminated face. Elsie picks up the night light and moves toward the door. She feels the golden warmth coming from Our Lady's heart strengthening her resolve; her essence spills out onto Elsie's hands, making puddles between her knuckles. But she must be busy tonight, Elsie thinks, because as soon as she gets as far as the door, the light goes out.

Elsie runs down the stairs, hurtling her body head-long into nothingness. Behind her the demons follow at a close pace, leaving a charred smell in the air from where they burn the carpet with their incubus feet. She runs straight into the kitchen where her grandmother sits at the table. Above her head a ceiling lamp casts a beam of light at the floor.

"Elsie," Her grandmother says, startled. "Elsie, what's wrong?"

Elsie looks behind her to see if the demons have been bold enough to come into the kitchen, but sees no sign. They are afraid of her grandmother.

"Did you have a nightmare?"

Now Elsie notices her grandmother's face: blotchy and red, like a collection of sores strung together by skin and fine wrinkles. Her lips are loosely arranged in the centre below her nose, as if they have been used to sop up a spill and freshly wrung out. In her hand are the remains of a balled-up Kleenex.

"Yes," she says, because she can't think of a better way to explain.

Violet motions for Elsie to join her at the table. Some of the curlers on her head have come loose and are dan-gling down over her ears. They are both silent for a moment, then Violet speaks. "We're quite a pair, the two of us. We've got to learn to stare our demons right in the face."

Elsie has never been told anything like this before, especially not by an adult. Her grandmother knows about the demons? And what's more, they are after her too? She stares at the table and waits for Violet to finish her milk, wondering what she can say. When they get back upstairs Violet helps Elsie plug her night light back into the socket. She helps her arrange her bed covers into a semblance of neatness, ignoring the dark marks on the carpet that Elsie knows will be gone by morning.

In the evenings after school Elsie goes for walks with her grandmother to the end of her street where the road ends in a path through the farmer's field. The field is covered in tall, stellate grasses with exploding seed heads and wart-shaped growths that her grandmother calls tumours.

"They're like a plant cancer," she says, walking along the path. "If you open them up with a knife you'll see a whole bunch of worms in there eating away at the plant."

Elsie dislikes the idea of tumours. Who wants to have worms eating them up? She has seen the pallid men and women sitting off to the side during mass in pews reserved for the sick and dying; they have tumours in their lungs, in their brains; they are too feeble to rise for communion so the priest must leave his place in front of the big red Bible and place the bread directly on their tongues.

"Did Uncle Russ have cancer?" Elsie asks. The thought just occurred to her. "Is that how he died?"

"No," Violet says. "Your Uncle Russ died in a car crash. He was just sixteen."

A teenager, thinks Elsie, who has been warned.

They follow the muddy path to a place where the river bends gradually into patches of grey rock. Elsie has heard her father call this line of stone the *Niagara Escarpment*, which makes her believe that the destination of the river is the dreaded Niagara Falls, the place where heathens and crazy people ride the jagged lurching cascades in nothing but a barrel. She herself never swims in the river for fear of getting swept all the way to Buffalo.

When they reach the concrete bridge jutting out across the water Elsie decides they are far enough away from the house to ask the question she has been saving up. "Why did Uncle Russell have red hair?"

Violet turns around to look Elsie in the eye, and for a moment, Elsie feels as if she should know the answer. In her grandmother's hands is a willow twig, bent in half. Violet starts walking again. "Well Elsie, it has something to do with genetics. I don't know that much about it, except that I was his mother, so I suppose he got it from me."

Elsie understands how things like this can be passed down from generation to generation. At school they are learning about attached and unattached earlobes. "But my dad has brown hair, and so does Uncle Lawrence. You were their mother too."

"Well, it doesn't always come through in everyone you know. It's not as clear as all that. Anyone can produce a redheaded child providing they have the right genes. Which is lucky for me, because those kinds of things used to matter a lot more to people than they do now."

Elsie is confused by this last comment, but she doesn't

say so. This is as far as she has ever gotten on the subject of her Uncle Russ and she is afraid that if she asks too many questions, her grandmother might decide she is being nosy.

"Russ was just a different sort all round," says Violet. Her voice is jagged now, the way Elsie's gets when she has been in the cellar for a long time. "He had his own way of doing things, and being the oldest, he had a harder time of it. He was in love with risking his life, which ended up being his downfall."

Elsie knows about downfalls, there are lots of them in the Bible: Sodom and Gomorrah, Lot's disobedient wife, Delilah, and of course Eve, to name a few. Downfalls are bad and always result in more or less the same thing: total destruction, or life as a pillar of salt. If permitted to carry on in human form, the lives of the fallen are usually overshadowed by excruciating pain. They are lucky to get away with a body covered in boils.

Elsie stops walking because she has figured out her grandmother's secret: Russ wasn't conceived by the Holy Spirit, but some human man, perhaps Violet's dead husband. Even worse, Russ was conceived by the devil. He whittled his way into Violet's womb and out popped Russ, red as the fires of hell. Violet herself may be a direct descendant—what did her father call her, *my red-devil?* That would explain why Marian's face darkens when Violet is around. She is afraid of getting infected.

"Well Elsie, shall we turn around?" Violet stands at the bank of the river, looking down into her shimmering reflection. The water is rushing with spring run-off, swelling up and over the edges and into the surrounding field.

"O.K.," Elsie replies. When her grandmother's back is once again turned, Elsie takes a handful of water and splashes it in her direction, hoping that in the absence of real holy water, a muddy river will do.

"Oh," says Violet. "It feels like rain."

Elsie is sure that God will understand.

On the second Sunday of Violet's visit Elsie stands at the front of the church with Marian's hand on her shoulder. She wears her good white dress with white knee socks and brown sandals; her hair has been brushed flat and curled towards her face with a hot iron. On the back of her neck are the burn marks from when Elsie forgot to hold still. Next to her, on either side, are the other boys and girls from Elsie's class lined up with their godparents. Some of the girls, the Italian ones, wear long lace dresses to their ankles and starched veils attached to their heads with pins; their shoes are gleaming, polished that morning with the chalky white brushes that they use to brighten their ice skates in winter. They wear white lace gloves with two sets of pearl buttons sewn along the wrists, and seamless leotards made from silk. Around their necks are golden crosses. The boys wear suits: reversible polyester, or itchy tweed. They have their hair cut short, their bangs done straight across using a ruler and a pair of sewing scissors. Their godfathers are larger versions of themselves, with bigger, itchier suits, and ties long enough to use as blindfolds in Blindman's Bluff. The godmothers are different. They wear colours: magenta, aquamarine. Most of them have hats with jaunty brims; shoes like mint candies, pointed or open-toed. They wear tan leather gloves, or no gloves at all, and have painted fingernails done in subdued tones to accent their delicacy.

Violet and Clifford sit behind the lineup, halfway back on wooden pews. Elsie can't see them because she and all the other children have their backs to the audience. The church is filled with misty-eyed mothers who hold personalized versions of the New Testament in their laps, reserved as presents for when the sacrament has been completed: *For Jenny, On Her First Communion.*

In front of Elsie is Father Thomas, with thinning hair and wide purple lips, who was recently assigned to Our Lady from his home in Poland. Most of his body is concealed by flowing robes and long sashes with fringes on the ends draped about his shoulders like curtain ties. Once in a while two pink hands emerge from their hiding places at his sides, and he raises them in the air to conduct the audience. Elsie can only make out parts of what he is saying over his accent, but everyone around her responds:

Blessed be God forever.

She is a little nervous about receiving Communion, and forgets to pay attention. Something isn't right. She told her mother this morning that she felt sick, which was a lie and her mother knew it. "All the more reason to go," she said. "You need to be thoroughly cleansed." Elsie didn't go in the cellar because there were too many people around and there wasn't time, but she wasn't trying to be cheeky. She had a bad feeling in her stomach, one that came up all the way from her soul and sat searing on the insides of her body. What it brought was a message: *Don't go, you are not ready.* Elsie knew what this meant: *You are not acceptable.*

On her shoulder she feels the sharp hand of her mother squeezing her bones, and there is the sacrament, held up before her like a small off-white prize.

"Say Amen Elsie," says her mother, in the voice she reserves for company.

"Amen," Elsie manages.

Then it's in her hand, light as paper, as pinfeathers, a coin-shaped slice of bread with a cross stamped in its centre. She raises it to her mouth as she has seen her mother do so many times, and slides it onto her tongue. Instead of moving between her teeth like it should, the bread sticks, fuses to the roof of her mouth like a piece of skin left behind on a cold metal pole. Marian's fingers dig into Elsie one more time. "Sit down," she hisses.

When Elsie gets back to her seat, between the other grade twos who beam at each other and crinkle their powder-puff noses, she looks up at the crucifix hanging over the altar. *I just ate your body,* she says to the bleeding Jesus. *Because I am a sinner and you had to die for me so I could eat you. I am a bad girl.* Then she is crying. She tries to stop, but the tears flush down her cheeks; hot, salty rain. One of the Italian girls in the bridal dresses offers her a white hanky, but Elsie is going to be sick. The weight of the bread inside her stomach is making her sink, making her heavy. The demons are leaping for joy in the cellar because look! Elsie is riddled with sin. Nothing can save her, not even a piece of Jesus. She gets up and runs to the back of the church where she vomits into the vestry.

"What in heavens name?" says Violet outside the church.

[110]

"I feel sick," Elsie says. Her face is green, like the new young grass sprouting up all over the lawn.

"What's wrong?" her father asks.

Elsie doesn't know how to explain.

Violet bends down to where Elsie is hunched over a patch of dandelions. Her breath is minty, like toothpaste. "Now Elsie, are you upset about something? You didn't feel sick this morning."

Elsie feels her stomach turn and tries not to retch. She knows the service: *This is my body which will be given up for you.* The whole reason she is sick is that she's been rejected. Her body is too full of dirt and sin and the bread couldn't find its way down. The demons have her. But she doesn't want Violet to know what a sinner she is.

"Maybe we should take her home," Clifford says.

"No," says Marian, moving in, straightening Elsie up and handing her a Kleenex. "It's natural to feel sick the first time you receive communion. That's the Lord battling off all of the evil inside of you."

Elsie watches the cars drive by on Church Street and turn the corner, knowing that her mother is right. In her case, there was just too much evil: the Lord was overcome. Her grandmother looks at Clifford, a startled, questioning look, and walks away briskly towards the car. Elsie can hear the sound of her shoes clacking against her heels as she crosses the parking lot. Clifford sighs and catches up to her at the curb where they begin to argue, quietly at first, then louder.

"I don't want to confuse her by always contradicting Marian," her father says. He is exasperated now. Elsie has hardly ever seen him this way.

"Well if that woman doesn't confuse her, I don't know what will."

Elsie sits on the piano bench in the study, crammed in between her father's bookshelves lined with hardcover books, and her mother's sewing table. In front of her is the mahogany piano, richly oiled and smelling of lemons. Its graceful curving pillars taper down towards the floor where it meets the olive green throw rug that Marian placed beneath the bench to keep Elsie from scratching the hardwood. The piano lessons were suggested to Elsie's parents by Miss Pollard, who felt Elsie might benefit from learning to play a musical instrument. "She is a very introverted child, " Miss Pollard said on parent-teacher day last fall, while Elsie waited outside the classroom door. "She lives in a world of her own. Learning the piano may bring her out and give her a sense of accomplishment." Marian did not like the idea. A piano was hardly the place to start. It was too expensive. But then Miss Pollard had suggested that Elsie might accompany the choir by playing songs at Mass. "I know they are always looking for pianists," she said optimistically.

Not long after that two men in coveralls hauled a piano up the steps to Elsie's house. Some of the paint was still worn on the porch, where the piano's wheels had rubbed against the boards. Elsie went in to the study to look at the new piece of furniture.

"Well Elsie," said Marian, with a shammy in her hand. She was already shining the wood where the movers had smudged it with their greasy fingers. "You are going to learn how to play the piano." She often told Elsie things like this, things that she would do and wasn't it wonderful? Usually the things involved standing up in front of a prayer group and having her sins cast out by a circle of the bent-headed faithful, or taking a trip to the mission where Marian handed out copies of *The Book of Worship* to people off the street. Elsie wasn't sure about the piano, but she smiled anyway. What exactly would she have to do?

Since then Elsie has practiced every day for half an hour. She is working her way towards beginning her grade one *Royal Conservatory Songbook*, although Marian has requested that she first learn to play hymns.

When she sits at the piano she keeps her back straight like a board, and her hands arched over the keys, *as if you are holding a potato*. She concentrates on the music book opened up before her like a voluminous bolt of cloth, wracking her brain for the proper note, the proper positioning of her fingers. As she plays she moves her hands carefully down the keyboard, cradling the sounds that come from strings wired tightly to an inner metal frame; she visualizes the felt-tipped hammers striking these strings, converting their vibrations to music along a wooden sounding board as big as the whole inside of the piano. She can alter the noise that the piano makes simply by pushing the pedals beneath her feet. There are two of them down there, within reach of her tippy toes: *the damper pedal,* and *the sustainer.* They are often called, although somewhat incorrectly, the "soft and loud" pedals. *Piano e forte.*

Sometimes when she plays, Elsie pretends she is doing calisthenics with her fingers, stretching for the high G, then rotating and dancing back down the width of the octave. She lets the sun pour in the window and shine on her face, lets the sensation of hot light warm her up, loosen her bones. She can feel it kiss her with promise.

When Elsie has managed to pick her way to the middle of "Here We Go Gathering Nuts in May," Violet comes in to the study and stands smiling next to the sewing table. She is wearing her travelling suit, the pleated slacks and knitted striped vest that she arrived in two weeks ago. Elsie knows what this means: her grandmother is leaving.

"Elsie, I am taking your grandmother to the airport," says her father, who enters and leans on the bookcase. "Would you like to say goodbye? She's going back to British Columbia."

Elsie slides down from the piano bench and walks over to her grandmother. She doesn't want to say anything at all, but she does: "I don't want you to go."

Violet's face is cheerful, avid. She has powdered down her freckles more seriously this time, and outlined her lips with a pink lining pencil. Elsie can tell that she doesn't want to stay. She is deflating with relief.

"Remember to look those demons straight in the face," Violet says, her hair glittering in the sunlight.

Elsie thinks she could be brave if only her grandmother would stay on living in her bedroom. They could fight off their demons together, just the two of them. Alone she doesn't think she is up to it, she is so small, so easy to consume. She is so easily led into temptation.

"I don't want you to leave," she says again.

By now Marian has joined them in the study. She takes Elsie by the hand and presses her fingers together.

"Your grandmother has a plane ticket," she says. "It's time to say goodbye."

"Maybe you can come and visit me in B.C.," Violet adds tentatively, trying to force a smile. "You would like it there Elsie. I'll bet you're a dyed-in-the-wool west coaster. I can show you the sights."

Elsie likes this idea. "Can I go with you now?"

"Elsie," says Clifford. "You know that's not possible. You have school to finish. Don't you want to move up to grade three with the rest of your class?"

"No," says Elsie.

"Well you should," says Marian. "You have responsibilities. You are a part of this family and you need to contribute. Now say goodbye and let your father and Violet get on their way."

"I can't," says Elsie, her voice shaking. "I want to go to B.C." She lunges at her grandmother whose face is both startled and terrified, hoping to grab hold of something secure: a leather purse, a shin. Tears fall from her eyes as she moves, but she doesn't get very far; her mother's grip is too tight. "I want to go with Violet," she screams.

"That's quite enough Elsie," says Marian hotly, forcing her onto the couch, onto her lap where she pins down her limbs and breathes against her neck. "You will control yourself right now." But Elsie doesn't control herself; she can't. Something is rearing up inside her heart and sealing off her windpipe; something is infecting her innards and causing her to gasp for air. She's afraid, that's what she is, and she can't do anything about it.

"I think we'd better go," says Clifford, picking up the suitcases. "This is probably for your benefit, mother. Once we're gone she'll calm down."

[115]

Violet looks at Elsie struggling on the cushions. She smiles weakly and adjusts her scarf. "Goodbye Elsie, I'll come back. I'll send you postcards. Please don't be mad." But Elsie can't hear. She has gone to the place inside her head where everything is safe.

"Elsie," Marian says when the door is closed. "Listen to me. I want you to listen." Her voice is measured, edged with steel. She cups Elsie's head in her palm and forces her to look her in the eye. "This is your house, the place where you live, and I am your mother. You belong to me, Elsie. Me," she repeats, thumping her chest. "And you will do what I say. Until you are an adult you are at risk, you need protection from the kinds of things that trapped me. Evil, Elsie, do you understand?"

Elsie doesn't answer, but she listens without breathing. She can never disobey her mother for long.

When Marian is gone, Elsie watches from the window as Clifford loads her grandmother's things into the Lincoln. She stands on the ottoman and puts her hands on the glass, feeling ashamed. Violet is talking freely now, her mouth opening and closing in the clear blue background of the sky. Her hair is extra brassy in the sunlight, with wisps of grey fluttering around her face like the legs of spiders. Elsie can tell they are having an argument. They should be gone by now. Her father's face is stern and flustered. He climbs into the front seat and puts his arm over the window sill, waiting for Violet to do the same. Finally she is in, and the car starts with a muted roar. Together they head off down Magnolia Avenue, until Elsie can see nothing at all. Somehow, while disappointing her mother, Elsie has failed to be good enough, or attractive enough to her grandmother. Somehow she has managed to drive her off, back to the mountains, where, she imagines, demons can't climb high enough to live in your cellar.

10

For her own story Violet has to reach back, into the shadows of time and the warped records of history, because look where she is: she's eighty-six and in a nursing home! She can't walk down the hallway on her own two feet; she can't sing "Has Anybody Seen My Gal" without sounding like a bad impersonation of Ethel Merman. And if she has a hankering for huckleberry pie, she might as well pray to the Virgin and all the saints rather than asking the Avondale kitchen staff. "Oh Mrs. Leggett," they say disapprovingly, offering up their chopped applesauce wrapped in vulgar shoe-leather pastry, "That would be special treatment." What's wrong with special treatment? Violet wants to know. Being special used to be an advantage. How much things have changed indeed!

Her story is complicated, she thinks, knotted by the pitfalls of love, the land mines of politics, and chock full of people in fedora hats. Or maybe that was a movie she saw somewhere?

Still, if she had to tell her story sometime, the story of how she got here despite various cuts and bruises, minus two tonsils and an appendix, but with all her own teeth, she'd start way back in the house on Chesterfield Avenue, the other house that she used to live in with her mother and dad and Matthew, before the city let developers tear it down and replace it with a coffee shop and the Hong Kong Bank of Canada. She'd start right there because that's as far back as she can remember. And she's tried to forget.

Violet lived on Chesterfield Avenue for most of her life. The street ran parallel to Lonsdale, the main street of North Vancouver. At one end of Lonsdale was Grouse Mountain, a hulking, snow-speckled peak that you could climb if you were full of puff; at the other end was Burrard Inlet, a lean leg of the Pacific Ocean, its shoreline interrupted by the Wallace Shipyards and Pete Larson's hotel jacked up on blocks of wood covered in black oil. This was North Vancouver during the First World War: a series of dirt streets carved out of the side of a mountain, a loose collection of bald spots resembling sores where pioneering men and women had chopped down the trees so that they could see the ocean. Between the bald spots, on the edges of Lonsdale and Chesterfield, ran wooden sidewalks split from cedar or fir; slippery when wet, they kept the bottoms of dresses dry, and more or less away from the mud.

People walked up and down the streets all day long searching for sacks of feed or sales on cotton broadcloth. Men in grey flannel suits with their jackets unbuttoned to the navel, or Prince Albert overcoats and rounded felt hats, sauntered across the rubble of the road to peer in windows with their hands behind their backs. Women in ankle-length frocks with demurely puffed sleeves, cinched bodices and mighty pea-cloaks hiked uphill with their skirts in their hands, looks of determination stamped into their faces. The latter were strangely sexless, corporeal, their unseen curves pressed into angular piping and tailor-made seams. Everyone carried black umbrellas with shellacked wooden handles and sharp metal points at one end (you never knew when it might rain), and was fastidiously well-groomed.

Lower Lonsdale was the business district. Cast-iron lamp posts with pyramids of electric lights alternated with telephone poles and their menace of wires. The buildings were brick, cinnabar red or new gamboge, with hand-carved triglyphs and continuous sets of windows, or board-and-batten timber with green trim and false fronts. Rectangular signs jutted out over yellow awnings: Paine Hardware, McDowell's Drug's, Simpson and Wight Ideal Florists, The Flat Iron Store. There was also a dressmaker's shop with its own corsetiere, and a place to buy penny candy.

At the foot of the mountain where the Vancouver ferry docked every twenty minutes for Gastown, an electric trolley ran all the way up a jagged stair-step track, across a ninety-eight-foot wooden trestle to the Capilano River. This was the place Violet first learned to swim, the place that turned red in the fall with salmon making their way to the spawning grounds. At the mouth of the river was the Capilano Indian Reserve, formerly known as Homulcheson, sleepy and portent, once just a summer home for the Squamish, now lived in year round.

Violet's own house is a modest Edwardian with an off-the-centre porch and symmetrical windows. In the front garden hollyhocks climb trellises to the sun and flutter like dainty wings in the morning breeze. The blinds are drawn, but her parents are not trying to hide anything. It's only Monday. Laundry day. Violet's mother, Lila Spencer, is in the backyard scrubbing the family sheets on a washboard. Her hair is pinned up in a tight bun on top of her head to prevent stray wisps from falling into her eyes. When she is finished she will put the sheets in a pot to boil on the back of the wood-and-coal McClary range which sits on her reinforced kitchen floor, then remove them with a wooden paddle, transfer them to cooling pails, and wring each one out by hand. She doesn't go in for those newfangled washing machines with the oxidized copper basins and hand-agitators that Paine Hardware is selling for the ridiculous price of one hundred dollars, or one dollar down. She has heard about how they tangle shirt sleeves into unimaginable knots.

Violet's father, Jack Spencer, is also home. He is in the corner of the parlour trying to get some work done.

"Daddy, how did we get here?" Violet asks. She stands halfway into her father's study, her body bisected by a heavy curtain partitioning off his wooden roll-top desk from the rest of the parlour. As she speaks, she plays with the curtain's tassels which smell like pipe tobacco and old earth: Daddy's smell. She wears a long-sleeved dress, a white pinafore with an empress waistline; high ankle boots pinch her six-year-old feet into ladylike points.

"We came on a steamship." Her father speaks without looking up from his ledgers. "We came in 1912, and just missed sinking on the *Titanic* by two months. Only the people on that boat were going to Ellis Island, while we were going to Montreal, which is also an island."

"Why did we leave England?"

"Well Violet," with politeness, "every time Daddy turned around there was a priest in his parlour. Montreal was not a damn sight better, so we landed here, on the golden mountain." Jack is dressed in his business clothes: a taupe jacket with matching waistcoat and trousers, and a pair of polished lace-up shoes. Across his stomach, from the pocket of his waistcoat, a chain stretches to a wooden button where it is fastened with a golden clasp. Violet knows that the chain comes from the watch with the train on the back.

"You came first, all by yourself?" she says with admiration and concern.

"I came six months ahead to find us a home and a job. You and your mother followed on the train and I met you at the station in Vancouver."

Violet stops playing with the tassels and considers this. Looks up at Jack. She likes to watch her father in his study even though Lila tells her to let him be. She knows there is a possibility that one day she will draw back the curtain expecting to see Jack in his suit—his hair combed neatly away from his forehead and held in place with the transparent cream from the bathroom—and he will be gone. His straight-backed chair with the hand-tooled ebony swirls and the firm leather insert will be empty, cold. The usual scatter of papers on the surface of his desk will be packed away into a box by her mother.

Or this is what she imagines, based on her mother's

stories of the past. *Your father likes to go his merry way,* she says to Violet while they clean the floor, or scrub the drapes with bristle brushes, *he can't be pinned down.* Violet thinks of her father as a butterfly beating his wings against the window pane, trying to escape the deadly fingers of collectors by moving towards the light; he is a delicate insect covered in incandescent powder, one whose inevitable fate is to have his body pricked all over with dressmaker's pins and displayed in a glass case at the Museum of Natural History. Her mother warns Violet to be good, to please her father, but at the same time she hardens and chokes on her words: *He used to be away all the time, coming and going as he pleased.* Then she sighs complacently, wipes the hair from her face with the back of her hand, and says, *But now we have the war.* The war is another thing all together.

Violet knows that the war keeps her father in their Chesterfield house, sitting in his chair, his nose aimed at the ledgers on his desk like the sharp end of a soldier's bayonet. Unlike other fathers who are sucked up by the war, hauled overseas in steamships with deafening fog-horns and crow's nests which aren't really for crows, Jack has plenty of work to do in North Vancouver. She knows this, but she asks him anyway, just to make sure.

"Daddy, are you going back to England to fight the Kaiser?"

Jack removes his reading glasses and looks down. "No Violet," he says. "I am not going to war. Canada needs all her engineers here."

Jack is a mechanical engineer, which has something to do with building and fixing things. Violet has been told by Jack himself that before the war, he worked mainly with cars, but because the Dominion needs all the help it can get, he now works at the Wallace Shipyards. Sometimes he works on wooden ships, *The Mabel Brown*, or *The Jessie Norcross*, which Violet imagines are named for famous ladies who died at sea; sometimes he works on other, darker things, things he doesn't like to talk about but which are nonetheless necessary to help our boys in the fight against the Huns. *Metal shell casings*, he tells her, when she pesters him enough. The words are dusky, with sharp edges; they come out of Jack's mouth with hesitation and reproach, so that Violet imagines they must stand for some clandestine military secret she should never reveal. Her mother, however, tells everyone she meets. *Bullets*, she says, narrowing her eyes. *Jack is a blessing to the Dominion.*

One of the benefits of the end of the war is that Jack will be able to return to working with cars. *Cars are the beginning of another life*, he says to Violet. *They will change the way we do things completely.* Already there are over three hundred registered cars in the province of British Columbia and the number is climbing every day. Jack tells Violet these kinds of things at dinnertime with a pleased look on his face. Right now his Hudson is parked outside, in the alleyway behind the Spencer's house. It has four skinny wheels which look to Violet like Christmas cookies but are called pneumatic tires, and a brass steering wheel interposed between the dashboard and the driver. The engine starts in less than two minutes, and has two fabulous gas-powered speeds that Jack controls with foot pedals the size of serving spoons. Violet's mother has a fear of cars, and will only drive in the Hudson if Jack promises to stay below ten miles per

hour, and if he refrains from using his horn. She is behind the times, Jack says, and doesn't like to spook the
horses.

On Sundays Lila walks down the hill to St. Edmund's
Church. She wears gloves and a chip-straw hat with a
wide black band, and carries her copy of *A Catholic's
Pocket Manual* in her leather handbag. Violet does not
have to go to church, because her father said so. "Violet
is a busy girl with many things to learn," he said to her
mother, a long time ago. To Violet he whispered sideways out of his mouth, "You have better ways to spend
your time." At first Violet thought she might be missing out on something important, something she needed
to know, so she peeked inside Lila's *Pocket Manual* and
found pictures of sad-eyed men and women with holes
in their hands. The men were badly in need of haircuts
and the women were on the verge of tears. Most of them
had no shoes, and some displayed bleeding, prickly hearts
that you could see right through their clothes. Violet
could read by then, and she made out the first line of
one of the prayers: *Oh Lord, let me have a perfect sorrow for my sins.* But just because she could read, didn't
mean she understood everything.

It is on these Sundays, while Lila is at church, that
Jack and Violet drive down Keith Road in the Hudson
until they arrive at the Capilano River. If the weather is
especially nice, they turn right onto Capilano Road and
head north to the suspension bridge. The total drive is
almost four miles, and it takes them over half an hour.

Along the way they pass other people out and about
for Sunday excursions: jacketed, well-bred gentlemen

waiting graciously at intersections for the streetcar which shunts its way up Capilano Road like a giant, hot-waxed beetle. Touring jitneys crammed full of picnic baskets and passengers decked out in their Sunday clothes—porkpie hats for the men, muslin lace for the women—with signs bolted to one side shouting encouragingly in yellow script: "Ride to the Canyon for five cents!" (Drumming up business is a challenge during the war, Violet has heard her father say, and companies have had to resort to gimmicks: buy one fare, get a second for free; bring a lady and you get half price. Others have folded all together, preferring bankruptcy and anonymous debt to the public scorn doled out by community members who believe that a man shouldn't make his opportunities with a war going on. What else should he do? Jack says to Violet, let the country go to ruin?)

Another thing about the war: Capilano Road has turned into an obstacle course, with washboard ruts and clay boils the size of prize-winning watermelons. Although it wasn't much better before, according to Jack, at least there were boys with pick-axes and shovels to do the work. *Now there are just old men*, he says, grinning. *Old men like me.* Violet doesn't think of her father as old: he is almost thirty, with cinnamon brown hair and only two teeth missing. True, he wears old men's suits—crisp white shirts and brass-plated cufflinks—but he doesn't act like them. He doesn't growl or heave when he gets up from armchairs; he doesn't mutter phrases under his breath when he walks along Lonsdale.

Jack steers around the cavities in the road and the horse patties which have piled up into steaming nodular pyramids, whistling to the tune of *Let Me Call You Sweet-heart*. He is not easily dismayed. When other drivers approach, facing off against the narrow roadway punched like a wasp-waisted trench through the forest, Jack is always the first to pull off, nudge the hood of the Hudson into the bushes and let the other car pass on the side. He does this gallantly, without hesitation, reminding Violet that *We must never forget our manners*.

The other cars are dirtier than Jack's; they are noisier. They are ancient Stanley Steamers with coffin bonnets over their unfortunate boilers, and steering handles that you crank to the right or left to control the wheels. Some of them are Pierce Arrows, Packards, or Model Ts, which Jack scoffs at after they've passed because Henry Ford is a pacifist and not willing to support the war. Nearly every one of them is painted black and has high fenders that look like batwings.

If Jack and Violet come upon an unlucky driver stuck in a mud hole, or smashed into one of the barrel-thick roadside trees, Jack always stops the Hudson and gets out to help. If the driver is a man, Jack will joke with him and call him "Guv'nor," then fasten his tow-chain to one of the axles, tell him which way to steer, and pull him free. If the driver is a lady, Jack will remove his jacket, get underneath the car and tinker around until he finds something, then exclaim "Here's your trouble!" with a voice full of satisfaction and surprise. He'll ask the lady to step aside just for caution's sake while he gets her automobile back on the road single-handedly. Sometimes, if the ladies are the young, squealing kind with flow-ered broad-brimmed hats and gossamer eyelashes, he will give them a complementary copy of *200 Practical*

Points for Motoring. "Read it carefully," he'll say. "A lady should never be without this kind of advice."

Violet knows the manual: it has long, boring lists of what to do in case of any situation. "For one wheel smashed, replace it with a skid made from a purloined fence post. For two wheels smashed . . . " She wants to know what to do in the event of there being no fence posts for hundreds and hundreds of miles, but the book doesn't give any indication. It is published in England, where everyone, she supposes, has broad farm fields surrounded by fences. She herself rarely sees a farm, but her father tells her about the ones around Abbotsford that he visited in his *wandering days*: luminous spring-green sheets of grass dotted with Dalmatian-like cows, cones of freshly stooked hay looking like the roofs of thatched cottages. *200 Practical Points for Motoring* also has inky black drawings of motorists—usually men—and their cars in compromising positions: upside down, inside out. The drivers in the book have radiators that overheat at the drop of a hat; they have steering wheels that jam and cause collisions with phone booths or cows grazing precariously on boulevard plants. They are the kinds of motorists with no common sense, who should not be allowed out in public, Jack says. But he carries a stack of these books in the back of his trunk, *just in case*.

Jack also carries other things, just in case, stowed neatly away in the Hudson's various compartments: a tin of gasoline, a kerosene lantern. There is also extra packaged food tucked into little paper envelopes, which tastes like salt and chalk when you add water, as well as water by itself, and ropes and blankets. Jack says you can never be too prepared when you go out on the road, and his well-thought-out plans are why he always gets home on time. *Well,* he says grinning. *Almost always.*

This Sunday the sun is shining in the sky like a glorious lemon. Motoring down Keith Road, Violet stands with her hands next to the steering wheel, her face pushed out over the engine like a mermaid carved into the prow of a ship. In a few years' time glass windshields will block driver and passenger from riding this way, partitioning off bodies from the outside, but for now—Oh wind. Fresh air the colour of emeralds, scents like a million roses unfurling in spring. Wild mint. Violet watches as walls of spirea and foxglove zoom by, their pink clusters of bells and soft pompom petals making streaks in the air. Giant fir trees pass on both sides, and plants she has begun to know as salal, Oregon grape, and huckleberry; all the ingredients for her mother's wild berry pie that's as sweet as homemade jam.

Jack drives with the skill of a royal chauffeur and Violet is a princess, her white shift billowing, her bloomers full of sky. He leans into the quilted upholstery, hollering, "This is the wave of the future Violet. In twenty years you'll be able to go as far as White Rock in one day's drive. Nothing between you and those mountains but a strip of roadway. Path of freedom. All those people you see walking, well, they won't have to have blisters ever again. The milk wagon will never be late, and the Chinaman won't have a sore back hauling his fish up Keith Road hill."

"Will I have a car Daddy?"

"You sure will. There'll be roads enough for everyone—from North Van to Hope, to Alaska even." He jerks the wheel to avoid a mud hole, adding, "And smooth too."

At the gates to the suspension bridge a gentleman collects Jack's money: ten cents to enter and view the gardens. To cross the swaying bridge two hundred feet above the canyon floor. If you dare.

The first garden is afloat with blossoms: daylilies, lavatera, rainbow marigolds, double-petal roses dripping like strawberry-flavoured whipping cream. Farther on rhododendrons and azaleas make up the top layers of terraced beds—their soil held in place by boulders brought up from the riverbed—a backdrop for wooden benches flanked on three sides by blazing heather and gloriosa daisies.

Violet likes this part of the park. She likes the ladies in scarf-covered hats who stand with parasols under cottonwood trees and sip tea from china cups. She also likes the men who congregate in bunches with their jackets over one shoulder, talking about the war and smoking cigarettes. Most of them are her father's age, with their own picnic baskets full of fruit pies and finger sandwiches, and families of three, four, or five. Some of them have enlisted despite being married, because they need jobs and want to help out. They are waiting to go overseas with grand impatience, her father says. They are afraid the war will be over before they have a chance to fight.

Others are already back from the war—from the 1st British Columbia Regiment, or Princess Patricia's Canadian Light Infantry—although these men are rarer, more precious. They are gathered around by the waiting men, goaded and egged on until they reveal stories of capture, of dangerous escapes across *No-Man's Land* from enemy camps. *Second Battle of Ypres,* they say, and all mouths go silent. *Like hell struck with a hammer.* When Violet's father overhears these stories he sometimes shakes his head regretfully, woefully, looking at Violet as if there is a hidden message she is supposed to decipher. But she doesn't know where to begin; adults are full of secrets.

Some of these men back from the war are so precious they have to stay home in the daytime to rest and take naps. They have to be kept away from loud noises and out of the brightness of light which hurts their eyes because of the poison gas. Violet has heard that these men have plasters on their arms and legs, or turbans of bandages wound round their heads to keep their brains inside. The ones that got the turbans too late—after their brains were already lost—are locked up in Essondale so that they won't bump into things.

Jack puts down the picnic basket and unfurls a woollen blanket on the grass. "Marvellous," he says, looking up at the sky. Violet knows he is referring to the day, the day in general, and she warms all over because her father is so easy to please. Together they remove their jackets and coats, and sit down to eat: egg salad sandwiches on Lila's bread. Tea from the iron cantina. Violet starts with a butter cookie, picking off the orange peel jewel in the centre and hiding it in the grass; then she sighs. She can't wait forever.

"Can I go across Daddy?" she says.

Jack eyes his daughter's face, chuckling. "Go and get 'em," he says.

This is her favourite part: the crossing. The crossing

alone. She is a big girl and she can prove it, just watch. She clambers to her feet and runs on ahead. At the edge of the bridge a man in suspenders and a grey flannel work shirt stoops down to her level. Violet can smell his chewing tobacco.

"Are you going to cross this bridge all by yerself miss?" he says.

"Yes sir," she says. "I am six years old."

The man waits for Jack's nod, then stands aside. "Well then, I s'pose that's all right then."

Violet launches out onto the bridge which sways languidly over the canyon. She is not afraid of falling, of the bridge coming unglued from its supports like a poorly-licked stamp; she knows that the whole thing is held up by cables, a thick one and a thin one on either side, which span the canyon's width like uncoiled metal snakes. At each end these cables are cemented into concrete blocks the size of the North Vancouver ferryboat, and buried in the ground beneath a tower of dirt and debris.

When she gets to the middle of the bridge, Violet slows to a trot. Her father warned her about stampeding. Two ladies in white blouses with ruffles at the neck and sleeves and cameos pinned at their lily-white throats watch Violet with amusement. "Look at her hair!" one of them exclaims. "She's as red as a fire engine." "What a cute little thing," the other says, guffawing from her extensive bosom.

Violet's face flushes red, making things even worse, and the women squeal with delight. "Oh my! What a little darling!" they say. Violet can't stand it; she is not a little darling, and she doesn't have anything in common with fire engines. They are blood red, the colour of cherries, while Violet's own hair is distinctly saffron, a word she learned from her father. "I'm not a darling," she tries to say huffily, but there is a shriek from the ladies, and a weight on her back like a load of stones. Before she knows it, Violet is knocked down flat.

From the edges of her vision she can make out a black shape on her back, four matchstick legs and a large head pressing her stomach hard against the bridge's planks. The ends of her dress are being tugged at surreptitiously from behind by a growling dog.

The canyon is now directly below her. Violet's head and right arm are wedged through the cables, into the open air. Her ringlets hang in suspension over the Capilano River, which rushes onward despite her predicament.

Jack is alerted to the scene by the shrieks of the women. He sees his daughter hanging mutely over the gorge—God love me she's too close, she could fall, fall forever—but before he has a chance—

"Get," Violet says to the lump on her back. Wriggling her arm free from the cables, she swats the air behind her, joins her fist with the dog's head. "Bad boy," she says.

Jack watches his daughter belt a Labrador Retriever, then stand up and walk back to where he sits gaping.

"Daddy, I'm all dirty in my front," she says, her face tight with concern.

He takes her to his chest, hugging, and smiles faintly. "That's my girl, my red-devil angel. You tell that dog who's boss."

Instead of being scolded for getting dirty, Violet eats French Vanilla ice cream at the Tipperary Tea Gardens, an extra expense these days because of the rationing. Jack orders her an adult-sized bowl with pralines and syrup, while the waitress apologizes. He wanted to get Violet a maraschino cherry.

"Sorry sir, but you understand with the war, we're right low on specialty items like that."

At home Violet's mother bathes her knees in salt water and sits her in the parlour with a book.

"I mean it Lila. That girl is going to be a boxer," Jack says to his wife.

"I hope not Jack. And don't you try teaching her. It's not for ladies."

Lila speaks without raising her eyes to her husband. Between her fingers clink two knitting needles: socks for our brave soldiers overseas and the dear departing young men set to leave next week; grey strands of wool disappearing into a column of stocking stitch. Violet thinks her mother should have chosen green wool to match the trees. She can't imagine the place without forest that everyone calls *the front*, where broad fields of stumps and mud choke with sleeping bodies; parts of bodies. Red wool—the only colour sure to match. Lila is a member of The Women's Institute knitting group, *For Home and Country*.

"She's a go-getter. Right Violet?"

"Yes Daddy."

"Stronger than this feller here." Jack squeezes the toes of his baby son gurgling in the bassinet at Lila's elbows. "This Matthew. What kind of crazy apostolic name is that Lila? Don't know why I let you talk me into such a thing. I hope his nose will straighten out, he looks as if you've been ramming him into walls. He is the first family member born on Canadian soil though, albeit blue at birth. Must have felt the cold."

"Matthew will be strong. Give him time."

"Oh, he has all the time in the world, this one. It's easier when you know they're coming. It was different with little Violet. I didn't know what I was getting into when we stepped behind the market back in Liverpool for a goodnight kiss—"

"Jack." Lila's face is stern now, cranked up and away from her knitting.

"I'm not complaining though."

"We both planned this family, you and I."

"Think what you like."

Lila returns her knitting to the carpet bag at her feet and goes into the kitchen. A repressed sniffle escapes behind her.

"Daddy?" Violet approaches Jack from her spot in the corner, trailing blankets. "Why is Mother angry?"

"Your mother and I are just having a little disagreement."

Violet considers this. If that is the case, they have disagreements quite often, usually about things she doesn't understand. Most of the time her mother leads the way. She wants to go back to England and see her family. She wants to move away from the north shore and into the city. Sometimes she says things about another woman, one who doesn't seem to have a name (Lila calls her *that woman*), but who must be important because Jack's face always turns red and he goes out the front door. Violet is afraid that if her mother keeps being disagreeable, Jack

[135]

will go out and never come back. She tries to make up for her mother's poor behaviour by being good, but there is only so much she can do. "Don't you like having a family?" she says.

"Oh Violet, I do indeed. Nothing could be better. But you my red devil, you started the whole thing, and, well, let's just say you were an accident."

Violet returns to her book. *Accident*: Jack's word for crashing cars, or when he falls down the stairs after a night out with the boys. *Accidentally on purpose,* he says, rubbing the bruised spot on the top of his head. Either way, it doesn't make sense.

11

Violet sits at the table waiting for her father. She is eight years old, and is learning to cultivate patience, not to mention manners, and should not start eating until everyone is seated; cultivation is what her mother calls her efforts at encouraging Violet to sit still with her back straight, to pick up only one utensil at a time at the kitchen table: *cultivation*. Like a vegetable, Violet thinks.

Instead of taking a seat the way Lila asks him to, Jack stands in the centre of the kitchen reading the latest edition of the *North Shore Press*. Violet can see the black headlines printed in dramatic letters at the level where Jack's head should be. Instead there is a swatch of newsprint cutting him off at the shoulders: *World In Uproar!* Beneath the words, Premier John Oliver sits in his tweed suit in Victoria drinking tea from a bone china saucer.

Violet knows the word *uproar*. Last week her school was closed because of the Spanish Influenza. Public meetings of the Women's Institute were also banned, adding to the commotion and personally vexing her mother.

Although the war is almost over and men are returning from Europe, Violet's father slinks angrily through the house. One year of prohibition this month.

"I go out to the North Vancouver Men's Club and all I can get is near-beer and a shot of lemonade. Women can vote but I can't have a glass of wine. They call this progress?" Jack says vehemently.

"Jack, come and eat your dinner," Lila says. Next to her sits Matthew, who is smart enough to hold his own fork, but not smart enough to find his mouth, so Lila feeds him, gently, making a cooing noise that remind Violet of pigeons.

"Why does he get to eat first?" Violet asks.

"Because he is too young to have manners," Jack replies.

Lila shakes her head. "I have to feed Matthew first so that I can eat with the rest of the family," she says. "But I said grace for him," she adds, carefully wiping his mouth.

While Violet waits she looks at the table. True, there is no liquor present, only mashed potatoes, peas and carrots. Coffee boiled with eggshells for the calcium. But liquor was never much a part of their dinner routine before the dry law; it belonged in hotel restaurants and back street pubs where sailors and men in overcoats spent their spare time. But according to Jack, you can't even find a drink in those shady places. "I have to find a blind pig if I want to have a good time," he says, exasperated. "What is this country coming to?"

"What's a blind pig?" Violet says. She can't imagine.

"Never you mind," says her mother.

Violet knows her father is only pretending to be mad,

the same way he does every Saturday night. He walks around looking anxious and short-tempered, leaning on door jambs with his shirt sleeves rolled to the elbows, on the verge of cussing. Then he goes out with his pals and comes back slurring his words. Of course he's allowed to drink.

Still, she knows things are about to change. Everyone is talking about the end of the war, how it can't possibly go on any longer, how the boys will be back and there will be celebrations, jobs. Prosperity, that's the word. Violet's father has been pacing around the house for a week now, forgetting to change into his suit and go down to the shipyards. He doesn't agree with everyone else; he doesn't like prosperity. *The war is as good as over,* he said to Lila, *and when it is, I'm going to have even more time on my hands.* Violet's mother had looked cross at this statement and remained silent. *I just need a few months,* he said. A few months for what? Violet wanted to know.

Jack puts down the paper and comes to the table. "A man needs a little recreation Lila," he says.

Violet's mother wipes Matthew's face with the corner of her apron. "Of course Jack," she says.

"You know, I have a good mind to call off your meeting. Just so I wouldn't be cast out of my own house. Or better yet, I should just stay here in the parlour and see what you all talk about."

Lila stops chewing. "It wouldn't interest you Jack."

"You're right there, I'm sure."

Only once has Violet tried alcohol. Two years ago, when she was six, her father gave her a sip of his whiskey sour. She knew right away why he called it a sour:

her entire face puckered up like a lady eating lemons. But her throat felt warm, with raspy edges. Her mother, however, had disapproved. "You can't give her things like that Jack," she said crossly. "She might get into the habit."

Although men were allowed to go out on the town and drink, ladies were not; it was not in their code of ethics, according to Lila. Along with the rest of the ladies from the Women's Institute, Violet and her mother have taken the temperance pledge. "For self conquest, the sake of others, and for love of Christ and country, I do hereby pledge myself to abstain from the use of alcoholic liquors as a beverage, from the use of tobacco, profane language, the reading of bad books, and to devote earnest efforts to securing the prohibition of liquor traffic."

Because of the bans on public gatherings, the Women's Institute has dwindled to a scant few congregating in vacant neighbourhood living rooms. Violet likes to help out when her mother hosts these meetings, on nights like tonight. Her job is to scrub the sterling cutlery and the silver tea service with tooth polish until she can see her face: a serious freckled girl biting down on her bottom lip with concentration.

Each member of the Institute brings some sort of sweet ingeniously whipped up that morning without the luxury of cane sugar or excess lard. The list is usually predictable: Mrs. McDowell, angel cookies; Mrs. Little, cheese twists. If Mrs. Mahony feels creative—as Violet hopes she will—she'll bring miniature hermits squeezed through a cookie press, an invention every woman in the Institute envies for its cleverness. And Mrs. Clayton Marshall, the newest member, will settle with jam tarts, an easy standby during this time of trial, the pastry being made from leftover bacon fat and the filling picked last evening in her backyard blackberry patch.

When members of the Institute begin arriving after dinner, Jack has already left to play cards at the men's club. They come on foot, walking down Chesterfield Avenue in feathered hats and kid gloves, their girths reduced by corsets. Violet imagines them as tight, uncomfortable balloons waiting to burst. One by one, they file into the Spencer's parlour—the blinds yanked up for it's the weekend—and sit their spreading bums on parlour seats. The early ones choose the upholstered wingbacks while the latecomers get the stunted ottoman.

"Oh Lila dear, thank you for your kindness."

The beginning of these meetings is marked by pleasantries: *How-do-you-do-Mrs. So-and-So,* and *How-is-that-lad-of-yours-with-the-croup? My the day is bleak but our Lord prepares us for these hours.* This always progresses into the louder parts, when, Violet observes, the ladies remove their gloves and satchels (keeping on their hats), and the air fills with a seamless haze of barking voices.

"My dear it was a squaw, an Indian woman in rags, shawls once upon a time, knocking right at my door. In broad daylight. She had only two teeth in front, and eyes like slits. Younger than myself and asking for food for her grandchild."

"What did you do?" Voices aghast.

"I sent her on her way of course. Closed the door. Lord knows what kinds of lice and disease live in her clothes. No use giving anything out because they carry coal you know, to mark your house for all to see."

A nodding of heads around the parlour.

"They say it won't be long now."

Violet knows they are talking about the war. They've been talking about it for as long as she can remember. *The War to end all Wars*, they say, tightening their lips and clucking like hens. Violet can hardly imagine not being at war; she can't recall a time without it. "They're low on men, and winter's coming." Sighs and silences. The clinks of cups and saucers. "I guess we are some of the lucky ones." Violet has also heard this many times. She knows that most of the ladies in the Women's Institute are the wives of important men who need to stay in Canada to keep North Vancouver running. Her mother tells her this all the time. "Where would we be without McDowell's drugstore?" she asks, although Violet doesn't have any answers. "And without Mr. Little, where would your father buy his clothes?" Violet thinks her mother could make Jack's clothes, the way she makes Violet's dresses and pinafores, but she doesn't suggest this. She knows by the tone in her mother's voice that she is not supposed to answer her questions.

The ladies of the Women's Institute are also lucky because their sons are too young to go overseas. Many of them are still in diapers. Violet has heard them talk about this also. At first the idea bothered them, particularly Lila, because their families could not fight battles and be decorated. Matthew would never have a chance to earn a Victoria cross; he would never have a royal medal presented to him in front of the Prime Minister. But now Violet notices the ladies have changed their minds. They don't sigh wistfully and talk about what their sons are missing on the fields at Ypres. Instead they knit ferociously, and count their lucky stars. *The Lord watches over us,* they say, nibbling on crumpets.

Some of them are not so lucky: Dora Marshall is what Violet's mother calls a *war bride*. She married Clayton Marshall overseas, and came back to Canada when he was wounded. He wasn't fighting on the front, like some of the boys from North Vancouver, he wasn't even a soldier. He was in the Medical Corps, and took some shrapnel in the eye. "Now, he can't very well patch up someone else when his own eye has been wrecked, can he?" Lila said to Violet's father. Clayton Marshall was the Spencer's family doctor, before he went to France and came back with an eye patch and a crooked grin. "That's not all that's wrong with him," Jack replied. "Now the poor sod couldn't sew up a pair of knickers."

Part of the Women's Institute pledge is to ease the suffering of war brides. Violet knows this because she has heard the ladies reciting it in her mother's parlour, before Dora Marshall even came along. It is because of this pledge that Dora gets special treatment. "Here is a recipe for salmon steaks," the ladies tell her politely. "You'll just love it I'm sure." They also tell her where to shop, *not at the foreign market of course,* and teach her about cleaning rugs: sprinkle two handfuls of crushed tea leaves onto the carpet, then sweep briskly with a broom.

Dora nods timidly and looks down at her hands, which are softer than Lila's and free of wrinkles. Sometimes her face turns red and Violet knows she is being difficult again. The trying part for the ladies of the Institute is that Dora is from France, and sometimes she forgets her English. "She makes things hard for herself," Lila says, "by speaking French at home with her daughter. She'll never learn English that way." Violet can tell when her mother's patience is being tried, by the crease in her forehead, something she herself has inherited. Lila folds her hands silently and coaches Dora on how to speak. At the same time, she pities her along with all the others. *There, there,* they say, when Dora forgets; they look at her with sympathy, then at each other, patting her hands with their own and offering her their handkerchiefs. *It's not your fault.* Who's fault is it, thinks Violet?

At the end of the evening Violet clears the dessert plates from the parlour and scrapes the crumbs from the tablecloth into a hand-held pewter dustpan. She likes to be useful, and wants to put her mother in a good mood so that she will be civil to Jack when he comes home three sheets to the wind. On her way out of the parlour door, Dora Marshall bends down—a hat like a turkey platter lolling on her head—and says to Violet, "My Gracella will be starting at your school. She is just your age. I hope you two can be friends."

Violet nods solemnly, because it is the polite thing to do.

The Lonsdale School is a multistoried brick building with arched entryways and a flat roof. It sits on the top of the hill overlooking the inlet and the steamers which pass from the shipyards at the foot of Lonsdale out into the Strait of Georgia. On the front lawn of the school is a cluster of big-leaf maple trees with gouged bark and hanging branches that litter the flower beds. Next to the trees stands a white wooden flagpole with the Union Jack proudly drawn up into the skyline.

In Violet's grade three class, Miss Whiteley presides

over wrought-iron desks with wooden hinged seats that lift up to reveal hasty initials done with a pen knife, and balled-up spruce gum crammed into sticky nooks. Ink pots fit snugly into holes in the desks' top right hand corners; too bad if you're a lefty.

If Violet had the choice, she would rather stay at home with Lila and bake pies. Even though she hates the lard-and-flour crust that forms on her hands and makes them look rotten and diseased, she would rather roll out pastry than be confined to the classroom where row upon row of pupils are made to sit ramrod straight like a bunch of corpses. The classroom smells like moulding sandwiches and runny noses, with traces of ageing shoe leather and Miss Whiteley's own putrid, dirty laundry smell sprinkled in for good measure.

In the morning there is math class, or *'rithmetic,* as her father calls it. Violet sits hunched over in her desk, trying to obliterate the voices of the rest of the class as they chant ceremoniously: *three times two is six, three times three is nine, three times four is twelve, three times five is fifteen . . . .* The chant is excruciating, mournful, as though they are muttering a curse over and over into the schoolroom void, filling the musty air with a never ending drone. *As in ghost stories,* thinks Violet, who tries to remember to move her lips.

Miss Whiteley notices this lack of enthusiasm, and smacks her yardstick on the front of random desks to get her students into the lesson. "You must do better!" she shouts. "Remember our poor brothers overseas!"

Violet doesn't know what memorizing times tables has to do with fighting in the war, but she is used to the association. Miss Whiteley uses the phrase a lot.

She also can't decide which is worse: boring math class, or even more boring, writing. *Penmanship,* Miss Whiteley calls it. After a lunch of biscuits and cold chicken, Violet's class must churn out ream after ream of handwritten letters, *Ps* and *Qs, Rs* and *Ls,* painstakingly looped into slender curlicues and graceful arcs and set between straight black lines. Even though she tries, Violet's letters always look squirrelly around the edges, slanting and embarrassingly wobbly in all the wrong places. Miss Whiteley says that Violet's words look as though they have been written by a child, and Violet wonders what she means, because of course they have.

She also points out other things about Violet, which Violet doesn't think is fair: her muddy socks from sloshing in puddles, her broken shoelaces; and more and more frequently, her red hair. According to Miss Whiteley this red hair has something to do with her bad temper, which, she says regretfully, *is not at all ladylike.* She says these kinds of things after Violet pinches a boy for putting a frog on her seat, or pushes a sissy into a puddle. "You will learn to control yourself," she says in front of everyone, but talking directly to Violet. "I will help you." *Thanks heaps,* Violet thinks, mortified and all the angrier. She knows Miss Wittless—as the boys call her in the schoolyard—is dead wrong: her red hair is a gift, a treasure. Her father told her so himself.

When the quarantine is over and the school reopens, Gracella appears at the front of the classroom. Miss Whiteley introduces her to the class as *Grace.*

"Everyone," she says. "I would like you to welcome Miss Grace Marshall to our school. Grace has recently moved to our wonderful district from France, all the way across the sea in Europe." Grace curtsies and says, *allo,* then sits down behind Violet.

"My father won't let my mother send me to Catholic school either," she whispers into Violet's ear across her desk. Violet raises her eyebrows, because how did she know?

Grace tells Violet that her real father was killed in the war, in the very first month. He was the first casualty for France, and was decorated even though he didn't have a chance to do anything out of the ordinary. Grace says she doesn't remember much about him except that he had thick black hair, and he could play the violin. His favourite song was *Au Claire de la Lune,* which he sang to Grace when she was just a baby. Grace's mother has a bronze medal with his name engraved on the back that she keeps hidden in the toiletry drawer of her vanity, in with her underwear and stockings, although she doesn't have to hide it, Grace says, because Clayton can't find his own backside. She says that her mother met Clayton—she pronounces his name *C-la-yton*—at a hospital in France, when she went in to see about a sliver. She had been waxing the hardwood floors when she caught her finger on one of the grooves. Even though Dr. Marshall was supposed to be there for soldiers, he told her how to force the sliver out by soaking her fingers in warm water and salt. After that, they got married.

"A year later 'ee was 'it with shrapnel," Grace says. "It got 'im in the eye, and in the 'ead, and now 'ee just walks around smiling."

Violet likes Grace immediately: the way she talks, stretching out her words, sharpening them to a point, then putting them away like newly folded linen. She cannot say the letter F, and forgets entirely about her H's. *'Ow are you today?* she says, tilting her head, puckering her lips. She tells Violet that she has an accent.

"I do not."

"You sound like dee Americans."

"No I don't. You're the one with the accent."

Grace has long black braids and blue eyes, "A French speciale," says Mrs. Marshall. "Almost as rare as red hair." She wears pressed jumpers with blouses underneath, and cardigans with knitted belts and covered buttons. Violet decides that Grace is clever, because she can speak better English than her mother. She took lessons in school back in France and traveled across the English Channel twice to visit Buckingham Palace. The only thing Violet doesn't like about Grace, but she overlooks because she is an ally, is her mother's cooking: fish soup, pancakes thinner than paper with wild mushrooms wedged between. The skins of the mushrooms are slippery and yellow; they remind Violet of leeches.

"They are chanterelles." Mrs. Marshall says. "They come from outside, in the forest, right Gracella?" Violet picks them out and piles them into the corner of her plate to make them look smaller. She does not want to offend.

Together Grace and Violet look through the Eaton's catalogue that Mrs. Marshall keeps in a drawer by her bed. The catalogue is red on the front, with a black-and-white drawing of people in carriages riding through the streets of Toronto. When Violet and Grace get the chance to sneak into Mrs. Marshall's bedroom, they slip out the catalogue and go straight to the pages marked *Ailments*.

"Ooh, look at that!" says Grace, pointing to a pen-and-ink drawing of a woman from the rear clad in nothing but her underwear. Around her shoulders, her waist, and between her legs, runs a thick fabric-covered brace with various sets of buckles. The title of the item is Comfort Brace. "I'll bet that is just frightful!"

"Most definitely," giggles Violet. She reads the description aloud: "For the trials and ailments specific to ladies . . . trials and ailments!" she shrieks. Neither of them know what the comfort brace is for, but they know it is hilariously funny.

On the same page are some mushroom-shaped rubber devices that strike Violet as faintly obscene. Rubber nipples, the title says, and Grace keels over laughing. "Extra nipplesss," she says, dragging the 's' for effect. "In case your own get sore!"

After this they move on to the corset page, which is almost as good. All the women have real heads pasted on to pen-and-ink bodies, giving them the appearance of patchwork ghosts; some of their necks are drawn too big, and their heads look mismatched, or shrunken. Most of them wear petticoats and undershirts and stick their bosoms out as far as possible in one direction, while countering with their backsides in the other. The effect is one of strangely contorted profiles which Violet thinks look too much like the pictures of vampires she has seen in storybooks.

"Look," says Grace, pointing to one of the women. "They're still selling bustles. My mother says those are right out of fashion."

"Yes," Violet says, nodding. "We wouldn't wear those if our arses were on fire!"

Violet understands that although Grace is a foreigner, she is not as foreign as some of the children at her school. She is not as foreign, for instance, as the Chinese boys in the grade five class, who were born in British Columbia, but are still considered foreign. She is also different than the Native children who Violet has seen playing on the mud flats of the Capilano River, and who go to school at St. Paul's on the mission reserve. Violet doesn't know where they come from but figures their homeland must be far away, maybe even as far as Russia, because of the way the ladies from the Women's Institute talk about them. *Indians*, they say, in hushed tones, as if the word itself is a hex. They are not enemies, exactly, like the Huns, but they are also not allies. They are like the poor orphans in the pictures Violet has seen of war-torn Europe: Slavs with kerchiefs on their heads, long print skirts and shawls around their shoulders. They feast on fish which they spear from the Capilano River; they live in shacks towards the bottom of the hill.

Every morning Violet and Grace walk to school together. They meet each other in front of the drug store and head up the wooden sidewalk to the top of Lonsdale holding hands. Today Violet has her red hair drawn back at the sides into a blue bow, with the bottom left long in ringlets. Grace is in double braids with little wisps feathering out around her face. They carry their slates in their free hands, and boxes of slate pencils.

"This school is nothing like mine," says Grace. "Mine was strict."

"What was it like?" asks Violet, wishing she had been to France.

"We had to wear uniforms, plaid skirts with fringes on the side. And we were not in with the boys, except at recess."

Violet thinks she could do without the boys who chase her in the schoolyard and call her *carrots*. She throws dirt in their faces, or kicks them in the shins when she can catch them, but she would rather spend her time playing with Grace.

"We had longer hallways, as long as your street, with air raid tunnels beneath. When the Central Powers flew overhead a siren would sound and everyone would go underground and huddle together in a tunnel."

"That sounds poopy," says Violet, who likes to teach Grace bad words. Really it sounds exciting—she has never been underground—but she knows from her mother's friends that the war is *horrid*. The only thing she can think to do is make fun of it.

Grace crinkles up her nose and shrieks, giggling uncontrollably. "Poopy!" she says, skipping with exaggerated steps down the sidewalk. "*Trés trés* poopy!"

During history class Violet lets her mind wander. Miss Whiteley stands at the blackboard with her butter-coloured ruler pointing out battles on a map of Upper and Lower Canada. The front of her skirt is smeared with chalk. Above her head is an octagonal wooden clock with a brass pendulum that ticks painfully slowly. Violet can't stand it. School will never be over.

As Miss Whiteley speaks, her mouth opens and closes like a small sea creature expelling water; Violet can see the words gush out, and get carried off in the ensuing tides. They dash against rocks, splinter apart, and are reworked into a more exciting scenario: ravishing English maid with decoy cow fouls invasion. Creeps through woods occupied by sleeping soldiers who leer even in their dreams—it's her red hair they're leering at—and reaches the fort in time to sound the bell. All is saved except that the soldier can't take his eyes off—

"Violet, stand please." Her teacher's voice is like a yardstick to the knuckles.

Violet removes the flat of her hand from its groove in her chin and stands to face Miss Whiteley. She hopes she wasn't drooling.

"State the name of a famous person in contemporary history working to better the lives of humanity."

The first thing to her mind: "Miss Margaret Sanger."

Miss Whiteley is cautiously surprised. She does not recognize the name. "And what efforts does Miss Sanger make to better the lives of people today?"

Violet hesitates. Miss Whiteley would have to ask. She has overheard her father say it, what is the proper word? "Miss Margaret Sanger is a dedicated advocate of the birth control movement in America, Ma'am."

Scandalous. The older pupils in Violet's class turn crimson and squeal with delight and superiority. They know about girls like Violet. They have heard from their mothers. *Free thinkers.*

Miss Whiteley remains still for a whole minute, then picks up her ruler. "What you have said is inappropriate and uncouth. Perhaps you would rather spend your time more fruitfully, as you have obviously learned nothing from our lessons." She circles around Violet's back, guides her to the corner, and forces her to sit in a dust-covered corner. "Please count these specks of dirt. I will expect your calculations to be complete by the end of this class."

Violet stops herself from sneezing as her backside hits the floor. Then she reconsiders, and sneezes anyway—that terrible itch in her nose is rage. She looks at Miss Whiteley's stern face, grits her teeth, and decides at that moment that the bun piled high on her teacher's head looks exactly like a turd. Her foot goes to the dusty corner and stomps, her heel smears away the dirt. "There is no dust," she says, through sniffles. Her face is a hot flame.

After school Grace catches up with Violet. "You were brave," she says, putting her arm around her shoulders. Violet switches her slate from hand to hand, avoiding the sores where Miss Whiteley's ruler hit. All she did was clean a dusty corner. What's the big deal?

12

When Violet comes home from school on Friday her father is in the kitchen drinking a cup of coffee. She knows this is a sign, this afternoon repose; her father never sits in the kitchen except at mealtimes.

"Ho there Violet!" he says, enthusiastically. He is wearing his work shirt, the one he wears to plant the garden in, and stovepipe trousers held up by braided suspenders. His hair is a loose tangle on his head.

"Hello," she says.

At Jack's feet is a collection of items Violet has only seen in the garden shed scattered across the dirt-packed floor, or stacked up into perilous towers behind the rakes and shovels: tin cups with wire handles, an enamel kettle and matching spongeware soup bowl, a set of nesting pots tucked into a green army sack. There is also a jellyroll of blankets held together with leather straps and a wooden frame backpack the colour of winter mud.

"Violet," Jack says. "Daddy is going away for a little while. On an adventure."

Lila is at the sink peeling potatoes. Violet can hear the thin curling scabs of the potato flesh hit the porcelain with a slap. This part is a ritual in the Spencer family: her mother at the sink on Friday afternoon soaking a stack of Russets or new spring Norlands in frigid, twice-used water, scrubbing off the dirty boils, digging out the eyes and lime-green poisonous bits where the potatoes got too much sun. The potatoes form the tastiest half of fish-and-chip Friday, a tradition that Lila insists upon.

As she peels, Lila jerks her hands and presses hard on the knife, harder than usual, Violet notices, as though she is striking a drum or a hollowed-out gourd with musical sticks. She bends her head sharply downward, in the exaggerated pose of a leaking scarecrow.

"I want you to help your mother," Jack says, indicating Lila's presence with a toss of his hand. "You will need to be a big girl and take care of Matthew for me."

Violet doesn't want to take care of smelly Matthew, who poops in his diapers and spills his food. That is Lila's job. She's the mother. "I can't," she says. What she means is *I won't*.

Lila turns around and regards them both. Her lower lip hangs pitifully off her face by the barest threads. "See what you are leaving me with Jack," she says, the knife pointing limply in Violet's direction. "It's your duty to stay."

Jack sighs. "I just need a couple of months."

"That's a long time Jack. Longer than you think."

"Well it's the only choice you've given me Lila, you and your beliefs. There's more dignity in the other, but you won't have it."

Lila's face crumbles. "You know I don't abide by divorce."

"So this is how it will be for now. There's plenty of money from the shipyards. That will hold you over until I get back. I'm going to be cooped up all winter. I need to take this time to get away for a while."

Now Jack looks at Violet and she can see something in his face: the look that children get in the schoolyard when everyone ignores them, when no one wants to play what they want to play. She has also heard the word *divorce* and it scares her. Why can't her mother behave? Jack rarely raises his voice but he is almost shouting now. There are veins in his forehead, rising up like earthworms after a heavy rain. If her mother stopped whining and snivelling—behaviour deserving of punishment according to Miss Whiteley—Jack might reconsider. He might not go.

Violet figures that he is off for one of his "holidays," the ones Lila told her about while they scrubbed the floor. She can vaguely remember a time—at the beginning of the war before Matthew was born and the shipyards started to boom—when he sat in the very same chair, a paper envelope in his hand. He was rougher then, with whiskers sprouting and mud on his collar. He had just come back from someplace far away. *Look*, he said, emptying the contents of the envelope onto the table. *Gold*. Violet had been disappointed, expecting something shiny and miraculous. Something that you could look in to and see your face. Wasn't gold supposed to be magical? Wasn't it supposed to be solid? Instead she saw flakes: fine particles no bigger than dirt on the floor. A little mound of them stacked by the careful fingers of her father into a dusty cone. A sneeze could blow them away.

"Are you going to look for gold?" she asks.

"Yes," Jack says, a smile tugging at his lips, because at least Violet, his one and only daughter, understands him. "Yes Violet, that's part of it."

"Then I want to come with you," she says. She is older now, she could carry the pots and the blankets; she could fight off the mosquitoes and protect him from scurvy, feed him the nubbly rosehips that are mentioned in her third-grade reader.

The edges of Jack's face melt into a tender grin; Violet imagines keeping him there like a wad of dough, sculpting his features into a permanent look of contentment and rapture so that he would never again be cross. "You have to go to school Violet, and to help out your mother. You have to be a big girl."

I am a big girl, she thinks, which is why you should take me. Instead she says, "You might get hurt Daddy. You will be lonely."

Jack reclines and looks at the table. His face changes again, almost instantly, as though he were trying on masks: sorrow, dreadful woe. The expressions whiz by Violet at an alarming rate, but she takes them in and memorizes the furrows, the drawn-up mouth. She stores them up for later.

"What makes you think he's going to be alone?" Lila asks, biting her lower lip. Her own face is sharp, her lips barbed. She forces the words through tears and a throat full of anger.

Violet knows that she isn't expected to answer. She also knows she will be left behind.

13

Lord, thinks Violet to herself in the Avondale lounge, *was I ever that young?* The midday news has played out its weary sensational cycle of floods and car wrecks, of serial-killing chipmunk-faced children in baggy trousers and sweat tops, and here Violet sits in her wheelchair, dabbing a tissue shamelessly at her nose. Oprah Winfrey is on the screen, her coffee-coloured face made up of nothing but infinitesimal dots the size of pin pricks, her great pumpkin lips entreating her guest to continue with her story. "Go on honey," is what she says, in her solicitous, I-support-you-one-hundred-percent voice of angels. "We understand." Her guest, clad in a continuous black velvet jumper the texture of cat hair, hesitates for a moment then resumes her tale.

Oh Please, thinks Violet, who doesn't believe in all this spilling your guts; it's too revealing for her, and too fraudulent. Some women have no dignity at all, which explains why she sees them running around in see-through blouses with gauzy necklines, or reflective silver mini-skirts that make them look like walking ads for aluminum siding. *Fashion my arse,* she thinks. Don't they know that most of those clothes are designed by men? *Let them try wearing it for a change.*

She looks around at the other residents to see if any of them caught her sniffling. Most have given up on consciousness, opting instead for the numbness of sleep. Three or four lurch forward in their chairs, swaying tentatively on chrome edges, their hands curled inward like the paws of dead mice. Some of them snore as though they are slurping the tail ends of milkshakes through straws. *Typical afternoon at the Avondale,* Violet thinks: *sit, doze, drool.*

As for her father, well, what can you expect? He was a wanderer, he could not be *pinned down.* Within a year of the war she was used to his pattern of coming and going like the good weather, retreating into the mountains when daylight savings was on its last legs, returning when the rain set in. Without fail he appeared on their Chesterfield doorstep every November, his sack of rusting mud-laden camping gear looking like a weather-beaten hood ornament, his own face redder, grubbier, as though he'd been sleeping in ditches. He brought presents from the places he'd visited: trains or soldiers for Matthew who grew despite his exclamations that he should slow down, and wool for Lila that came in three colours and smelled of the heavy-sweet oily smell of lanolin. Always he saved Violet's for last, drawing her to his knee, hiding it behind his back in one of his tight-fisted hands. Sometimes, if the present was small enough—a miniature wooden doll, or a two-inch dug-out canoe with totemic designs and a slender keel—he might pull it from her ear, saying in his surprised adult voice, "Well, what do you know?" Her favourite gift was the pipe that he'd whittled himself from a pin cherry tree, sticking a branch with his jack-knife and hollowing out its centre. Violet imagined him sitting by a serpentine river, humming as he worked. She didn't care that she was not allowed to smoke.

Admit it kiddo, she says to herself, *you adored that man.* And what was wrong with that? Even if he was smitten with wanderlust, he still provided for them; he had priorities, an honourable thing in this day of negligent fathers and their missing child support payments. He was funny, a real dynamo. *He was there when we needed him and that's all that matters.* And let's face it, Violet wasn't the only one who adored Jack. He didn't spend those adventures alone, she surmised later on, when she was old enough to understand the term *other woman* (entirely different than *lady*). He took along the person he loved (Violet once saw the picture in his wallet), a woman who wore breeches and lace-ups and miner's shirts; who had cropped flyaway hair and no children. Violet realized in retrospect that she herself was probably a liability to Lila, a lead weight around her muslin-clad neck: *an accident.* If she had never been conceived, would her mother have gone off with Jack, clambering in caves, sleeping in smoke-filled canvas tents that smelled like wet leather? Would he have married her at all?

She couldn't help finding fault with her mother for being so bitter when Jack returned, for treating him like something that the cat dragged in. *Hello Jack,* she would say, neck stiff, eyes locked into place like hardened, embedded stones. No hugs, no embraces; not even a pat on the back. Days went by until he was allowed to sleep in his own bed for goodness sake, the one he built with his own two hands! At the time this had angered Violet, and she refused to help her mother with the housework: *let her do it herself if she thinks she's so great,* she said to no one in particular. The house was not pleasant, those first few days, not the kind of place a house should be.

Now she knows that her mother was only being human. Jack wanted a divorce and Lila wouldn't consent. Violet likes to think, in retrospect, that her father would have supported the family despite a divorce, but she doesn't really know for sure. He always told her the age of prosperity was upon them, and that it was full of possibilities. As a girl, this excited Violet. It was only as a woman that she realized the possibilities he was referring to were for himself.

ROAR

14

The snow starts to melt on Thursday. Elsie sits in her grandmother's kitchen sipping jasmine tea from a china mug covered by the vines of wild blackberries. Violet has a whole set of these mugs—bone white with gold-rimmed handles, dainty too-narrow bottoms and fluted openings like the centres of daffodils—which she stows neatly away on brass hooks beneath her kitchen cupboards. Each one is decorated with slightly different forms of prickly vegetation done in natural muted watercolours and titled in elegant script at its base: salmonberries, thimbleberries, and—one that Elsie doesn't recognize—cloudberries, a copper-white creeper with serrated leaves. Elsie drains her tea and turns the mug upside down to read the fading inscription: *Wild Forest Berries of Canada, Made in England.* Her grandmother always did have an affinity for English china.

Today she will meet Tia downtown. Luckily the buses are almost back on schedule, or so she has heard from the local traffic-woman, cheerfully bidding her listeners good luck as she gets into her own chartered helicopter and buzzes above the city to check on car jams. Of course she's cheerful, Elsie thinks, she doesn't have to be seen. She's just a voice on the airwaves, and a disembodied one at that. Elsie sighs and gets up from the table, swishing her breakfast crumbs onto the floor and into the corner with her foot. She will sweep as soon as she can find the broom.

In the bathroom she looks at her face, smiling as optimistically as she can. "Hi," she says to the mirror image which looks far too rumpled, too distorted and splotchy to be her own reflection. "I thought you were younger." She fills the sink with water, scrubs her cheeks and chin with a face-cloth, splashes water into her eyes to reduce the puffiness that is developing there like a fresh bruise. Last night was rough. She was into the photo albums again, the ones of her father, of Daniel and herself on their various trips, Sauble Beach, Algonquin, Montreal, and earlier on, when they had money, Graceland and its giant billboards mounted along the highway, Elvis smiling immortally from white teeth: *Welcome to My World.* Although the act of looking up these memories is self-indulgent, Elsie can't help herself; she is a voyeur of her own past. Despite the fact that she knows how everything turns out, she always hopes, somewhere in the back of her head, that the ending will be a surprise.

Take last night: she ended up crying like a baby, snotting up her grandmother's blankets with her own pathetic longings. *I did the right thing by leaving,* she told herself, wiping her eyes, *I do not want to go back.* But she was less certain than before, less certain than

[166]

the day she packed her duffel bag, cramming its denim pouches with underpants and mismatched socks, while Daniel slunk around the apartment looking wounded. That day she was sure of herself, as sure as she had ever been.

She gathered up her toothbrush, her special shampoos for the auburn-haired, relishing the idea that Daniel would soon be alone, helpless; that he would grovel his way across the country, whimpering for Elsie to rescue him from his newfound desolation.

Since then conviction has been leaking out of her like air from a balloon. So much effort has to be made just to get up in the morning, to butter her toast instead of eating it dry, because who really cares anyway? Certainly not Elsie. She is looking more and more like the bag ladies that she sees scavenging in waste bins on Granville, ragged around the edges, unloved, with the dredged up scarves of dead people wound around their necks to keep the spirits at bay; except that the scarves she wears belong to Violet who is still alive and kicking, and who has more associated spirits than the Old and New Testaments put together.

After smoothing her eyebrows back into place (she does not want to look like an oversized Brook Shields), Elsie brushes her unruly hair into the usual layered attempt at chic, which ends up instead looking like a fierce mushroom. She does like the colour, the reddish tint, and it's her very own, her saving grace. In high school her unusual height could have put her in the same class as the freaks, the kids who bobbed down hallways wearing second-hand tuxedos thinking they were cool, or girls with stainless steel braces encircling their heads like the rings of Saturn. Elsie was the tallest girl—a beanpole, a towering scarecrow—but her hair was the colour of cinnamon, and people liked her.

Today she goes for the natural, slightly dishevelled look, and leaves her hair loose around her face. She can get away with this facade of carelessness for a few more years, why not indulge? On her cheeks, chin, and forehead she dabs liquid foundation in lacteal triangles and rubs them in until they banish her freckles; she follows with a mellow sorrel line beneath each eye and a thin layer of Vaseline to beef up her eyelashes (a trick Violet taught her for when the chips were down). She tops it all off with a spritz of hair spray from a non-aerosol bottle (why add to the destruction of the universe?) and a dash of honeysuckle oil behind the ears.

Elsie dislikes riding the bus during the week because she is inevitably shoved into a stranger's armpit, or seated at crotch level with nothing but zippers to fill the view. More often than not, her size compels her to stand, to press herself against the emergency glass windows or the space reserved for wheelchairs—she displaces a lot of usable room. Standing taller than the average passenger, Elsie's outlook is somewhat unique: a parade of scalps and heads kerchiefed against the rain; a selection of flattops, pageboys, bald spots, and ponytails concealed or sculpted into place using the outdated and cutting edge techniques of a whole history of coiffeurs. She passes the time by making mental notes on how *not* to part her hair.

When they hit Burrard Street Elsie gets off the bus and walks away from the mountains, past the inner city arboretum filled with dormant rhododendrons, past the Bentall building, a smoked sepia version of the mirror-covered skyscrapers taking over the city. At the building's entrance scores of well-dressed business people move around one another, tilting, scowling, sandwiches in hand; they are like the giant herds of woolly sheep Elsie has seen on farms, shuffling from one trough to another at mealtimes, with looks of purpose and cautious greed. Where are they all going? Elsie wonders, and why in such a hurry? The coast is supposed to be laid back, slow paced; but too many easterners have infiltrated the province, filling up its condominiums, its up-market co-ops, reproducing like rabbits. With them has come the need for coffee bars on every corner, the advent of waterproof socks (they are not used to the weather, the intermittent sun), but even they have been altered by the climate. Instead of Harry Rosen suits, Burrard Street is flecked with men in purple dress shirts, hand-tooled belts holding up their sardine-coloured chinos. It's Bloor Street gone slack, minus the monotones of grey and black, the unending stream of slicked-back hair.

When Elsie locates the restaurant it is almost noon. Blinking in the sun, she stands for a minute on the sidewalk beneath a wooden sign that hangs from burnished copper wires bent haphazardly into hooks. The sign is an orange circle eclipsed by a rising sun which smiles maliciously, knavishly, as though it is up to something. *Greenhouse gases*, thinks Elsie, *skin cancer*.

Inside, L'Orange is a modern attempt to stylize fast food and make it once again desirable. The tables are black iron with faux marble surfaces, and are tall, as in jazz bars, with matching padded stools that give Elsie plenty of room to dangle her legs. The walls are done in three colours, salmon, ochre, and something approaching magenta, overlaid and smeared with a rag. Elsie knows the technique because Daniel tried it once in their own apartment; tried, but did not succeed. Instead their walls looked as if they had been whipped with a wet towel, leaving behind the great bleeding scars of carmine paint that he'd chosen on impulse. *Towel burn*, Daniel called it, *oh well*. Elsie felt as though she was living inside a wound those last few years. In more ways than one.

At the back of the restaurant some of the well-dressed people from Burrard have formed a line-up beneath menus drawn by hand in colourful chalk on overhead blackboards. They laugh and pitch as if they are out on recess, waving their arms in the air in the cryptic, obscure messages of stockbrokers. Behind a glassed-in counter, servers wearing aprons and hairnets and latex gloves take orders as they are shouted above the din: *one Revitalizer, hold the honey, two Indonesian chicken wraps heated to go*. Elsie squints at the menu, reading the ingredients. Carrot juice, it seems, is making a comeback.

She is looking for someone in lime green; Tia told Elsie what she would be wearing so that she would have an easy time picking her out in a crowd. Elsie can see two women in this colour: one at the cash register fumbling with her purse, and another in a lime-green chest-hugging sweater on her way to the washroom. Both are older than Tia should be, and neither seem to be looking for company.

Elsie sits down at one of the corner tables and stares bravely out the window. In Brimstock she never cared about being alone; she went out frequently after Marian's death to clear her head, putting on one of her best scowls so that everyone would know she was by herself on purpose. Being alone in Vancouver is somehow different; here she feels the way she felt as a child: outcast, peripheral. She always attracts the wrong kind of people.

"Elsie? It's got to be you."

Elsie turns to see a woman in a leather skirt and a lime green coat with a gigantic belt buckle cinched at its middle. The woman is smiling a terrific smile from a perky mouth the colour of cherries, and is smaller than Elsie, much smaller. *She's from the same gene pool?* Elsie thinks. *Incredible.* "Tia," she says.

Tia stands for a moment wrestling with her coat and Elsie wonders half-heartedly, *Should I hug this woman? She's one of my only living relatives.* Instead she stays seated and watches. The coat isn't leather, but some synthetic material; in all probability, highly flammable. "How did you recognize me?" she says.

"Oh, we have family pictures, you know the kind. I think your father sent us one when you graduated."

"Yikes," says Elsie, remembering the photo. "I had quite a hairdo."

"Impressive," Tia says. She adds: "I'm sorry about your father. I got the card too late to come to the funeral. I had just started a new job, things were pretty harsh at the time."

Elsie catches the word *harsh,* a coastal euphemism. She can't bring herself to use it, still trying to shed *awesome* and *decent* from her high-school days. Instead she goes for the wishy-washyness of Brimstock: "Well, yes. Things are better for me now too." *Better how?* she wants to know.

"I hope heart conditions don't run in the family. Everyone on our father's side seems to die young," Tia says.

She is referring to Clifford and his father, Elsie surmises, but she forgot one thing. "What about Violet?" she asks. "She's eighty-six? That's not so young."

Tia looks down from the blackboard menus, her small red mouth parting in the centre. "What? Oh, Violet. Yes, she's still going isn't she."

Still going. Like a watch, or the Duracell battery commercial. Elsie realizes Tia is not going to want to discuss what she wants to discuss: that Violet is both of their responsibilities, that they are her closest relatives, and although Elsie is the executor, they are both in charge.

"Have you seen her?" Elsie says.

Tia straightens and rearranges her coat on her lap. "Seen her, I don't even know where she is. The Avonlea, or something like that. She's all the way over in North Van."

Exactly how far I came today to eat lunch with you, Elsie thinks, but she's careful not to think it aloud. She's beginning to feel like the better grandchild: Tia has lived in Vancouver for years. "The Avondale," she says. "On Marine Drive."

"Oh," says Tia. Then she changes the subject: "You have to meet my boyfriend Jeff. He is a real sweetheart."

They bring their lunches back to the table and sit on the stools, supporting themselves with their elbows. Elsie watches Tia's mouth open and close like a goldfish eating tiny flakes, like a bird pecking at suet or millet seeds at the bird feeder. She sees a family resemblance, after inspection: the tilt of the head, the way she furrows her eyebrows. Elsie, however, is the one with the red highlights. A genetic branding of the Spencer family.

"So," says Elsie, wanting to get back to the subject of responsibilities. "You know that Violet has given me the power of attorney over her estate? I don't know the total contents of the will, but your father did say that both of us were named. He spoke to her about it before the stroke. The estate excludes the house, of course. For that she has other plans."

Tia sighs and sips her juice, a muddy green concoction of ground-up celery and apples. "Yes. My father told me I was getting something. He also said she didn't have much to leave. The only thing of any value is the property. Did you know she was offered three hundred thousand for that seedy place? For the land of course, not the house. They would just tear that down."

"What did she say?" Elsie says.

"No, of course. She wants to keep it. Apparently she has plans."

"So I'm told," Elsie says. She has heard about these plans from the lawyer, although not all the details. For those she has to talk to Violet.

"Anyway," Tia continues. "It doesn't really matter. She's still alive, so dividing up money is a little premature. And she was flat broke before she had the stroke. No bank account or anything."

You obviously haven't looked in the chimney, Elsie thinks, but this she also keeps to herself. Instead she nods, adding: "There is her pension," she says. "Which I've been using to pay the Avondale—it's only a partially subsidized rest home. The monthly balance goes towards the utilities and the upkeep of the house."

Tia leans back in her chair and stretches her neck and shoulders, moving her head around in a small, low-impact circle. The motion reminds Elsie of an aerobics class she attended back in university, during the year that she temporarily lost her senses: line-ups of women just like Tia, feline, petite, poised in front of a mirror making chugging sounds with their bodies, and a teacher, coarse, muscle-bound, shouting from the centre of her pink, huffed-up face, *Come on girls! Three more, two more! Keep it up, keep it up!*

"Well," says Tia. "I'm glad it's not me in charge of things. I'm too busy right now. I'm nearly burnt out as it is."

Elsie nods, relieved at Tia's lack of interest. There will be no family squabbles after all.

"She was always closer to your family anyway, until that unfortunate thing happened with your mother."

"What unfortunate thing?" Elsie asks.

"Well," says Tia, hesitating. "That fight. The one that made her stop talking to you, stop visiting."

"I didn't know it had been on the evening news," Elsie says, surprised. How many things does Tia know about her family? Her own parents rarely talked about their relatives.

"My mother was sorry for you, you know. She always talked about getting you to come stay with us after Marian died. She thought you might like to get away, but I guess it was too far, too complicated."

"Well," Elsie says, reprieved. Somebody had cared

after all. "We managed. It probably wouldn't have worked out with school and all. And my father needed my help around the house. My mother, as you might have heard, was in charge of all that."

"Yes," says Tia. "But I never got the whole story. My parents didn't have much to say on the subject of your family. It's like nobody ever talked."

"It's an epic," says Elsie. "Remind me to tell you sometime."

"Well," says Tia. "I've got time now."

Elsie shifts, nervous now that she is being asked to reveal something. She has never shared the full story of her mother's death with anyone, save Daniel, and he had been drunk. She's not sure that she is ready to tell someone who might be listening.

But Tia doesn't look like anyone Elsie has known before: someone with ears, with interest. Someone who won't use the story against her, to have her admitted, committed. To laugh in her face.

"It's O.K.," says Tia. "If you want to leave out the tough bits."

The tough bits are the only bits, thinks Elsie, but she makes a mental note to skip anything that smarts. She breathes deeply and takes a sip of her coffee. She begins at the beginning.

Marian's death came as a surprise to most of the people in Our Lady of the Immaculate Conception Parish Church. Elsie's mother had never missed a Sunday Mass, nor had she ever called in sick to the convalescent homes or the hospital. She was staunch and purposeful, a woman with direction and vigour who could not be put down by a trifling cough or a pitiful swelling of the throat. So when she was admitted to the hospital on the day of Elsie's Confirmation, even Clifford was astonished. Elsie, it appeared, was the only one who saw her mother's death coming.

Elsie was in the seventh grade at Our Lady Elementary when she noticed the first indication. She was taller by then, with feet the same size as her mother's; she stood on the fringes of her class photograph with the grinning afro-headed teacher, away from all the other girls who were dressed primly and seated on benches. The teacher in the photograph was not Miss Pollard, but a man named Mr. Noseworthy whose unseemly red face was tinted by blood vessels that came to the surface of his skin like catgut threads floating in a puddle.

The boys who had once scared Elsie with their parking-lot antics now seemed shrunken and unfathomable, dwarfed to an impracticable smudge on the recesses of her childhood. They had been replaced by a new line-up of upper-grade boys made awkward by puberty, their faces and necks blemished by pimples, their chins sparsely coated with the downy hairs of kittens. Above the tallest of them Elsie stood, a sheepish, reluctant beacon, lean as a fence post, taller than anything for miles, and wishing, with all her heart, that God would deliver her from her sins of vanity and make her stop growing.

With the allowance that she gets from her father, Elsie buys a pair of cotton pants from the Long and Tall section of the Sears catalogue. She begins to slouch, just a little, to take the edge off her shoulders and reduce her height by several inches. Although she is no taller than a grown woman with healthy roots, Elsie is thirteen years old and too thin and flat-chested to fill out regular garments in Ladies' Wear. Most of the dresses come with molded breast-cups, or broad, fanny pinching waistlines that leave her feeling like a scarecrow playing dress-up.

At school she is rarely teased. Although the boys in her class are roughening around the edges, exposing themselves to older adult forms of entertainment and conversation, they too know about courtesy and politeness; they too know about hell. They leave her alone for the most part, skirting around her in the schoolyard, avoiding her at lunch, singling her out only during gym class when the game of the day is basketball.

During health class these boys are ushered out of the room into another corner of the school, and Elsie, along with the rest of the girls, learns how babies are made. A woman in a white lab coat hands out mimeographed booklets stapled at the sides, *What Every Catholic Girl Should Know*, and explains the meanings of various clinical-looking diagrams. Elsie is not surprised by the content—the headings in the booklet are familiar words printed in block letters that she has heard from Marian's lips many times: *Hygiene, Sanitation*—but they are followed by recommendations that strike Elsie as a little on the slack side. According to *What Every Catholic Girl Should Know*, sexual intercourse is permitted in the eyes of the church when a couple united in holy matrimony is trying to conceive a child. In addition, this intercourse, with its black-and-white diagrams, its various jellies and painful-sounding instructions, is designated as the only way to create babies. The booklet decidedly leaves out all information on immaculate conceptions. Elsie decides not to show the book to Marian.

[177]

At home Marian develops a cough; she heaves into the sink with the same dry hack emitted by a dog straining a leash. Circles unfold beneath her eyes like pools of tar. When Elsie cleans out the wastebasket in the bathroom she finds clumps of her mother's hair scattered in among the Q-Tips and white Kleenex, the brittle strands like cunningly placed birds' nests hidden from predators. She overhears Marian and Clifford talking in the kitchen.

"I've been feeling tired," her mother says, "that's all."

"You should take a rest. You're working too hard. You don't have to do so much."

"It's not me who decides these things, Clifford. You should know that by now. I should be doing more. Think what might happen to Elsie if I didn't."

As winter approaches, some of the grade seven girls start sitting out from Elsie's gym class, complaining of cramps to embarrassed Mr. Noseworthy. They perch languidly on benches at the perimeters of the gymnasium floor, laugh a secret, clandestine laugh in the change room, and say, with a shake of their freshly brushed hair: *I have to sit out this whole week. My Aunt is up from Red River.*

Elsie can't bring herself to admit to Mr. Noseworthy when *her* aunt is visiting, because admitting would be telling, and telling such things is inappropriate. Instead she participates, week after week, month after month, slapping a hockey puck with a plastic stick, thumping the base of the perilous white volleyball with her fist, feeling queasy, head-achey; feeling soiled.

When she turns fourteen she is ready for the sacrament of Confirmation. Marian and Clifford come to the Church of Our Lady to witness the bishop smear grease on her forehead and pronounce her an adult in the eyes of God. After tea and digestive biscuits, they pile into the Lincoln and head for home. Marian looks directly ahead and says in a bodeful voice, "Take me to the hospital."

From the back seat Elsie can see her mother's hair brushed carefully over the thin spots, falling in a dull sheen to her shoulders. She can see the milky-white flesh of her lower neck peeking out over her cotton print dress, spotted faintly with lesions. All of this is tinted a sickly green by the woven green hat roosting on her head, and the sun behind it, streaming in the window.

"What?" Clifford says. "You're not thinking of working?"

Her mother continues looking ahead at the street, straightening her shoulders. "I'm ready now Clifford, I wasn't before. Take me to the hospital."

Elsie's mother is in a private room in Brimstock General Hospital. In the centre of the room is the bed, a plump, tight-sheeted mattress surrounded by chrome supports, and a feeding tray on a single arm that swings back and forth above her body like a dentist's light. Next to the bed, on the side closest to the window, is a small table covered in plastic drinking cups that the nurse fills with water and hands to Marian three times a day so that she can wash down her pills. The pills are also there, next to the drinking cups, in plastic bottles of various sizes that look to Elsie like film canisters, except that they are translucent, harder to open, and covered on one side by the doctor's messy handwriting.

On the other side of the bed, on top of a leaner table made from pressed wood, bunches of flowers multiply in one-litre glass jars: arrangements of carnations, gladioli, and festive curled ribbons stacked one against the other with small wistful cards nesting inside their foliage. *May God be with you Maryanne. Get Well.* The flowers are from church organizations—the Catholic Women's League, or the Knights of Columbus—and from the staffs of the Brimstock nursing homes where Marian did her charity work. There is also a stuffed elephant from Elsie's father, with a diamond-shaped tag that says in sequined letters: "For My Wife."

Elsie is told by a straight-browed doctor with a stethoscope springing from his chest pocket that her mother's lungs are full of liquid. He explains the stages of pneumonia, which he says is the cause of Marian's present suffering, and tells her that her mother is a fighter. He also tells her that pneumonia is not caused by going outside without your hat, as Elsie once believed, but rather by a complex series of circumstances that—in her mother's case—have something to do with helping the sick.

"Your mother caught this disease through honourable actions," he says to Elsie sternly. "Don't you let anyone tell you otherwise."

To Clifford he gives more details. "We didn't take the precautions then that we do now. Now we wouldn't let a volunteer near that kind of situation." He also uses the words *virus* and *tainted blood*, brushing his hair back from his forehead so that Elsie can see the lines of sweat erupting from his pores. He gives them both a set of latex gloves and masks to wear when visiting Marian, and tells Clifford not to kiss her on the mouth.

When Elsie enters her mother's room she sits on the chair beside her bed and tries not to act scared. She knows that Marian is a strong woman, and that God put her on earth because Elsie needed discipline, but she also knows that her mother is sick—very sick—and that without her she will have to take charge. She just doesn't know if she has the strength.

"Elsie," Marian says from chapped lips. "I made it. I want to make sure you understand."

Elsie, who doesn't know what it is she is supposed to understand, nods out of habit. The elastic on the mask is cutting into the backs of her ears and she wants to take it off and throw it out the window; but she knows this kind of behaviour is inappropriate. She has been in the hospital enough times to know how to act.

"Don't you see?" Marian continues, lifting her head anemically from the pillow. "Now that you are safe I don't have to fight."

"Fight?" Elsie says, who wants to understand.

"Yes. You are safe now, an adult in the eyes of God. Elsie. I don't have to fight any more because now you are responsible. Now you," she adds, "will be the one to answer."

Elsie crosses her hands in her lap and looks at the floor. Her mother's face is not the way she remembers, stern, with points of stress knotted around her eyes and throat; with dark patches of skin flickering like small shadows in the space beneath her ears, and her lips, thin and liver-coloured, rigorously engraved. She is no longer a fearful sovereign with severe limits and painful eyes, but more like a spider, only faintly menacing.

Two weeks later Elsie is called from school to visit her mother, who has taken a turn for the worse. When she enters, Marian is already looking in her direction; the brown beads of her eyes roll across Elsie's face, surmising. Beneath them the circles have deepened to ghoulish craters, yellowing around the edges like sores. Her hair is loose and oily against the pillowcase; it looks to Elsie like the tangled lengths of jute used in rug-making and macramé.

"Mother," she says, wishing to break the stare. Her eyes are even more vacant.

Marian's lips part and a gasp flutters out. Or is it in? Elsie can't tell. The sound is desperate, sarcastic; a derisive sucking. Elsie steps forward and places her gloved hand on the covers. Beneath is her mother, diminished, weak: *in the flesh*.

Marian's mouth opens again. This time the sucking is louder, more ferocious. "You should have tried harder," she gasps, forcing out the words as though her mouth is full of wool.

Elsie steps back, shocked.

Her mother's inanimate torso gathers momentum, rising, rolling; her arms begin to shake, her legs, her feet, begin to rattle; everything convulses as if agitated by an earthquake.

Her voice goes on, higher now in pitch: an ascending squeal. "I won't go with you," she says, eyes widening with hatred. "I won't go."

"Go where?" Elsie says.

Marian looks at her and hisses: "Stupid girl. She's not talking to you."

Now the voice is not Marian's; it comes from her lips, but it is not her voice at all. Elsie does not recognize the sound at first, there is too much rasping, too much unexplainable laughter. She stands with her hands at her sides and listens. "Heavy," it giggles, "She's very, very heavy."

With a thrust Marian's body flips hard against the chrome railings of the bed. Elsie sees a contorted grin where her mother's mouth used to be, hears the cackle fading from the room like a smothered recording. Then Marian's body rises up beneath the sheets, beneath the scabrous chenille bedspread and carefully arranged heating pads placed against her hips and shoulders; her knees are poky volcanoes, her chest a heaving mountain range spewing out hot air and dry threats. If Elsie could see below the sheets, she would estimate six inches of space lies between her mother and the bed, but she is in a state of shock and nobody will expect her to get this part right. Instead she stands processing the events; she can't be sure of anything.

With a thud her mother's body slams against the mattress and is deposited like a discarded banana peel on the bed. Her neck is cocked sideways, an afterthought, a footnote, so absently attached to her body that Elsie can tell her mother's flesh is no longer inhabited. Behind her the door opens and Clifford enters jangling his keys. He is followed by the doctor.

Elsie feels a pair of arms go around her shoulders and hears her father's voice. "Elsie," he says. For the first time she realizes she is crying. "Elsie, come with me."

She slips her hands into her pockets and feels their emptiness, realizing with horror that her mother was right: she forgot the salt. The salt to drive away the devil, to safeguard her mother's soul. She removed the shaker months ago, when she stopped making rounds at the hospital, and now she is useless against the power of evil. All she has is her bare hands.

"Come on Elsie," says Clifford again, leading her to the door. "She's gone. It's too late."

And he's right: but only partly. It is too late for Marian, for her mortal self; but she isn't gone. Not completely. Elsie knows she has failed, and this time the consequence is her mother's soul.

15

This is what Elsie tells Tia, more or less, crouched over her double espresso in the chaos of L'Orange. She tells about her mother's illness, about how afraid people were of the word *AIDS* at that time. Back in the early eighties the disease suggested some illicit dealings with the devil, some you-get-what-you-deserve responses from community members who stepped up onto their soap boxes and began loud declarations upon hearing the words *sexually transmitted disease.* The doctor's warnings to Elsie had been in earnest. People would not go easy on the truth in her mother's case, even if she had contracted the disease through honourable actions. There would be uproar, name-calling; there would be ostracization. The cause of death was generally accepted as pneumonia, a truth not entirely suspect considering it was the final illness to overpower Marian's already ravaged body.

What she does not mention in her conversation with Tia are the voices. She does not want to end up in a loony bin prematurely, a youthful unmarried Violet with arm restraints and tape across her mouth. She does not want to summon the voices back by giving them room to breathe. Both Tia and Elsie know dementia runs in the family, but only Elsie knows it runs on both sides.

She also refrains from mentioning other things, things she cannot talk about but remembers all the same, as she pays the bill and says goodbye to Tia, accepting a farewell hug, her body stiff in this unfamiliar lock of affection; as she walks from L'Orange to the bus stop and sees that she has missed her bus.

"Damn," says Elsie, as the 210 pulls away from the curb, leaving behind only pavement, the smell of fuel and inner-city decay.

"There'll be another," says a man in a T-shirt, leaning against a pole. "Relax a little. Take some time to think."

"I don't need time to think," mumbles Elsie as she sits on a hard wooden bench and sighs into her coat. But she has it all the same. She will have to wait half an hour.

Four months after Marian's death, Elsie is called to the principal's office. She sits with her legs crossed beneath her chair, waiting for Mr. Jarvis to finish talking on the telephone. As he speaks his lips fill up like a balloon, and he scribbles messy notations onto a piece of paper. Outside the window she can hear the janitor mowing the lawn. The smell of the impending summer holiday seeps in through the glass. She knows what the summons is about: last week she told Mr. Jarvis that she wanted to attend Brimstock Secondary even after he advised otherwise; he said she would be making a grave mistake choosing the public school instead of the blessed Catholic one.

"All right," says Mr. Jarvis, hanging up the phone. "I just want to make sure you know what you are getting into, because there is still time to change your mind. The forms won't be available until tomorrow. I want to be absolutely sure that you know Brimstock High is completely secular."

"I know," says Elsie, who has given her choice some thought. Lots of thought.

"There will be no spiritual support at a secular high school, nor will there be opportunities for spiritual fulfilment. In fact," he says, tapping his pen on his desk. "There will likely be no Catholics at all."

"I know," says Elsie again, who has made up her mind, and Mr. Jarvis frowns. He was hoping to bring her around, she can see that now, and she feels slightly traitorous for letting him down. But she is an adult, at least in eyes of the church, and this is her decision.

"I just want to make sure," he adds more delicately, "that this rebelliousness is not the result of your mother. Your mother was a saint in many ways Elsie, but you should know at the same time that she wasn't exactly *normal*."

"What do you mean?" says Elsie.

"She wasn't," says Mr. Jarvis carefully, "like other people in the church. Like other parents. She was a little eccentric, Elsie. A little severe. What I'm trying to say is that you shouldn't be giving up your faith because of your mother, because, with time, you'll find the Church is in fact very liberal."

Elsie looks at the wall beside Mr. Jarvis's balding head where two framed portraits gaze back at her with regret: Pope John Paul II and Queen Elizabeth. Both of them wear elaborate crowns on their heads and gowns like wedding cakes, but only the Queen is smiling. It is a tense smile, like the one on the two-dollar bill, jacked up by prudery and elocution lessons. Elsie knows that she too is disappointed.

"I'm not giving up my faith," she says solidly. "I just want to try something different."

"Well that's fine I suppose," says Mr. Jarvis, leaning back in his chair. "Providing you keep going to church."

"Yes," says Elsie, answering. But to which question she's not sure.

The next day she stands in line in front of the secretary's desk and fills out the forms by herself in small upper case letters, throwing glances behind her back in case of an unexpected lightning bolt. She realizes she is going against her mother's wishes, and that because of her choice, she will not be able to apply to the seminary when she graduates, but she is propelled forward by a small voice that speaks timidly to her inner ear: *Go Elsie, Go!* The voice cheers her on, applauds her, and at first she is suspicious of its zealousness (perhaps it is the devil?). It takes some time before she recognizes that the voice is her own.

At high school she sees her first counsellor, an astute woman with tightly permed hair and small breasts that point out from behind her polyester ruffles like wan torpedoes. She asks Elsie if she has regular periods, if her *immense sadness*, as she calls it, is worse at certain times of the month. She also asks if Elsie thinks of death, and if at night she dreams about her mother. Elsie sits politely through these sessions, hands folded in her lap, feet crossed at the ankles, nodding and shaking her head as though she were mute. She doesn't have a great deal to discuss with the woman and so spends the time examining her face, her plucked-thin eyebrows, the fine black hair protruding from the mole on her upper lip. The woman is eager to help, Elsie can tell that much; she can smell the sincerity and beneficence leaking out from her perspiring face like animal musk.

Seeing a counsellor was her father's idea. He worried about the impact of her mother's death, about her growing silences. *A woman*, he said to the high-school guidance department, *make sure she sees a woman.*

"What do I want with a counsellor?" Elsie said when she heard the news. "I'm just fine."

"Of course you are," Clifford said. "But there will be things you will want to talk about. Female things that I can't help you with."

The counsellor shares her father's opinion on the subject of *female things.* "Sometimes," she says to Elsie during one of their sessions, "there are things in our female bodies that confuse us, make us feel mixed up. Sometimes these things make us feel sad too. These things are just hormones, and they are completely normal."

Elsie listens and stares. She knows she is supposed to smile with relief at this point. Isn't every teenage girl's dream to be told by an authoritative figure that they are completely normal? Not Elsie's, she already knows about hormones: she read about them in National Geographic. Hormones are not her problem.

"In a few years," the counsellor continues, undaunted, "your body will have regulated itself, and these little *mood swings* will be a thing of the past. Then every day will be as bright and sunny as the next, and you will look back on this time and see what valuable life lessons you have learned from your experience."

Elsie sits on her hands. Her counsellor's speech sounds suspiciously like the textbooks she has seen in the library under the subject heading, *Puberty—Making the most of it*. She looks at the posters fastened with thumbtacks to the pink walls of the office, charts of the male and female reproductive systems with wormy blue tubes, screw-jiggy sacs; breasts and scrotums and penises done in cross-section. *Oocyte. Alveolus. Corpus spongiosum.* She reads the explanatory paragraphs on follicle formation, on fertilization of the ovum.

"Is that," she says, pointing to one of the posters, "the only way babies are made?" This is a bold question, the boldest one she has ever asked, but after spending her weekly sessions surrounded by body parts, she suspects it is acceptable.

"This here?" the counsellor says, standing. "Why yes, of course. Sperm and ovum, male and female." She turns to Elsie and stutters. "Didn't you learn this in elementary school Elsie?"

"Yes," Elsie says, flushing, embarrassment creeping into her cheeks. She has been deceived. "I just, well, I just thought there might be another way, that's all."

"No," the woman answers. "This is it. And don't be embarrassed. Sexuality is a wonderful thing."

This is the first time Elsie has ever heard sexuality referred to as *a wonderful thing*. No one, not even her teachers in elementary school called it that. But as her days at high school progress, she begins to discern several new things on the subject that she never noticed before. First of all: there are girls like Elsie who are average, who wear clothes from Eaton's or the Bay picked out from the young ladies department with the help of their mothers. These girls skip down the hallways, or bound, their loose hair swaying attractively across their shoulders. Then there are girls with thick wool cardigans and revealing net tops, with tight jeans and low-hitched breasts and hair tarted up into crusty wings; these ones tread heavily, as if they are wearing horses' shoes, or slink past the lockers and classroom doors with their red surly mouths cranked into sneers, trailing husky perfumes and the closeness of sweat trapped too long inside nylons.

To Elsie the difference between the two groups of girls seems to be the clothes they wear and how they wear them, but even that is not always definitive, because at high school there is an overall increase in the exposure of skin. A certain amount is acceptable, Elsie can see, no matter who you think you are, so long as it is in fashion magazines or on television. The second group, however, effuses the dark scents of sexuality; they pour them out of their orifices like berry syrup or strong, intoxicating nectar, and brandish them on the outsides of their bodies. This brandishing, Elsie gathers, is done in a sort of one-way code, a language of signs and watchwords meant to be picked up by boys or men, and not by girls like Elsie who can use it as a weapon, as evidence, paste it to the backs of the other girls like a kick me sign—only in these instances the sign would say *bad reputation*.

A bad reputation has to do with being slatternly; it has to do with cheap jewellery bought at the five-and-dime, and late nights in farmer's fields or in the back seats of cars nudged spontaneously into deserted parking lots. Although Elsie has a lot to learn, she understands that bad reputations have to do with flaunting sexuality as opposed to concealing it; sharing yourself with others like a public depository for pop bottles, instead of keeping things to yourself. But what she doesn't fathom is this: when is sexuality wonderful? The fine line that seems to delineate the girls with the bad reputations from the ones she sees pushing baby strollers legitimately down Broadway seems to be a wedding ring, a husband. When you have one of those two things, Elsie gathers (although preferably both), a mortal sin becomes *a wonderful thing.* Her counsellor goes even further: *a partner whom you love,* she says, handing Elsie a copy of *Our Bodies, Ourselves* and smiling wistfully like a Victorian lady. *You don't have to be married at the beginning.* Elsie isn't sure about that last point (there are some rumours about the counsellor), but figures she has some time to think about it.

Elsie is in the locker room after gym class. She has just finished playing her first game of field hockey in which teams of girls in short plaid skirts chase a bright orange ball around a field. The object of the game is to hit the ball into the opposing team's goal while artfully blocking the way to your own. Elsie's team captain was a muscled blonde with thunderous calves and a voice hoarse from yelling, who told Elsie that her size was an asset, and that she should be able to stop anyone bent on scoring. She made Elsie the designated team blocker, and told her to stand in centre field with her legs apart.

Unfortunately Elsie's inexperience got in the way: she ended up crushing her own toes.

The locker room is a windowless rectangle lit by sizzling fluorescents and a floor of tightly grouted slabs speckled like trout; its walls are tiled in five-inch aqua tiles, and the ceiling is white stucco. On three sides of the room, aqua lockers with slatted vents spill their contents into the open air: T-shirts, blouses, vanity pouches, mirrors with sticker hearts and lips, bras, slips, underwear, panty-hose, curling irons, barrettes, posters of Charlie's Angels or the Dukes of Hazard taped endearingly to gouged metal. The most important wall, the fourth, is lined with a broad mirror where the bulk of Elsie's gym class now stands, curling their feathered hair away from their faces in attempts to look like Farah Fawcett. They apply frosted purple lipstick and press their lips together in a smirk of satisfaction. Some of them wear belts with wide buckles, and halter tops that do up into bows at the shoulders; others wear plaid shirts drawn with metal snaps into a knot above the navel, and T-shirts beneath, their names welded across their breasts in fuzzy, transferable letters: *Christianna*, or *Mary-Rose*. The colours are sassy this year, rough-and-tumble: shocking puce, sexy pink, and the earth tones, orange, buff brown, dandelion. Sleeves have been drawn in, shortened, and finished at the edges with strips of elastic material cut on the bias; shorts are even shorter, with slits up the sides, necessitating the shaving of legs right up to the bikini line. Exposure of the navel is permitted, in most cases, providing there are no visible hairs or stretch marks, but tube tops are absolutely forbidden at Brimstock High;

there was already an embarrassing incident with the principal's wife.

Most of the girls in Elsie's class wear running shoes over pompom socks, or the latest thing, clogs, with burnished brass rivets hammered around the soles and designs of the wild west burnt into the leather. Some of them wear train track braces which they fit with elastic bands; others wear make-up and hair spray. They spend a lot of time talking about movie stars:

"I think Shaun Cassidy is the cutest."

"I think Matt Dillon."

"Yes, he is a babe."

"What about Robert Redford? He's still handsome, he's my mother's favourite."

"Of course he's your mother's favourite. He's as old as she is!"

Elsie waits for the girls to finish their proceedings so that she can change in privacy. She doesn't feel comfortable exposing herself to strangers, especially ones who squeal and roll their eyes at every misplaced hair, saying drolly through pinched lips, *gross me out the door.* Instead she sits patiently, copiously, burying her nose in the latest homework assignment, going over her history notes; better they should think her studious than what she really is, which (Elsie has heard them say mockingly to other girls) is prudish. *You're such a prude.* What can she do? Marian always called it propriety.

Today Elsie is reading *Pride and Prejudice* for English class. She is only halfway through and already she is in love with the dark and mysterious Mr. Darcy who artlessly seeks the hand of ignoble Miss Bennet and is refused point blank because of his pride. *Have a little sympathy*, she says to Miss Bennet, who in her opinion is too harsh, *he's just a man*; but she knows everything will turn out all right in the end. She has seen the movie.

When she reaches the chapter where Miss Bennett visits Darcy's estate at Pemberly, she hears the humming. The sound is faint, mawkish; it rises in the room like the abominable squealing of an old washing machine. Elsie turns to see the familiar light gliding determinedly toward one of her classmates poised with a curling iron in front of the mirror. As the light grows brighter, the orb at its centre descends and alights on top of the girl's head. Elsie is almost sure that she can make out a twitching pair of lips in the centre of the light; a pair of lips! That's a first. And this time the light is not blue at all, not even turquoise, but sickly green.

Elsie stares back at the apparition, engulfed by her old feeling of terror. Do those lips belong to someone she knows? They are not the lips of the Virgin as she always believed; they are too flawed, too quivering. They belong to a real human being.

In the mirror the line-up of girls has dwindled to a hazy backdrop of mute actresses. Elsie can tell that none of them sees what she sees: they gab and squawk at each other in unbreachable silence, tossing their feathered bangs back over their ears in a pantomime of real life. Elsie wants to be there with them, on the other side of this experience, laughing, sharing, unaware, but she can't break through; she doesn't know how.

At the centre of the orb, the lips part, forming a slit in the green light. *You must try harder*, they say to Elsie. *Try harder.*

Elsie starts to shake. It has been so long since her last vision that she was beginning to believe they never occurred. She is nobody special, certainly no candidate for prophet: why do they appear to her?

Try harder.

"I am trying," Elsie snivels, confused. "I did try."

No, the voice says. *No you didn't. You must do better.*

"How?" says Elsie. "What should I do?"

You know what to do. How to behave. You must try.

Elsie reels with desperation. She does not know, she needs some clues. How can she change if the only advice she ever gets is *try harder?* "I am useless," she says.

Excuses.

"I'm not meant to be a messenger," she says. "I'm not capable."

Excuses excuses. Try . . .

She notices something in the mirror: the apparition has no reflection. But she does, Elsie does. She is staring at her own crumpled face. By herself. She exists. All this time, only she has existed.

For the first time Elsie knows the voice, the lips. She has seen and heard them before. In the hospital, the day her mother died. They have been the same lips all along. She stares hard in their direction, fixes her eyes on their implacable quivering. There is iron in her blood. No, she says, tentatively. I will not. Her voice feels as though it has dried up, as though no sound comes out when she tries to speak. I have tried my hardest. My hardest. I will do no more. It is not my fault.

The lips curl into an emblem of disgust. *You hateful girl,* they say. *Hateful, hateful girl.*

No, Elsie intones. It is not my fault. You are not real.

I don't believe in you. You are not real. She must not be afraid. Food for the demons.

I am, they say.

Why don't you get lost, Elsie continues, staring harder. Get lost.

The lips open into a cavernous sinkhole and screech out into the locker room. *No,* they say, their voice diminishing. *You can't do this.* But she can; and she does. Elsie forces her fingers into her ears to block out the noise that has been following her around for far too long, ever since she can remember. She pushes against her eardrums until the voice is squeezed entirely from her brain, until the lips sputter relentlessly out from their spot on her classmate's head. In a flash of green they are gone.

"Ow!" the girl screams, dropping her curling iron.

"What's wrong with you?" one of the others says. "Did you get frightened by your own reflection?"

"No!" the girl says, bending into the mirror. "I just burned myself real good, that's all. It's like my curling iron came alive and bit me." She parts her hair and touches the white scalp beneath. "Ow. That smarts." Then she sees Elsie gaping at her in the reflection. "What are you looking at?"

Elsie stammers. "Nothing. I—nothing really. I just hope you're all right."

"Oh," says the girl, softening. "Thanks. What's your name anyway?"

16

When the bus finally comes, Elsie is fortunate enough
to get a seat: it is two-thirty, just before rush hour. They
approach Lost Lagoon, shunting between stops so severely that Elsie fears she may get whiplash, then plunge
headlong into the uproarious green of Stanley Park. *Yes,*
thinks Elsie, *I am nearly there.*

Although geographically speaking, Stanley Park is on
the south shore, Elsie sees it as the gateway to North
Vancouver—a resplendent tunnel of red cedar and fir, a
summary of the lush forests that once covered the entire lower mainland but were chopped down to make
room for the homesteaders. It is a prelude to the gardens, the felicitous boulevards of crocuses and snowdrops
that even now, in January, poke their brash heads through
the soil in an announcement of spring. For what it's
worth, Elsie prefers the north shore; it is cleaner,
becalming. She likes how she can leave Lonsdale and hit
residential neighbourhoods instantly, without first walking past twenty blocks of marginal kitsch, bargain base-

ment stores and their blow-out sales, warehouses, fur outlets; she likes how the fountains still have children splashing for quarters, and how there is evidence of all ages—old and young—strolling along the sidewalks. There is something ghostly about the way Vancouver proper is monopolized by the middle-aged; there is something lacking.

When she crosses the lane and climbs the stairs to her grandmother's back porch, Elsie sees the cat waiting patiently on the landing. He has a new scar on his ear, a clean red slice through the fur. "What have you been up to, hey?" she says. "I wondered where you'd gone."
The cat meows in response, and follows her inside.
"Well," Elsie says, hesitating. "I guess you can come in."
She fetches his dish from the porch and puts it on the kitchen counter. While she ruminates over what to feed him, the cat slides under the table and sharpens his claws on a Rubbermaid container. "What are you doing?" she says. "Don't you know you shouldn't scratch things?" She bends down to shoo him away, then realizes what he is after. Removing the lid of the container, she finds a sack of no-name cat food, and a plastic scoop in the form of an old drinking cup. "Oh no," she says. And she has been making him sleep in the snow. "Looks like you do belong here after all." The cat purrs in response and slips between her feet, massaging her shins with the pressure of his rib cage. For some reason Elsie finds the gesture touching. He does not appear to hold a grudge.

After the cat's meal, Elsie sits down at her piano and dusts off the keys with a handkerchief. Her lessons will begin tomorrow, and she wants to look organized. She gathers a stack of dictation books to her lap and reads over the lineup of pupils on the agenda for the morning: Sabine, Thomas, Miranda, Bronwyn, Caleb. These days her classes are mixed: girls and boys, with names taken from the Bible or other ubiquitous works of literature resurfacing their timeworn heads. Elsie is careful to get the pronunciation of these names right. She does not want to be responsible for contributing to any childhood complexes.

Secretly she longs for her early days at the conservatory when the most trying events were temper tantrums, a snivel into a hastily dug up Kleenex. The girls she taught were not all perfect students, not by any stretch of the imagination, but they were more or less reserved, controllable; with them Elsie knew what was expected of her: a pat on the back, a discreet hand placed encouragingly on the shoulder. She was a gentle, but insistent presence in their lives; willful, but easy to please.

Lately, however, a piano renaissance has swept through the country. Well-meaning parents of all backgrounds are clamouring to enrol their budding prodigies in music lessons. Some of the more daring ones choose the violin, if their houses are large and sufficiently insulated to sustain two years of merciless screeching before Junior can carry a tune; others opt for the easy way out: *Aunt Agnes has died and left us her piano and Sarah has always wanted to learn, haven't you Sarah? Well, don't mind her, she'll like it soon enough.* Elsie has heard too many of these conversations for her liking. She knows from Music Psychology that it takes a certain kind of child to play the piano: someone who can span at least five keys, or better still, a whole octave, someone who is not overly gregarious, who is self-sufficient, and who has good eyesight. She might also add, someone who is an only child in a family of supportive grown-ups, but does not, because she has her living to think about. Her pupils at the conservatory did not all fit this description, but most were temperate enough so that Elsie could impress upon them some basic understanding of piano ethics. The present ones, Elsie fears, will not be so easy. There are too many who are energetic beyond reason and who are demanding of results. During registration they fidgeted on the piano bench, kicking their feet up against the sounding board, or they pounded on the keys in a hyperactive staccato. In these cases it is always the mothers who mediate: "What can I do to get Monika interested in playing?" they say, the ends of their noses swelling with genuine frustration. "What is your secret?"

"No secret," Elsie says. "They have to want to do it first."

This is as far as she will go nowadays; the answer lets her off the hook by volleying responsibility back to the child, and is ambiguous enough to get the parents thinking. She stops there because she knows what their reactions will be if she puts all the onus on them. Once, while she was at the conservatory, Elsie boldly questioned a mother who insisted her daughter take lessons, when the girl clearly found them torturous: "Why does Chantal want to study piano?"

The mother thought for a moment, flushing red in the face. "Because," she said finally. "What kind of question is that? She is just a child," she shrieked. "She doesn't know what she wants. That's where you come in."

Ever since then Elsie has been careful to tread lightly.

On rare occasions Elsie has glimpsed her pupils' fathers: at impromptu recitals in church hall conservatories, or at her own, meticulously organized performances where students are showcased before one another and their respective parents. They sit, close-mouthed, bleary; silent, reserved, encouraging, like caged exotic birds wearing undersized jackets and uncomfortable shoes. They remind Elsie of Clifford, the way he was after Marian's death when both of them tried to give the other what it was they needed themselves.

When Marian was alive, Clifford existed on the edges of Elsie's life. True, Elsie always knew where to find him—at his office at the Department of Highways, or in his easy chair in the living room—but when she approached him with a question, his answer was inevitably the same: "Ask your mother Elsie. That's her area of things." When Marian was alive everything was her *area of things*. Clifford was a figurehead who behaved appropriately when scrutinized, and who appeared every Sunday, hair combed, shirt ironed, to navigate the Lincoln down Magnolia Avenue and into the parking lot of the Church of Our Lady.

After the funeral he was attentive. He took Elsie out for ice cream on Saturday afternoons. He bought her a whole set of *Encyclopedia Britannicas* bound in imitation leather with embossed gold letters on their spines, and set them up in her bedroom on shelves next to her world map desk. "There," he said. "Now you can find the answers to all your questions."

Elsie knew he meant well, that these gestures were his way of saying *We'll be fine, you and I. We'll make do nicely;* but at fourteen she was bright enough to know the answers to her questions were not written in any encyclopedia. She took cursory glances at the books, looking up places she hoped one day to visit: the banks of the Arno in Florence, Salisbury Plain where her ancestors had organized monoliths of stone into calendars preempting the Flintstones by two thousand years. She unplugged her Virgin Mary night light and slipped it into the bottom drawer of her bedside table.

On Sunday she came down the stairs to find him at the stove, spatula in hand.

"Good morning," he said, looking up from the cast-iron frying pan. "I'm making us an omelette with green onions and tomatoes, the way you like it."

Elsie's heart broke; the kitchen was a disaster. On the cutting board and all across the counter were the entrails of tomatoes, scattered like dewy birdseed. The floor was coated with a fine mist of crumbs and various beneficial nutmeats that had spilled from a loaf of seven-grain bread and were now stuck to the bottom of her father's socks (she could see them when he lifted his feet). In the oven on a warming plate was a stack of charred toast.

"Don't mind the smell," Clifford said jovially. "I'm not doing anything illicit. It's just the tea." He pointed to the back of the stove where a fractured tea bag had spilled its contents on to the element and was leisurely roasting like a lump of wet sawdust. "Everything is almost ready."

Elsie poured herself a glass of orange juice and sat down at the table. She could live with the mess, now that she was over the initial shock, but at the same time it bothered her; this wasn't her father at all. Why couldn't he act normal?

"Dad," she said, turning her head. "I want to go for a walk this morning."

Clifford slid a piece of the omelette onto a plate and placed it in front of Elsie. "Well that's a good idea," he said.

"No," she said, taking a breath. "I want to go for a walk, instead of going to church."

He sat down opposite Elsie and regarded his breakfast, rubbing the end of his nose with his forefinger. "Well," he said. "Mmm."

Elsie had seen that look before: dismay, earnest confusion. His mouth was pinned shut and inside poked his tongue, gouging the limits of his freshly shorn cheeks. "Mmm," he said again. He picked up his fork and stabbed the omelette. "I don't see why not."

Together they walked along the river, Clifford strolling with his hands in his pockets, remarking on the level of the water, the profusion of bumblebees so early in the year; Elsie gathering milkweed pods, breaking them open, and releasing their contents to the wind. She didn't mind his company, she liked it in fact, as long as he didn't ask her too many questions.

"You're doing all right?" he said, tilting his head.

"Fine," she said.

"And at school, everything is good?"

"Yes."

"Well then, I'm glad."

His questions weren't particularly intrusive, not on the surface, but Elsie knew what he was getting at: *How are you taking all this? Am I doing enough to get us through this?* He felt responsible for her happiness, for her well-being, and he would blame himself for everything if she didn't pull through and get on with her life. She had to buck up and forget, to appear contented, normal. She made a vow to put everything behind her, to be an adult, a companion. She wanted to be someone her father would no longer have to worry about, so she compressed her past into a wound the size of a pin prick.

"There," she thought, cracking open a milkweed pod and watching the downy umbrellas bob and glide on invisible thermals. "I'll be fine."

Four years later she stood in front of the mirror in her brocade gown and elbow gloves, fastening the bulk of her hair into a bun. Around her neck was a single strand of pearls, knotted at one end into an opalescent snarl.

Outside the bathroom door Clifford sat waiting in his suit. He was ready first, of course; there wasn't much for him to do except slip on a clean shirt and yank up his pleated trousers. Together they were going to the Daddy Daughter Dinner Dance, an important prelude to Elsie's high-school graduation where all the girls from grade thirteen would make an appearance with their fathers; the final appearance before they moved on to bigger, greater endeavours involving careers in nursing, education or child care; before they trotted off to university or college and found themselves men of their own.

Elsie knew what to expect: bunches of girls in taffeta or Celanese mesh, looking frowsy and buffed and recently plucked from a tissue box; sentimental clouds of pink and tangerine. She steered clear of fringe, of excess gusts of satin, of midriff half-skirts that made her resemble a decorated blowfish (with her height she couldn't be too careful), and went instead for the classic look: the little black dress. She knew what Marian would say about her choice: *You look like you're going to a funeral. Like death warmed over.* Black was not one of her mother's favourite colours.

But this was a funeral of sorts. Elsie was bidding goodbye to Brimstock High, to all her classmates, friendly and retroussé, to the teachers and their tedious discussions, the counsellors with their misplaced concern. She was walking away from vacuous hallways, from changing rooms and gymnasiums, from classrooms that smelled like lemon-scented floor wax and bathrooms with ever-clogging toilets. When she left the front doors of Brimstock High on the last day of classes, she would not have to come back. Ever again. Now there was cause for mourning; there was also cause for rejoicing.

Many of the girls in her graduating class belonged to a clique of well-dressed prefects that dictated school fashions. Their parents owned local clothing shops or drug stores, or were lawyers, or town counsellors; their brothers and sisters were important personalities in the youth community—captains of football teams, fall fair queens—and were well-respected for their good-naturedness, their ruddy enthusiasm. Already some of the girls were talking about engagements with high-school sweethearts, or plans to enter university sororities.

Elsie had few close friends, save a handful of girls on the periphery of popularity who dared to spend their evenings studying. With these she had an understanding: when projects were assigned, she would help them, contribute by being part of their group because who else had the time to do all that work? Elsie did, naturally; she had no boyfriends, no momentous dances or birthday parties to attend. She was gifted, they said, with the ability to understand and gather information more quickly than any of them; shouldn't she share those gifts, saving time for everyone in the long run?

But even these girls Elsie found dull, insincere. She couldn't rally herself to get excited about the same things, to condole with them on their tragedies. Instead she was bored, obdurate; she attributed her lack of kinship to her situation as an only child.

"Dad," she said, inserting the final bobby pin into her hair. "I'm ready."

The high-school gymnasium was decorated with scalloped streamers and handmade paper chains painstakingly cut from construction paper. Cafeteria tables were drawn back against the walls and covered with punch bowls, snack platters with cheeses hardening at the edges, and dusky, insipid grapes. At both ends of the tables someone had stacked plastic wine glasses into translucent pillars which posed like pieces of conceptual art.

Elsie and Clifford stood against the stage where the other fathers congregated under a banner that read *DDDD 1982: Congratulations My Girl!* The men wore pinstripe suits and coal black polished shoes, or brown corduroy combinations with suede elbow patches. All of them had ties slung about their necks, lengths of silk or wool or polyester with diagonal stripes, polka-dots, airplanes, maple leafs, or more expensive paisleys; they were broad wedges that looked to Elsie like foreign ciphers, or narrow windsocks dangling in the stillness.

"I work in plastics," one of the fathers said sipping at his drink.

"My business is clean water," said another.

At the opposite end of the gymnasium the daughters spoke in thrilled tones about hairdos and cleverness of dress. When the music started up, they moved toward the fathers with some trepidation, and paired off reluctantly, keeping their partners at arm's length.

The records were chosen to suit both generations: Chubby Checker, The Beatles, Neil Diamond, The Jackson Five, The Pointer Sisters, Ike and Tina, Abba, The Bay City Rollers, The Bee Gees. When "Precious Moments" came on Clifford leaned toward Elsie.

"Well," he said. "Shall we dance?"

Elsie accepted her father's hand and they moved toward the swaying crowd. She didn't mind that they had different rhythms, both of them were so unused to dancing; she just wanted things to run smoothly so that her father would feel adequate. She would be leaving soon, after all; she wanted everything to be positive.

"I'm sorry," Clifford said, nodding to the other daughters on the dance floor. His face was sheepish, wounded. His mouth turned down at the edges as if countered by weights. "I didn't know we were supposed to get corsages. I would have got one, had I known."

"That's O.K. Dad," Elsie said, collecting her spirits and forcing out a smile. "You know I'm allergic."

Elsie selected the University of Western Ontario for its proximity to her father's house. She had considered the east coast, Mount Allison or even Dalhousie, but couldn't imagine leaving Clifford entirely by himself. Instead she chose London, an undersized city on the railway, a half a day's drive from Brimstock.

"You take care," he said, patting her on the shoulder as she boarded the train, his eyes subdued by looks of befuddlement and fatherly love.

"I will," said Elsie.

"If the food is bad, just call me."

"Thanks."

"And I mean that."

"O.K. Dad."

Clifford did mean well. Before bringing her to the train station he gave her two dozen ballpoint pens and ten pairs of socks. *I'm not going to the North Pole*, she had said, touched and impatient at the same time. *It's not that cold. I know*, he said. *But you take care.*

"Take care of yourself Elsie," he said again.

Elsie climbed onto the train and rocketed west. The edges of Brimstock gave way to farmers' fields, cows out to pasture, crops of corn, alfalfa, fall rye. In the bleakness of the morning air, the train's whistle sounded, chasing Elsie to the brink of her new life: *woo wooo*, it said. *Woo wooo*. What Elsie heard was something else, something grievous and neglected that she meant to say to Clifford: *You too, you too.*

But she never did.

17

Shit, thinks Elsie. She's crying again. She brushes away the tears with the edges of her sleeve and glances at the keys. Plunk. Plunk plunk. She plays the first five bars of Beethoven's *Für Elise, poco moto,* and stifles her desire to bawl. She used to believe, when she was younger, that *Elise* was German for Elsie. The idea that a young woman like herself could be the inspiration for such heart-wrenching, glorious music made her feel validated in some spurious way.

The song was also a favourite of her father's.

Plunk plunk.

"What am I doing?" she says aloud, stopping. "I'm making things worse."

She swipes the cuff of her sleeve across her cheeks a second time, and picks up in the middle of Scott Joplin's *The Entertainer.* "There," she says. "Nobody can cry at this old rag." Elsie has witnessed nearly every one of her students massacre *The Entertainer* at some point in their studies. If she wants to drown out emotion, this is the song to do it.

"He's dead and that's that," she says firmly.

It's not your fault. You did everything you could.

"Right," she says. "Everything."

Your father chose his own life. You are not responsible.

"Yeah," Elsie says, unconvinced. The internal dialogue belongs to one or more of the counsellors who attempted to tell her, at various times in her life, that she was suffering from *misplaced guilt*. A remnant of her overly-religious childhood. They said that many people felt abandoned after the death of a loved one, and that this abandonment was easily mistaken for delinquency on the part of those left behind. She was not, according to the counsellors, culpable for anything. *People die,* they said, holding out their metaphorical hands. *Nobody knows why. It's normal to feel at fault.*

"What if I am at fault?" she says to no one in particular.

Now Elsie. He died of a heart attack.

"I know. But I gave him high blood pressure."

You didn't. That's nobody's fault—

"But I didn't prevent him from getting it. I didn't prevent her—"

Nobody's fault . . .

The song ends with a broken triad. Elsie gets up from the piano bench and stretches her legs. Beside the piano, on a fold-out television tray, she has arranged her students' theory books in alphabetical order. "Now where was I?" she says, collecting her thoughts, looking over the mess in the living room. Today was supposed to be her day for cleaning, for mounting at least a facade of cheerfulness and organization in her grandmother's front room, but she seems to have lost her place.

She picks up the stack of photo albums that were the

cause of last night's sob session, and hauls them into the bedroom with the intention of stowing them away in the closet. On the top album is a picture scotch-taped to the cover: Daniel on his twenty-fifth birthday standing with his arm around Elsie's shoulders. Both of them are wearing sombreros and holding margaritas out to the camera, but only Daniel is smiling. His mouth is a graceful willow-whip; wretchedly charming.

What did women think of his mouth? she wonders. The thought is cutting, shameless; it made her feel better, at one time, to conjure up Daniel and *her* together. She had to have some glimpse into what went on behind her back. She couldn't help herself. *What was it like?* she hears herself saying. The memory slaps her; it stings.

Seven years, thinks Elsie. *I must be nuts.*

Daniel materialized in introductory music class during Elsie's second term at university. She must have been nineteen going on twenty, with feathered hair and cotton pastel blouses marked all over with unobtrusive floral prints. She has a vague memory of berets worn askance on windblown heads, of billowing corduroy skirts. She trudged through drifting snow three times a week, across the interlocking paving stones of the main campus path, to the sloping lecture hall vaulted and dank and smelling of wool socks.

For the first few weeks, Elsie didn't notice anyone; she peered hard at her teacher's blackboard scrawls, mentally erasing the dull frosh static from her brain. Every eye space on campus was cluttered with advertisements directed at new students: *Barbecue Bash '84, If you aren't there, what will you talk about Monday?* She had already received two pamphlets regarding testicular cancer in her on-campus mailbox; *Everything you need to know to stay a man.*

The professor of Introductory Music was tall like Elsie. He had big teeth, a sharp nose, and a face made up of drastic angles that raised his eyebrows into points as if stuck there by pins. He looked like someone out of uniform, a lion tamer, a contortionist; slightly arty, with a French twist. His paisley shirts were always neatly buttoned, tucked into casual, multi-pocketed slacks held up by black suspenders. Even though the sixties had trotted through the academic system, snipping ties and plunging copies of *Wordsworth* in the toilet, demanding free speech, subsidized marijuana greenhouses and unadulterated hedonism, professors in jeans and knapsacks driving orange Volkswagen beetles had yet to infiltrate the scores of tenured old men presiding at Elsie's university. Her music professor was a rarity, a fill-in for some classical fart on sabbatical. That's what she heard Daniel call the previous instructor, *a classical fart.*

"What makes a fart classical?" she asked him pointedly. Elsie spoke to few strangers, especially ones with ratty suede vests and furious dark hair; in the past, when she had tried smiling at strange men, her face opened up like a handbag and all sorts of miscellaneous goods fell out, splattering into the open air where they roared and bounced, then curled up into an irretrievable ball. She was a ripped seam exposing too much skin; too much for a first conversation. But this time she had been caught off guard.

[213]

"What?" he answered.

"Classical music is never *farty*," she said, pacing herself. "You probably only listen to the muzak versions in bank lineups."

That was how they began—Elsie's fluky tongue managing to stay inside her teeth, and Daniel, surprised at her challenge, bringing her home to see his record collection. Previously she would not have gone home with a stranger, but something about Daniel encouraged her not to back down. She had to see for herself.

Daniel lives in a three-story brick house with soaring white ceilings, a hulking staircase, and foggy sheets of cellophane stretched across the windows and sealed with a hairdryer. Next to the door on a feeble rubber mat, forty pairs of runners with broken shoelaces and belching tongues lie dormant in a heap. Some of the larger ones have hand-written messages like *Anarchy is good for you*, or *Meat is Murder* printed across the toes in thick black marker. He leads Elsie into a narrow carpeted room previously used as a parlour or dining area; a built-in china cabinet now holds stacks of LPs. Along the top of each wall, running lengthwise, a plate rail traces the lofty distance between corners, faintly reminding Elsie of baroque cottages nestled in the English countryside, except that Daniel's is holding crushed cans of *OV*.

Elsie trips over a bean-bag snake, enormous and soggy, in the centre of the room. She notices a split seam, an overflow of dainty styrofoam pellets. "Your roommates are a tidy bunch," she says, alarmed at her own forthrightness.

Daniel grunts an acknowledgment and lifts a thin album from the stacks: Stravinsky, *The Rites of Spring*. He eases the disk from its dust cover, places it on the turntable, and pushes the automatic start button to release the arm and spin the record. He does this precisely, solemnly, as though handling consecrated objects.

"Now this is music," he says, relaxing. His shoulders drop beneath his striped shirt, revealing creases in his neck. He bends zealously into the notes, as if by some will of his own he can climb into the melody and ride it like a midway roller coaster. "Not like some of that shit Sullivan plays."

Elsie notes the word *shit*, a vestige from her childhood: *poop*, *scat*, all those one syllable inappropriates her classmates emphasized with such abandon when adults left the room.

"I mean," Daniel continues, "I like him—Sullivan— he tries to make the class hip by playing Dylan, Hendrix, the Sex Pistols. But he's lacking something, if you know what I mean."

Elsie does know. She's seen Mr. Sullivan flop in earnestness, smiling too deeply, too widely, with too many teeth. He doesn't notice the snickering first-year students snorting behind his back when he closes his eyes and gutturally hums along. They have yet to be invited to coffee in the faculty lounge, have yet to experience the slap of a drunken professor's hand on their newly formed academic shoulders; a slap of camaraderie that indicates brotherhood, sisterhood, a kindred knowing of intellect. Mr. Sullivan's attempts are premature, wasted on fledgling students still afraid of the principal's office. He tries too hard. He cares: this is his downfall.

[215]

"You must like music," Elsie says, sensing it is her turn to speak.

"I'm in a band. Bass guitar. But I'm actually studying art."

Studying as opposed to doing; the line between the two becomes increasingly obscured when enrolled in institutions such as Elsie's university. You start out directed, knowing you like nothing better than the moan of woodwinds warming their metal casings, the creak of piano pedals in a damp, underground module, down, up, down, up, thudding against the floor, only to be told *theory first year, practical second*; you then submerge yourself in rudiments, in the histories of tubas, the bleak beginnings of organs crossing the Atlantic in poorly made galleys, arriving in Quebec mice-nibbled and out of tune; you try to focus, stand with your ear to the wall when senior students rip across keyboards, sending out trills, arpeggios, beautiful uproarious crescendos, and concentrate on the idea that one more essay on Mozart's cocker spaniel will increase your awareness of your instrument.

You begin to wonder why you are there.

"Oh," Elsie says. "You mean in the art building?" Art in the art building, a good assumption.

"Yes," Daniel says. "Mostly I paint. But first year we do everything. Sculpture, print, and of course, Art History."

Daniel's building, the art building, is solid orange brick with green awnings, heavenly skylights, and a solarium where sculpture students battle lumps of white plaster into abstract organic shapes resembling extracted molars. Elsie walks around it every day on her way to the

Student Union Building, barely noticing the shifting forms on display in the courtyard: a giant bat welded from rusty tractor parts, an emaciated aluminum man with fangs and claws and an erect penis. Things no longer demanding respect simply by their ability to shock (someone had hung a banana peel on the man).

"Yeah. I'm working on a project right now. Do you want to see?"

Elsie nods, banishing her mother's voice from her head, the one that warns about strange men who say things like *Do you want to see, little girl? See what I have?* But she breathes an audible sigh of relief when Daniel moves into the kitchen.

In the sink there are so many dishes that some have been piled on the floor. Teflon pots, casseroles, griddles, woks, colanders all sit expectantly waiting attention. On the table three cutting boards with various stains offer half-chopped carrots, wizened tomatoes, and petrified crusts of bread. Glasses, some empty, some half-full, perch on every available surface; there are mugs on the stovetop, on the refrigerator, on the chairs; there are shot glasses with a matching toppled decanter, crystal and plastic wine goblets full of cigarette butts. There is an eggplant impaled on a fork hanging from the light fixture.

Elsie feels her mother rolling under her feet. "Did you have a party?" she asks.

"No," Daniel says, then, "these are mine." His arm shoots upward, fingers splayed, indicating a space over their heads.

At the far edge of the room, between a window and the suspended eggplant, tree branches protrude from the ceiling, pushing through the drywall like claws through a glass of milk. Each grey branch ends cleanly, as though a forest decided to grow down from the second floor, hungry for dirt, grass, the opposite of whatever is in the sky.

She wants to ask *why*, but refrains. Their delicate tips graze the top of her head, caress her hair like fingers. She should say something encouraging, she should sound impressed. Suddenly she is nervous. What is she doing here, in this person's kitchen? She has no business, she'll put her foot in her mouth as usual, she knows nothing about art, is a total fake. She wishes she were alone, then notices Daniel glowing.

"Wow," is what comes out. Open to interpretation.

Daniel moves towards her, smiling, floating on his droopy socks, his rolled-up pant legs. He takes her hand, holds it to the branch, rubs the bark lightly. "Soft, isn't it?" he says, almost a whisper. His hands are warm, like a comfortable bath, old pajamas. They are what Elsie needs, what she wants. She's doing all right, hasn't swallowed her tongue. She's inhaling his smells of flaky soap, illicit oils. She likes the sound of his voice, the weight of his sighing. His mouth, too, she likes that.

18

Every Wednesday at lunchtime Elsie meets Daniel at a bar called *The Paradise*. The building is downtown, part of a heritage complex of chipped brick facades with stone cornices and leaning wooden flagpoles. The rest of the complex, with its charming barber shops, a bulk food store specializing in ethnic spices and gourmet coffees, and a bank, has been restored to its original rust and white grandeur reminiscent of autumn leaves; but *The Paradise* is the colour of cement, with turquoise and pink highlights flashing from the sidewalk like a neon marquee; on the heavy oak door, two pink flamingos embrace in a steamy tango.

Elsie chooses their usual table hidden from the main room by inflatable plastic palm trees and a large potted fern packed with cigarette butts. The black stucco walls are bumpy and cold, like chopped asphalt, or—Elsie imagines—lava rock; she peers out from their uniformity feeling somewhat like a lizard in a cave. All the tables in *The Paradise* have this effect, making you feel shadier, riskier, more illicit than you actually are. The shabby olive carpet filled with the grit of winter boots could be the sort of moss or lichen Elsie has seen growing around the Great Lakes; the kind that takes ten thousand years to grow a square centimetre. How could anything have such patience? Elsie empathizes.

The favourite table is Daniel's. He loves its mismatched chairs, its surface embedded with miscellaneous postcards from all over the world. Most of the cards look flea-bitten or mouldy where moisture has been trapped below the glass, but Elsie doesn't want to deaden his enthusiasm by pointing this out. He is so easily damaged.

"I love it here," he said on a previous Wednesday. "This place is such a dive. Full of real life." Daniel is convinced *The Paradise* is frequented by drug dealers and ex-convicts who gather behind plush room dividers making delivery arrangements and bootlegging alcohol. "Look at that guy. I'll bet he's the ring leader."

Elsie looked at a fat man in a wilted hat playing cards. He was a regular, one of the many indiscriminate men Daniel fingered in his theories of conspiracy. She wondered what he thought of the university crowd pouring in between lectures and on half-price nights to smoke and yell and pound the tables. Probably he thought Elsie's generation was a bunch of no-good loudmouths with too much time and money to waste on flashy hair dye and metallic silver eye make-up. Probably he didn't care.

"I'll bet," Elsie seconded.

"I'm serious. And it's a damn shame. He's probably somebody's husband you know. Everyone has their own personal tragedy, you just have to look hard enough."

"Oh," Elsie said. "What's yours?"

Daniel shrugged his shoulders. "My father, I guess. The asshole."

"What about him?"

"He made off with my mother's best friend. The one with the silly-cone tits and the bleached blonde wig. Can you believe it? He lives in a big stone house in Toronto that he never paid a cent for. One of these days she'll get sick of him and give him the boot."

Elsie looked at the table where Daniel was making circles with a stir-stick. She didn't know what to say. Silly cone tits?

"Geez. Parents are for the birds," Daniel filled in. "Do you picture yourself with kids?

He caught her off guard. Was she being tested for something? "I haven't thought much about it, to be honest," she said.

"That's smart," Daniel said. "One less delinquent. Personally, I know I'd be a terrible father."

"Why do you say that?"

"Because," he said, taking a sip of his drink. "I work with toxic chemicals all day long. I'll probably die young."

Today Elsie orders a pitcher of beer to share with Daniel: a dark one, one with pith. "You should almost be able to chew it," Daniel had said, meaning he liked a thick ale the colour of pond water. Each time he tries a new beer he tosses a penny into the glass and lets it settle. If the penny remains visible, he flags the waitress. "You call that ale? That looks like cat piss."

Elsie takes the pitcher and pours gingerly, tilting the mug away from her chest to cut down on foam. She drinks in small sips, letting the beer prick her tongue and slide down the back of her throat. In just four months Elsie feels at home with alcohol. This must be some sort of accomplishment; she marvels at her ability to adapt. At first the yeasty flavour had reminded her of bad coffee souring in the pot; she'd concentrated on the ruddy liquid, on the delicate breaking of bubbles, thinking *Do you know what this means? For me to be drinking?* Daniel didn't know about her strict childhood; he had no idea of rules. His own mother was a psychologist with an extensive liquor cabinet. She invited him to smoke joints. How could he understand?

Most of what she knows about Daniel bewilders her in an exciting way: he shares a house with three other men who grunt obligingly at Elsie from behind the refrigerator door—a house with innumerable cracks in the walls and a clattering radiator covered in wet socks; he eats pasta two times a day, soaking the noodles with Louisiana hot sauce, ketchup, or tomato soup, all of which are cheaper than bona fide spaghetti sauce; he sleeps on a mound of blue and grey comforters gathered in the middle of his bed like a beehive, riddled with Kleenexes, discarded turtlenecks, and a tape deck with a makeshift antenna fashioned from a coat hanger. Lying on his sheet-starved mattress, Daniel listens to *Tubular Bells* and CBC's *Nightlines* each evening, believing that unsettling noises keep the brain alert in sleep.

Some of these things he tells Elsie during their Wednesday lunches at *The Paradise*. Other things she picks up. She imagines him at night, curled into his soft blankets with his arms flung into the air, frozen in some dramatic gesture, his cheeks paled by the slate darkness of the room. This is the part of him she wants to access, the lone Daniel, uncluttered by party-going housemates, by stale lecture halls full of loose-leaf notebooks, tenuous scribbling, the fug of wet jackets, scarves, mittens dampening the air; but there is an unwritten rule, a limp piece of paper stuck to his forehead: *Go Back, No Entry.* Elsie can wait. But for how long?

Each time they meet, Elsie greets Daniel with a contained smile. She nods at appropriate intervals and cocks her head in a reassuring way, making light remarks about music assignments and the mind-numbing rock bands he imitates on his bass guitar. When Daniel brings his friends along—people with names like Moose, Bug, Rooster, or Sid—Elsie tries even harder to be straight-faced; other people always see the evidence. Evidence of what, she does not know. It is not lust that she feels for Daniel, although that is part of it; what she feels is deeper, more exhilarating.

Daniel's friends are nice enough, but when they are around Elsie finds herself blocking them out. They wear old dress shirts with pointy collars, faded pants from the Salvation Army; they look like outport fishermen in black wool caps with fancy embroidered braid-lines, and navy pea coats with moth balls in the pockets. When Elsie asks them if they are artists, they say they are *on the verge.* They tell her this apologetically, full of disdain and remorse, as though they are the butt of a cruel joke involving formal education.

Today Daniel arrives late, with one of the half-artists trailing behind him.

"Hi," he says halfheartedly, and slumps into his chair.

"Elsie, see if you can cheer this guy up," the artist

says. "He's low, and I've got to make class in ten minutes."

Elsie smiles. "Sure." She is glad when he leaves.

"What's up?" she says to Daniel.

"I'm flunking Sullivan's. I've already missed two assignments and if I don't get them in by Friday they're going to kick me out." Daniel's hair hangs into his eyes; he hasn't shaved in days and Elsie can see the barbs of his whiskers jutting from his neck. He wears a loose T-shirt, hand-dyed jeans, and a silver-plated pocket watch attached to a leather thong and pinned at the chest.

"I don't have time for essays with all my studios. Essays are shit."

"But you can fight it. Talk to Sullivan."

"I have," Daniel sighs. "He wants to help, but he's no authority on anything. He's just a nice guy who wishes people like me didn't get into trouble."

"But Daniel, they can't kick you out. You're a genius, your paintings, everything you do is beautiful. Can't they see that?"

Even now Elsie doesn't know if she meant what she said; of course she thought *Daniel* was special, his eyes, his slightly dented chin. Shouldn't everyone else think so too? But she surprised him, laying his talents on the table like a bolt of impeccable cloth; he stared at her, surmising. Was she too obvious?

When they get back to his room Elsie stands by the door while Daniel arranges the covers. She hasn't said a word all the way to the three-story house in case she has misinterpreted what is happening; in case she has understood.

Daniel puts his hands on her shoulders. He kisses her softly like he is lapping up a bowl of milk; he undoes her cardigan and pulls it from her wrists.

Elsie has learned some things about sex since her introduction to the reproductory organs in the counsellor's office; most of these tidbits come from books that she reads (now that her reading list is no longer censored), or from people she meets at school. Their general attitude is this: sex is like falling into water. Does that mean it is supposed to be suffocating, Elsie wonders, or easy? As far as she is concerned, that means you can either drown, or tread water. Which is preferable? When she tries to kiss him back she smashes her teeth on his; when she thinks about reaching for his fly, she knocks her forehead against his chest.

"Relax," Daniel says, and soon Elsie feels the same lapping sensation moving down her thighbone. He maneuvers her onto the bed, runs his fingers along her knees. He makes her feel like a still life—a pile of apples, a stuffed bird under a lamp—arranging, rearranging her for the perfect light: *Portrait of two legs and a watermelon,* Elsie thinks. Then the lapping dips so that Elsie feels a small part of herself rising with his tongue, a tiny seed growing inside her, awakening, reaching for sun. *Wait,* she wants to say, *how do you do that?* Daylight flickers at the windowpane.

19

They move into a basement apartment with brown and yellow tiles and beige trim that comes away from the doors when leaned on. Elsie gets a part-time job at the Royal Conservatory giving piano lessons and uses an inheritance from her father to finance Daniel's undergraduate, and then his masters degree. His thesis is a ten-by-two-foot rectangle of acrylic paint fastened to the wall by tacks. To create it, Daniel applies over three hundred layers of Day-Glo colour to a piece of masonite, then peels the mass in its entirety from the backing and hangs it on the wall. The whole thing has the woeful look of an abandoned piece of skin; it looks to Elsie like a gigantic, sun-dried tomato.

At the conservatory her own students are well-bred girls under eleven. That is the cut-off age, the age when girls discover soap operas; the age when they start pinching their lips together like fashion models and squealing at boys after school. At eleven they no longer care about words like *andante* or *allegro;* they are no longer interested in the slow romp of waltzes, in *tarantellas*. They scoff at the stickers Elsie puts in their notebooks. They learn how to glare.

Elsie gets out of bed at six-thirty every morning to make coffee. She irons her blouses which are no longer modest pastel jobs, but flowing peasant tops, gathered and collarless and dyed earth brown or pine green with things like cabbages, beets and reindeer moss. She reads novels in the bathtub, with mud on her face from a bog somewhere in France.

At eight o'clock Daniel comes to the table, his hair dreaded and black, and mutters a greeting like, "Life is nothing but a chance encounter between an umbrella and a sewing machine." He plants his eyes in a magazine, in the back of an imported second-hand record album, or in the garish, offensive advertisements from cereal companies.

"What do you mean?" Elsie might say.

"I mean, there's no point in trying to make sense of anything. We can't control life anyway."

"Perhaps not. But that doesn't give us the right to bury our heads in the sand."

At this Daniel groans, or looks sternly at his reflection in the blade of his knife and states methodically, "I'm going to be just like my father."

Not if I can help it—Elsie notes, cheering up. Their mornings together are a ritual. Daniel's recurring pessimism relieves her, almost comforts her; his moodiness means that she is still in charge, that he needs her to buoy him up. The prospect of being needed thrills her. She understands his negativity: its presence means things haven't deteriorated beyond her uncanny ability to fix. *Security* is the word, why doesn't she just use it?

Daniel backs up her theory of usefulness. "You are good for me Elsie," he tells her one night.

"Like Wheaties?" says Elsie.

"Like an apple a day," says Daniel. "All these years my father has treated me like a wacked-out peacenik, and my mother like a case-study. But you are so straight-forward. You're not hiding anything. Sometimes that's hard to get used to."

Elsie smiles and wishes she could tell Daniel that she is hiding something, she just doesn't know what. Instead she slips into bed and smoothes the covers. She counts her blessings.

In the morning when she awakes he is studying her face. "What are you looking at?" she asks.

"You," says Daniel. "Do you know that your lips twitch when you dream, and that your eyelids roll back and forth inside your head? It's like a whole other life going on in your subconscious, one that I don't know anything about."

Elsie shrugs and stretches her arms. "I probably don't know much about it either."

When fall comes Elsie has a new crop of students with names to memorize. Daniel gets a job two days a week at a nearby Beckers store manning the cash register and restocking shelves with boxes of baking soda and Archie comics. The rest of the time he allots for painting; or at least, that is his plan. He has some exploring to do, some evolution as an artist. He points out to Elsie that three days a week should be just enough for him to develop his style and find his niche, and explains that the time will give him the chance to discipline his talent, as though it were a pet that needed housebreaking. He also says, his lips forming a serious string of luscious candy, that he might not be able to meet his half of the expenses for a few months, inferring that surely Elsie, with her instructor's certificate and her three years of experience full-time in the workforce, will be able to toe the line until he makes a name for himself.

Elsie doesn't mind paying the bills. This is the nineties right? She is an open-minded woman. She understands that while Daniel was scratching away at his masters degree, she was working her way up the conservatory ladder to a position with medical benefits and a modest dental plan. This gives her security, not to mention (although Daniel alludes) an unfair head start. If he needs an opportunity to create a market for his art, the same way Elsie ferreted out the possibilities for her musical talents, she is all for providing the necessary support. Anything she can do to be helpful. She brings home some pamphlets from the local chamber of commerce on market research and how to sell your product, and leaves him to the creative process. She imagines he will spend his days stretching canvases across knotty pine one-by-twos, or mixing up viscous blobs of acrylic or oil paint on his improvised TV dinner palette and applying them to the stark white blanks with his collection of sable brushes. These are the kinds of things he did during university, when he was completing assignments for his teachers or preparing for a student exhibition. What he does now, however, is different; just the opposite in fact, if that is possible. He explores *non-marketable* art.

"Capitalist art is for pigs," he tells Elsie one evening when she returns from work. "It's a sham." He holds up a canvas doused in strokes of deep umber, criss-crossed with the spatterings of what looks like the remains of their tube of toothpaste. "This is something," he says, considering, his hand on his chin. "I'm really happy with this one."

"It's great," Elsie says, feigning interest and hanging up her coat. She has seen worse. The painting is a small rectangle the size of a sheet of foolscap. It reminds her of a mud puddle. "You should do a series." She knows better than to ask the question, *What is it supposed to be?*

"No," Daniel says. "The idea is to keep moving on to new things. To never get caught up in the confines of one medium. Too many artists get bogged down when they find something that works. They get stuck. Look at Robert Bateman. That guy can't paint his way out of a hole now that he's a big shot. He's doomed to tickle out finches and pussycat whiskers for the rest of his life."

"So the object is not to sell?"

"The object," Daniel says, intensifying, "is to work for yourself. Selling usually means catering to the public. Do you know what kind of person the average art buyer is? A rich moron with a house full of too many walls. That's why people buy art. To cover up their putrid walls. Do you think I want my art hanging in places like that?"

"But if those are the people who buy art," she says, "don't you have to give in, just a little, to make a living?"

Daniel shoots Elsie a hurt look. His dark hair drips to his ears in beetle-black tendrils. "Yeah," he says. "And I'll sell my soul while I'm at it."

The last thing Elsie wants Daniel to do is sell his soul. Isn't an important chunk of it supposed to belong to her already? She is his other half, his *lover*, his girlfriend. According to all the famous love stories this position automatically gives her dibs on some intimate fragment of his tormented innards, like mineral rights, like mortgages. Letting any part of him go might mean disposing of something that is rightfully hers, some scrap of passion or adoration that he has yet to exhibit, but which is nevertheless there, hidden inside him like a metal plate or a swallowed penny just waiting to be excreted. She can't let him kowtow to the mainstream if it means losing him, bit by bit, in a capitulating dribble. She loves him, she wants him (what would she do without him?). Besides, she has to respect his principles even if she doesn't understand them. It's not his fault that respecting his principles also means disregarding her own.

So Elsie works. She likes her job. Most of the time she wakes up smiling, although this happiness is not so much a product of her satisfaction with her career but of her situation in general; being needed. She will help Daniel get on his feet, and then, she supposes, they will get married. She hasn't thought much about the second half of her plan, because people nowadays take their time getting to that point; they ramble through relationships and life in general as if walking blind through a park. But marriage still seems to be the natural progression of things: the place that people end up after they are sick of wandering and being bitten by collarless dogs; or, Elsie thinks despite herself, the place where they end up when they have exhausted all the other possibilities.

Helping Daniel consists of more than providing financial support, it also includes furnishing him with inspiration. During the evenings and on some weekends he has her dress in old clothes that he picked up from the Salvation Army or the Good Will thrift store: gabardine coats with fitted shoulders, or hats with discouraged looking accessories wilting off their peaks like broken tail feathers. He asks her to pose in these get-ups in the lees of various run-down store fronts with her hands outstretched or her face smudged dismally with mud, and then he takes her picture. His idea, he tells Elsie as he shoots, is to capture the demise and decay of modern society. He has abandoned painting temporarily in an attempt to slough off convention and replace it with the unvarnished boldness of silver gelatin prints. Too much attention is given to the pretty, to the picturesque. Too many galleries are filled with the placid debris of somebody's rendition of a Sunday afternoon whose only purpose is to soothe you like a lullaby. "That stuff doesn't make you think," he scoffs as he readjusts the chin strap on Elsie's pillbox hat. "It just puts you to sleep. The last thing we need is more valium for the soul."

Elsie nods when Daniel talks like this, because she doesn't know what else to do. Usually she agrees with him, more or less; either that or she tries to see his perspective. She knows he has led a different sort of life than she has; he was born in a city, or on the edge of one, into a place called Brampton where shocking things happen all the time. She has heard about some of these things on the news: children bringing guns to school. An army of upset workers from the Mars Bar factory spreading nougat all over the road. Brampton was once its own quiet place with a town clock and a city hall, but now it is just an extension of Toronto, which Daniel says is a good thing. "Except for the malls," he says, gritting his teeth. "They stretch all the way to bloody Yonge Street."

Coming to London was a step back for him; he expected to see action, unrest. Instead he landed in never-never land with a bunch of well-groomed whites who waited for the light to change before crossing the yellow line. "I should have gone to York," he says to Elsie, packing away his camera. "They could have given me a chance. At least there I would have been at the centre of things." Elsie recognizes the reproach—the subject is a sore spot with Daniel who wanted to stay in the city and go to school, but was turned away because of his poor academic record. She can't share his frustration, however; after all, if he went to York University they never would have met. Doesn't their relationship cancel out the negatives of living away from the front lines? It does for Elsie. She sits still on a crumbling set of stairs with her feet jammed into a pair of Mary Janes, inhaling the traces of mothballs and pipe tobacco leaking from her clothes. The part that worries her isn't that she can't say the same for Daniel—she knows better than to speak for him—the part that worries her is that she is too afraid to ask.

When he has exhausted the possibilities of photography, Daniel moves on to sculpture. He spends several weeks scavenging local garbage bins for miscellaneous items to add to his collection in the laundry room: a bathroom sink, a pair of women's stiletto heels covered in threadbare satin, a roll of rain-soaked Berber carpeting, the steering wheel from a 1954 Massey-Ferguson tractor. He purchases a hot-glue gun and fuses smaller objects to bigger ones, so that instead of one pile of junk he has a series resembling the models of atoms or intracellular molecules that Elsie has seen on her trips to the Science Centre.

All through this Elsie works. She teaches hard-nosed little girls how to spread their fingers across the keys like the oscitant wings of a butterfly; she teaches them the meaning of *arpeggio*, and opens up the recesses of the piano to show them the parts, saying in her glib voice: "These are the dampers and these are the hammers." If the girls are older and more advanced, she plucks on the metronome and watches them sweat beneath pale blue turtlenecks as they rush to keep in time, encouraging them with the tapping of her foot against the hardwood floors.

After work she returns home and finds explosions in her living room. Scrap metal on the chesterfield. Papier maché in cracked Tupperware juice jugs oozing onto the kitchen table. One day Daniel even replaces their curtains with garbage bags cut open and stretched across the windows like drum skins, puncturing the plastic with the sharp end of a pencil so that only a few threads of light filter into the room. "It's a commentary," he tells her when she finds him in the darkness. "There's one hole for every nuclear submarine in the Canadian navy." Elsie nods mutely, because what else can she do? At first she thought he wanted a reaction when he presented her with his finished products, and she would try, giving legitimate opinions on the expression of the abstract that she lifted from one of his art history textbooks; but soon she realized he was not interested in what she thought, not immediately anyway. He was still concentrating, looking straight ahead. Saying *It's a commentary* was a form of practice for Daniel; he spoke the words heavily, as though he were delivering a sermon. Sighing, she picks up his black socks that lie strewn about the apartment like licorice slugs and forces them into the clothes hamper. She is not a neat freak; she just appreciates order. Clutter that you can navigate without a map and compass.

"You're weird," Daniel says looking up.

"What do you mean?"

"I mean the way you pick up my clothes every day before dinner. And the way you clean the toilet—it's weird."

"Why?" Elsie asks. She is beginning to feel defensive; the skin around her neck bristles as if she is standing under a cold air vent.

"Because," Daniel says. He likes to answer her questions with *because*. Sometimes that is all she gets. "You don't just clean things up. You also mumble."

Elsie does not like the fact that she has been mumbling. She does not want to turn into her mother. How long? she asks Daniel, but he is vague, waving his fingers in the air like a magician. More and more often he speaks to her this way, obliquely, shrugging his shoulders, cupping the air with his palms as though he could contain it like liquid, like a rock, use it to wall himself off from Elsie's bootless line of questioning. He is becoming ephemeral, sullen, curling away from her cold feet in bed; he is losing solidity for Elsie who appreciates a good conversation now and then.

She understands his moods: he hasn't been able to

get an exhibition, not a solo, not even at a third-rate gallery where the majority of the paintings are on velvet or the outsides of handmade cookie tins. He did have one sculpture done in relief accepted into a community art show a few weeks back, but when he and Elsie went to the opening ceremony, they found his piece at the end of the gallery, hung slightly askew over the heat vent. The blast from the warm air had peeled off his name tag and stuck it to a nearby fern in an oriental pot. People were milling around the heat vent with plastic cups of Blue Nun, admiring the plant.

By the first snowfall Daniel has given up his three days a week at home and is volunteering at the campus art gallery hoping to make connections. A group of women artists on the verge of completing their Ph.D.s are capturing headlines for the university, touted as *groundbreaking* and *fringe* by various low-budget art magazines coming out of Toronto. Although they work individually in various mediums (Elsie has heard Daniel call one of them a *fibre artist*), they are collectively known as The Dinner Party.

"They've got talent," Daniel says to Elsie. "They need some encouragement. They've also got an advantage that I'll never have."

What he means, Elsie gathers, is that they are women; being a woman artist at this time in history gives them an edge. They can talk about anything in their art work—masturbation, childbirth, rape, periods, slavery, genocide—and not be accused of insensitivity. Nothing is outside their realm of subject matter because they are no longer the subject, as they have been for so long. These

[236]

women are behind the canvas, not on it, and therefore they are entitled; the avenue of their birthright is a mile wide.

Within weeks Daniel is the head curator of The Dinner Party's graduation exhibit. He is the personal lackey, the organizer who makes arrangements for deliveries of crates of Poly-Filla and cartons of cheap wine. His tasks include drawing up a list of important people to invite to the opening night, people like the mayor who is rumoured to have Mafia connections, and a sanguinary art critic living in the next county. He is also supposed to write an expository essay on the importance of the art show for publication in the show's catalogue.

"I can't write this essay Elsie," he tells her one evening over a bucket of fried chicken. They are lounging with their feet on the coffee table, eating off paper napkins. "You know how I nearly flunked out in second year in Sullivan's. If it wasn't for my painting, and the fact that my student advisor is buddy buddy with my asshole father, I would never have made it this far."

"Yes you can," she says. "Your writing is fine. Besides, who reads these things?"

"Everyone," Daniel says, insulted. "Everyone important. I wouldn't know where to begin, and it has to be done by Friday." He moves closer to Elsie and forms his mouth into an earnest pout, aiming his eyes at her heart. "Can you help me?"

Helping Daniel means writing the essay, but Elsie doesn't mind. She is relieved in a way, despite the fact that she doesn't have much time. Curating the show has given him an impetus for getting out of bed; she can see the colour returning to his face, the feeling to his limbs. His former lacklustre coating has been replaced by a blush of determination, filling up his body like a pint of new blood. By agreeing to write the essay, Elsie can not only make a contribution to this pattern of well-being, she can appear philanthropic while satisfying her own intentions.

She sits down at their kitchen table on Friday morning and clears away the residuals of Daniel's latest effort, an unfinished cardboard replica of the CN tower. Before the show, he had been planning to take the sculpture by train to Toronto and set it on fire in Queen's Park in a gesture of contempt for the provincial government. He got the idea from an American novel where one of the main characters is shadowed by the FBI for blowing up reproductions of the Statue of Liberty. Elsie places his Exact-o knife on the kitchen counter and slides the dust and paper scraps to the floor. *Thank goodness for The Dinner Party*, she thinks. *Thank goodness* and not *Thank God*. Despite various attempts to shed her religious past, Elsie draws the line at cursing. There is more than God's wrath to consider. There is her mother's.

She lines up her stack of books on the table and reads over the titles: *Femininity and Domination. The Struggle of Women in the Artistic Realm*. Gardner's *Art Through the Ages*, Volume Two. And of course, *Women, Art and Society*, the definitive lay person's text on feminist art criticism, according to the heavily made-up librarian. She flips through their pages, licking her thumb and index finger to moisten the edges, and takes meticulous notes. Although Elsie has never written an essay on art before, she figures it is more or less the same as writing an essay on music: pedantic, meandering, and slapped full of big words. After an hour of perusing, she pencils out an introduction:

The history of notable women artists is the history of exceptional female figures who transcended the hierarchy of gender to contribute to a patriarchal system of artistic creation. Their history is one of deviance from cultural norms, and like The Dinner Party, many elements of their work were considered shocking when they first appeared.

In the next sentence she throws in a *therefore* and an *in so far as;* she looks up the words *objectification* and *phenomenology* and scribbles them on a scratch pad in case of emergencies. When she has completed the introduction, she consults Daniel's curatorial information, a manila folder containing five artist statements and a newspaper article on The Dinner Party's unique use of everyday items such as toilet paper and bedspreads. There is a picture of two of the women in the article—*Miriam* and *Terese,* the caption imparts—standing next to an organically shaped armature wrapped in burlap. Both of them have cropped hair, and smile out towards the camera with toothy grins. Elsie notices the article says little about the work itself. Originally she had wanted to concentrate the essay on the contents of the show, but Daniel forbade it.

"You can't mention the art work directly without giving things away," he said. "The women are taking a step in a new direction. They want to keep their theme hidden until the opening so that people of all ages turn up. If you let the cat out of the bag, the show will be seen as exclusionary."

"But I need to say something about what they do," she said, frustrated. How could she write about a show she'd never even seen? "You want this thing to be good, right?"

"Yes, but it's important to keep a lid on things. The women want this to be a smash when it opens, to blow away convention and all that."

As far as Elsie could tell, the only purpose of art seemed to be the *blowing away of convention*. Daniel repeated this phrase interminably, with his eyes on fire, stating in the same breath the relative impossibility of ever doing such a thing. She was beginning to think he was a masochist. "Is that even possible?" she said. "I thought you said everything had been done."

"It has," he sighed, irritated, as if explaining something definitively simple to a small child. "But not in London. Nothing has been done in London. This place is like Europe in the Middle Ages. Just talk about their backgrounds a little, what they are up against as women. You know, embellish. You're good at that."

Elsie raised an eyebrow. "I am?"

"Yes," Daniel said. "You do it all the time."

When she has completed the handwritten draft, Elsie organizes her notes into a neat pile and types out a good copy on her electric typewriter. The words flash across a narrow band above the keyboard, *image, material culture*, like the disembodied fragments of a poem. She likes the way they sound, even if they are somewhat pretentious, because they are open-ended, new. One thing she has learned from her research is that the words of art are in a state of revision, clamouring collectively for a breath of fresh air; this has resulted in a transformation of terminology, an attempt to recreate an entire language free of sex-specific and repressive baggage. She likes the way the new words read, insisting belligerently to be heard, and the old ones, she likes the way they curl up and wither, tentatively gripping the page. You never knowing when they will be left behind. Her fingers move proficiently over the keys, picking out the letters in a whir of zinging metal. Thanks to the nuances of genetics, Elsie cannot only span twelve notes on the piano with relative ease, she can also type faster than a whirling dervish. She draws the last page out of the typewriter's black spool and adds it to the essay, clipping the completed work in the top left-hand corner then depositing it on a table in the hallway. Daniel should be turning up in the next few hours from his stint at the gallery; he will want to retrieve the essay and take it to the copy shop as soon as possible to have it ready for the opening tonight.

Elsie is proud of him, if not a little jealous. He has worked hard. He has taken his duties seriously and seen the job through to the end. For the past few weeks Daniel has been a man with a mission, and that mission has had nothing to do with her. She is so used to bolstering him up, supporting him like a back brace, that she can hardly bear to see him doing things for himself. She knows this is an awful thought. The feminist art critics would sneer: *Who do you think you are, his mother? Get a life.* She laughs when she hears these sorts of ac-

cusations, quietly, secretly, with a touch of piercing bitterness, because what kind of mothers did these women
have? Nothing like Marian, she wagers. Who do they
think they're kidding?

The painful part about Daniel's involvement with The
Dinner Party is his absolute commitment. Even when
there were wine-and-cheese invitations, or chances to
visit with friends, even when there was a *Star Trek: The
Next Generation* marathon on late-night television he
remained steadfast in his goals, filling out forms, snipping announcements from the *Free Press* to put in his
scrapbook chronicling the show's progression. Instead
of sharing meals with Elsie he left notes by the phone,
ducking out before she got home from work: *Hanging
the show, back later,* or *Sleeping at the gallery, don't
wait up.* He put the launching of those five women above
every other thing in his life, and Elsie wants to know—
although she knows the question is inappropriate and
niggardly—would he do the same for her?

She returns to the kitchen to fix herself a snack. After
six hours of work her stomach feels like an open-pit mine.
She runs the water from the tap onto her hands to clean
off any traces of lead (although she knows most pencils
are made from graphite nowadays, there is always potential), and puts the kettle on the stove for a cup of tea.
Likely there won't be anything exciting in the refrigerator; they have both been too busy to shop. She settles for a package of steamed noodles and a dollop of
peanut butter spritzed generously with soy sauce; pro-
tein and carbohydrates will keep her sharp for her
evening lessons at the conservatory. While she is searching for the chopsticks—wedged as usual between the

chesterfield cushions after take-out—she digs up an unfamiliar wand of lipstick.

Lipstick is one thing she never wears; her lips are big enough without smothering them in waxy crimson. Who wants to look like a made-up gorilla? She removes the cap and stares at the end, worn down to the quick of its plastic (cheap) casing: deep theatrical red, the same colour children use for rendering fake blood on their necks and faces when they are dressing up for Hallowe'en. But this one is authentically female, with the embossed initials of the cosmetic company, *CM*, and little red smudges all over its base. Elsie looks at the smudges: a peanut-sized thumb, an arrow sharp forefinger. The prints are too small to be Daniel's.

She roots further and unearths a pair of lace underpants tucked slothfully beneath the back of the chesterfield, shocking red with a lace gusset and petite bows sewn along the bikini line. She holds them close, turning them over in her hands, then at arms length: size eight. Even if she could squeeze her bum into pants this small (although you can hardly call them pants—two triangles connected by an impoverished set of shoelaces), would she dare to sample lace? Marian told her early on about the bacterial possibilities for synthetic undergarments—*breeding grounds* she called them in the store, fingering a rayon pair of panties covered in Winnie-the-Poohs. *Don't even think about it.* To this day Elsie has a hard time shaking off the influence of her mother's sanctions, but she would have tried for Daniel's sake, if she'd known he had a *thing* for transparent fabrics. How ridiculous that he should leave them here in their own furniture, in the chesterfield Elsie bought herself through an ad in the paper. Elsie is in the habit of straightening up the living room, surely he would have known she would find them. Or perhaps that is his plan; perhaps he acted carelessly on purpose with the intention of being found out. Innocent Daniel, with the libido of a neutered St. Bernard (not to be cruel, but he isn't overly attentive); or rather Daniel and *she,* squirming recklessly on the couch, together, a triumphant *they.* Because there would have to be two of them.

20

How could she have been so thick? So completely taken in? Elsie lies in bed with the covers up to her neck. A purple duvet slinks over her body, hugging her backside in an overdone lump. What she sees is not exciting: an aloe-vera plant on top of a milk crate, a raku pottery candle holder with iridescent cracks; she can make out the corner of one of Daniel's posters, a promo shot for the Rolling Stones Steel Wheels tour, supposedly the band's last, but already cancelled out by another one that took place this year; she can also see a portrait of herself in the corner, resting against the milk crate. The portrait is done in oils, or at least the underpainting is; brash strokes of greens and blues thinned to a toxic dribble by linseed and turpentine, never filled in, never finished. Daniel gave her the portrait for her twenty-third birthday, close to their second anniversary, saying, "I wanted to finish it, but I didn't have the time. I will though. Soon."

Soon. Elsie wonders if Daniel's definition of soon is

close to hers: in a short time, before long. She wonders if he has ever felt for her the kinds of emotions she has felt for him, the burning kind, the ones that singe. The ones that leave your stomach tangled in a French knot, and your heart begging outside your lungs. Because if he hasn't, if he has simply been cruising all this time, waiting for something better to come along, someone with ravishing hair and smaller pelvic bones, she will die; either that, or he will die. Someone, it seems, will have to give up their life.

The worst part about the whole thing is that she never saw it coming! Not when he started spending longer hours at the campus art gallery, taking along his dinner in a grease-stained paper bag; not even when he spent the better part of his evenings at home checking the insides of his nostrils for hairs. He never wore aftershave, and then all of a sudden, there it was on the bathroom counter in its brisk amber bottle with polished brass plunger—*Wolverine*. How obvious and insulting. Why didn't she see it before?

What she wants to know now is which one: Miriam or Terese? Wanda or Beth? She can't remember the fifth woman's name, but that will be remedied soon enough. Somewhere in the apartment Daniel has left a stack of flyers for Elsie to post on her way to work. The flyers list the names of all the women in The Dinner Party, and give a sneak preview of the exhibition without actually showing any pictures of the art. She wonders if the owner of the lipstick and the underpants looks anything like the girls she used to see hanging around Daniel's painting classes. Soot black hair, chocolate skin, ribcages like immovable cellos. What right does someone have to look like that? In the seven years that they have been together, Elsie has only been to a handful of openings, predominantly student exhibitions at the artist's co-op where Daniel hauled his melting canvas baguettes for post-hour critiques and coffee with pie-eyed, spur-nosed graduates. The women there congregated in bunches, leaning against boiler pipes, wearing black impervious jeans and balancing their belted hips over pairs of army boots. When asked about the boots, one of the women told Elsie they were *to maim,* heaving her toes at the base of the pipe. She also showed Elsie her switchblade, stashed in a zippered pocket below her elbow, which Elsie knew was illegal. *Stashed* was the woman's word—*just in case.*

Thinking about these women is not enough to get Elsie out of bed; if anything the thoughts paralyze her further. Her arms and legs feel like gelatinous spaghetti, her feet like gumshoe rubber. She lies frozen, drenched in lethargy, crouching under the covers like a shrewd mouse until Daniel walks in the door.

"Hey," he yells from the hallway. "Thanks for the essay. I have to split to get the catalogue copied. I know you're getting ready for work. Wish me luck."

Elsie opens her mouth to speak but such a thing is an impossibility. What will she say? There are too many options.

The tactical approach: *You're in love with her, aren't you?*

Or the outright crass: *What was it like, screwing another woman?*

Then there is sympathy, compassion, the old-fashioned method condemned by modern women because it never got their mothers anywhere: *Try me, I might just understand.*

As far as Elsie is concerned, none of them are any good.

"See ya later," Daniel says, closing the door behind him.

Silence invades the room. The words that stick in Elsie's head: *You didn't try hard enough..* She starts to cry.

How could he do this to her, after almost seven years? And how could he do it with *her*, a rawboned sylph with buns the size of new potatoes? If bottoms were the scale on which they were to be measured, Elsie could not possibly compete.

She had been planning to say something to make him stay, a confrontation, an insult, but something held her back. Something new and slightly abnormal. She struggles to suppress the idea but there it is: relief.

Relief because she no longer has to convince Daniel, bleary-eyed and late for work, to comb his hair into a serviceable cap; she no longer has to entreat him to scrape the burnt-on crust from their saucepans—leftover from his cooking endeavours—into the monster-like garburator buried in their kitchen sink. Relief because she no longer has to prop up, to cajole; to wheedle or coax. She is a free woman for the first time in her life and she can stop the compromises, the niceties, the infinite attempts to be agreeable and full of mirth, because now that Daniel has cheated her and she is on her own, the only person she has to please is herself.

Feeling this way is like waking up after two hundred years and meeting yourself in the mirror; it is like breathing in pure oxygen through a larynx fixed by restorative surgery. It is also easier to take, making the end of their relationship a choice, her choice, rather than a fact that is imposed. But just for the record she wants to know who he has been seeing. What kind of woman? She plans to visit the art show tomorrow, when the crowd has dispersed and Daniel is in bed with the characteristic hangover, and all that is left in the gallery are the remains of yesterday's cheese trays, and the ruins of creativity that everyone calls art.

21

At the art gallery Elsie wears a baseball cap with her hair tucked inside, and a pair of denims; she wishes she had chosen something less noticeable, however—black and yellow gumboots, or a rubber nose—when she sees how other people are dressed. One woman has purple pigtails knotted at the edges of her scalp like plums; another wears checked overalls strung over her shoulders by a rattling pair of chains. The spot above her eyes is shorn and smooth, and in place of her eyebrows the woman has painted chevrons.

The show is hung in a series of white rooms adjacent to the art building where Daniel studied sculpture and painting when he was an undergraduate. Over the main doors, a large banner painted by hand onto bed sheets proclaims *The Dinner Party: A Graduate Retrospective of Five Women Artists*. Elsie walks about the rooms in her sunglasses, feeling like a spy for the French Foreign Legion. The baseball cap lessens the effect somewhat. Oh well, she thinks. At least no one will see the bags under my eyes.

It is a crisp November Saturday, the day after the opening ceremony. The crowd in the gallery is small and predominantly female. As she suspected, Daniel was hung over when she slipped out of bed this morning, and didn't flinch when she told him she had things to do. "O.K.," he said, wincing under the weight of a headache. "Good luck."

She took the bus to the campus and snuck into the gallery without reading any of the explanatory billboards mounted on the entry wall. Although she has every right to be here, she doesn't want to be recognized until she gets what she came for: a clue, a confirmation. Hanging around the entrance is asking for trouble. Someone might try to solicit her help as a docent or a volunteer; they might think she is interested in making a donation to the Purchase-A-Picasso-Print-Fund. Someone might realize that she is connected to Daniel, and then she would have to make conversation and pretend she is in control of her life. (She would have to lie.) She is better off moving around fortuitously, like a mosquito.

All of the art in the show seems more or less abstract. Three-dimensional sculptures of roughly textured rope or shredded material. A collage of Barbie heads pasted onto a scrabble board over the letters B-I-T-C-H. Paintings, prints. Installations. (Elsie has heard Daniel call them installations, as though they were dental fillings or bathroom fixtures.) She approaches one of the ones that takes up nearly half a room, keeping her distance to get a good look. The construction is gigantic: a seven-foot cavern breached by cascading velvet curtains. Billowing strips of pink and red cloth spilling from circular supports. At the centre, where the sides of the cavern come together in a soft arch, a sign that says *Touch me here* dangles seductively on red lace ribbons. Elsie thinks she recognizes her living-room curtains.

She takes a step closer and reads the name plate on the wall: *"Roar," chrome, silk and polypropylene fabric. Miriam Benjamin, 1995.* The surrounding red tints the label so that it too looks dark and bloody. Checking over her shoulder, she makes sure she is alone. A woman walks by in orange lipstick. Nobody else is around. She takes another step, putting her hand on the velvet, beneath the sign, making a tentative brushing motion with her fingers. It feels all right, like dense woodland moss. Sumac branches. It feels like something newly born, with baby fur around the ears. She moves her hand a little further, stroking. There is a slight attraction.

"Quite a ride, eh?" The woman with the orange lipstick says, startling Elsie from behind. "Not everyone touches it you know, but when they do, they sure don't stop in a hurry. Miriam did a great job, don't you think? It's a portrait of her lover. How does it make you feel?"

Elsie lowers her hands and retreats a few feet. She knows the woman, but in different clothes; in a different hairdo. It is Miss Pollard, her teacher from Our Lady of the Immaculate Conception. "Pardon me?" she says.

"Doesn't it give you the chills? The first time I saw the whole thing completed I was knocked down flat. I think it really made a big impact with the straight population last night. The ones who touched it, that is."

What gives Elsie the chills is seeing Miss Pollard without her frilly dresses, without her lips drawn on in virginal rose. "Straight population?" she says.

"Yes," the woman says. "The conservatives, the

heterosexuals. London is full of them, or hadn't you noticed?"

"Of course, it's just that—"

"Oh don't worry, I'm only joking. We had a great turnout last night and I think some of the older folks were a little taken aback when they found out they were attending an art show put on by gay Christians. But that was our intent, really. I think some of them were even disappointed. They expected more tattoos."

Elsie opens her mouth, then changes her mind. She can't believe this woman is Miss Pollard. She is older, but not that old, and slim, with a slight puffiness around the eyes. She wears her hair short, in a shingled bob, and her ears pierced with a series of small rings.

"It's even kind of a shame that the opening is all over. We have been planning for so long. Doing so much work."

"You mean," says Elsie still processing, "that all the women in the show are gay?"

"Queer, dyke, whatever you want to call them. Why?" says Miss Pollard. "Didn't you read the write-up in the front foyer?"

"No," says Elsie. "Actually I just came in to look for Daniel. I thought he was dating one of the women showcased in the retrospective, because he always seemed to be coming here."

"Oh," Miss Pollard says. "If he is that's news to me. Daniel helped us with the show, that's why he was around—although I don't know if I should call it helping."

"Why not?" says Elsie.

"He isn't very organized, for one. And he hardly ever

showed up. We had a lot of tense moments when he didn't pull through, which makes things tough when you're trying to plan."

"Oh," says Elsie. "I'm sorry." And she is, but not for Miss Pollard. She's sorry for herself, who seems to have lost control somewhere along the way. She is like a shamed mother whose child urinates in a public place. Somehow this is her fault.

"Don't get me wrong," Miss Pollard continues. He's a great guy. We appreciate what he did do, writing that great essay for our catalogue. But when you're paying someone, you expect him to show up on time, meet deadlines. Daniel doesn't do that. He's got a lot of issues to grapple with, if you know what I mean."

"No," says Elsie, her face reddening. Daniel was paid? "I don't actually know him that well." This time the lie is only partial. They seem to be talking about someone else, not Daniel, *her* Daniel, who always said he didn't have time for deceit.

"Well," says Miss Pollard. "He's working on them. But I would say responsibility is key. He needs to grow up a little, get out of adolescence."

Elsie tenses and looks at the wall. She has had the same thoughts about Daniel, more than once, but always convinced herself she was wrong. Other people felt this way? "I should be going," she says.

"I'm Wanda," Miss Pollard says, opening her orange lips. "Wanda Mortimer, although I'm in the process of shedding the last name, bad marriage and all. I work at the Children's Resource Centre down the road, teaching kids that have been roughed up once too often."

Elsie nods. "Oh," she says. She tries to imagine Wanda

praying, her hands folded in a gesture of devout holiness, but the orange nail polish gets in the way. "I'm only telling you this because you look familiar," Wanda says, tilting her head. "I thought I might know you from work or something. What's your name?"

"Violet," Elsie says, before she can help it. She still prefers to remain incognito, especially in front of someone who knows her mother. Knew her mother.

Wanda shoots her a serious look, studying her through her sunglasses, then shrugs her shoulders and laughs. "I guess I was wrong," she says. "But it's nice to meet you all the same. I hope you enjoy the rest of the show. Say hi to Daniel when you find him."

When Elsie gets home Daniel is sitting at the table eating cold cereal, a flaky mixture of bran and oats sugary enough to appease his sweet tooth. He wears his blue and red striped bath robe hanging open at the navel; he has no chest hairs. Elsie watches him chew, his jaw cracking like a wounded animal. He sulks over the newspapers, mumbling out the headlines. Now that the show is over, he is looking for a full-time job.

"Daniel," she says, "whose lipstick is this?" She holds up the offending tube.

"Lipstick?"

"I found it in our living-room couch. Between the cushions."

"That's Miriam's," he says, chewing. "It's leftover from her installation. I brought it home thinking I'd try out a few canvases. You know, de Bouffet style. Scribble a little."

"And," Elsie continues. "Whose underpants?"

Daniel swivels around in his kitchen chair and scowls. "I know, they're gross. Miriam bought a whole case of them to line that cavern of hers. Lace scales. I was going to cut some of the spare ones up and use them for something. Maybe drape a few of them over my CN tower to make it burn better. Why?" He looks at her, his mouth an innocent butterfly.

"Oh," Elsie says. "Never mind."

22

Ridiculous, Elsie thinks, sitting in her grandmother's basement. How did she get down here? She was looking for something, a screwdriver or a pair of pliers to change the light bulb on one of Violet's ancient lamps, when she was assaulted by memories, her grandmother's and her own. Her grandmother's are easier to take, of course, because they are more tangible and more removed. Next to her feet a Little League catcher's mitt from some wartime baseball association huddles on the floor. On the laundry tub behind the washing soda, a collection of cloudy milk bottles rattle in their wire cages. Each of these items, Elsie suspects, is linked to some everyday event in Violet's life, events which seemed at one time as if they would go on forever, but which gradually slowed to an unforeseen halt. Elsie knows the feeling. She thought Daniel would always be there, smug and familiar, like a mole. She thought the two of them would prance on into the future living happily ever after, because if you are good and eat all your vegetables aren't you supposed to come out a success? A winner? Everyone says so, but then again, most of them are Protestants. Elsie is beginning to see the benefit of Marian's view of life, and of Catholicism in general: no matter how well you behave you might still be the target for random acts of misfortune; you might wake up penitent only to find your body covered in boils, your wife sold into the slave trade for a sack full of slugs. This is God's way of saying *Pay attention, don't lose track, life is not a bowl of cherries;* his way of keeping you on your toes like Stalin in the reign of terror, because life is suffering and only the truly tenacious make it to heaven.

At least if Elsie had stuck to her mother's outlook she would have been prepared. Instead she is bitter. No, not bitter, but hurt. She is riddled internally with hairline cracks and if anyone were to touch her now she would instantly fall to pieces. *That is the consequence of your behaviour,* Marian would say if she were still alive. *Now you must accept your fate.* Elsie is trying, she just wishes her fate would hurry up and do something decisive. She can't stand all this brooding.

What do any of her experiences matter anyway? She is here now, in British Columbia, inside a body that performs familiar enough observances: it hums, it bleeds, it pains, it growls. It demands to be fed and watered and taken into the open air. Perhaps one day it will meet another body with similar wounds and the two of them can do the whole damn drama together, a unified couple of daredevils. But this time she will do things differently; this time she will keep her eye on the door.

Until then (and she won't waste her breath thinking about *when*), she is free. Or is she? There is still the problem of memory, cunning and deep, slavish and lucent, clutching on to the back of her neck with hands just weighty enough to damage her windpipe. Since moving to the coast Elsie has learned that memory is traitorous: hanging around when you want it gone, drifting away when you are desperate to keep it locked up in your bosom. Freedom, ha! What was she thinking? What she needs is something to numb the ache, an ice cube or a packet of frozen peas, but she must choose her medicine carefully, she doesn't want to end up on a street corner like the growing numbers of steely-faced adolescents she has seen on Georgia, with their stratagems for lifting small change. She must take extra care of herself, because there is nobody else to look out for her blunders.

She stands up to relieve some of the tension in her legs. Her socks are coated in cat hair and a fine, nebulous dust the colour of chalk. Somewhere in London Daniel also sits, in front of the television, twitching the converter, pressing it firmly with his crooked thumb, or he paces in front of a canvas (before Elsie left, Daniel attempted a half-hearted return to painting), his hair clinging to his head like an erratic bird's nest. His eyes are vacant sockets of gloom; his mouth is a mournful dance performing in the middle of his face. He has lost all will to go on because Elsie, the one woman he entrusted with his soul, crushed it under her boot like the dwindling end of a cigarette.

Or this is what she believes when she is being delusionary. Instead she moves back in time and remembers the truth.

"I spoke to Wanda," she says to Daniel. "At the gallery."

They are at the kitchen table eating breakfast. Darkness wallows outside the window, enveloping the house that contains their basement apartment, the hemlock trees on the back lawn; pushing up against the bricks and the doors and the beige horizontal blinds that Elsie bought to replace the curtains, swathing the room in nihilistic mist. The month of October is waning, Elsie has seen Hallowe'en costumes for sale in the drug store. Daylight Savings will soon make it official: they are on the road to winter.

Daniel is wearing a pair of black jeans fringed at the cuffs, and a T-shirt that says *Metaphysical Graffiti* in spray-painted letters. He puts down his knife and looks at Elsie.

"Oh." The word is not a question, but a statement. An implication against Elsie who has been flexing her feminine claws and sticking them into his private business. Snooping is something Daniel despises. His stepmother was a snooper.

"Do you want to know what she said?" says Elsie.

"You want to tell me," says Daniel, shifting his eyes to the table. Looking away.

"She said you were getting paid," says Elsie. "For your work on the show. And that you hardly ever turned up." She tries to speak without warbling. She is nervous now, confrontational. She can feel her hackles raised, the hair on the back of her neck erect and bristling.

Daniel places his toast on his plate and consults his cup of coffee. No response.

"So why did you tell me you were volunteering?" says Elsie.

"I didn't," says Daniel. "You assumed and I neglected to correct you."

Elsie hardens: so that's how it was. He didn't care enough to fill her in. Her knowledge and opinion were inconsequential, just as *she* was inconsequential. She crosses her arms to conceal her shaking. "What else have you neglected to tell me?" she says. "Where you were all those nights you were supposed to be at the gallery?"

Daniel looks at her in disgust, his features sharp and indignant. "Where do you think I was?"

"I don't know," says Elsie, because she doesn't. She has no idea. If he offers something close, something even half plausible, she is willing to barter. She doesn't like the alternative. "Well?" she says.

"Why don't you ask Wanda?" Daniel says, overennunciating his words like an impersonator. "You two seem to be close."

"I'm asking you," says Elsie.

"Well I wasn't here," says Daniel. "Being here is about as exciting as living in a shoebox."

Elsie looks at Daniel and feels the pinch of abandonment: he was bored. Despite all her attempts to cuddle and cherish and catalyze inspiration, Elsie was boring, the same way a rock was boring, or a documentary on the life of Canadian parliamentarians. She shifts in her chair and tries not to fall to pieces—she can't afford to come apart this early in the morning—and then she gets mad. She tried so hard. How can he be so mean? "Why didn't you tell me you felt that way?" she says, shaking harder.

"You don't take me seriously," says Daniel, sipping at his juice. "Just like my art: you think it's a hobby, like quilting or making ashtrays. You think I should give up everything and go into pothole repair just like your father."

"Daniel," says Elsie, stunned now that the accusations are going the other way. "I never said that."

"But that's what you think. A normal job. One like yours. Well I can't be a teacher Elsie. It would eat me up."

Elsie checks herself to see if she feels eaten. She can't tell any more. She's too tired. Maybe that's the same thing. "So this is my fault?" she says. "The fact that you lied? The fact that I thought you loved me?" She is breathless now, her lungs ache; but now that she has pierced the air with the word *love*, she can't go back.

Daniel sighs and looks out the window. The sun is coming up, filling the streets with colour. He doesn't usually get out of bed this early in the morning, but today he has a job interview at Mac's Milk. "Love doesn't exist, not really," he says. "It's a societal construct invented by Hallmark so that people will get married and send greeting cards. There's passion and there's tenderness, but not love like in the movies. That's all bullshit."

Elsie's heart muscle seizes up and she feels a tremor building at the back of her throat. If Daniel is right she doesn't want to go on, get up from the table and clear her plate, wrap her scarf around her neck and go out the door, walk down the street like a cleverly automated mannequin; if Daniel is right she can't go on teaching little girls to manipulate sound, believing that the ability to generate music is an acceptable substitute for the fact that Elsie is love-starved.

"I don't believe that," she says, rising from the table and depositing her napkin on her plate. Moving towards the coat rack where her three-quarter rayon anorak is hanging like a piece of skin. Knowing for the first time that she does believe in love, in every kind of it in fact, and that like any other person she is entitled to her share.

"Elsie," Daniel says, lifting his eyebrows in a concentrated look of impatience. "You'll be early for work. Where are you going?"

"Away," says Elsie, opening the door.

"Look," he adds, sighing as if punctured. "I was with Miriam, hanging out at the Paradise. All we did was talk."

The Paradise, Elsie's Paradise. How long has it been since they went there together? Months? Years? Somehow this information doesn't matter to her anymore. She doesn't care. The Daniel in the kitchen is not the same one she remembers, the beautiful one with dark tendrils who laughed at the world. Who made her laugh at herself. This Daniel is hardened, cynical, an old man home from war. If she touches him she will get burned, or worse, shot through the heart. She can't take a chance: she has never been good at recovery.

"That doesn't matter," she says, cinching her coat at the waist, walking out, because she is good at that. "Not anymore."

After work Elsie starts packing. She is amazed at the number of pieces of furniture that they have crammed into a one-bedroom apartment. Where will she live? What will she take? Before leaving to visit his mother, Daniel made it clear to Elsie that he does not plan to move anywhere—their suite is close to the campus and downtown galleries, not to mention affordable to heat—and that leaving is her idea, so she should be the one to go.

With this in mind Elsie purchased a copy of the *Free Press*, extracted the accommodation section and spread it out on the floor. So far there is nothing that attracts her, but she has to find something. She has no girlfriends to stay with and Daniel will only be away until the end of the week. The sooner she can leave, the better. Less chance of changing her mind.

Although on the surface she knows the break-up is painful for both of them, she also knows they will benefit from the exercise. Isn't that how things are done? Get a little perspective, see the holes, patch them up? She thought so at the time. She believes in stepping back from things and using her head; but instead of a clear panorama, what Elsie gets is one recurring image:

During the second year of university Daniel took Elsie to a film festival in Toronto. They drove a friend's car all the way to an obscure corner of the city and parked in front of a brown brick house with a sagging porch.

"Where are we?" Elsie said as they got out of the car.

"At the festival," Daniel replied.

As far as Elsie could tell the festival was not funded by corporate sponsors. It was run out of somebody's living room, and had the aroma of stale cottages that have been shut up for the winter. Everyone sat on threadbare couches, a man with turbulent eyebrows nursing a bottle of whiskey, girls in leather mini-skirts, a silent couple (heterosexual), and a woman with pupils the size of nickels who approached Elsie, put her hand on her arm, and said in an earnest voice, "The Coke bottle man is after me again." The movies were put onto a projector by another man with black hair who came out of a revolving door that looked as if it led into the kitchen; they were projected onto a filthy screen that hung limply on the end wall. The images were black and white: a psychedelic spiral, a gorilla and a woman wearing a toga doing some sort of Russian dance. Then there was a cloud, ants skittering on the beach, a floating grand piano. A man appeared with a razor and cut a woman's eyeball in half. Elsie watched the films wondering if they were on the correct speed, but thinking at the same time, would it make that much of a difference?

No matter how rational she attempts to be looking back over their lives together, all she can think about is that film festival, and the way she felt sitting next to Daniel on the fetid upholstery. Disembodied. Surreal. If she's being honest, and she might as well try that for a change, she has felt that way for the better part of the last seven years.

Two days later Violet's lawyer calls and tells Elsie she is the acting owner of a two-bedroom house on Chesterfield Avenue in British Columbia. He also says she has the power of attorney over her grandmother's estate, and that there are cheques to be signed, bills to be paid. He can put off BC Hydro for a few more weeks, but after that, a visit to the coast would be recommended.

"O.K.," says Elsie impetuously. "I'll buy my ticket today."

Her logic is simple. Things with Daniel have been tenuous, inert, but there was a time when they were better, a time when they were in love; or at least she was. Perhaps if she were to leave, to break into a new environment, the two of them would be rejuvenated. Ready to try again. Perhaps Daniel would follow her to the new frontier and together they could work on maintaining that level of emotion that seems necessary for the sustenance of love. Either way she will benefit. If he comes they will have another shot, a chance to start over and do things right. If he doesn't, then what has she been doing for seven years?

What was I doing? Elsie thinks, looking out the window of her grandmother's basement through wrought-iron bars. On the lawn she can see the cat marching purposefully toward the fence line. If only she had such direction. *You were living kid,* an internal voice replies, *the only way you knew how.* She turns to regard the mess. *But now,* she insists, one hand pressed to her hairline. *What am I doing now? What am I doing here?* The voice has an answer, but as usual, one that offers little comfort: *That, my dear, remains to be seen.*

She moves back into the rubble and picks up a box that has spilled its contents onto the floor. One of the items is a small rectangular container carved by hand in the likeness of what looks like a frog. The legs and arms run up the sides in perfect symmetrical green, and are accented by parallel lines alternating in red and black. Inside the container are keepsakes: a lock of red hair taped to a piece of cardboard, a ring. There are also two photographs, one which Elsie recognizes from her father's photo album left behind after his death. The shot is Uncle Russell at age sixteen. He stands with his arms crossed, smiling charismatically out at the viewer. Behind him is an old car with fenders so large they appear inflated. The other photograph is of a man not much older than Russell, with a similar smile, only this picture must have been taken earlier because of the man's clothes, and the way his hair curls on top of his head like a puff of whipped cream. He too is looking out at the viewer, exposing his willowy portrait to the camera, but his hands are in his pockets and his face appears smudged. Behind him Elsie can make out a sign: Burrard Dry Docks Inc. The back of the photo says only *1927* in faded handwriting.

She takes both of the photos upstairs to add to the collection of what to keep, putting the rectangular container and the lock of hair back into the cardboard box. She has heard from some of her more far-out acquaintances that keeping bits of people after they are dead—things like hairballs and toenail clippings—encourages their spirits to linger. Although she is not superstitious, she doesn't like the idea of carrying around a part of someone else's body, especially if that someone else is no longer on the planet. The thought gives her the creeps. She would rather take her chances with the photographs.

Upstairs her grandmother's house is silent. There is a slight buzzing coming from the refrigerator, but apart from that, the padding of Elsie's feet against the flooring is the only discernible noise. She looks into the kitchen where yesterday's dishes are stacked in the sink, unwashed. Her inability to rally herself for the cleanliness cause is evidence against her; if she had not been so preoccupied, so inadvertent in her approach; if she had not been so single-minded, or *single* for that matter, she would have done a better job of manufacturing a facade of control. Even the dinner was a sham. She had made a half-hearted promise to eat well, swearing off the platters of noodle elbows and spaghettini and other overdoses of carbohydrates that had recently been keeping her afloat, preparing an uncharacteristically green salad with two colours of bell peppers. She followed this with a plate of steamed cut broccoli next to slices of whole wheat toast, but when she sat down at the table she lost her appetite. Gone. The dinner looked too vibrant, too herbaceous and spry to be enticing. She thought instead of new-mown lawns, of Weed and Feed. She settled for the toast, and a thin layer of peanut butter to cover the seeds.

Now the colander sits in the double boiler like a stainless-steel UFO. Elsie manages to clear the dishes from the sink with a minimum of spillage, and runs them under the hot water to loosen the grit. She does like vegetables, that is not her problem. She did not lose her appetite on the account of finicky eating habits. Living with Daniel meant acting on behalf of vegetables everyday, saying in the joyous voice of other people's mothers, *Delicious salad, why don't you try a few bites?* It meant working with the innovations of sauces and glazes to conceal the inherent dullness that Daniel associated with anything yanked directly from the earth. Cooking for herself is not the same. She knows the flavour of beets, of calcareous brassicas and their leafy Elizabethan collars, and she does not mind the taste, the zing of raw vitamins; or rather, she didn't used to mind, up until a few months ago. Now, after years of catering, she finds them boring, and she cannot bring herself to jazz them up. Why go to all that effort when there is only herself to impress?

But that is not all. What is really bothering her is this: she is alone, doomed to wander the streets, peruse the shopping centres, hop on the bus, cross the bridge,

[268]

take her meals like a bachelor from a lonely one-serving saucepan, all by herself. Day after day. Night after night. Alone. And now that all the bank tellers have gone instant, she doesn't even have the satisfaction of making conversation while she pays her grandmother's bills.

Of course she anticipated this loneliness when she left the apartment in London, but she also believed it would be short-lived, because somewhere in the back of her head (or her heart) she thought their story—hers and Daniel's—would end in happy reunion. That's how it works in the movies: the heroine boards the plane, the train, the heli-jet, to cross some vast expanse of tumid, boiling geography, only to be intercepted, at the last minute, by the hero, who despite the guards and guns and metal detectors makes it to her side just as the music is climaxing, in time to mouth across a sea of faces blotted out by their ordinary apparel and dull complexions, *I won't let you go alone.* But Elsie is alone. That is her problem.

And at least part of this is her grandmother's fault. Her grandmother, who walked out on her own family.

She goes into Violet's bedroom and rummages through her drawers, throwing things on the floor instead of shifting them neatly to one side. She slams photographs of the Leggett family face down onto Violet's vanity, and tears the covers and linens off of the bed.

"What are you hiding?" she says, lifting up the mattress. "Why did you go?"

She goes into the room that would have been her father's, once upon a time, shared with his brothers until he was old enough to leave home. The room is dark and spare, outfitted with a set of drawers, a thin bed pressed against off-white walls. In the corner is a cedar chest, engraved and smelling of old wood. Elsie opens the lid and begins to sort the contents: blankets, photo albums, lace-edged tea towels, bits of old newspaper, table cloths. As she sorts she feels the anger turn to frustration; she doesn't even know what she is looking for.

She is interrupted by a knock on the window.

"Yes," she says, opening Violet's back door.

"Hello," the woman says. "I brought cookies." She holds out a tin of Danish shortbreads and removes the lid, revealing small homemade rounds that look to Elsie like they have been rolled and cut with a knife. The woman is the same one that came over on Elsie's first day and reprimanded her for Violet's stroke. Her dark hair has been pulled back into a bun, and she wears a silky dress with a cross-your-heart neckline.

"Oh," Elsie says, surprised. "You didn't have to do this. This is awfully kind of you."

"They are for Mrs. Leggett. You take them to her."

Elsie stammers. The woman is not being neighbourly, she is not even smiling. She is pushing the tin forward with her small hands.

"You take them to her. Say they from Mrs. Wang. Mrs. Wang down the street."

Elsie nods politely and the woman is off, shuffling down the alley in her slippers. She takes the tin into the kitchen and removes the lid, sampling a corner of one of the cookies, which are arranged delicately on a layer of wax paper. Almonds. Butter. Mrs. Wang has gone to a lot of trouble. If Elsie doesn't take them to Violet she supposes they will go rancid, take on the flavour of old socks, of blue cheese on stale crackers, and if she eats them herself, she will likely get sick; either that or gain twenty pounds. How does Mrs. Wang manage to stay so thin eating treats like this? Elsie looks at the table where some of the legal paperwork given to her by her grandmother's lawyer waits to be completed. There are questions she needs to ask Violet, but making her understand will be difficult. Will she even recognize Elsie? Will she know she has a house? Still, Elsie can't turn everything in until she knows the details, and for now it appears there is only one way she is going to find out. She just wishes she didn't have to do it herself.

23

Sometimes, before her stroke—although Violet would never admit this out loud—her mind betrayed her. She might be speaking to some stranger on the bus, or, heaven forbid, an acquaintance from the old neighbourhood, when all of a sudden her train of thought would disappear. Gone. She would stutter and haw and have to make a joke about losing her mind until she could pick up on whatever it was she was saying.

If the acquaintance was old like herself, they would laugh along with her and say in a conspiratorial tone: "I know exactly what you mean dear." But if they were young, a bank teller, for instance, or the clerk in the pharmacy, they would look at Violet with mild concern. "Mrs. Leggett," they would say. "Are you feeling all right? You don't seem quite like yourself today."

Violet hated these statements. Of course she wasn't herself; she hadn't been herself in fifty years!

At the Avondale things are worse. Nurses ask her obtuse, mortifying questions—*Mrs. Leggett, when did you last move your bowels?*—then wait like indulgent parents for her to scribble out her answers on the stenopad; attendants push her to and fro, clipping her elbows on the edges of banisters, leaving her marooned in the loony ward next to maniacal patients who speak incoherently to coat racks. Nobody gives her a chance to explain herself; to tell them that, save the odd bout of amnesia, she is perfectly sharp.

She is just a little tired, for God's sake. That's all.

What galls her the most are the memories. Despite the fact that she misplaced her keys once in a while, and that she sometimes, though very seldom, called Lawrence *Russell*, she was always perfectly in charge of the past. Even now she can recall every minute of her formative years as though she recently saw them replayed at the movie theatre in surround sound: her mother at the sink peeling potatoes or turnips, her father, the coniferous, balmy smell of him, lingering in the parlour with his feet on the ottoman. If she closes her eyes for one instant, she can conjure up the exact texture of her husband's favourite pastry, and the feeling of his bedtime kisses: wet, a little on the mushy side, but comforting nonetheless.

And then there are the Saturday night dances, the smoke-filled ballrooms, the breakneck music working its way into Violet's legs, infecting them with the need to dance. *Five foot two, eyes of blue. Oh, what those five feet could do! Has anybody seen my gal?* She can still remember the sensation of his arms around her waist, the way his skin bristled when she touched him beneath the pine trees, lightly at first, because she was scared, while the music sang on, leaking out

[273]

from the dance hall into the summer night. *Blue skies . . . smiling at me . . .*

Contrary to what people think, lucidity is not always an advantage. Those memories hurt, they slice into her heart. If Violet is not careful, her memories could tear her apart, ripping slowly from the inside like a set of small thumbs; peel her down like an orange. She is scared of letting them out, of dealing with them any more than is necessary, because if she does let them surface she will have to face them head on. Then what will happen? She might go completely mental! Or worse, the memories might dissolve entirely, and leave her without a history, stranded and alone, just like everyone else has done in this life.

No thank you.

She looks out the window of her private bedroom and onto the Avondale grounds. On the grass, patches of melting snow fall into puddles; a German Shepherd bounds toward a fire hydrant and sniffs out his competition.

"Mrs. Leggett," a nurse says, poking her head in the door. "We're starting the slide show now. We thought you would be particularly interested because there are a lot of old-time photographs of the north shore. From the twenties and thirties. Can I wheel you to the lounge?"

Violet has seen the posters for the slide show scotch-taped to the walls of the lunch room by volunteers from the historical society: *Golden Years on the Golden Mountain.* A retrospective no less. She knows the pictures will likely be mundane newspaper reproductions: the mayor's house, the Capilano Hotel before it was drowned by the Cleveland Dam. A shot or two of the dry docks during the war. Still, she's curious.

Why not? she thinks, turning herself from the window. "Oh good," says the nurse. "We knew you wouldn't let us down. You're one of our oldest north shore residents you know. One day you'll have to tell us all about those times. They must have been quite something."

Yes, Violet says to herself, because who else can hear her? *They were. Quite something indeed.*

By the time Violet entered high school it was 1925 and North Vancouver had grown. Wooden sidewalks still lined the edges of Lonsdale and Chesterfield, but medians had been inserted at intervals along local streets to protect pedestrians and oncoming traffic from the fateful careening of overzealous motorists (who, incidentally, were becoming more numerous than even Jack had ever imagined).

Lila Spencer continued her Sunday jaunts to St. Edmund's Catholic Church for purposes of worship, and kept up her ties with the Women's Institute. In the wake of peace, the ladies of the institute transferred their efforts to the improvement of community morals through a series of lectures on *mental hygiene.*

"We must be models of restraint and orderliness," Violet overheard her mother say on more than one occasion. "We are citizens of a new, unbridled era. We must check this wild abandon while it is still in its infancy."

Violet knew that the *wild abandon* her mother was referring to had something to do with the selling of alcohol in government-controlled liquor stores. Jack visited these places often (he called them *John Oliver's drugstores*), and picked up a flask of whiskey or a bottle of rum before heading off to the North Vancouver Men's

Club. To Lila's chagrin, and to the chagrin of Catholics all over the lower mainland, liquor was back, but at least you needed a permit to buy it.

Her mother's definition of *wild abandon* also included the behaviour of women. Somebody somewhere had got the idea that women could walk up and down the streets with skirts above their knees, flaunting their legs and ankles, shamelessly exposing the backs of their necks. And now, everywhere you went, women were tramping down sidewalks in dresses like flour sacks, their hair shorn, their brazen faces dotted with rouge and the chocoate lines of an eyebrow pencil. The streets were full of skin: arms appeared from sleeveless ready-to-wear frocks cut neatly from voile or artificial silk; calves and thighs emerged from one hundred years of darkness beneath ground-hugging hemlines and gadded about in flesh-coloured lisle stockings. Store windows featured inexpensive locknit underwear—an exciting alternative to dull cotton—available in a decadent array of colours. "I don't know what's come over us," Lila said to Violet one night. The concern on her face was lifted directly from a tragic movie. "We seem to have no propriety at all."

Violet liked the new styles and didn't mind a sip of liquor now and then. She was fourteen going on fifteen; she wanted to experiment a little. If that meant sneaking a sip or two of Jack's whiskey, slipping her body into a slinky sheath, and acting boyish, she was all for progress. She liked the way she looked smoking a cigarette, although she didn't smoke them at home, and she preferred a spot of rouge to the repeated pinching of the cheeks. In addition she was redheaded, fair; without make-up her own eyebrows were virtually nonexistent.

"What's the big deal anyway?" Violet says to Grace as they walk down Lonsdale towards the beach. At the foot of the hill ladies in shawls and low-slung dresses gather near the waterfront to catch a glimpse of the HMS Renown, the official ocean liner of His Royal Highness Prince Edward of Wales. Every few steps Grace stands on her tip-toes and strains her neck towards the crowd.

"He's just a man," Violet continues. "Like any of the other ones around. He doesn't have blue blood, or anything."

"Oh I don't know, I wouldn't mind seeing him. He's very handsome, even if he is thirty years old," Grace says. "Besides, he has a lot of money. And one day he will be the king. Just think, if we were lucky, he might pick one of us for a wife!"

"Hardly," Violet says, grimacing. "He's twice our age and he only goes for married women."

"Violet!"

"Well, it's true. Didn't you hear about Lady Furness? Everyone and his dog knows about her."

For her own part Violet doesn't see what all the fuss is about. In all the pictures she has seen of him, Prince Edward is a tall severe man with a sharply tipped nose and transparent, slippery hair. His eyes are cold and glazed-looking, and his ears stick out from under his hat like the handles on a trophy. He looks like some of the boys at North Vancouver High School: petulant, brassy, with ironed wool trousers and a hermetically sealed waistcoat. Violet hears her classmates mooning over these boys when they line up for the bathroom: *Isn't he a handsome one, with such nice manners! And*

when he looked at me, well, my heart simply dissolved.
She can't stand their milksop yearnings, their brains full
of fluff. She is too smart for that kind of thing. She has
better ways to spend her time.

What she likes to do when she isn't in school is this:
walk down to the second canyon on the Capilano River
and descend a precarious wooden ladder to the beach.
Splash around in the arctic water until her lips turn blue
and her legs are numb, then float downstream like an
oversized salmon and sun herself on the rocks. She can
also do this at Ambleside, the closest saltwater beach, if
she feels like walking that far and putting up with the
shrieking children who bury their parents in sand and
run around in their birthday suits. If she doesn't feel
like swimming she might go downtown to the dress
shops to look at material—woollen tweed, or if she's feeling audacious, sheer silk—or stand in front of the face-
less, armless, severed-at-the-thigh mannequins to figure
out what kind of dress she wants next.

On week days Violet and Grace wear plain print
housedresses with flat bras underneath to flatten their
profiles; they roll their stockings to the middle of their
knees or slightly above, fasten garters around each of
their calves, then roll down the tops of their socks to
hide them. On week days they go to school.

But today is a Saturday in June, a real scorcher, as Lila
says, and they are in breeches and sailor tops with matching sailor hats. Their hair is cropped short to the ears
with the ends done in spit curls and the tops waving
gently across their scalps like ripples in a puddle. Beneath their clothes they wear Jansen white wool bathing suits—brand new—and little mini-belts which clasp

about their waist to keep the wool from sagging. They walk towards the ocean with the hopes of cooling off.

Because her mother is able to sew, Violet's clothes are homemade. She usually asks for dresses with low flapper-style waistlines, and sashes or ties that she can draw in at the hips. Sometimes these dresses are made from rayon or georgette, with handkerchief points or floating panels extending beyond the hemline; at other times they have shoestring straps and fall to the ground like a pillowcase. Lately, however—on two occasions now—Violet has requested three-quarter trousers with buttons at the knees. These are the kinds of clothes she can wear on the weekend, hiking through the bush along the canyon, or down to the beach at Ambleside in West Vancouver. Ambleside is where they are going today.

"What do you think of these breeches?" Violet says, holding out her pant legs. "They seem a little wide."

"I think they're the cat's pajamas."

"You would, wouldn't you? You're my hero."

"They look sharp," Grace insists. "You better believe it."

"O.K.," Violet says. "But only because you said so." She can trust Grace's opinion because she has lived in Paris.

"Oh Violet," says Grace swooning into a lamp post. "Will we ever be saved from our boring lives? Will Douglas Fairbanks give up on America's sweetheart and come to our rescue?"

Both Violet and Grace have been to the Empire Theatre and the Lonsdale Movie Hall. They despise Mary Pickford, her sweet angel nose, her lips like melting jujubes, and favour instead women who are wild and naughty and who take chances. They have seen Clara

Bow cackling in her crepe de Chine underwear, and Theda Bara in practically nothing at all. Violet knows that she herself will never wear a corset.

"Don't bet on it kiddo. If he hasn't yet figured out that America's sweetheart is Canadian, he's not worth the effort."

"Violet," Grace says, rolling her eyes. "You're so droll."

Violet stops with her hands on her hips. "Yeah?" she says smirking. "So's your old man."

When they reach a wide boulevard filled with flowers, Violet and Grace turn off Lonsdale and walk along a dirt road towards the waterfront. As they descend the hill Jack pulls up beside them in his new car and leans on his horn.

"Ladies," he says. "Care for a ride?"

In the front of the car Lila and Mrs. Marshall sit wedged between parasols and picnic baskets in lamp-black dresses. They fan their faces with the flat of their hands, and mop their brows with hankies. "Gracella," says Mrs. Marshall. "We thought we would find you here. *C'est bon.* We can all cool off together."

"The heat is dreadful," Lila seconds. "Ridiculous for June. We thought you had the right idea."

Violet and Grace climb into the back seat and smile at their good fortune. Why sweat it out walking when you can catch a free ride? Jack's car is the latest in automobiles: a Ford Touring model with electric lights, demountable wheels, and isinglass windows. There is a certain amount of prestige to be had, riding downtown in a car like that. Besides, thinks Violet, with a feeling of satisfaction, how often do Grace and Mrs. Marshall get to travel in such luxury? Dr. Marshall drives a cheap old flivver, and he's always running into telephone poles.

"So Dad," Violet says, leaning against the upholstery. "I guess Henry Ford isn't so bad after all."

Jack shakes his head and laughs, smiling into the windshield. "No Violet, I guess not. Even pacifists can make a good car if they put their minds to it."

Ambleside is less crowded than usual. A small collection of women recline on woven mats beneath striped umbrellas; they wear bathing caps like aviation hats and hold their hands above their eyes to block the sun. Men stand talking in the sunlight in groups of two or three, dragging on cigarettes, laughing and slapping the tops of their knees. The ones in swimming wear full-piece bathing suits that become completely transparent when wet. When they have had enough of the water, they make hasty beelines for their towels placed strategically on the sand.

"Better luck for us," says Jack, eyeing the rash of choice spaces. "Everyone's greeting that jug-eared prince."

While he unloads the baskets and arranges the parasols, Violet, Grace, Lila, and Dora Marshall head for the change houses, slapdash boxes of wood resembling privies. They file in, two to a room, mother and daughter. Inside, the floor is damp and mottled with sand and blades of grass. They peel off their outer layers, hats, tops, breeches, and sandals, and whittle down to their skivvies.

"Give me a hand," Lila says to Violet as she struggles with her corset.

Violet is nearly undressed herself and can't wait to be seen in her suit with the microscopic diver embroidered on her left hip, that latest in fashion symbols. She can't wait to feel the water surge around her body. Unlike Lila who paddles in a circle like a duck with her rump in the air, Violet is an excellent swimmer. "Just a minute mother," she says, pulling her sailor top over her head and smoothing out her overskirt. Then she looks down.

"Mother!" she cries, parting the wool slit at her abdomen.

Lila looks. "Oh good heavens!"

Between Violet's legs is a bloodstain, a swatch of violent red that lights up the white wool of her bathing suit like a fresh kill in snow. What has happened? Suddenly she is scared. Did her appendix burst? She did have that dreadful stomach ache last night before bed.

"Good heavens," Lila says again, riffling through her bags. She hands Violet a segment of cloth, faintly plush, like a towelette, and shows her how to fold it and keep it in place with a series of straps. It looks to Violet like the comfort brace from the Eaton's catalogue.

"Mother," she says, incredulous. "I have to wear that?"

"Of course Violet, we all do at one time or another. It's just lucky I brought extra ones. I'm not far off myself. You'll have to change back into your clothes and keep this on until we get home. You can sit under the parasol with your father."

"You mean I can't go swimming?"

"Heavens no. What are you thinking? You'll have to make do."

Violet can't believe it. She watches as her mother puts on her own bathing suit, a black-skirted set of bloomers and a matching top with puffed sleeves, and fastens her bathing cap around her skull. She's starting to look like the pictures Violet has seen of Queen Victoria.

"Another thing," Lila says, looking Violet sternly in the eye. "From now on stay away from the boys."

Violet has no idea what she is talking about.

It's not that Violet doesn't know about periods. She is fourteen going on fifteen, a late bloomer in many respects, but let's face it, she has heard the rumours. It's just that she didn't expect to feel like this: swollen, overbasted, like a turkey stuffed with too many croutons. She imagined something more romantic, an ailment, a classical, paling sickness that would keep her bedridden at least for a month. Not this tidal bloating, as though her body had its own salty regimen and every four weeks decided to empty itself by slow leak; as though someone had seen fit to kick her in the stomach and leave their foot there, pressing.

Another thing: she didn't know it happened so often.

What she did know was this: her mother's bland references to *that time;* her secret daytime boilings of her own soiled towelettes on the back of the stove in a cast iron pot and Jack coming home from work, his nose to the air, sniffing, "Christ Lila, what's for dinner?"

What she knew you could put in your eye.

Still, she is glad to be privy to the kinds of details that are hushed away from children and men when they come into the room (as though the two are of the same order, both in need of protection), the details that permeate the conversations of ladies from the Women's Institute, or of all ladies for that matter. Everywhere she goes Violet starts to see the evidence: women sitting on the beach in flowing caftans, hats like tight-fitting overshoes, refraining from dousing themselves in the ocean despite the smouldering heat; service girls in the library complaining of stomach aches, holding their hands to their abdomens in limp expressions of forbearance. Now that she knows the meanings behind the whisperings, the secret intonations and gaunt curlings of lips, she doesn't understand how she could have missed them before!

But there is more than that: these strange undercurrents go beyond Violet's experience. They delve into the realm of sex. Sex isn't something Violet has thought much about, in down-and-dirty terms. How could she? No one talks about it outright, but the clues are there, rattling beneath the surface.

There are warnings: discreet insinuations doled out at all-women pot-lucks over dry crackers pasted together with egg salads and jellied meats. Warnings from other girls' parents, or friends of her mother's, who smile pleasantly while chiding town girls who *give it away*. As if *it* is something unrenewable, something that could run out if a girl wasn't careful. Something completely valuable to everyone else but the woman who owned it.

Violet isn't exactly sure what *it* entails, but she won't let anyone know. She doesn't want people to think she is a poser.

At the same time she has heard these murmurings applied to the subject of babies.

"I suppose Mrs. Paine will be delivering soon," Lila might say to Dora Marshall, when she thinks they are alone. *Delivering*, like a sack of mail. Only recently has Violet learned that her mother means *giving birth*, words which she heard Dr. Marshall speak with some embarrassment at the Women's Institute annual picnic. If she doesn't pay attention, turn her ear towards the finer points of her mother's conversation, Violet will never find out anything at all.

This goes on for some time.

Violet dons her fall coat, swaps it for a woollen tunic, then slides back into her breezy sweaters. The fruit trees on Lonsdale blossom with spring. On her sixteenth birthday she eats chocolate layer cake with sugar frosting. Lila serves generous slices on the Belleek china tea service, and brews a pot of coffee in the stovetop percolator. For her presents Violet gets a pair of black patents with two-inch heels from Jack and Lila, a beaded purse on a chain from Grace, and a model airplane from Matthew, which he built himself from a kit. Everyone sings *For She's a Jolly Good Fellow* one octave too high, and blows on the coffee so they won't burn their tongues.

"Well Violet," Jack says, pouring his drink into his saucer to let it cool. "You're a young lady now."

"Yes," Lila agrees. "So you'll have to behave like one."

"What do you mean by that mother?" Violet asks, knowing full well the comment has something to do with the way she has grown. The way she combs her hair, neatly at first, setting in the curls, then mussing them carefully with the tips of her fingers. She is aiming for the ravenous look that she has seen on movie stars: purposeful imbroglio, fiery dishevelment. Instead what she gets is the rabid look, but it will have to do.

"I just mean that you'll have to be careful of course. Take care of yourself."

"I thought I already did."

"What your mother means Violet," Jack intercepts, shuffling his feet beside the table, a smirk playing with the edges of his mouth, "is that you'll have to keep your legs crossed."

"Jack!" Lila snaps.

"All right, I'm just joking Lila, have a little humour. I know that's what you meant, you're just too prim to say it. Of course Violet already takes care of herself. She's a smart girl."

"Yes," Violet agrees, not wanting to pursue the issue. "A smart lady."

On Saturday nights she starts attending dances. She walks down to the third street pavilion arm-in-arm with Grace to swing to the gramophone while Lila and Mrs. Marshall participate in whist drives; or she catches a ride in a jacked-up buggy crammed with other girls to the Horseshoe Bay Dance Hall to move to a real live orchestra. The boys who once seemed crude and unruly have grown older, have become men, with dazzling smiles and rugged bones that jut from their skin like husky scaffolding. They part their wavy hair slightly off centre and wear it long on top in heartbreaking curls that look to Violet like crimped leather. Together Violet and these men dance cheek-to-cheek dances like the one-step; they wiggle like frenzied insects to the kind of jazz that leaves their bodies humming hours after they quit the dance hall. Violet likes the way the men smile at her with mouths full of clean white teeth, but she wants to find a partner who's not so easy to wear out. She herself could go on forever.

This evening Violet and Grace are with a group of friends from school. They rode along the winding gravel road to Horseshoe Bay in the back seat of a convertible borrowed from somebody's old man, and arrived gasping from laughter, clutching their cloche hats with both hands. Together they stepped down from the running board into parking lot craters; they inhaled the glorious fish-soaked air that wafted in from the salt chuck and blessed their faces with rain.

Now Violet is on the dance floor by herself in an orange crepe dress with spaghetti straps. Around her neck two strings of artificial pearls descend the front of her body to her navel. She wears slave bangles, and diamante clips to embellish her chemise. The remainder of her group is resting, but Violet can't stop. Once the band starts she is no longer a human being of flesh and blood, but a rhythmic bird that belongs to the music; her toes are made of melody, her hips are built from swing. She moves her arms and kicks her feet until they are nothing but a blur of orange and gold, flying, leaping, flapping around her body like sets of dim wings. She crosses the dance floor, once, twice, face flushed, bones alive; she circumnavigates the hall, a tenacious frigate, blasting through waves of sweat and muscle ache, testing the limits of her own endurance as if by will alone she can keep joints supple, her feet tap-tap-tapping.

"Thatagirl Violet," someone shouts, encouraging. "Keep it up!"

As she moves she takes the band with her—a piano, drum kit, and sax—they follow her loops and whirlabouts by matching their tempo to her delirious

[287]

pace. They tilt and lean on stage until they are on the edges of their instruments, until they are wrung out and flattened like spoon-drop cookies. The last note is marked by Violet's heel landing on the hardwood, a synergistic period, a finale, and the dance hall breaks into applause.

Around Violet's face, curls bounce out and up in an explosion of saffron. Her lips are moist (she has eaten off her lipstick again), and her cheeks are flashes of victorious crimson. She shrugs her shoulders, laughs, and takes her seat next to Grace. Compliments follow her to her chair.

"Violet, how do you do it kid? You're amazing."

"Violet sure has rhythm."

"She's the Charleston queen."

Tell me something I don't know.

She's not trying to show off, she just loves to dance, to let the music carry her away. Thank God for Milton Ager, she thinks, or Bessie Smith; she's grateful that her generation has shed the ballroom glides, the elaborate underwear and the starched petticoats of her mother's era that rustled under tulle during lunchtime dances at the Royal Corset Company in Liverpool, girls paired off with girls. That was probably the only fun her mother ever had, before she met Jack. How dull it must have been!

When Violet wants entertainment she doesn't have to look far. The whole north shore is crawling with dance halls, with movie houses and open air pavilions and theatres-under-the-stars that anyone can enter for a couple of pennies and instantly convert their lives from drab to fantastic. What a time to be alive, Violet thinks, she wouldn't trade it for anything.

"Excuse me miss?"

Violet whirls around to see a man smiling at her. She has seen him before, walking up Lonsdale, whistling jazz tunes, his hands in his pockets. She noticed him because his hair was red, is red; the colour of fire engines.

"You are a fine dancer miss."

"Thank you," Violet says.

"I was wondering, if you aren't too tired," he says, tilting his shoulders. "If you would care to dance with me?" He extends his hand towards Violet and grins. "That sure would make my evening."

Violet looks at his hand, at the pearly, spatulate fingernails arching like shells on the ends of his fingers; at the faint, russet arm hairs quivering like sedge-grass. Then she looks at his face: beaming, an open flame. Her heart lurches for the first time. "Let's go," she says.

Together they heat up the dance floor. Two red devils.

Here Violet has to pause. She's coming to the tricky part in her story, the part she doesn't like to think about—although her husband knew—he was not that slow-witted. Sitting in her wheelchair in the Avondale social lounge, quoined in between an ancient southern madam in flamboyant kimonos who thinks she's Josephine Baker, and a partly cognizant grandmother of twenty-six, Violet straightens her aching back and watches the slides flash onto the wall like wartime newsreels. Volunteers from the historical society have cleared away the debris masquerading as interior design from one end of the room—waist-high glass bottles in plaited casings, a series of watery etchings in metallic silver frames—to free up space for their presentation. Curtains have been drawn across the windows, cloaking the room in insubstantial darkness, which despite being a little on the filmy side, is enough to put everyone to sleep.

Violet, however, is paying attention. How could she help but look? What they are showing are pictures of her old haunts, of the buildings that she passed—somewhat blithely because she thought they would always be there—on her way to school or to the beach. The high school on St. George's and 23rd. The first North Vancouver Hospital. She can't believe Pete Larson's hotel is now the site of a waterfront park, neatly mowed and dotted with shoreline rip-rap, a place where melon-scented yuppies take their colour-coordinated dogs to void their colons, where people conglomerate, old and young, to watch the ships steaming their way up the inlet towards acres of infill and giant piles of sulphur. She can't believe the streetcar has been extinct for almost fifty years! Someone has looted her childhood, ransacked her memories; someone has torn down her dance halls and replaced them with Starbuck's, with glamorous tattoo parlours and their silver-laden body artists.

If this slide show has done anything, it has made her feel old.

(She remembers the time she had her cataracts removed two years ago; they had been building up for some time on her pupils so that when she went outside to catch a bus or pick up a few items at the Safeway, she felt as though she was looking through a fine layer of gauze. After the doctor removed them, one at a time with a laser-tipped scalpel, and her eyes recovered, she looked in the mirror. "Oh God!" she screamed, throwing her hands to her face. She was covered in wrinkles.

She didn't leave the house for days.)

But the reason she wants to pause is not one of vanity, it is this: she wants to get things straight. She was not a dolt, despite how she might have acted; she was just young, uninformed. She didn't understand how things worked, how her body and all its morose caverns, its sweet-talcumed flesh powdered over with a hanky and streamlined with Vaseline, she didn't know how it functioned. No one told her a thing, especially not Lila, and in those days there were few places to go to find out.

What was my mother thinking? she asks herself as the slides roll by. *That I would learn by divine inspiration? That God himself would let me in on his glorious secret?* She did not, however, learn by divine inspiration. She learned instead by personal experience. What happened was simple, but not so easy to deal with when it came right down to things: her period—that bloated feeling of distension that ran her ragged every month—stopped coming.

"Oh Violet, you're a real star. How could you have been so dim?" Violet sits on a boulder at the entrance to the shipyards. As she talks she pulls at her stockings with her thumb and forefinger, forming minute puckers in the silk along the insides of her shins. "I mean, what were you thinking? That you could make it go away? That you could think real hard and change the inside of your body? Hah! You're a real shuckster."

Above her head a narrow billboard is tacked to the lintel of the entrance, proclaiming the newest name of the shipyards: *Burrard Dry Docks.* Men in dungarees and work boots pass under the sign and throw her innocent smiles from faces smeared with grease and coal dust. Around her the debris of their efforts lies like the ribcages of dead animals: bits of wood, raw planks, lumber of various lengths and sizes stacked into waist-high piles, metal girders and sheets of black iron. Violet can't tell which items are the dregs of old projects waiting to be dumped into the ocean and which are top-of-the-line supplies. All she knows is that she is surrounded by wreckage, which, considering the state of her life at this very moment, should make her feel right at home.

Instead she is uncomfortable; she fidgets. She is the only woman loitering around the shipyards this evening and she worries what people will think of her. She worries what *he* will think of her when he finishes work and finds her perched on a boulder like a crippled seagull. Usually she waits for him in her parents' parlour, sneaking glimpses out the curtained window, peeling back the blinds to see the street. Or she walks down Lonsdale to the viewpoint on the hill where she can make out the indistinct shapes of men moving around the shipyards like blots of grey ink. He has worked at the shipyards ever since she met him, ten months ago now, caulking the hulls of ships and inserting rivets into carefully punched holes. Because it is November and darkness falls before the end of his shift, she can sometimes place him in the rubble by following the red-hot rivets on their way from the shipyard forge to a canvas-bottomed bucket where their flight is stanched by another man in a woollen shirt. Here the rivets are gathered up with tongs and passed on to the spot where *he* stands, smiling (she imagines), his red hair molded by sweat into the inflexible comb of a rooster.

"He is a hard worker," Violet says. "Which proves something." Just what it proves, she doesn't know, except that perhaps he is faithful? Persistent? He cares about his job, his lot in life. He cares for her too, because he told her so.

The shipyard whistle blows, signalling the end of the working day.

"Take a deep breath Violet," she tells herself. "He won't let you down."

The only reason she knows for sure that she is pregnant is because she asked. Not Lila, not on your life, but Dora Marshall. She concluded that surely Dora who was twice married and French to boot would tell her what she needed to know. And she did. At the thought of their conversation Violet's face reddens. They met last week in the Marshall's front parlour when Grace was away helping her father.

"How long has it been," Dora said kindly, leaning forward from her Duncan-Phyfe gossip chair, her ivory hand on the varnished tabletop, "since your last time?"

"Three months," Violet answered. She had practiced saying her answers bravely, with a straight face. She did not want to cry, no matter what happened.

Dora crossed her legs and readjusted her skirt on her knees. Her face was warm, full of sympathy. "Then Violet, you know how it works. That you have to *be* with a man."

"Yes," Violet said, colouring.

"Well," Dora continued. "Have you been with someone?"

Violet hesitated, clenching her hands in her lap. Her red hair was loose, held away from her face by a narrow headband. "Yes," she stammered. She could do this. "That is, I might have been."

"*Tantôt*—" Dora said, gazing into Violet's eyes. "You are a good girl not to talk openly of this, but you see, this is important. Did he have his pants on, or off?"

Violet coloured further; her hair emblazoned her face with an unqualified blush. She had never spoken like this to anyone. "On," she said courageously. "At least, partly. You see, it was dark, but they were mostly on, I'm quite sure."

"*Mon Dieu*," Dora whispered, slipping her hand around the back of Violet's head and drawing her forward. "You *are* a good girl, don't you understand? Mostly on is not enough."

Violet's mouth went limp.

"Now, don't fret. All will be well."

"O.K."

"There is something you must do, before you go any further. Do you understand?"

"Yes," Violet said. She thought she did.

"*Bien*," Dora said, taking her hand. "You will have to tell him."

And so here she is, sitting on a boulder, avoiding the oozing puddles of creosote, the ashen guano of shoreline birds who swoop at her head and threaten to make off with her hat. A couple of mottled seagulls not yet sporting their adult feathers heckle over the remains of a crab next to the shipyard pilings.

"I will tell him today," she says loudly in their direction, hoping for some response. They pay her no attention.

She stands up and straightens her skirt, a checked wraparound with a half-inch fringe, and paces a circle on the wooden beams. She thinks about the way he touched her: gently, with an unspoken indolence. His mild, unembarrassed hands found their way across her body, underneath stockings, girdles, garters, and starched pressed underwear. Violet never flinched, although she didn't know what he was doing, or why his lips parted the way they did when all she felt was a thrusting numbness. At first she had been excited, after she got over the initial confusion, but the episodes graduated into silent moments where Violet concentrated on the trees above her head. She found their familiar needled arms a comfort.

She realized that what she was doing was not necessarily proper, she did not need a diploma to figure that out; but she also knew that she was not the only one sneaking into the thicket at Horseshoe Bay, clearing away salal and patches of salmonberry for a smooth place to lie down—she heard those other voices—she just didn't comprehend the result.

Now that she does understand the state of her body she is sure he will act like a gentleman, and, as Dora explained, ask her to marry him. He is two years older than Violet, nineteen to be exact, and is sure to be capable of supporting a family.

"I will tell him," Violet says, forcing a smile. "And we will see what he says."

Beneath the sign the beginnings of the shipyard crew are funnelling out from the dry docks. The ones closest to Violet tip their hats as they pass, smiling in her direction and lighting cigars or cigarettes. Some of them carry tin lunchboxes with shiny handles and hinges, and swing them by their sides to make them creak. Others run their fingers through their hair and hot-foot it up the hill, intent on making it home in time for dinner.

Violet extends her neck out from her collar and looks at the faces as they flash by in the late afternoon light. She is not sure which is better: to appear as though she is waiting for someone, a brother perhaps, or a fiancé, or to appear aloof, with her legs crossed and her scarf arranged nonchalantly across her shoulders. She feels frightened, and out of breath. If only she had volunteered at the town hall players, Violet thinks, she would be able to control herself right now. Don't actors practice at things like that? Emoting, projection. Instead she is quivering faintly like one of Lila's jars of marmalade, one that refuses to set, but instead shakes and oozes inside the glass. Where is he? she says to herself. He is almost never late.

Half an hour after the crowd has dissipated Violet is still sitting on the boulder. "Maybe he called in sick today," she says aloud. "Although that is unlikely when there is work to be done. Or maybe he left early to run errands for the foreman. I've heard that the foreman is always asking for favours like that." She picks at the empty barnacle shells fused to the boulder, and considers her options. "I could wait a little longer," she says to herself. "Or ask whoever is left at the shipyards if they have seen him today." But she can't seem to make up her mind. Both options seem equally useless. Why wait when everyone has disappeared, and similarly, why venture into the shipyards when everyone who was working today has obviously gone home? She looks out at the ocean spraying gently at the shore, blackening the sand with fragments of wood and ruddy detritus, shifting under the darkening sky. She doesn't want to walk home alone.

"Do you need something Miss?" says a voice. A man has come out from the shipyards and is addressing Violet with his hat in his hand. "You waiting for a reason?"

Violet smiles and plucks up her courage. Surely he will be able to help. "Yes," she says, folding her hands. "I'm waiting for someone but I didn't see him come out yet. Has everyone left?"

"Yessir," says the man. "What does he look like? You might have just missed him."

"Well, he is about this tall," she says, holding her hands in the air above her head. "With bright red hair and freckles. He usually works the full day shift, then leaves for home with the rest of the men."

"Miss," says the man. "You're not talking about the one who had the accident?" His face tenses, hangs down in jowls. "The accident this morning?"

"Accident?" says Violet, feeling faint.

"Oh Violet," says Lila Spencer in the living room of her Chesterfield house. "There was nothing to be done. It all happened too fast. What an accident!" Violet is sitting next to the fireplace in her parents' parlour, staring at the flames. Lila is applying cold cloths to her forehead. "Four tons of sheet metal," she says, continuing. "That place is a hazard. Why, I heard just last month that Mrs. Donafield's eldest boy lost three of his toes when a steel girder slammed into him. Just like that. And another time somebody was knocked clear into the ocean when a timber came loose from its chains and fell crashing to the docks. That particular fellow was lucky to be alive. Everyone at the Women's Institute agrees. We have petitioned, we have given talks on safety in the workplace. But who comes? Not the Wallaces, for goodness sakes. I'm just thankful that Jack got out of there when he did."

Lila dips the cloth into a basin on the floor next to Violet's chair and wrings it hard between her fingers.

"And now you are affected," she says, brushing hair away from Violet's face. "Four tons! We can just thank the Lord that everything happened as fast as it did, so that he felt no pain. They say he was crushed instantly, Violet, and first thing in the morning too!" Violet sighs. As if the time of day should make that much of a difference.

"He was a good man Violet, but it wasn't meant to be. He's in a better place now. A wonderful place."

Violet makes no comment, she has lost her tongue. Forming words with her mouth, stretching her lips into various shapes—that all seems too complex. She stares instead at the hand-hooked throw rug beneath her feet, a splash of rose on the wooden floor, and listens to her mother prattle on like a strangely high-pitched tea kettle. She is sure that somewhere between the heckling of the seagulls at the waterfront, and the confusion that ensued after she realized what had happened, that she heard a scream. A violent sigh, like the reeling of the waves. She remembers the noise: the indescribable sound of a ghost. She just isn't sure if the scream was hers, or his.

24

Violet married Hobert Leggett. The ceremony was short-ened to a few suppressed words mumbled by a Justice of the Peace on the Spencer's back lawn, and a plainly deco-rated sour cream cake dotted with yellow daffodils. Vio-let's wedding dress curved slyly around her abdomen and knotted into a bow at her navel; her mother chose the material, cream crêpe de Chine, a decent colour close to white, and measured around Violet's middle in stern, unuttered disapproval.

"What have you done?" her father had demanded when she recovered enough from her shock to know that her troubles were just beginning; that she must, sooner or later, reveal her secret. She chose a Tuesday evening, one week from the accident, when both her parents were sitting placidly in the parlour.

"I don't know," she answered lamely.

She watched her father's lips twitch, the only mark on his impeccable image, and felt her heart plummet. She had let him down.

"Oh Lord!" Lila said, breaking into sobs. "We are all ruined. Violet, how could you? We will be shamed, the laughing stock. What will people say?"

Jack sprung up from his spot on the wingback, flinging one of Lila's cross-stitched satin pillows across the room in the process. "They'll say nothing," he declared firmly. "Nothing at all, because my Violet is a princess and she's going to stay that way, despite everything. Everyone else can go to the devil."

"Jack!" said Lila aghast, her face twisted into a suspended bawl.

"Now Violet," Jack continued, ignoring his wife's rebukes and pacing in front of the fireplace. "This little mistake of yours will be all smoothed over if I have anything to say about it, but you must promise to help me. If you do what I tell you, everything will be fine. Do you understand?"

Violet nodded meekly.

"Good." He stopped pacing and clamped his hand to the mantle. A stray bundle of hair had come loose in the commotion and was lolling in the centre of his forehead. Jack pawed it absently. "The first thing you need to do is this: never mention this redheaded fellow's name again. Not to anyone. I don't care what people say, he never existed. Not in relation to you he didn't. Do you think you can do that?"

Violet stared at the ground. "Yes," she said.

"That is the important part," he resumed. "Because he wasn't around long enough for people to make the connection. And people have short memories when there is a wedding to celebrate."

"A wedding?" Lila said, snivelling. "Whose wedding?"

Jack straightened his shoulders and brought his hands to his lapel in a gesture of deep-seated cleverness. "Violet's of course," he said. "She still needs a husband. And I think I know a man that will do nicely."

Within a week Hobert was sitting down to tea in the Spencer's house, picking poppy seeds from his teeth with his car keys, smiling bravely at Violet between shortbreads and matrimonial cakes. He was twenty years older than Violet, thirty-seven to be exact, and towered over the Spencers at six-foot-six like the tallest mast on a wooden schooner. His skin was coarse, checked with blue veins and the deep shadow of a beard that seemed to grow in front of Violet's eyes, and his hands and feet were unwieldy and soft, like improbable sets of flippers. When he looked at Violet he reddened slightly, bashfully, and readjusted his tie. He wore a three-piece tweed suit the colour of tired onions, and held his hat in his lap like a gentleman.

Violet did as she was instructed, crossing her legs, keeping her boots together, but she didn't try to love him. She didn't try on any feelings in the beginning, because having them seemed an inconvenience. She nodded politely, noticing how his thick hairs rose from his scalp like inchworms checking the wind, and sat largely in silence. She didn't want to further disappoint her father, who had hand-picked Hobert to be her husband, and who sat like any father-in-law-to-be in his parlour wingback, smiling eagerly, initiating conversation for the blushing young couple before him. Except that Hobert wasn't young, nor was he devastatingly handsome; there was no consideration for his looks, which were not flamboyant or plain, because looks were incidental. He was respected in town (he owned a company that manufactured portholes), and remained single simply out of busyness. He had never had time to court a wife—he had spent his young life in the pursuit of independence and success—but was now prepared to turn out a family. Violet nodded for the duration of each meeting. Her head felt like a pendant bobbing furiously on the neck of a hanged man. She continued nodding when Jack mentioned the date of the wedding.

She gave birth to Russell in the month of May, 1928, in a clapboard two-story hospital with enough beds for twelve patients. A nurse in a starched white apron wheeled her into the maternity room on the first floor and left her panting, her legs in the air. When Russell came, the pain was excruciating. She was too small on the outside, and even smaller on the inside. The doctor guided her through her labour pains and slit her from stem to stern. After thirteen hours, Violet was a mother. Hobert, it appeared, was a father.

An unfortunate occurrence for the both of them was that Russell resembled his father. He had red hair, a conclusion Violet might have been able to foresee had she known anything about the probability of genetics, and green eyes framed in freckles. Hobert's own head was covered in hair as black as your hat. His descendants were a mix of Greek and Serbian, large hulking men with dense clouds for beards, women with hefty bosoms and horses' bones. There was, however, one oblique Anglo-Saxon remittance man that had married into Hobert's line and left behind the name Leggett. Violet came to see this man as responsible for her first son, whose watery skin and squat profile was uncharacteristic, to say the least, of the remaining Leggett family.

Together they lived in a house on Chesterfield Avenue, six blocks up from the Spencers. Part of the bargain between Jack and Hobert, Violet surmised, was that she and her developing family were never to be taken from North Vancouver, and were not to stray far from the neighbourhood in general. Despite handing her over to another man, Jack told Violet he could not see her gone forever.

Hobert cooperated and purchased a brand new house backing onto an alley. He fenced off the yard so that Russell could play unattended, and planted a cedar tree in front of the living-room window to commemorate what he called "their everlasting union." Violet also cooperated, maintaining to anyone uncouth enough to ask that yes, Hobert was indeed the carrier of unique genes and weren't they lucky to have such a variety in their family? She never mentioned the name of Russell's father to anyone, not even to Grace, and because she had consulted Dora Marshall not two weeks before her wedding, even Grace's mother assumed Hobert—however misplaced as an object of desire—was Violet's true love.

She has kept that promise to her father to this day, and is not about to break it.

She did do one thing: she kept a photograph of the man with no name tucked away in a hand-carved box that Jack had given her after one of his many adventures. The box was yellow cedar scored with the Cowichan design of a frog, and she sealed it with an elastic band and slipped it under her commode. In the early years of her marriage she would draw the box out at intervals and look the picture over while Russell lay napping; she did not cry or snivel over this man, she would not betray Hobert like that, but she did wonder how her life would have been different had he been standing in another place, on another plank altogether, on the day of the accident. Would the two of them have been married? Would they have lived in a waterfront tenement and raised a pack of redheaded hooligans? Would this man, with his sublime smile and radiant eyes have made her any happier? At one time she would have said yes, definitely yes, but now she is not so sure.

Married life was not the way she expected it to be, but it was also not unpleasant. Every day Violet rolled out enough pastry for two pies. She beat together eggs and vinegar, warmed the fat between her fingers, and flattened the dough with an old green bottle corked at the end and filled with cold water. As the north shore changed, so did Violet. Buildings went up and fell down. Wooden sidewalks were removed and replaced with concrete. Violet's own body swelled with the bulk of two more pregnancies and she gave birth to Clifford, then Lawrence, in the heat of the depression.

The bread lines were long those years, and camps of unemployed hungry men sprouted up on the outskirts of the city. Because they had some savings, Violet's family was not as badly off as many; Hobert cashed in some of his bonds, sold a property in the highlands that he had been saving for the boys. Jack and Lila contributed what they could to the running of the household. Still, the manufacturing of portholes was not high in demand,

and by 1937 Hobert had donned a pair of dirty trousers, grabbed a shovel, and set out to work on the roads for food stamps. Violet maintained a small kitchen garden in the backyard and took in ironing. She knitted herself jersey wool dresses and cardigan jackets, and hand sewed porridge-coloured flannel suits for outings. During the week she listened to the news on the radio: men were marching into Vancouver from relief camps, drunk on loganberry wine, irate, demanding work; mill strikers were attacking scabs and smashing mill windows in protest over wage rollbacks. Car owners wanting to claim relief had to turn in their licence plates and give up driving.

In the evenings, Violet drew the blinds against the street and did crossword puzzles; she let the boys listen to their favourite shows: Clifford and Lawrence liked *Orphan Annie* and *Jack Benny*, but Russell was too old, too gregarious to sit still for a few laughs and the voice of a high-pitched whiner. He preferred *The Green Hornet*, with its sound effects, its spurious plots and deep-throated mysteries. He sat entranced on the living-room floor and formed his hands into small guns. "Bang!" he said, mouthing the words as they drifted from the speakers and into the air. "Now we shall see justice be done."

Violet watched her children carefully; none of them displayed any knowledge that Russell was different, aside from the obvious physical anomalies. They played together in the front yard, in the back; they ripped apart her kitchen, tracking mud and sawdust across freshly waxed floors. They grew like weeds, bursting through their shoes, passing them down the line like hot potatoes until the soles were worn thin and Lawrence's toes poked through the leather like burrowing caterpillars.

"Please," Violet would holler at them when they ran in the house, knocking over furniture, scattering their toys. "Take your games outside. My house, my clean floor!"

"O.K. Ma," they would say on a good day, slamming doors on their way to the lawn. They were used to her complaints, her moments of frustration. She liked to keep on top of the chores, the stacks of shirts and underwear, the dirty dishes that collected within a millisecond of the last load, but mothering three boys made her goal a near impossibility. Still, she hated to see them grow so fast. From the moment their bodies fell from hers, the distance between them widened like a chasm. And that space, she realized, would only ever get wider.

Through walks and births and Hobert's business luncheons, Violet rolled out pastry and flattened it against the counter. Her hips widened to meet the cupboards as she slapped the dough, scalloped the edges, and filled it with apples, huckleberries, and salmonberries, whatever was in season and not too far up the mountain to reach on foot. Hobert was a gentle, appreciative husband. He bought Violet the latest things: a sewing machine with a motorized pedal, an ice box for storing salmon and giant cuts of pork. Violet supposed he even loved her. Once in a while she would catch him watching her from the back of the kitchen, her face dusted with flour, her hands covered in grease. His eyes would twinkle like luminous moths and he would step forward, smooth out her exploding hairdo, and kiss her on the forehead. She knew she was lucky: she had a successful husband, a house full of lace curtains and chintz sofas; her best friend Grace lived within walking distance, and her garden was full of blooming hollyhocks.

But still, those years were hard.

Lila was the first to go, struck down with tuberculosis and obliged to spend her remaining days in a Kamloops sanatorium. Next followed Matthew, who died an officer in the British Columbia Regiment on the pursuit to Rouen; he had a chance to fight after all, but nobody knew if he died bravely, or cried like a baby. The final death to touch Violet and riddle her body with grief was Russell's, just sixteen and smashed almost as flat as his father, his first father. They peeled him from the car and shunted him off to the hospital but it was no use. "He went quickly," A police officer told Violet and Hobert. Jack said, "There are too many cars on the road for anyone to drive safely anywhere."

The day of the funeral Violet stood in the cemetery holding Hobert's hand. In her other hand she held Lawrence's, a small collection of fingers jammed into a fist. Clifford stood off to the side, several paces away from the hole in the ground, exercising his independence by pushing his own hands deep into his pockets and staring at the grass. Not one of them was crying. Not yet.

The weather had also decided against mourning and instead flushed the sky with sun. Birds sang in the tops of the apple and willow trees surrounding the cemetery, and Violet thought she could make out a faint sun-dog softened by clouds. Next to the grave site, patches of late-coming dandelions toppled on thin stalks. The only indication that autumn was underway were the traces of burning leaves seeping up from the waterfront and westward from Grand Boulevard, wafting in on a mellow breeze and playing with the ends of Violet's hair.

Around the Leggetts stood most of the population of North Vancouver; or at least, that's the way Violet remembers things. The Marshalls were there, straight ahead, and so was Russell's teacher despite the fact that Russell had planned on dropping out and taking a job at the shingle mill. There were also several faces that Violet thought she recognized as Russell's friends, both boys (stone-faced) and girls (quietly sobbing). The rest of the crowd were strangers, pale faces in a sea of charcoal and grey, with features like toy dolls that Violet could invoke and shut off simply by closing her eyes.

At the edge of the crowd was the North Vancouver band leader fronted by his band. They came to all the funerals then, Violet remembers, especially the funerals of youngsters who had been taken prematurely from the community. They were standing in military formation with their boots pressed tightly together.

Lawrence's nose was running, and Violet wiped it with the black monogrammed handkerchief her mother had given her expressly for funerals. He had been the first one to break down, bursting into tears when Hobert told him gently—after the accident—that Russell wouldn't be living with them any more. He had gone to another place.

"Why nawt?" Lawrence had demanded, his furious face upturned from his toys. "Why nawt Daaad?"

"Because he's dead," Clifford had answered, his rock hard face breaking Violet's heart.

When the minister read the eulogy Hobert started to cry. The tears were large and cautiously spaced, etching trails of shine on his cheeks as if silently made by slugs.

He pressed Violet's fingers together in his hand, and stared straight ahead. Violet had not seen him cry like that, out in public, but at least he was dignified; at least he didn't blubber.

She held her head up, under her black veiled hat with the off-the-centre velvet bow, and forced her mouth flat across her face so there would be no quivering. The edges of her shoes were cutting into her heels, and she shifted uneasily on the grass. Tomorrow there would be blisters. She knew Russell's death was an accident—a careless one, but still an accident—but that didn't change the fact that he was gone, an idea she could not fathom. Of course no one was ever prepared for death, she knew that by now, but surely one should be able to bank on the fact that children outlive their parents. They were here to take over; that was their job. But in her case she was not so lucky. At least there were still two of them to carry on.

When the coffin was lowered into the hole, the band began to play. Violet's back went rigid.

Oh Danny Boy, the pipes, the pipes are calling . . .

She couldn't stand it: of all the songs! Of course they were only trying to help, to pay tribute, but didn't they know she couldn't handle this kind of noise: the crying brass, the way the horns moaned like smooth lamenting gypsies? In her hand Hobert's fingers felt like a lump of pastry, of ham. A lump of nothing because Violet's own hands were dead meat, flesh without life or blood. Empty. She stood and stared, at the dandelions, at the hole in the ground as neat and linear as a cigar box, as a crate of

[309]

oranges. She thought to herself, *Russell is going into that hole.*

Next to Lawrence Clifford hunched his shoulders. Violet thought he looked smaller than usual, unprotected, holding his features in that wince of his and bracing himself physically with his arms as if walking into a strong wind. She thought she could see a lump forming in his centre, a hard lump like a golf ball; layers and layers of rubber bands wound tightly around a core of empty space.

The summer's gone and all the roses falling,
It's you, it's you, must go, and I must bide . . .

She swallowed hard and tried not to cry, but the second chorus started and she was unable to hold back her tears. That night she cried again on Hobert's shoulder, and then alone into her handkerchief after she put the boys to bed. She tried to concentrate on the idea that life was supposed to go on, to continue as before, but she was less and less sure how to make this happen. She watched Hobert for an example, for an indication of how to behave, but most of the time he seemed to be watching her.

After Russell's death and the end of the second world war, Violet's outlook on life changed. She didn't feel carefree anymore, she didn't feel like dancing. She made an attempt to swing to Glen Miller's *In the Mood* when Grace got married at Horseshoe Bay, but she didn't feel *in the mood;* her feet wouldn't cooperate. Her legs, her arms, even her shoes were weighted down with some immutable sorrow.

One development she did welcome was the lengthening of skirts; after all the time she spent scrubbing and waxing floors, her knees puckered and drooped like a set of baggy underdrawers. She didn't like the hairstyles, however, or the way women made up their faces. Now she had to sleep with metal rollers forced in behind her ears and along the back of her neck to get a half-decent wave. She had to pin back her bangs at the peak of her scalp and expose her gleaming forehead, and powder down her effervescent nose. Due to the post-war shortage of artificial silk, she had to shave her legs from the knees down and draw a line up the back of her calves with an eyebrow pencil if she wanted to have the look of a decent pair of stockings.

When Hobert brought colleagues into their milk-paint kitchen, bulbous wealthy men who shined their windshields with silk handkerchiefs and combed their sparse hair with bits of tortoiseshell, Violet heard the ocean inside her. The sound started below her pelvis, hissed slowly upwards towards her head, and ended in a gurgle at the back of her throat. She felt like a lithe tunnel filled with salt water, an endless drain clogged with fleshy debris and sharp-ended organisms that cut her on the inside whenever she exerted herself. If she were to open her mouth, to reply to the men who complimented her on her housekeeping abilities, on her marvellous slipcovers, a mad gasp would rise from her innards; they would hear the fiendish sucking that pleaded daily for moisture, and recognize the sound: grief. She kept her lips tightly corked. She served turnips and glazed hams, whipped egg whites into stiff, sugary peaks. She passed flour and lard through her fingertips and smoothed bolts of pastry into uniform, cascading ribbons.

After thirty-six years of marriage and 13,140 pies, Hobert died of a heart attack. His arteries were so full of fat that his doctor suggested they might have been reserved for the war effort, had Germany not already surrendered. But they were in luck, because a war was brewing in Vietnam.

Violet pared down the clutter in her house. She removed Hobert's clothes, his neat lineup of shoes standing like army cadets in the closet, and placed them in the basement in cardboard boxes. She was not up to full-fledged organization; not yet. She stacked them haphazardly in corners, behind an outdated sawdust burner donated by Jack, behind buckets of sample portholes with brass fittings, and other boxes of unidentified rubble leftover from the days when Clifford and Lawrence were single.

Hobert's death had left her a widow, but it had also left her comfortable. He had a small insurance policy which she used to pay off the newest refrigerator—a massive enamel Astral that growled like a tiger from beside the cupboards—and enough money in a savings account for Violet to pay the yearly taxes, plus meet her expenses for food and electricity. Those savings, however, would not last indefinitely, and Violet decided to get a job. On Tuesdays and Thursdays she walked five blocks to the local tailor; she worked cheerfully hemming men's trousers and matching buttons to their shirts from a vat of strays the size of a bathtub. On Sundays she made dinner for Lawrence, now Larry, who came over to have his shirts pressed and to mow the lawn. Around a plate of steak and potatoes, Larry told Violet about his wife's pregnancy, about her tender nipples cracking in the summer heat. About how Alexandra wanted to name the baby Priscilla if she was a girl, because she had always been fond of Elvis, but that she might settle for Tia, because the other was too many syllables.

"What about a nice name like Elsie?" Violet said, thinking of Clifford. She missed him since he had taken up with that woman and moved all the way to Ontario. He had always tried the hardest to make her happy.

"Mother," Larry said impatiently. "We can't name her Elsie. That would be two Elsie Leggetts in one family. Too confusing."

"Oh yes," said Violet. "Of course, I was only kidding."

After tea and angel food cake (Violet had abandoned pastry for non-fat alternatives), Larry usually worked in requests for silver tea trays, for hand-embroidered cushions dyed with sumac berries and decorated all over with roosters. Alexandra's ankles swelled, her varicose veins made standing difficult. The solace of Violet's heirlooms—some of which would likely go to Larry's family anyway and were rarely used by Violet—would surely ease his wife's discomfort. Violet heard Alexandra's persistent voice behind her son's requests, slipped meekly in between spoonfuls of sugar. She saw Larry's vulnerability, his gently limp nostrils sculpted on to his ridiculous face, and she offered them up: dishes to be scoured clean by modern cleansers and automatic jet dishwashers; rugs to be trod on by unwashed feet, crudely trimmed toenails. She handed over the Chippendale settee, the hand-monogrammed pillow shams. She loosed the entire set of almond-tinted bone china decorated with orchids.

"Thanks mother," Larry would say on his way out the door, his arms full of boxes. "You know we'll take care of these."

Violet didn't know; either that, or she didn't care. She had lost her interest in things. When she polished her silverware, she noticed her severe, inverted face stretched absurdly around the bases of her spoons. Her chin had sharpened to a bony point, and her eyebrows disappeared into the sunken cliff of her forehead. Somehow the edges of her skin seemed doctored, as though someone had seen fit to edit out her austerity, and replace it with a downy replica. She hated this feeling of being tampered with; the thought that everyone believed she needed appeasement. *Take them,* she thought. *Take everything.*

When Jack fell ill, he refused to be moved to the hospital.

"I'm too old to die in a white room," he told Violet from the parlour of their old house. "And not pure enough either."

Since her mother's death, Violet had seen her father with several women, many of whom lasted long enough to alter the flavour of the front room where Lila used to concentrate on her knitting. The walls were less sombre now, and were redone in fanciful wallpaper. Modern flower arrangements replaced the stand-up portraits of Lila's relatives and reached for the ceiling from fringed runners. The original woman, the one that accompanied Jack on his adventures, had died, Violet guessed, before Lila. Jack kept photos of the both of them in the back of his wallet.

"What do you need Dad. Can I get you anything?"

[314]

"Oh Violet," Jack said, "I'll be fine. I just need to rest, that's all. You're a good girl."

Violet smiled. *A fifty-nine-year-old girl.* She covered his feet with one of Lila's afghans and made him a cup of tea. At the doctor's orders she served him applesauce and runny oatmeal watered down with milk.

"What are you feeding me?" he would roar on the days when he was particularly impatient.

"You know it's for your own good Dad. The doctor said so."

"That Dr. Marshall doesn't know his behind from a hole in the ground. Never has. I want steak and potatoes, Violet. You know how I like it."

"Dad," Violet would sigh. "Dr. Marshall has been dead for years."

"Of course he has," Jack would reply, squirming like an infant. "His brain leaked out of his head during the war and now there is nothing left but stuff and nonsense."

When she wanted someone to talk to who would truly listen, Violet turned to Grace. Grace whose long black braids used to shine like licorice whips but were now a dusky grey wound into a pert bun; Grace whose skinny chicken feet had swollen out over her shoes because of high blood pressure. Grace's house backed onto the same alleyway as Violet's, and even though her husband was still alive, she understood Violet's lethargy. She too had been through tough times over the years, losing her father first, then her mother. In addition she had no children. This left time on her hands.

"Come on Vi," she would say, ringing up on the telephone. "Let's go to the pictures."

The Empire Theatre was gone by then, demolished into a pile of brick and timber and replaced by a blocky tower belonging to an insurance company. Now they took the bus to Park and Tilford where flashy marquees winked on and off in continuous rows of light bulbs: *Easy Rider. A Love Story.* A whole new selection of talkies. Violet brought a stack of tissues in case they should encounter a plotline with an emotional finale. Ever since the second war she seemed to be on the verge of tears.

On her seventieth birthday, after Jack passed on, kicking and snarling and making raspy exclamations concerning modern cars, she decided to visit Clifford for a second time. She had been to Brimstock for a short visit six years earlier, where she was introduced to Marian and Elsie and the town in general. The visit had not been ideal: Clifford's wife was too fussy for Violet's liking; she had followed her around with a dish cloth and a bristle brush, giving her lectures on the importance of cleanliness. *Who does she think she is?* Violet wondered at the time. *Mary Poppins?* Elsie had been equally perplexing: a quick growing weed with a flea-sized voice and a body like Howdy Doody. She was overly timid, and spoke to Violet in careful measured sentences about miracles from heaven and her piano lessons. Still, Violet was willing to give them another try. She was becoming more adventurous with age, and she needed a holiday. Did she ever.

25

Violet gets off the plane in Toronto airport and walks
the dank, slender hallway to the arrival gate. Along one
side of the terminal, tinted windows diffuse light from
the outside, cloaking the air in opaque, half-hearted illumination. Ahead of her, women in lengthy print skirts
edged with lace scuttle forward on high heels; they lug
overstuffed vinyl suitcases with enormous stainless-steel
buckles in their toothpick arms, or yank them along on
squeaky wheels like resistant toy poodles. From where
she walks—comfortably in her orthopedic shoes—Violet can see their narrow backs filamented with bones,
their long straight hair cascading to their bums like burnished waterfalls. Although some of the male passengers
mimic this pace—the ones in three-piece suits with suede
patches on the elbows and sardine-coloured ties—most
of them are more listless, strolling along in checked polyester. Some of them wear hats: Panama silk if they are
rich, or beige-brimmed corduroy with a button in the
centre if they are not, round and soft, like a kaiser bun;

their pant legs are wide on the bottom, the way Violet remembers them from the twenties and thirties, Oxford bags they called them then. Today they are bellbottoms.

As she rounds the corner where the terminal joins the waiting area, she sees a wall of faces beneath a flashing electronic signboard spelling out the details of her flight: *Arrival time for flight 411, 3:02 p.m. Passengers deplaning via gate number 2.* Smiles light up as faces are selected from the lineup. Arms are lifted in gestures of welcome. One or two people stand with messages printed carefully on poster board. She sees Clifford towering at the back of the crowd, his arms crossed. If it is possible, he has grown; either that or she has shrunk. Which is worse? she wonders. Both ways she is older.

"Mother," he says, striding forward as if on stilts. He bends down to take her bags and kisses her on the cheek. Violet sees his face looming toward her own; there are grey hairs germinating on his eyebrows, a network of thin veins working their way to the surface of his cheeks.

"Oh Clifford," she says, struggling for an appropriate greeting. "I'd forgotten how flat this place really is, and how barren!" What she meant to say was that she was glad to see him after such a long time, but he caught her off guard. All she could think of was her view from the air, the way Toronto looked: a bit of rubble marooned at the mouth of a souring lake. A boundless expanse of turgid earth carved into hollow blocks by roads. The last time she was here, six years ago now, it was April and everything had been bursting with green. Now it is March, only a month earlier; everything smells like mud.

"Yes, it is a little bleak right now," he agrees. "You

[318]

just missed the snow. But we'll have some more to cover everything up before too long."

Oh, Violet thinks straightening her purse. Snow: is that a good thing?

The drive to Brimstock is also not something she remembers, even though she must have done it at least twice during her last visit. Toronto is stretched out like a rubber band across the landscape, reproducing its castle-brick houses, its strip malls and their giant, fibre-glass letters that scintillate above parking lots, in all directions. On the edges, the city thins into stunted warehouses where tractor-trailers congregate in military formation to load and unload goods; it dies down into turnpikes, billboards, on and off ramps that jettison cars into the sky like the take-off strips for spaceships that Violet has seen on television. She looks out the window as the buildings disappear, finally, and are replaced with flat fields of dry stalks; with greener fields full of cattle and their stoic looks of contentment. She asks Clifford about his family.

"Everyone is fine," he says, tapping the steering wheel. "Marian is busy with her charities, as always, and Elsie is doing well in school. She is away for two days at a music competition, but she will be back on Wednesday."

Violet smiles and tries to conceal her disappointment. Two days alone with Marian. Will she survive?

"There is one thing I should mention," Clifford continues. "It's nothing serious, just that Elsie is a little self-conscious these days, particularly about her height. It would be better, I think, if you didn't mention it. O.K.? If you tried not to say anything about her being so tall."

"Of course Clifford. I won't."

"Good. Because she's at an awkward age, twelve, almost thirteen. We've all been there."

"Certainly," Violet says, even though she can't remember being there herself. She is thinking instead of the way Clifford has changed, the way he is beginning to resemble Hobert, his gorilla hands, his legs like parallel obelisks. She looks at him peripherally, across the electric blue interior of the Lincoln, and almost starts with recognition: his hair is a deep stratum of soot flecked with salt-and-pepper wisps; his girth has widened around the middle. She can see that he wears his brushed leather belt on the last hole, pinched up and inward with some difficulty. These are the endearing characteristics she remembers about her husband, the traits that made him all the more distinguished as he aged. On Clifford they are alarming. She looks at him and feels time creep over her like a slow sickness. What has she been doing all these years? She is so happy to see him.

"Mother," says Clifford, and she realizes she is crying softly. "Do you have a cold?"

"No," Violet says, getting out her Kleenex from the inner pocket of her purse. "But I think I may be developing an allergy."

The house on Magnolia Avenue looks the same, but the vegetation around it has grown. Clumps of perennials cut back almost to their roots form woody circles in the soil. An ornamental cedar clipped into an immaculate sphere sits on the soggy lawn like an oversized soccer ball. On either side of the front steps, two lilac bushes taller than Violet remembers clamber up towards bedroom windows. Inside the house has been given a fresh coat of paint, the chalk-white colour that reminds Violet too much of monasteries or the residential schools she has seen in documentaries. This effect is compounded by the crosses over every door: plaintive crucifixes made from wood, metal, or carefully looped vegetation that Violet suspects is left over from Palm Sunday. (Her own mother carried out this tradition, fashioning leafy crosses for many years, until arthritis got the better of her hands.)

"Violet," Marian says, as they walk in the door.

The word is not so much a greeting as a statement of fact. Violet translates: *You are here.*

"Hello Marian," she says. "You are looking well." Marian, to be honest, is not looking well, but Violet is trained in compliments and doesn't know where else to begin. *Jesus Marian, you look like hell?* That would not go over smoothly in this house.

Marian wears a loose striped blouse with a bow at the neck; her navy blue pants are wide at the cuffs, and droop slightly like poorly measured curtains. Violet wonders why a woman so careful about housekeeping would neglect to take in clothes which are obviously too large; then she notices a puckering around Marian's lips, her cheekbones jutting—just a little—from her flesh. She realizes Marian has lost weight.

They both stand in the hall smiling painfully at no one in particular.

"Well," Clifford says, breaking the silence. "Shall we have a glass of juice before dinner?"

Violet is once again set up in Elsie's room on the fold-out cot. Marian gives her a set of clean towels with pale flowers embroidered at the edge, and points out the way to the bathroom. "We keep the lid down," she says firmly, motioning to the toilet.

When she is alone Violet organizes her clothes in the empty drawers provided courtesy of Elsie. She sets her slacks on the bottom, layers up her sweaters and sheer print scarves; she hangs her collection of skirts and blouses on the wire hangers in the closet. After she has unpacked, she removes a chocolate bunny from her suitcase, and hides it in the bottom of a second drawer beneath her socks and underwear. Normally she just sends Elsie a card at Easter time with a five-dollar bill tucked inside; this time, however, she wants to give her a real gift, one that she can eat. She chose the chocolate bunny on the advice of the sales girl in London Drugs. "Girls just love this one," she told Violet, holding out the purple box trimmed with sweet peas. "It has a pink heart for a nose and is filled with caramel." Violet laid down her money knowing the gift would probably give Elsie cavities, but figuring at the same time that a little sugar once in a while should be acceptable—even to Marian— if it is followed by conscientious brushing.

Without Elsie the room seems hollow. Four angel-white walls. A spartan desk-and-chair set made out of pressed wood. Perhaps Marian aimed for this effect on purpose (Clifford has no preferences when it comes to decorating), spreading the pious austerity of the first floor to Elsie's room with the intent of keeping her cloistered like a nun. Perhaps she believed that maintaining control over the walls and floor that surrounded her like blank slates would enable her to affirm a sort of power over the rest of her daughter's life. With this idea, Violet empathizes. She may be a grandmother, with corns and portly reading glasses, but she still remembers the desire to keep her children babies, the impulse to guard them close to home and prevent them from becoming adults. *I have news for you,* she thinks for Marian, *it doesn't work.*

Elsie, however, has made small marks on this intimidating tableau. Between framed prints of Jesus and his apostles giving sermons to the crowds, and a wistful looking nature calendar inscribed with psalms of the month, Violet sees a poster tacked carefully to the wall: *Star Wars. The struggle against the dark side has just begun.* In the centre of the poster a women dressed in flowing robes clings fiercely to a man in an equally flowing karate suit. They both hold futuristic weapons and look out into the abyss of the picture plane, their mouths set into foreboding arcs. Except for the weapons, Violet thinks, and the fact that one of them is a woman, they are not wholly different from the apostles.

The overloved stuffed animals that Violet remembers from her last visit have been gathered together in a plush wad and placed in a wicker basket. There's the lamb Elsie offered Violet when she was having trouble sleeping; there also is the Virgin Mary night light, still on the bedside table, blinking chastely like a street lamp. Some of the more childish knick-knacks have been whisked away and replaced with scholarly and religious items: a map of Canada in three startling colours, unrolled and weighted open with bricks; a music box stamped with the Queen of England and her three handsome but muppet-like sons. On a shelf above Elsie's desk, Violet sees a scant collection of books. *We Celebrate the Eucharist. Religious Songs from the Last Century. From Bach to Tchaichovsky: 50 Classical Pieces for the Piano.*

She takes one last look in the closet, stumbling over a pair of enormous sandals, then rubs her kneecaps where she skidded on the carpet. On a shelf above Elsie's clothes she sees a familiar box. This is one of her own well-meant gifts, hand-painted and made from red cedar (she loves the smell) that was once used to store smoked salmon. Inside is a bone china cup and saucer packed meticulously in styrofoam, which she sent Elsie on her last birthday. The pattern is *Dreamtown* by Johnson Brothers. The gift was meant to be an initiation of sorts: in Violet's day young ladies collected cups and saucers for their trousseau, although Violet herself never had the time. Their bridesmaids held cup-and-saucer showers to aid them in stacking up their china troves, and everyone oohed and aahed over the various designs while nibbling on shortbreads. She wanted Elsie to use the cup, to enjoy the luxury of drinking tea from china that you could see through when held to the light. She also wanted her to feel that she was becoming a young lady now, at twelve years old. Instead the gift is packed in its original wrapping and stashed away in the closet.

Violet returns the cup to its place in the box and starts to arrange the styrofoam. It is then that she notices the letters, her letters, the familiar bespeckled stationery and touristy postcards that she fired out to Elsie over the years with the hopes of maintaining contact, however oblique, with the grandchild that reminded her the most of herself; they are stacked up one by one in a careful pile and held together with ribbon, wedged in between the packing materials and the edge of the carton like secret messages from the underground. With them are pictures: black-and-whites of Violet horsing around at Ambleside in her white wool bathing suit; Violet as a new wife with Russell bundled in her arms like a swaddled infant Jesus.

"Where did she get these?" she wonders aloud.

It is possible she gave the pictures to Clifford in a moment of motherly bravado, or that he pirated them himself from the boxes of photos stacked in her basement. But that would not explain why they are now stowed furtively away in the depths of Elsie's closet in a time capsule of letters.

She looks at the shots and their scalloped white borders, and feels a flush of pleasure rise in her cheeks. They are evidence of something: Elsie's interest in her family. More specifically, Elsie's interest in Violet. She leans on the shelf and smiles to herself. Perhaps she still has a chance.

The next morning Violet rises and wipes the sleep from her eyes. Sun is streaming in the window, between the cotton-polyester blended curtains flyspecked with pale vegetation, onto the plush wall-to-wall carpet. Violet swings her feet down to the floor where the pile is particularly worn and a patch of baldness is developing in the rug like a bad case of hair loss. *Day two*, she tells herself. Not that she is counting.

After she has put on her bathrobe and encased her feet in a new pair of slippers, she descends the stairs for breakfast. Marian and Clifford are talking in the kitchen.

"All I'm asking," Clifford says in his hushed voice.

"Is that you show her where things are. After that you can go about your day. She knows you have things to do. She won't get in the way."

"If I show her where things are, she'll just mess up the kitchen. You said so yourself that she was a lousy housekeeper."

Violet catches herself on the stairs. How cruel. She knows she was a little lax in the housework department, forgetting to wash Hobert's shirts for important sales meetings, leaving the dishes in the sink to harden and petrify into porcelain stalactites, but surely she'd got better? Surely by the time Clifford was old enough to remember she had outgrown her naive approach to housework; and if she lapsed a little, as all women do at some time or another, why would he tell Marian? She didn't think he cared about those things.

"That's not what I said," Clifford whispers defensively.

"Well," Marian says. "I don't have time to entertain. You know this week is my busiest time of the year. I have plenty of work to do already."

Violet hears Clifford sigh. "She understands this Marian."

"How could she? She has no morals."

This is too much for Violet. She bustles into the kitchen coughing from the bottom of her lungs and pulls on her ears in a gesture of temporary deafness. "Good morning," she says loudly, cheerfully. "I see the sun is shining." She moves toward the teapot to pour herself a cup, humming gaily to the tune of *Rhapsody in Blue*. The act is for Clifford's benefit: she does not want him to know that she overheard his private conversation, however accidental. He would be wounded beyond repair. Plagued by guilt. As for Marian, the lying charlatan in a blessed wimple. Let her wonder if her uncharitable opinions have been discovered; let her also repent.

"Hello mother," Clifford says.

"Good morning," Marian adds. Both of them drop their hands to their sides.

Violet smiles and a silence invades the kitchen. Her lips part with the intent to say something good-natured, but she can't think of anything. She isn't as capable a pretender as Marian. She stares into her tea cup and fumbles with the handle.

"I should be going," Clifford offers, walking briskly in the direction of the coat rack. Making his escape. "You can have anything you want for breakfast mother, if you don't mind helping yourself. We have the usual: toast, eggs. I think I saw some sausages in the refrigerator."

"Thank you Clifford. That will be just fine."

"Actually," Marian interjects. "I just used the last two eggs in my Easter cake for the church social. I also put the sausages in the freezer yesterday because we have given up all forms of meat for Lent this year. Did you forget Clifford?" She turns toward her husband who looks at her sheepishly from beneath his feathered eyebrows; he says nothing. *Come on Clifford,* Violet thinks. *You can do better than that.* But Marian continues, "By now those sausages are likely frozen solid."

"Oh," Violet says, seething internally. Then calmly, a master of disguise, "I guess I'll have cereal."

The two days with Marian are equivalent to ten years. Each morning Marian emerges from her room fully dressed; she has a breakfast of dry toast and weak tea, slides on her woollen pea coat, wrenches a second-hand plaid scarf around her neck, and tops off her head with a hand-knitted red tam that looks to Violet like a maraschino cherry. In less than ten minutes Marian is transformed from a virulent housewife into a murmuring, threadbare sundae redolent with all the odours of a thrift store basement. *Eau de mothball,* thinks Violet, despite herself.

Around lunchtime she returns looking more dishevelled. She slouches into the house, replaces her coat neatly on the rack, and makes her way to the sink where Violet has been careful to wipe up any crumbs remaining from breakfast. Here Marian scrubs ferociously, stabbing her hands into a sink full of water as though they are on fire. While she scrubs she whispers something that sounds like a medieval canticle. Violet can only make out some of the words, which don't strike her as at all biblical, but then again she's no authority. *Dirt,* she hears Marian say. Or, *Purify.* Over and over the words sputter out of her mouth, half-chewed by her wriggling lips which work the centre of her face into a twitching fury.

Violet tries to make herself look busy. For two days while Clifford is at work, she tiptoes around the house, colliding wordlessly into Marian in the hallway; she makes an effort to appear at ease and worthy of attention by sitting down opposite Marian both days and participating in silent noon-hour lunches. Together they stumble, first through grace (Marian bowing her head solemnly and mouthing the words *Bless us Oh Lord and these Thy gifts which we are about to receive from Thy bounty through Christ our Lord, amen*), then through a meek plate of food that apparently constitutes a meal in the household: a sweating wisp of orange cheese pressed between two sheets of white bread the thickness of rice paper. A mug of leftover tea. Bread-and-butter pickles on the centre of a plate like the Zen appetizers Violet has seen recommended in health food magazines. *Lord,* Violet thinks. If she wants to be an ascetic she's on the right road. Starvation and supplication. No wonder Marian is wasting away. How does Clifford manage to stay alive? But she nibbles hungrily on her crusts and says nothing.

After lunch Marian goes upstairs to pray. Violet goes out for a walk in the fields behind the house where other houses are starting to appear, their concrete foundations squared off and fit into place, their flesh-coloured bricks rising like temple ruins from mud puddles. The last time she was in this field, she was with Elsie. Together they picked their way along the swollen river in their summer shoes; they knocked over last year's seed pods and spilled their contents to the earth. Although she can't remember the details of their conversation, Violet does recall Elsie asking questions, several questions, which struck her as rather mature topics for a six-year-old girl. What had she been told about her ancestry, Violet wondered at the time, to prompt such curiosity?

On Wednesday afternoon Elsie returns from the competition. She walks into the house with her arms clamped around a leather duffel bag and places her shoes neatly on a mat beside the door.

"Hello," she says to Violet.

Violet smiles enthusiastically from her spot on the living-room chesterfield. At first glance, many things about Elsie have changed. Her hair is substantially longer, not to mention her arms and legs, and her mouth is a giant slash of rose against ivory cheeks. She wears a kilt, bottle green stripes on a navy background, and a high-necked blouse with covered buttons. She is a beautiful young girl, a little on the tall side and somewhat awkward, but Violet can see how she will turn out. She stifles the urge to throw her arms in the air on the pretence of a hug.

"Oh Elsie," she says eagerly. "Look how much you've grown!"

Elsie presses her lips together and looks down toward her shoes. She doesn't answer until Violet changes the subject.

Together they sit down to a dinner of broiled fish sticks and tossed salad, three generations in one family—Violet can't help but point this out. Marian passes around a plate of baked potatoes drizzled with margarine and pepper, and gives thanks to heaven: *For what we are about to receive, may the Lord make us truly thankful.* Violet notices the difference between the grace Marian says at lunch time, and the grace she says at dinner, but she doesn't ask for an explanation. Instead she has another tactic to alleviate the tension. When everyone's plate is loaded, and all the napkins are carefully draped on their appropriate laps, she launches into conversation by asking Elsie about her competition. She figures this is a beginning, and an innocent one at that.

"I played some studies," Elsie says faintly. "They were just short pieces to get me warmed up, but I liked them a lot. Then I played *Gymnastiques,* which is very hard."

As Elsie speaks she smoothes out the surface of her potatoes with the back of her fork.

"And how did you do?" Violet asks.

"The judge told me that I was good," Elsie says. "He said, if I had more practice, that I could perform one day."

"Perform," Violet says looking around the table for fellow enthusiasts. Clifford, her preferred ally, has his mouth full. "That's wonderful Elsie. I bet you would be a perfect performer."

"He also said," Elsie continues, her voice strengthening. "That if I went to the right school, a music school instead of the regular one, that I would be able to do a lot better."

"A music school?" Clifford says swallowing the bulk of his bite and raising his eyebrows.

"Yes," Elsie says. "He gave me these pamphlets about all the different places I could go." From somewhere under the table she extracts a glossy bundle which she raises timidly to eye level, then waves gently like a fan. "He told me," she continues, placing the brochures in the centre of the table between the plastic tub of margarine and the mashed potatoes, "to give them to my parents. That's you."

Marian deposits her fork next to her plate and dabs her lips with the corner of her napkin. "We know that we are your parents Elsie," she says, throwing a brief glance at Violet. "You don't need to remind us who we are."

Elsie stares at her plate.

"And because we are your parents, we know what's best. Don't you agree?"

"Yes."

"Yes," Marian says. "Of course we do."

[331]

"But I also thought," Elsie says, lifting her head. "I thought—"

"What did you think?"

"That you might like the idea." Her voice is a wounded breeze, already partly extinguished.

Marian sighs and places her hands in her lap. Beneath her eyes, Violet notices sacks forming. She picks up her fork and continues. "You already know that you will be attending the seminary after high school Elsie. There's no point in studying music now if you aren't going to follow through with it in the long run. Did you think that you could do both?"

Elsie is silent for a moment, then answers. "No."

"Well then," Marian says. "That's all settled."

Violet looks to Clifford for evidence of discussion, for evidence that he has been listening and disagrees with his wife's dictatorial methods. What she sees are his cheeks, slowly rising and falling with the force of his jaw; and his eyes, concerned black pearls occupied with the pressing matter of his fish stick. It appears to Violet—who does not claim to be an expert on family dynamics—that there will be no music school.

26

After dinner Violet retires to Elsie's room to find a warmer pair of socks and a respectable hat. Dinner sits like a diving bell in her gullet, but she doesn't like to criticize: at least she wasn't given bread and water. What she's trying to find in her luggage is something that will make her look reputable, humble; something that will pass her off as the kind of woman she has seen sitting on the steps of the various North Vancouver churches, with prim veiled hats and pastel scarves masking the merciless jowls that hang down below their chins. Already she has the jowls, so she's on her way, but she needs something more to get the right look: a fox-fur stole perhaps, with beaded glass eyes and a vinyl nose, or a pair of brown patent heels with a wide instep. She has a plan to improve her image, to make her less of a blot on the family history. She is just not sure if her intentions are entirely honourable.

"Mother," Clifford hollers. "We're on our way to church. We'll be back in an hour."

"Not so fast," she says, grabbing a silky scarf covered in totems—it will have to do—and racing down the stairs. "I'm coming with you."

"Coming with us?" Clifford asks.

"Yes," she says, sliding into her coat and arranging the scarf on her head. "Is that so strange?"

Clifford looks at Marian. "No," he says. "It's just that—"

"Just what?"

"Well," he continues, sputtering like a waxed-up candle wick. "We go every night this week Mother. You needn't come if you'd prefer to stay at home."

"Yes," Marian adds. "We have been preparing since Ash Wednesday."

Violet smiles bravely, feathering her scarf; she is determined. "Well," she says, looking at Elsie. "I'd better get working then. There is more joy in heaven over the one lost lamb."

That week Violet goes to church five times. Each evening she dons a pair of dress slacks and a loose-fitting blouse. She hauls on her coat and piles into the back of Clifford's blue Lincoln, forcing her lips to employ a smile. She gets used to the rhythm of the priest's voice, the drone of the audience that rises like a Gregorian wail. Following the service is out of the question, since Violet has no idea what the priest is saying—his words are laced with a severe accent—but she learns to anticipate the changes: a hand goes up and everyone stands in a shuffle of boots; the priest retires to his throne and everyone sits on benches. Then there is the incense, the ringing bell, the wavering song that emerges from the priest's mouth and fills the vaulted ceiling like the hoarse crowing of a rooster. This too is a cue, and everyone kneels on inflexible wooden pews and bows their heads against folded hands. Violet imitates their position, her legs creaking, her palms fitted into a bony triangle, but she doesn't try and pray. Praying is something other people do, and the thought of trying it out doesn't enter her mind.

She continues this pattern for a week: on Wednesday she files up to the front of the church behind the rest of the Leggetts and drinks sour orange wine from a shared cup; on Thursday she removes her stockings, peeling them off her calves like a slender rind, and has her feet washed in a stainless steel basin by a balding deacon with bloodshot hands. Friday is different. They go in the afternoon, sporting lighter, softer clothes in honour of the weather; Violet even wears a skirt, which is a remarkable event in her recent life history (she had taken to pants to conceal the spider veins). The church is packed and they narrowly miss getting a seat. Children fidget in decadent outfits. Older ladies fumble through cotton gloves with pages of their hymn books. Violet has trouble seeing over a collection of elaborate hats, accented by feathers and crêpe-paper roses, to the altar where the white-headed priest delivers messages from an oversized red Bible. It is Good Friday, and Violet participates heartily, standing up, sitting down, kneeling, shaking hands, until she thinks her legs will give out.

All the while she observes Elsie, slyly at first, from the edges of her peripheral vision, then openly, because her granddaughter doesn't seem to notice. Elsie sits tightly against the shellacked wood of the church pews and stares upward, over the heads of the priest and his audience, her eyes like glazed jewels. At first Violet believes her to be looking at the stained-glass window that hovers like a portal in the end wall. The window is a modern design, an abstract wave of blue through yellow, with the shape of a fish in the centre. It cracks through the dark wood of the ceiling and leaks light into the colourless interior of the church. Soon, however, she realizes that Elsie is not looking at the window at all; her gaze is steadfast, that much is true, but she seems to be looking beyond the wall, or, Violet thinks incredulously, *through* it. She looks entranced by something, something that Violet, try as she might, is unable to see for herself. Instead she looks at the priest, at his purple lips and bratwurst fingers; or at the lineup of heads stacked in front of her like bowling balls. She imagines all the services like this one that her own mother sat through, year after year, in the gloaming air of St. Edmund's, and wonders, without conviction, if Lila can see her now.

On Saturday (Elsie tells her they call the service Easter Vigil), Violet burns a hole in her scarf with the peace candle that she is given to light up the world. She participates in a reenactment of the trial of Jesus, and along with the rest of the audience is obliged to yell out *Crucify him, crucify him*, in a mock attempt at being a bawdy crowd. Then comes Sunday, the final service of the week, which passes by uneventfully. After church, when everyone is back in the living room for lunch, Violet draws out the chocolate rabbit and pushes it across the coffee table to where Elsie sits.

"Here Elsie," she says grinning. "This was left for you last night by the Easter Bunny."

Elsie looks at the box. She picks it up tentatively and looks at Marian. "There is no such thing as the Easter Bunny," she says.

Violet loses her smile. This is not something she would have admitted at twelve, but then again, illusions like that were more easily maintained in those days. There was no television, no scientific dissection of rabbits in their fetal stages on the news at supper time. "No," she says. "Of course there isn't. I was kidding Elsie. I brought that from B.C."

Elsie stares at the parcel. Her hands are clamped around the gift as if it were a time bomb. Violet smells the sweet odour of shop chocolate seeping through plastic wrap. She thought Elsie would be more excited, but she's treating this like a test.

"Elsie knows we don't maintain secular traditions," Marian breaks in. "We told her all about our holidays from the start, so that she would not be deceived."

Violet's temperature rises at this accusation. No wonder Elsie rarely acts like a child, pretending she is a princess or a fairy or whatever children today idealize as glamorous. They pulled the magic rug from beneath her feet before she learned to walk. "I was simply trying to give her a gift," she says. "I did not intend to deceive anyone."

"Gifts in themselves are frivolities when there are people suffering in the world."

Violet stands up and feels her face flush. Even though her red hair has dulled to a brassy dun, her pallor has not followed suit: she still turns red with anger. What is behind Marian's constant needling? She is like a small child that desperately needs attention; she will pinch and kick and take potshots until she has thoroughly rattled everyone in her presence.

"We are lucky people," Violet says in an attempt to contain herself. "We do have everything we need. But having things does not necessarily mean we don't suffer." She is referring to something oblique, she doesn't know what exactly, but she can't stand self-righteousness, especially not in Marian. If she wants to compare war wounds, Violet has a sack of her own injuries to flaunt. What does she know about suffering?

"Luck," Marian says, folding her hands in her lap in a gesture of finality and satisfaction, "has nothing to do with it."

After dinner Elsie and Marian go upstairs. Violet can hear their murmurs reverberating through the walls as they pray, first Marian, then Elsie in dutiful response:

From all evil. Deliver us.
From thy wrath. Deliver us.
From sudden and unprovided death. Deliver us.
From the snares of the devil. Deliver us.
From the spirit of fornication. Deliver us.

The words are slippery whisperings that slide like a moan down Violet's spine; they remind her of school and of her arithmetic lessons, that melancholy chanting that used to fill up the bricked-in classroom and rebound off the walls: *three times two are six, four times two are eight.* She has nothing against praying, but she pities Elsie all the same. Clifford sits down in his designated chair and rifles through the newspaper. His windblown hair is a lurid beacon over the sports pages and Violet imagines running her fingers through the ruff the way she used to do when he was a little boy. Even now, after one week in his company, she has a hard time picturing him as *little*.

She picks up a magazine from a stack on the coffee table and scans an article that points to the evidence of Jesus in the world. The article is titled *Storm of Justice* and is written by a Father Lazarus who appears in the lower left hand corner in a white smock and a hat like a half a grapefruit. *There are miracles everywhere,* the father begins, *contemporary messages of Jesus that are delivered wondrously by his mother, Our Sacred Lady.* Most of these miracles, Violet gathers as she reads, are announced by the archangel Michael in his armoured vest. They can take place anywhere in the world, at any time. The miracles Father Lazarus talks about are dramatic: rainstorms where nobody gets wet; a statue of the Virgin that weeps blood and tears; a hidden spring of water that bubbles out of rock and heals cripples; communion bread that turns to flesh on the tongues of nuns; bleeding Eucharists; rose petals imprinted with religious icons. One picture shows a mushroom cloud, part of a French nuclear test explosion on the eve of the legalization of abortion in the USA; the caption below reads *note the form of Jesus on the cross.* Violet looks intensely at the image, but she has never been good at cloudbusting. Still, she is baffled by the article, by the magazine and its headlines hailing the end of the world: *The end is nigh. Satan is real.* That's all very well, she thinks, but what are you doing about it?

"Clifford," she says, laying the magazine on her lap. "Do you believe in God?"

Clifford lowers the newspapers and looks at her with

a complicated pleading in his eyes. What a question! She could have commented on the weather, or the way Marian had repainted the kitchen walls, but she has never really spoken to him about this kind of thing, and she wants to know: what does he think?

She herself hasn't thought about God much. People died: Jack, Lila, Hobert, Russell. The unnamed redheaded man at the shipyards. That is the way of nature; she doesn't need an explanation. No omniscient soul, no matter how benevolent, would put someone through all the mourning she's been through. Especially not one deemed by millions to be compassionate and loving; no one could be that sadistic. Or that cruel. It is easier to believe she is all alone: then there can be no bitterness.

"Hmmm," Clifford says. "That is a tough one."

Violet looks at her son, at his abashed features devilled into a wince of concentration. He resembles the fish her father used to bring home in buckets from the Capilano River, hooked at the lip, but still alive in a foot of water. "Keeps them fresh," Jack used to say when Violet questioned him. Still alive, yes, but limpid, stunned; looking victimized, their silver-grey eyes doomed to a bleary stupor by circumstances beyond their control. "Never mind," she says, returning to her magazine. She already knows what he is trying to say.

27

Another week passes and Violet spends time with Elsie after school and on the weekend. They walk the serpentine lilt of the river from the Leggett's backyard; they watch the houses in the farmer's field emerge from the rubble of two-by-fours and sheets of chipboard. Elsie tells Violet about school, and about her piano lessons. She talks about her friends, of which there seem to be few, and about her current teacher Mr. Noseworthy. Violet reciprocates with stories about her childhood in North Vancouver, telling Elsie how she got the strap, and how she and Grace used to snicker over ladies' underwear in the Eaton's catalogue. In those days, she says, underwear was thought to be disgraceful, the same as snorting or passing gas at the May Day picnic. You had to deke around the subject if you wanted to appear ladylike and get your message across; you had to call them *unmentionables*. While Violet talks she notices a look forming in Elsie's features: worry, laced with concern. Her entire face contracts, tightening, drawing in her lips, her eyes, her elemental nose, and her hands pinch into compact fists. She wonders, though not to Elsie, if the child has a nervous condition.

On Thursday evening she comes across Elsie's pamphlets. They are glossy letter-size circulars printed in sombre blues and blacks, with self-incriminating messages typed across their covers: *Could you be doing more for your child's musical abilities? Yes you could.* Under the headings are children posing resolutely with their instruments: girls in stately dresses, their hair done up in pigtails using coloured wool; boys pink-cheeked in pinstriped suits and dangling, lofty neckties, with eyes like baby seals and preternaturally coiffured hair. They hold clarinets, trombones, violins, or are perched rigidly on piano benches with their fingers on the keys. Violet laughs at the seriousness of some of their faces, the way they all look like miniature versions of members of the symphony orchestra; she reads the fine print. None of the schools are in Brimstock, not even close, but one of them, Lord Stanley's Conservatory, is located in Vancouver, a stone's throw from the park. Although the south shore is a fair leap from Violet's house on Chesterfield Avenue, the distance is traversable thanks to that infernal bridge, the Lion's Gate, which damned the North Vancouver ferry out of existence. She thinks about Elsie: perhaps it is time someone asked her opinion.

"Elsie," says Violet that afternoon. They are in the bedroom seated on the floor, reading from Elsie's sixth-grade reader. Robert W. Service: *There are strange things done in the midnight sun by the men who toil for gold—* "Would you like to go to music school?"

"I'm not allowed," says Elsie.

"But if you were," says Violet. "If your parents said yes. Do you think you would like it? Would you like to be a concert pianist the way the judge suggested?"

"I can't," says Elsie, her voice remote. "I'm going to the seminary in Montreal. Marian already said."

Violet sighs and turns the page. An illustration of the northern lights flashes blue and orange over a man on snowshoes. "Let's pretend," she says, "just for a minute, that you can do whatever you want. Anything at all. Music school. The seminary. Or maybe you want to be a nurse or a teacher. What do you think you would pick?"

"I can't," says Elsie again, drawing her knees up under her chin so that she looks newborn.

"Can't what?"

"Please—" she says, moving away from Violet, standing up. Her voice cracks, as if someone is squeezing her throat. "I can't think about it. It's too hard." She sits down at her desk and stares at the world map. A tear traces the length of her cheek.

But Violet can think about it, and she does. Helping Elsie get to music school may be her last chance to do something good for the girl. She is already getting an edge to her voice, the bitter despondency of teenagers. In a few years it will be too late: Elsie will be fully formed, unassailable. Violet closes the reader, and lets herself out of the room. She has to make an attempt.

"I was thinking," Violet says that night at dinner, "that if Elsie wanted to go to music school, she could stay with me and study at Lord Stanley's. I have room, and she could commute. I read there are buses that go directly to the school's front doors." She forks a tree of broccoli into her mouth and chews. It's just a suggestion. Where's the harm?

"I think," says Clifford. "That we have already decided to keep Elsie here Mother."

"I realize you have talked about it," Violet continues, "but you didn't ask Elsie what she wanted. I'm not trying to stick my nose into your business, but the girl has talent. It would be a shame to waste that on—well," she falters, trying to steer clear of touchy subjects. She doesn't want to offend. "To waste it period. Elsie, what do you think?"

Elsie looks at Violet, frozen, a deer in headlights. Her lower lip quivers.

"Elsie already knows what she will be doing," Marian says. "We decided that long ago."

"Yes, but I was asking Elsie," Violet says. Then adds boldly, "Perhaps she doesn't share your enthusiasm for her chosen path."

"It would be impossible Mother. The cost would be too much for us, and she would need a chaperone," Clifford interjects.

"I've thought about all those things," Violet adds smiling. And she has; she expected opposition, it's only natural in the beginning. "I'm willing to pitch in, do my part with the money, and I can be her chaperone."

"You?" Marian says. Her eyes begin to flare and she gathers her sweater closely to her shoulders as if she is feeling a chill.

"Yes," Violet says.

"You," Marian says, "cannot be trusted."

"Excuse me?"

"Marian," Clifford says, lowering his knife and fork, attempting to mediate.

"You," Marian continues, "will not take her away."

"It would just be for the school year," says Violet, a little too defensively. "And then she could come back home."

Marian slides back her chair and rises. The napkin on her waist falls to the floor. "Elsie is not going anywhere," she says.

"Can't we just discuss this?" says Violet, incredulous. Is Marian a dictator or what? She is offering to *pay* for the tuition.

"Well," says Clifford, relenting, "maybe if—"

"No!" says Marian. "Nothing will be discussed." She moves over to Elsie's chair and wraps her arms around her shoulders. A suppressed groan of anguish escapes her mouth. "Can't you see?" she says, addressing Clifford. "She's already lost hers and now she wants to take mine away."

Violet looks at Elsie who is solid with fear. "What is she talking about?"

"I don't know," says Clifford.

"You do!" says Marian, hoarse with grief, shaking her head back and forth. "She didn't take care of hers and now he's dead. That's payment for neglect."

"Neglect?" says Violet, a tremble in her voice.

"Neglect and sin. Russell was your payment."

So many years have gone by since Violet has thought about Russell and the complications surrounding his birth, that she doesn't know what Marian is talking about. "Russell?" she says, confused. An image of red hair, of delicate newborn hands flits by in her mind's eye. She feels her heart bleed.

"Yes," says Marian. Her mouth forms itself into a snarl. "A sin from the beginning. The wages of sin is death."

Violet feels the words slap her like metal gloves, winding her. She sits at the kitchen table with a carrot speared on the end of her fork, her mouth a diffused circle grappling with speech. How can Marian pick on Russell, poor Russell, who never had a chance? His little round head like a basketball, his milk-white skin covered in freckles like her own. He was her angel, the first one to be born, but now he is gone. What day is it? What hour? What has time done to her, forcing itself between her and the people that mattered most, reeling her away. Now those people are just photographs in her poorly organized photo album. They are gone, gone for good, and Violet is left behind doing forty years hard labour. She is left behind *here*.

But she is not entirely deflated. She is more than an insect to be crushed flat. She is a woman, a mother. She is an elder for God's sake. What happened to respecting your parents? Being seen and not heard? She puts down her fork and stands to face Marian, wanting to say something, not knowing how. She opens her lips wider, hoping that something will come out. Instead she realizes she is crying.

"Elsie," she says, remembering the girl.

Elsie sits trapped between her mother's arms, her mouth pinched shut, her eyes wide with terror and amazement. Marian squeezes her shoulders together, pressing her flat against the chair. One hand grips Elsie by the chin.

"She's hurting her, Clifford," says Violet. "Can't you

see? Help me." She crosses the room to where Marian stands murmuring over Elsie as if in benediction, then looks at her son. "For Pete's sake Clifford, just this once—"

"This once, Mother?" says Clifford. "Of course, this is my fault."

"I didn't say that."

"Did you stop to think of Elsie before you disrupted everything? Because that's what you're doing." He looks at Violet accusingly, as if she is the child and he the parent.

"Please Grandma," says a small voice. Elsie's. The one that matters.

Violet looks at her granddaughter, shaking now under her mother's grasp. For a moment she looks small again, six years old. She wants to help her, will do anything she says. That was her intent from the beginning, despite what Clifford believes.

"Please stop," Elsie says.

The clock in the kitchen bongs: a quarter after six.

"But Elsie," Violet says, her throat closing with hurt. "Don't you want to go to music school? To BC?"

"No thank you."

"There," says Clifford, moving in. "You see Mother? She doesn't want to go. Case closed."

Violet recoils. The eyes of her family are on her now, aimed, penetrating. She must act; do something definitive. What was it the Greeks used to say? (Hobert told her this) *Know thyself*. Some oracle. The only thing she knows for sure is that she is leaving this house and never coming back. She pauses for a moment, looks at her granddaughter, then she moves on.

In the bedroom she gathers together her blouses, her

skirts; she wrenches out her knotted socks from Elsie's drawers and squishes them into her suitcase. Once she is packed she clambers down the stairs to where Clifford stands frowning in the hallway. "Dammit Clifford, your wife's a bitch! Why don't you teach her some manners for a change?"

His answer comes out blurry, *Now Mother,* but Violet sees it for what it is: a soother. He's trying to calm her down by sticking her full of compliments and sensible, understanding one-liners. He hopes she'll relent, the cad, and slink back upstairs like a penitent sinner. Well he's wrong. She refuses, insulting Marian a second time and demanding him to have some backbone. What did she teach him when he was younger, to be a good-looking doormat? If he won't help her, give Elsie a chance, let him rot in heaven with Father Lazarus and St. Michael the archangel. See if she cares! She's already made up her mind. She walks out the front door and heads toward the airport. When she reaches her first pay phone she dials information and hails a taxi. By nightfall she is already on the plane.

28

Violet is back in the Avondale social lounge with a crick in her back. The lights flash on indicating the end of the slide show, and everyone opens their eyes, slowly, blinking back weariness. Some of them straighten their necks and pop their heads upward as if on poles, scanning the indeterminate furniture and anonymous plants for clues to their location. Violet recognizes their expressions: *Where am I?* they say to themselves, perplexed, mouths drooping. They have been wrenched from sleep, from familiar, padded childhoods or memories of their past, only to find themselves restrained in wheelchairs, or slumped over on unfamiliar couches smelling of mothballs and the surly combination of a thousand perfumes. When you spend sixty-eight years waking up to the same watermarks on the ceiling, you get confused when they are suddenly replaced with stucco tiles or plaster board; you think you have finally died and gone someplace. Not heaven, and not even hell, she wouldn't go that far (although she is tempted). The Avondale is more like *purgatory*: a waiting area, the spot between. A place where the food is bad and the attendants curt, but no matter how well you behave, you are doomed to remain until some magnanimous individual decides otherwise.

She loosens her grip on her chrome armrests and eases the tension out of her wrists. The exercises have paid off: she can almost make a fist with her right hand and lift it above her shoulder as though she were doing calisthenics. She still feels uncoordinated, however, a small child testing the limits of her body, shouting to her parents, or any adult that will listen, *Look at me! See what I can do?* Her own children did this, one by one, as they paraded from toddler to schoolboy, shrieking *Mom! Mom! I jumped from way up there! Did you see me? I can do it again.* They were enthralled by the surprises of their arms and legs, of their agile feet that could tiptoe and pounce with a little practice, and demanded that she witness their successes. Now Violet knows for herself how they must have felt: exhilarated, overcome. She knows it is no small feat to learn to walk when you have been incapacitated for so long.

Her own plans are to take up dancing when she gets out of the Avondale. She has seen women on television, *senior citizens* they call them now, performing a variety of unbelievable stunts that she would never have imagined possible when she was young: women clad in windproof rayon hurling themselves from planes; crones like herself, with greying hair and wrinkles, strapped into fluorescent climbing gear and straddling the peaks of Grouse Mountain. And then there are the protesters, the activists, chaining their knobby knees to the doors of office buildings or the gates of roads into old growth forests: *Raging Grannies,* some of them are called. Violet wants to rage, but in her own way. She wants to be left alone on a dance floor with a record player and a good pair of legs that don't buckle when she turns around. She wants to take off like a bird.

If she wants to fulfill her dream, however, she will have to get working. All she has at home is an AM radio with a broken volume control, and a conservative collection of running shoes. (All her pumps have been packed away in boxes and buried in basement rubble.) She also needs that new pair of legs, which is why she continues to exercise. She can already stand in front of the mirror, sans cane, for over five minutes.

Why God, she says, *do we end up back where we started? Children once more.* She doesn't expect an answer, but she is getting tired of talking to herself. *From diapers to Depends,* although thankfully she is not yet at that stage of irregularity. Exactly the opposite, in fact, hence the All Bran for breakfast every morning. If she could do her life over again she would slow things down, make every year the length of twenty, except perhaps the ones she spent in school. Then she would have the time she needed to get things right, to weigh the consequences of every action and their potential outcomes; to live fully. *Oh Violet,* she thinks, *you would probably do everything the same again.* Likely she would. She's human isn't she? As blemished and flawed as your average apple; but she can't help wanting a second chance, especially with Clifford.

Storming out on Clifford was meant to be a dramatic gesture, one she hoped would goad him into action; it was also a reflex. After the way Marian behaved, what else could she have done? She was shaken to her core. When she crossed the threshold of their house, and later, when she was on the plane devouring a complimentary packet of oversalted almonds, she believed Marian was a spiteful woman. Full of hate. But later, in retrospect, she decided that her daughter-in-law was likely mentally disturbed, schizophrenic perhaps, or at the very least, obsessive compulsive. And Elsie. *Please stop.* That girl had broken her heart.

But even though Marian had been cruel, Clifford, in Violet's eyes, was the worse offender. He stood by lamely while his wife ravaged his own mother, making no noise but a watery bleat when the insults came hurling from Marian's mouth. Worse, he supported her! This was what hurt Violet the most, what prevented her from contacting him all those years. She wanted him to apologize, but he would not. He would rather forget that anything had ever happened than admit to his shortcomings; he would rather forget that he had a mother.

She tried consulting Lawrence, calling him when she returned, to get his advice.

"That family is nuts," was all he had to say.

"But what about Elsie? She's going to end up in a mental institution. Either that or jail."

"Mother," said Lawrence. "All you can do is leave them alone. Let them cool off for a while before speaking to them again. As for Elsie, why don't you try writing her letters. At least then she won't feel like you are mad at her too."

So she did. Letters at Christmas, and on birthdays. Letters with scented rainbow interiors and lacy edges with golden sealers that she purchased at London Drugs and Osterson's Stationery on a regular basis. But some-how, letters never seemed like enough.

She pivots her wheelchair and points towards the door. Already a sinuous line of residents shuffling behind walkers and chrome-handled canes are on their way out, followed by others in chairs like Violet's whose powder-white heads slouch languidly to their chests in physical expressions of resignation. *Chin up*, Violet wants to say, loudly, the way Jack used to when he caught her crying or looking sullen. *You look like a procession of snails.* Jack was always one for cheering up. *Let's not have any sad faces*, he would say in his regimental voice. Violet only wishes she had inherited some of his ability to con-sole, then perhaps she would have been more inclined to rush in after Marian's death and help her son with the raising of Elsie.

Elsie must have grown a great deal in the past twenty years. Twenty years! Violet can hardly imagine. Her grave little mouth will have blossomed; her gangly ex-oskeleton will have sprouted breasts and softened, she hopes, into the receptive frame of a woman. She will have gone through a series of jobs the way girls do these days: a check-out clerk at the grocery store, a person in a clown suit waving frantically at traffic with a bouquet of balloons and a sandwich board reading *Breakfast All Day! $3.99!* She has gone to university instead of the seminary, that much Violet knows for certain, although she isn't sure what she studied: Archaeology? World Religions? Something obscure and unemployable no doubt, with tweed-coated professors and incidents of sexual harassment clamouring up to her ears (Violet watches the news). She's probably even married by now, Violet thinks, although surely Lawrence would have informed her. If he had known, that is.

She can't hide the fact that she was hurt when Elsie stopped answering her letters. Even if they were shoddy attempts to keep in touch, they were well-meant. Violet intended to reconcile with Clifford, one day at least, but in the meantime she saw no reason to punish Elsie for her parents' ill-behaviour. On the contrary, Clifford and Marian's shared ineptitudes were all the more reason for Violet to remind Elsie that she had other, saner family members on the sidelines. Even if they were hedonistic redheads with a taste for a gin-and-tonic and a love of jazz, they still cared for her; she still mattered. But Elsie didn't seem to want this kind of attention. Violet wrote off her dismissal as a gesture of teenage rebellion, her attempt, however misplaced, to slough off bad memories; she tried not to let it bother her. She still tries. The Avondale is full of enough grief already. Grudges cloak the rooms like layers of old wallpaper, pungent and yellow, unravelling at the edges so that their patterns are barely visible, their origins skewed. Grudges against children who signed the admittance papers, against husbands and wives who didn't know enough to fight; grudges against anyone and everyone who had the gall to act human, let down, die. Those are the worst grudges, the deepest; the hardest to overcome. Grudges against the dead, because how could they?

She wheels herself into the procession, folding her slack hand around the tire and sliding it forward, gently, so that she doesn't smite the woman in front. The action is not as hard as it was last month, when she could barely coordinate her fingers enough to grip a plastic drinking cup. Now she is almost capable of wheeling herself back to her room.

"Mrs. Leggett," the nurse says, passing with another resident in tow. "You have come a long way, haven't you? Look at how well you're doing."

Violet smiles and nods her head. If only Grace could see her now.

Grace went through the Avondale before Violet. Three years ago. She would have shuffled these very same hall-ways; she would have eaten the same cream-of-salt soup and slept on the iron plastic-covered mattresses with her feet tucked in beneath the covers. Compared to Violet's stroke, Grace's illness was more complicated and bleak: dementia followed by a brain aneurysm. There was no hope of rehabilitating her tired mind, so Grace told her, although Violet persisted in bringing her crossword puzzles and books on sharpening your memory, just in case. She couldn't just stand by and do nothing. Grace accepted her fate like an angel. She laughed at the old men with the monastic hairdos and the lobster bibs that shared her dining table, and had her hair done every Wednesday—*my last luxury*, she would say. All the nurses adored her, even when she started letting herself into the lunch room in the middle of the night, singing *Au Claire de la Lune*.

When she came to visit Grace, Violet promised herself she would never go in a rest home, not as a resident. Rest homes were unnatural places where everyone within a two-mile radius was old, either that or ill; the sterile environment infiltrated by television sets and rubber plants infected everyone with touch deprivation in addition to their original sickness, which more often than not was simply being old. When she walked into the foyer a dozen gnarled hands went out in her direction, straining against vinyl-coated braces, against numbness; she never knew how to respond. She didn't realize how cunningly doctors and children conspired to slip you in against your will. Now she does.

Living in the Avondale means constantly fighting against the surge of bleariness and goodwill that threatens to pull her down and turn her into a catatonic. The people here will do anything if she lets them: set her hair into a wave and fix it with Pollyanna bows; cut her toenails and rasp the corns from her feet; change her bed sheets, her undies, her pillow shams; pluck the fine white hairs from her eyebrows; cut her meat; latch her garters; apply her cold cream. The tide of good intentions and samaritanisms is so incumbent, so debilitating, that Violet has to kick and push for the privilege of brushing her own teeth. A privilege which used to be hers by automatic default. She has to mouth the word *No* and fix her brow with a despotic scowl, and then, if they still don't understand, she has to swat their hands away like a cantankerous old bat. She hates doing this, realizing that such gestures could be misconstrued, taken as evidence of lunacy, or at the very least, the spoliation of basic manners, but she can't help it, her hands (at least one of them) are tied.

At dinner Violet is served *chicken divan,* a flaccid breast with the bones removed, baked under a cheese sauce and cut into diagonal fillets. She begins to work into the meat with her fork when the woman with the salt intolerance takes a seat nearby.

"I'm quite put out," she says to Violet, her demeanour obviously piqued. Her white hair has been permed into a diaphanous mist that hangs around her head like morning fog. "My new roommate was supposed to move in today. To fill up the extra slot in my room. I live in one of the double apartments over in wing F, and my last roommate dropped dead over a month ago. The place is terribly empty, all that space, and I keep asking them, When will you fill it? When? I worry about being alone because of my heart trouble, and they just shrug their shoulders and talk about the paperwork. Well," she continues, chewing on a bite of chicken, "finally they tell me, yesterday, Mrs. Troy, you will have your new roommate. She's coming in from the Lion's Gate hospital. Isn't that wonderful? And I nodded yes, because I had been so worried. (I can't quite sleep at night when I'm completely alone.) But now would you believe it? She's not coming after all."

The woman looks disdainfully at her dinner and raises her fork in a gesture of impatience. "It seems she just up and died. Just before they were to move her. Can you believe the rotten luck?"

Violet shakes her head. She cannot. Some people have all the misfortunes.

"But the worst part," the woman continues, "is the way she died. It seems she was one of those religious types, so the family got the minister to tell her that she was being moved to the Avondale. They knew she wouldn't like the idea, she was dead set against nursing homes, but they figured, coming from a holy man, she

[357]

might just consent. Well, the minister tells her and she is all politeness, saying, Yes father. Of course father, nodding her head and smiling, but as soon as he leaves the room she takes the nearest plastic bag, puts it over her head, and smothers herself."

The woman looks at Violet from wide eyes, her cheeks filled with chicken divan. "Can you imagine? Of all the nerve."

Violet stares at her plate. Luckily she is excused from having to make comments on topics such as these by her crooked lip, because what would she say? *I understand her perfectly. I thought about plastic bags myself, but there were none on hand.* Truthfully she did not, she has never been that close to despair—although she has been close—but she would like to say it just the same, to see the woman's affronted reaction. Who does she think she is, claiming personal offence at the death of a stranger? She doesn't even know the woman and already she's using her for sympathy. *Of all the nerve.*

Her own meal has been hacked into ragged bite-sized amounts that look as though they have been previously chewed. Violet eyes the chopped carrots: almost appetizing. She is making progress, cutting with her left hand, holding her fork in her right, but she is still a far cry from the woman she was before the stroke. Perhaps if she were to get more practice, some physiotherapy; a little exercise in a local weight room . . . Now who is she kidding? Of course she knows her chances of getting out of the Avondale are slim; statistics don't lie, the idea is a near impossibility. She knows all that, but she can't admit it. She won't. If anyone should get out of here it should be Violet. Healthy, adept. Coherent as the evening news. If anyone should have that privilege, that return to normal life, she is the one. She alone has been trying hard. She alone is worthy. Perhaps worthiness is taking things a bit far—she has never been particularly angelic—but if points were awarded for longing, for yearning deeply, she is sure she would win, hands down. Why keep her locked up when she has been fighting so hard? Why end things now, because for her it would be the end, when she has so much left to do, to deal with? *God—if that is who you are—you can't be serious. You can't. Please. Just one more chance.*

She puts down her tea and stares at the tablecloth. She must calm herself, exercise control. If she breaks down at dinner time, in front of all those sets of eyes, those pudding-faces cast toward her like rows of lugubrious scarecrows, things will be more difficult than ever; she will never be able to show herself again. She must concentrate on the idea that she can return to her former life. However lonely and arduous things might have been, they were still better than what faces her now: death by inarticulate companionship, by slow and alienating trips to the social lounge where the only socializing is done with the television set, beneath dim lights. She will do everything she can to get well, or she will die trying.

So why does she feel like she is on a sinking ship?

DANCE YOU DEMON

29

It is afternoon. Elsie walks from the bus stop on Marine Drive, through the slanting sunshine, towards the Avondale Rest Home. As usual she is dressed inappropriately; the layers of flannel and cotton cling to her skin like cellophane, like a corpse suffocating in a body bag. Sweat pours down the space between her breasts. She navigates the sidewalk in a sweater-coat with wooden toggle buttons, in black cords with fuzzy rayon leotards beneath. In her hands are the discarded fleece mitts and scarf that she slipped on before catching the bus—how was she to know the temperature would rise to eighteen degrees? It is still winter, according to the calendar, but she neglected to listen to the news this morning, or at lunch. She'd been busy with students, manoeuvring their small hands over the keyboard and saying in her solicitous voice, *Pretend you are holding a potato.* Now she suffers for her negligence. She undoes the last button on her sweater and forges ahead.

Along the street, traffic lurches towards intersections.

Elsie catches a whiff of gasoline and looks down the sidewalk to where a man in shorts and a T-shirt pushes a lawn mower. Amazing, she thinks. The end of January and already people are mowing their lawns. Doesn't anything ever go dormant around here? This is something she has wondered before. Take this morning: she stopped in at the market for a box of cereal and a carton of milk. What she saw were watermelons, pomegranates, hothouse tomatoes and cucumbers spilling out of wooden crates; apples, waxy and slick as lipstick; oranges and grapefruits and their splendorous golden skins; there were also net bags filled with grapes, baskets of strawberries lining the counters like sweet red nuggets. So much fruit, and this, the middle of winter. Of course she has seen this kind of selection before, she did not grow up in the third world, but she did spend the better part of her life shopping at farmer's markets and roadside stalls where you took what was in season and didn't worry about stems or pill bugs (those were picked off at home), and concentrated instead on putting everything up for the winter; or down, in Marian's case, on plywood shelves in the cellar.

For Elsie, the incredible selection of fruit displayed in outdoor bins is one more indication that winter doesn't happen west of the Rockies. Look at the pansies, the snowdrops; look at the robin on the lamp post. Isn't winter supposed to bring on hibernation? Isn't it supposed to speak in chilly tongues to overeager vegetation and convince it to dry out, harden, turn brittle, fall to the ground in an explosion of seed? In Brimstock, and again in London, winter meant a change of season; it meant hard and dramatic adjustments to the elements: fur-lined leather boots, a snowmobile suit with a hood and a neck flap that padded and swished and made you feel like a multi-coloured marshmallow. The point of winter is that it is supposed to be cold.

It's not that Elsie has anything against mild climates, she is just a little surprised. Although there was a record snowfall last week, an anomaly for the coast at any time of year, the general lack of coldness throws Elsie into a state of confusion; she feels off-kilter, skewed; her circadian rhythm must be out of whack. The fact that the seasons in North Vancouver are more or less blended into one protracted twelve-month blur, where a profusion of green leaves, of candy-coloured flowers and over-anxious men in shorts can be seen at any time of year, makes Elsie feel displaced, as though she were living in Europe on a tulip plantation, or at the very least, south of the border. She is used to anticipating the snap at the end of the season when spring invades and things awake, dancing like jackrabbits in a sun patch, creeping like old dogs towards new grass; when everything sleeping becomes once again inhabited and whines with lust for a bit of warmth. That snap used to arouse Elsie's own senses; she would feel invigorated, spurred on. Now she will have to look elsewhere for inspiration.

The Avondale is different than she imagined. When she arrives, a woman greets her as she opens the door, pushing out into the afternoon with her arms full of paper bags. "Beautiful day," she says, grinning like a cat on ether. "Just look at that sun! Fabulous." Elsie wants to know what it takes to make someone that happy. The woman is laughing as though she is leaving a movie theatre, and not, in reality, a nursing home. Aren't nursing homes supposed to be gloomy? She always imagined them to be a cross between a hospital and the waiting area of a dentist's office. She had braced herself for the marzipan upholstery, the rockers and wood-framed chesterfields done in almond, grey, russet blonde, colours chosen from a Bauhaus catalogue but cut out of shabbier material with toothy naps. She expected macramé wall hangings with explosions of tufted wool, one or two overhead ceiling fans with rattan-and-veneer propellers that hissed above her like a slow but methodical intravenous drip.

What she sees is a terrarium; pheasant under glass. The receiving area of the Avondale is designed like a sunroom, with three sides enclosed by panels of smoked glass that extend overhead in a pointed arch; bamboo blinds are drawn across the ceiling sections to keep out the sun. Beneath the blinds are leafy banana plants in terra cotta pots, arm chairs with paisley printed chintz and legs of cherry wood. Elderly people sit in the chairs, tucked in between the foliage, laughing, knitting, playing cards; parents, grandparents, and once upon a time, Elsie supposes, somebody's children.

As she makes her way down the hall to the room number given to her by the front desk clerk, she does recognize some elements that she considers to be characteristic of nursing homes, not that she is an authority on the subject. A woman in an overwashed housecoat struggles by with a walker and smiles distantly at Elsie as she passes, her reaction time off by several seconds. Her scuffling is followed by the sound of incoherent dialogue. One or two exclamations; syncopated laughs. Then there is the smell of old clothing and lemon-scented floor cleaner, a gust of pastillish air freshener. Elsie notices billboards with neat printing across construction paper signs: *Craft Club & Tea Time, 10:00 a.m.* Just like elementary school, she thinks. The only thing missing is the dove of peace made from pipe cleaners.

Violet's room is at the end of the hallway. Elsie knocks lightly on the door and stands with her hands folded, waiting for an answer. (She feels like a sinner outside the confessional—*Bless me father.*) When one doesn't come, she pushes with the flat of her palm and enters, hoping that her grandmother won't mind the invasion. Likely, she thinks, or rather, she *knows*, her grandmother is simply unable to respond. Even if her brain permitted her to make sense while chatting, the stroke will disallow any conversation. Elsie counts her blessings. She does not want to navigate lengthy discussions on the price of butter during the second world war.

The inside of the room is more like a hospital: pressed-wood bed, matching table. There is a tartan blanket at the foot of the bed, a jug of lilies on the table. There are also two chairs with blond arms against the far wall, and a wheelchair in the corner. Violet sits in one of the chairs in a white blouse dotted with pastel flowers. Her hair is camel brown infiltrated by threads of silver that intensify around her face. She looks older, yes, but still familiar, like a well-dressed advertisement for life insurance.

"Hello," Elsie says, faltering. She should have rehearsed. She is terrible at these kinds of things. "It's Elsie, Violet. Clifford's daughter."

Violet gives her a look which Elsie thinks must be contempt, but is perhaps just impatience, and follows with a slow, compelling nod. Her eyes are bright. Her mouth works itself into a crooked smile, then returns instantaneously to the deadpan of her face.

"I brought you these," Elsie continues. One-sided conversations are more difficult than she thought, especially when she is being examined. She holds out the tin of almond cookies. "Mrs. Wang made them. Your neighbour. She wanted me to give them to you."

Violet nods and watches as Elsie puts the tin on her bedside table. Her face has been altered by time, but beneath the lines and puckers Elsie recognizes a softness that she remembers from childhood, a kitten mouth, a tentative oval face with deeply incised eyes, the eyelids like the wilted petals of a tea rose. The skin of her cheeks is loose and withered, but also carefully powdered, smelling of hot oiled flowers or simmering pot-pourri. Her posture is impeccable, and Elsie wonders at this considering the extent of her stroke; but then again, Violet always did say that the Hunchback of Notre Dame was far from appealing when Elsie tried to make herself look smaller by slouching. *Straighten up child!*

She takes a seat in the empty chair, leaning into the spine-pinching backrest, and folds her hands in her lap. Already she feels as though she is in an interview with one of her student's parents: her face is being given the once-over, her manners scrutinized. Despite how heartily she believes in taking command of these situations, Elsie rarely manages to bleat out a convincing word of authority.

"So," she says, not wanting to languish in impolite silence. "It is very sunny outside today. The snow is all gone." When all else fails, talk about the weather.

"Yes," Violet says, firing the word from a prudently shaped mouth.

Elsie looks at her grandmother, surprised. She isn't supposed to be able to talk. The lawyer told her that Violet's right side was badly damaged by the stroke, injuring her ability to perform normal functions like walking, talking, possibly even thinking. How much does she understand? She watches as her grandmother produces a notepad and pen from a pocket in her blouse, then writes, gently, deliberately, across the surface of the paper. She hands the message to Elsie.

Hard for me to speak. Stroke. I am working on it. How is the house?

Elsie is struck by her grandmother's lucidity; she expected incoherence, dementia, at the very least a little bit of babbling. "The house is fine," she says, gathering herself. Someone must have told her that Elsie had arrived, that she and her power of attorney were taking care of things. *Taking care of things,* she laughs privately at the implications of this notion. "I cleaned off the roof during the storm, to save the shingles and the rafters. Some of those older houses on the street caved in. I also shovelled a path in the backyard when the snow was so heavy, so that I could get back and forth from the alley way. Not that there was anywhere to go," she adds, remembering the storm. "Everything was closed for a few days."

Violet nods adeptly and processes the story without flinching. As far as Elsie can tell, she is in perfect command of her senses. They stare at one another for several seconds, then Violet flashes another message: *I'm glad you have come.*

Elsie smiles. The guilt is heating up inside her like a case of indigestion. Why didn't she come sooner? But she stops this train mid-thought, catching herself before she rehashes all those familiar patterns of shame embedded into her skin like tattoo ink. She doesn't need to explain. She is the innocent in this twosome. Violet is the one who should be making excuses, proffering answers to the questions that have weighted Elsie down for the last twenty years like coffin lead; and now that she is before her, sane, with evocative eyes and a mouth like a slantwise crack in a cement wall, Elsie has some things she wants to know. But how to draw her out? She begins politely:

"How are you?"

"Are you eating well?"

"Have you been feeling better?"

Violet scribbles her responses onto the notepad, each in their turn—*Good. Almost. Yes, definitely*—wielding her ball-point pen like an extra, dexterous finger. She is so skilled, in fact, that Elsie sees the understatement of her former message, *I am working on it*; she is indeed well on the road to recovery.

"That's great," says Elsie, searching for something else to say. Instead Violet scribbles her own message.

I'm sorry.

Elsie stiffens. "For what?"

For leaving. Your mother, your father, you.

Elsie digs her fingers into the chair. She doesn't want to talk about this, not yet. "My parents weren't the easiest people to get along with."

They were human.

"Yes."

So are we.

"I hope so," says Elsie, catching herself in a laugh. She doesn't feel like laughing, but Violet always did have that effect: making her smile. Back then. Now she finds her grandmother unnerving. In her wildest dreams she did not expect Violet to understand what she was saying, let alone relent so easily over a past that obviously, at some point, offended her to no end. But she needs more. "Why did you stop talking to them?"

Violet's face slackens and for an instant Elsie can see the pale line of the stroke traced down the middle of her nose, chin, and forehead like the edge of a clown's half-mask. She must have been matching the left side to the misbehaving right by maintaining extreme control of her muscles; now that her guard is down, one side of her face looks like a cunningly rendered *trompe l'oeil*. She inhales deeply, sighs, then writes a response: *Because I was wrong.*

"But something happened," Elsie continues, wanting more than an admission of guilt, wanting justification, or at least to understand. Her father died before she had the chance to clarify things; Violet is her only hope. "You left us and didn't come back even when Mother died, even when Dad wanted you to but was too stubborn to say so. I know that was you on the phone. You had a fight. I was there. I remember." She stares at her grandmother whose face quivers in the afternoon light. "What was it about?"

Violet turns her head and gazes fixedly out the window. Elsie can't tell if she is looking at the landscape, or at her own reflection, but after a moment she returns to the steno pad. *My mistakes.*

"Did this have something to do with Uncle Russell?"

Until now Elsie had no intention of asking such a question, had no recollection, in fact, that such a thing was an issue; but seeing Violet has brought back her mother's voice—*The wages of sin is death*—and several other clues that must have been stored up in her subconscious. A photograph. A bowl of mashed potatoes. The strange idea that Violet had, somewhere along the line, copulated with the devil. "It was something about his father wasn't it?" she says, persisting. "He wasn't your husband."

Violet returns to her notepad, and after some deliberation, scrawls the words, *He had red hair,* in battered script. Then she starts to cry.

Elsie is disturbed by the tears: what kind of person doesn't allow an old woman her privacy? Still, she's glad to know there is some truth to her memories; she mustn't have been totally deranged as a child after all. Hobert, her grandfather, was a definite crowtop.

"So the fighting, the silence, all about a bastard in the family. I can't believe it. All those years." Elsie sighs. "We're all nuts."

Violet flinches at the word *bastard,* then suggests: *We should have seen counsellors.*

"That doesn't help," says Elsie. "I've tried."

She looks at her grandmother's hands, two blanched turkey necks, one lying dissolutely against her thigh, the other pinched into a tight fist. Then she looks at her own: pink, the long fingers segmented by pronounced joints, the toothpick tendons couching beneath skin like sticks under water. She moves one of them forward to grasp Violet's in a gesture that originates from somewhere outside her body. Violet looks up at the touch, her tears snagged on wrinkles. Her mouth forms a circle. "Good," she says.

Elsie nods and smiles, holding on. She doesn't need to know what her grandmother means right away. She can see there will be time enough for discussion.

On the way out, Elsie is stopped in the lobby by a woman wearing a cotton suit. Her chin-length hair accents the monopoly that her enormous mouth has over the lower half of her face: a dictatorship of the oral, with lips and teeth made for a polar bear.

"Excuse me," she says, "Are you Elsie Leggett?"

"Yes," says Elsie.

"Oh Good. Your name was given to us by Mrs. Leggett's son, Lawrence. He said you were the new contact. I'm Claire, the supervisor."

"Hello," says Elsie. *The new contact?*

"Violet, you see, is making excellent progress, better than we could have hoped for in fact. We're all quite astonished, but she's very determined, and we think if all goes well, she will have recovered sufficiently in another few months."

"Sufficiently?" says Elsie.

"Of course," Claire continues, "she will never be as good as new, she is eighty-six, but with home care twice a week, and with someone helping her along, perhaps a volunteer from the Heart and Stroke Foundation, she should be able to function."

Elsie looks blankly at the supervisor's heart-shaped face, tracing the outline of her nose which juts out like a funnel from her cheekbones. Apparently she is missing something.

"What I'm saying is that she will be able to go home if there is someone who will sign the papers. Mr. Leggett said that someone is you."

Now Elsie understands. Uncle Lawrence has passed the buck. "Shouldn't that be Violet's decision?"

"In these cases," says Claire sweetly, "we like to work with the family to make sure they agree. She might not be completely independent for some time. There will be a considerable amount of responsibility on the relatives."

"Responsibility?" says Elsie. She feels like an echo.

"Yes," says Claire. "She may be able to live alone eventually, she is very tenacious, but she will need companionship, contact; she will need to be checked in on more often than we can provide." She pauses and looks at Elsie as if examining her ability to perform such duties. "Of course," she says, "you will need some time to think about it. That's why I wanted to let you know as soon as possible."

"Thank you," says Elsie, turning to leave, plagued by a thousand thoughts at once. Violet? Come home? What about her piano lessons, just nicely established? Her rearrangement of the living-room furniture? What about her solitude, her personal space—she needs it to heal. She knows the house is Violet's property, the product of decades of marriage to a porthole manufacturer, but she can't help feeling possessive; after all, she is the executor. She can't just up and leave after accepting money from a roster of pupils; and at this moment, she doesn't have anywhere else to go.

The walk home is placid: the sun is peeking out over the west, over Vancouver Island and the fiery, luminescent sea that looks like liquid silver heated to boiling and poured, red hot, over a spangled glacier. Beneath the bridge, ships wait in Burrard Inlet, casting their murky shadows onto the waves, lurking like U-boats in the harbour. Elsie watches as children run along the sidewalk in their school uniforms, wishing she could be ten years old again, but perhaps, in a different family. Instead of waiting for the bus, she takes a shortcut through Mahon Park, skirts along Fourteenth Street to Chesterfield, and down to her grandmother's house.

Inside, the piano sits presumptuously in the living room, a piece of furniture not easily disguised by trailing plants or knick-knacks. Traces of Elsie linger boldly in the kitchen, her half-hearted attempt at cleaning up after dinner, in addition to the pile of dirt nudged into the corner in the absence of a dustpan. What has she been thinking? Violet is not senile, not ill, she is just partially set back. She will want to come home in several months and resume her life, her habits, and Elsie is no nurse, not even a nurse-maid. She does know how to cook, that's a plus, but modern, spicy food with names like pad thai or pakoras. Somehow she doesn't think Violet would go for that kind of ethnicity. She might think Elsie was trying to do her in by slow poisoning.

In the middle of her ruminations, the phone rings. "Hello," says Elsie.

"Elsie," the voice says. "It's Tia. I'm having a dinner party tonight, and I want you to come. Sorry about the short notice, but you don't have an answering machine."

Elsie looks at her watch. Five-thirty, and she hasn't even fed the cat. "I really have some things to figure out Tia, I don't think—"

"Oh Elsie," Tia says, exasperated. "You said yourself that you never get out. Here's your chance. It's an engagement party for me and Jeff, so you have to come; I didn't say so right off because I didn't want you to bring any gifts. We have been living together for two years already. We have everything we need. Except you."

Engagement, Elsie thinks. How old is Tia? Twenty-five? Just a baby. "O.K.," she sighs. "But it will take me a while to get ready."

"That's fine, as long as you get here."

Elsie hangs up the phone. Two years of living together and already Tia and Jeff are getting married. Married! For some reason she finds the idea incredible. How could they be so sure? Two years is nothing: a mote, a dust-speck of time. Either they are overly optimistic, she thinks, considering the recent divorce statistics, or she and Daniel were out to lunch for seven years.

30

"Ers," says Violet, still half asleep. Sunlight filters in through her bedroom window, piercing her eyes like peppered daggers. One of the nurses forgot to draw the blinds again, which is perhaps a good thing: they are the plastic PVC kind with the toxic particulate that will shrink your testicles if you are a man; if you are a woman they have the potential to make you infertile, or some other sinister effect that Violet has heard about on the ten o'clock news, not that she is overly concerned with her reproductive organs—they have been dormant for quite some time. She does worry about her granddaughters, however—Elsie and Tia—in the midst of their child-bearing years. What kind of children will they produce, if they produce any at all? Boys with two-inch penises? Girls with premature breasts and ovaries shrivelled like the skin of old fruit? She makes a mental note to stop watching these kinds of reports even though she sus-pects they are important. They make her slightly para-noid. Every time she turns on the television there seems to be some signal of the end of the world; and with her luck, she will still be around to see it.

"Yers," she tries again, arching her upper lip. She is determined to be able to speak articulately by the end of the week, even if all she can manage is monosyllables. She has already had enough of the steno pad, and of the tiresome charades; both are wearing thin like old cloth. Using her voice again will be a challenge, because she does not want to sound tremulous and frog-like; the Avondale staff might think she has gone off her rocker, fancying herself an opera singer or a retired thespian, randomly croaking off notable soliloquies for the purposes of nostalgia. No, she must continue to practice in private if she wants to be taken seriously. A rest home is bad enough; she does not want to be whisked off to a mental institution.

The door opens and in comes the blonde-haired nurse. She looks at the bare window gleaming in its nakedness like the bright side of the moon and makes an overt 'tsking' noise. "Good morning Mrs. Leggett," she says. "I can see you are awake. Just making the rounds. How are you feeling today?"

Violet holds up her hand in a gesture of *Fine, thank you*, and nods her head.

"Good," says the nurse who is used to Violet's hand signals. "I wouldn't be surprised if you had a visitor today. Your granddaughter phoned this morning to ask about visiting hours. She said that she would be stopping by."

Violet considers this piece of information. Her first reaction: *It's about time.* But then she scolds herself. Let's not be uncharitable, or ungrateful. Children can smell those sentiments a mile away. Perhaps grandchildren are also equipped with built-in sensors. She does not want to scare off her first visitor in six weeks, especially if that visitor is Elsie or Tia. (She wonders which one.) This is good news. Stupendous. Exactly what she has been waiting for. She will do her best to appear gracious and appreciative, because when she gets right down to things, that is how she feels. *Thank you, oh thank you.*

"Which one would you like today?" says the nurse holding two of Violet's blouses up in the air, a sultry blue jacquard or banana yellow button-up covered in daffodils. Violet likes the way this nurse always gives her a choice then lets her fumble through the proceedings at her own pace. Some of the fustier ones try to dress her like a doll.

She points nonchalantly to one of the chairs where she has laid out her preferred outfit in a trim puddle of silk and rayon, and raises her eyebrows at the nurse. Must keep on top of things.

"Oh," says the nurse, surprised. "You are ahead of me today, and very organized."

Violet nods to be polite. So much nodding; she hopes her head will stay attached to her neck.

Together they remove her nightgown, Violet raising her arms to be disrobed, and the nurse sliding the garment over her head and shoulders. Then Violet sits while the nurse slips on her brassiere and camisole, fastening the snaps and hooks that are unmanageable at the best of times. When they come to the outer layers, Violet holds up her hand.

"You can do the rest?" says the nurse.

Yes.

"Mrs. Leggett, that's wonderful. I will leave you to it, but you must ring if you are having trouble. There's nothing wrong with a little assistance."

Of course not.

"We'll see you at breakfast then."

Today's blouse is cream on brick red, with vertical stripes separated into Navajo style triangles. Violet spreads it out on her lap, taking one sleeve in her hand, then tosses the right side over her shoulder and down the length of her arm. Now the hard part: getting the left side around her back and into its proper position. No easy trial when her good hand is immobilized within the rayon sheath of the material, but she completes the task with as little indignant grunting as possible, and sets out to fasten the buttons.

When she is fully dressed she hobbles into the shared bathroom and puts on her face: eyeliner on the brows, lipstick, a little rouge, face powder. There are some hairs on her chin which Violet plucks using a pair of tweezers, wishing she could transplant them to her bereft eyebrows; there are also what appear to be a few new wrinkles, although she stopped counting some years ago after the cataract surgery and refuses to acknowledge the possibility that her cheeks could get any slacker. She plunges a comb into the rat's nest on top of her head, and pulls down hard, wondering if she should get another permanent. The last one was tight and ridiculous—bestowed by an in-house hairdresser who clacked her gums and pierced Violet's scalp with bobby pins—but she isn't yet capable of setting her hair in rollers so she might just have to succumb. She would rather look like a laminated cauliflower than a head of wilted lettuce, although when she puts it that way, neither one seems overly desirable.

If she were in her own house she would have taken a bath before getting dressed, but she knows better than to attempt this alone, even in the Avondale. Taking baths has always been contentious for Violet. When she and Grace were in their late sixties, one of their acquaintances died in the tub and wasn't found for four days. There were stories of blue toes from the building superintendent, and of the body, waterlogged and peaked as a salted snail. Then there were the comments:

She was always such a private person.

She would have been so humiliated.

Did you get a look at the bathtub ring? Grime as black as your hat.

After the incident Grace and Violet made a pact: they would not let each other perish in such a disgraceful and mortifying manner. The first thing they did was clean the enamel surfaces in their bathrooms down to their alabaster foundations using scrub brushes and caustic glow-in-the-dark toilet products to illuminate the stain and lift off the rust spots. The second and more important thing was to form a schedule. A washing schedule. Whenever one of them wanted to take a bath she phoned the other to let her know. *I'm ready. O.K. dear, call me again.* When she was finished, she phoned back. *Everything fine? Yes, just dandy. All done.* This arrangement confirmed that things were as they should be—safe, normal, breathing regularly—and it went on for almost twenty years.

When Grace went into the Avondale, Violet was left to her own devices and resorted to leaving the phone off the hook. Her strategy was this: if anything happened to her someone would call and notice that something was amiss when the line remained busy for hours on end. This strategy was only feasible, however, if someone was trying to call her, an event that had not occurred with startling frequency in the past few years. Most of her calls were placed by public librarians reminding her of impending book due-dates, or by deep-throated telemarketers hoping to con her into a demonstration for vacuum cleaners. If those people received busy signals, they would probably just pay the extra fifty cents to BC Tel and put her on automatic redial. Still, her choices were limited.

Getting the cat was a similar measure of precaution. She didn't consciously seek him out—he chose her by showing up on the landing at sunset and demanding in his considerate but pressing way to be fed—but she did adopt him immediately when she saw how companionable he could be. She liked his red coat (they would have been a matching set a few years previous) and named him accordingly, with a slight feeling of release. How wonderful it was to have company again, and what was more, to be depended on! She needed that kind of tethering, especially after years of being a mother. Without anyone depending on her whereabouts, she might have ended up rummaging through dumpsters in search of her lost children, murmuring to passersby about the end of the world. She might have ended up prowling through strip-mall corridors, handing out her money to strangers on the street. The cat was her anchor; *is* her anchor. She must learn to stop thinking in the past tense.

Breakfast is a poached egg on an open-faced English

muffin served next to an underripe piece of cantaloupe with All Bran on the side. Violet eats cautiously, taking care not to dribble any of the yolk onto her chin or down the front of her clothes like an infant. Now that there is the possibility of a visitor she must pay extra attention to her appearance. There is nothing worse than having a conversation with someone who is lacquered with the remains of their morning meal, especially when that meal involves Hollandaise sauce.

The supervisor is in the dining room making the rounds with her clipboard, leaning over everyone's tables so her cleavage is visible. Whatever happened to modesty? Violet wonders. Out the window along with girdles and cloche hats.

"Good morning Mrs. Plotkin, Mrs. Troy. Good morning Mrs. Leggett," says the supervisor. "I see you are all looking well."

Such formality—*Mrs. Leggett*. Violet would like to hear her first name for a change, but she supposes that the supervisor and the rest of the Avondale staff put her in the same class as school teachers and turn-of-the-century grandmothers with wandering eyes and sourdough buns: elderly, conventional. A group that clings to the remains of their dignity through surnames that once— depending on the person—afforded some measure of respect or approbation to the woman that flaunted them. Why cling, Violet wants to know, when the rest of the time we all sit on the same pot?

She swallows her mouthful of muffin so that she can smile properly, and feels the hand of the supervisor on her shoulder. "You are looking spry today Mrs. Leggett," she says. "It must be all this nice weather."

Spry, Violet thinks, like a horse. *Hardly*. If only she could be spry, she would show them a thing or two about dancing on Saturday nights. (She watched them once, at the Christmas Ball, wheeling herself down to the lounge and concealing her chair behind a potbound, arborescent fern.) The way they do it now is laughable, their stiff-bodies hunched over at the neck and shoulders, dowager's humps protruding out like misplaced, oversized bunions, stockings drooping, pant legs dragging on tiles. The women dance with other women because at this age, men are a rare commodity; the ones that remain are obese, with bellies that perch on top of their belts like outsized whoopee cushions, or they are painfully slow, forgetting that they are the ones who are supposed to lead. *Who me?* they say, pointing to their pumped up chests, their faces wrought with looks of dismay.

Violet puts down her fork and glances up at the supervisor. Her hair is piled on top of her head like an unstoppable mound of candy floss, teased and molded into a sort of golden camel's hump. Despite her feelings on ostentatious hairdos, Violet would like to be able to make the supervisor stay put, just for a few minutes, so that she can enjoy her overeager grin. She supposes she likes the supervisor, or Claire, as she is called by the staff, because she is one of the few people that is bold enough to touch the residents. A hand on the shoulder. An arm around the back. Her touches are not just obligatory boosts to steady an uneven foot or keep a hip from cracking against a wall, they are gestures of kindness offered automatically to everyone because they are human. She supposes that the supervisor comes from a different generation than the nurses who are young and distant, who are more like doctors, ultimately blaming the patient for their idiocy, their culpability, for letting disease and ageing drag them down and turn them into drooling lunatics. The supervisor must have grown up with gushing parents who squeezed her like a lemon whenever she did something positive. She seems used to that kind of physical contact. Violet herself has never been one to dole out hugs and kisses. She had a family of boys for Pete's sake, and didn't want to turn out a crop of delicate butterflies.

Now, however, she can see the advantages of being affectionate. She has witnessed some of the dourer residents being transformed by the pink arms of grandchildren, their faces weepy and rapt, their mouths crimped into doughy grins; she imagines that they started this pattern of tenderness by being tender with their own children, and she would like to ask them, how did they know? Did they realize it would come back to them? She would like share the experience, but in her case it is too late. Once you reach a certain age wanting anything seems unreasonable, especially compassion, especially empathy. When Lawrence visited she could tell by his stance, his aloof, touch-me-not posture as rigid and dry as a stick, that he would not be moved, no matter how sentimental she became: *You had your chance,* he seemed to say from across the room in the armchair, *your turn is over. Now me.* She doesn't begrudge him this choice, this cold way of dealing in emotions as though they were a deck of cards; she can handle all that. She has had enough practice. What she really needs is someone to listen when she figures out what she wants to say. What she really wants is forgiveness.

Forgiveness because look at the mess she has managed to make of things, of her roles—daughter, mother and wife—none of which she auditioned for and all of which she fouled up by failing to rehearse. If only she'd had the foresight to practice, she thinks, she might have been better off. She might have been prepared. Instead she was selfish, with interests that seemed harmless enough at the time, but in retrospect were clearly the work of an amateur.

She knows now that Russell was a love child; that is what they would call him today. A child conceived out of pure love, or in Violet's case, confusion and adolescent fumbling. She loved him deeply when he was alive—all of his sixteen years—and she loves him now more than ever, which is hardly fair considering she is the one left behind. She also loved Clifford and Lawrence. She just had to warm up to them for some reason, they were such angry babies with ferocious heads covered in the soot-black hair of chimney sweeps that promptly fell out after birth. Their faces were pouty and wrinkled, and both of them demanded her attention by yanking on her skirts while she was trying to make pastry instead of launching their own fearless expeditions the way Russell did at the same age. So much about them was different, of course, because they were only half brothers, but something about her was different too: no matter how earnest her attempts to treat her sons alike, she always felt a nagging furor inside when she looked at Russell, as if he was somehow more a part of her than the others. On more than one occasion she has thought about Marian's accusation—*the wages of sin is death*—and cried herself to sleep.

When Elsie arrives Violet is sitting in one of the bedroom chairs with her cane placed conveniently against her leg. She is wearing a pair of hand-knit slippers that she bought at the Avondale's Christmas craft sale for fifty cents, and a relatively fresh coat of lipstick. Elsie's knock is a soft rap that Violet almost misses, having recently dozed off while trying to maintain her air of collected indifference. She straightens her back with a start, and reminds herself to keep her mouth closed until the appropriate moment.

On first glance she can't believe the woman in the doorway is Elsie—she must be six feet tall, with arms as long as pitchforks and a set of shoulders built like a rack for displaying evening gowns; but after closer inspection, she sees a resemblance to Clifford, and a silent, almost understated beauty. Her granddaughter is pleasant to look at. There is something stunning about her mouth, which is large and nervously set, although a little too low at the edges for Violet's liking, giving her the air of a depressed mime. She is wearing cords—a mistake thinks Violet, because of her height—which are neatly pressed and cinched at the top with a leather belt. Her hair has lightened considerably, taking her a shade closer to red, which could be the result of streaking or tinting, but is perhaps just from being out in the sun. Violet wonders, despite herself, what would Marian think of that colour?

"Hello," she says, moving forward. "It's Elsie, Violet, Clifford's daughter."

Violet doesn't know what to make of this. Of course she knows who Elsie is; she had a stroke, she does not have Alzheimer's. She nods, indicating what she hopes is understanding, and offers a short, controlled smile. Something about Elsie's eyes send shivers down her spine. Is that a trace of Marian she can see in there, behind the cross-hatchings of the iris and the powdery gilded flecks that look to Violet like gold dust spattered across a pane of glass? A trace of Marian's brooding reticence which appears contained but is in essence highly volatile? If so, Violet doesn't want to acknowledge the possibility; she has had enough damning for one lifetime. Enough grudges. She would like to get on with things. She hopes that she will have the opportunity.

Elsie sits with her hands on her knees and talks about the weather. Violet prefers this arrangement; she doesn't feel like such a shrimp when their bums are on the same level. She decides to take a chance and try out her voice. "Yes," she says, swathing her mouth around the sound, caressing it like a truffle. What a pleasure, and also a scare, to speak aloud to someone else! To communicate using her vocal chords! She is still a bit rough, there is a coarse edge to her tone, but she got the pronunciation right and that is the main thing. The best part, though, is the way Elsie's eyes have widened, opened up like a pair of Madonna lilies in full bloom. *She is shocked*, Violet remarks to herself with satisfaction. *She didn't expect me to be doing so well.* She takes out her steno pad and writes Elsie a message explaining why "yes" is all she can say, for now. She does not want her thinking she will be this way forever.

"The house is fine," says Elsie in response. Violet is relieved to hear that she cleaned off the roof, although she refrains from asking how she did it. (Where would she get hold of a shovel?) She had been a little worried about the rafters after seeing those pictures on the news, but now she sees that things were in relatively good hands. Relatively, because look at the bags under Elsie's eyes: she looks toilworn, wrung out. The lines of her eyelids are echoed by a series of intense ripples that divide and pleat her face like the crinkled edge of a paper bag. She must have too much on her plate; either that, or insomnia. Violet does not want to drive her away by putting too much responsibility on her shoulders. She would like to show her gratitude, but she would also like to get on with things? She writes the message *I'm sorry* and holds it in the air.

Elsie smiles a smile that Violet recognizes, a smile of guilt. A wash of tubercular white passes over the pallor of her skin where it stops at the hairline and breaks into a cold sweat. Violet has seen that look on her own children's faces and wants to know, where do they learn it?

But Elsie continues, giving Violet time to demonstrate how adeptly she has learned to write. If only she could have been half as keen in grade school, she might not have felt the recurring sting of Miss Whiteley's ruler across her knuckles. *Oh well,* she sighs. *Better late than never.*

As she writes Violet can see Elsie tensing up, pinching her hands into fists the way she did when she was a little girl. *A little girl.* How incredible that this woman was ever little! She watches her sideways out of her peripheral vision, thanking her lucky stars for twenty-twenty surveillance and the development of advanced cataract surgery. If this meeting had taken place several years ago, Elsie would be nothing but a strapping blur.

"Why did you stop talking to my parents?" says Elsie.

Resolve goes out of Violet: she is being confronted, now, at long last, and she can't seem to get her thoughts together. Poor Russell, poor Clifford, poor Lawrence; poor Jack and Lila and Hobert and Grace, each of whom deserved better treatment from a younger Violet who knew about loving and could have done right if it weren't for the damn mesh of confusion and embarrassment that crippled her like a war wound. She should have supported Clifford when Marian died, or sooner, if she had any scruples. She should have forgiven him, because who else is left when children fall away into the jaws of history and you are left by yourself, dogged and unhesitating yes, but uncompromisingly alone? Who else indeed?

Elsie it appears, in Violet's case, is left; and for now she will do nicely.

Because I was wrong, she scribbles on her steno pad.

"But," Elsie continues, wanting more; and Violet doesn't blame her. She owes Elsie; she can tell by the pleading in her knitted eyebrows that she has been told nothing by anyone else.

"Did this have something to do with Uncle Russell," says Elsie. "The fact that his father wasn't Granddad?"

Violet loses control of her face, of her body; she feels winded, inert. Of course Elsie has a right to know this information. The reality of the illusive red-haired man cost her several things in her lifetime, one of which was certainly a relationship with her grandmother. Another may have been a cohesive family unit, although with Marian and Clifford that last one was probably never a real possibility. *Look*, she wants to say but can't, *I made a promise never to tell, never to say his name in relation to myself and Russell. I can't just break that prom-*

ise. I won't. But the promise to Jack—now gone and buried—was mainly not to mention his name. *His* name. The red-haired man: his fingers, his thumbs. His slick feet tapping and swooping like a sandpiper trailing the edge of the surf. Why is he so clear in her memory, when other, dearer, more important people have faded imperceptibly into the past? The way of history, she thinks, a cruel, bewitching trickster until the end.

He had red hair, is what she comes up with, which is an obvious enough admission, and she hopes, relatively decisive; harmless, she thinks, and as painless as a root canal. True, she could have told her about the cat, giving her a clue that way (her imagination was slim when it came to naming pets, and he does have such a lovely saffron coat), but that would be too close to telling. Too close. Elsie will have to make the connection by herself, if she can; and if she can't, there will be no love lost. Names aren't what matters, in the end. It's the faces attached to them that are important.

She feels a warm hand on one of her own, and suddenly she notices she is crying. This breaking down in public is happening far too often for her liking; she will have to learn to control herself, but right now she can't be bothered. Tears spill onto her cheeks. She has no excuse, really; she is just tired. Relieved. She even lets herself smile freely, allowing her mouth to find its own new parameters, however loose, and croaks out a message. *Good.* Somehow more things are possible than she thought this morning. There are more possible endings. Now she will just have to wait and see what they are, because she can't always be in control.

After Elsie leaves, Violet decides to take a walk to the social lounge. She does this by leaning on her cane, her good hand the fulcrum for her careening body, and waddling forward with her weight on her knees. She isn't so bad that she has to hide in the closet; she can do this after all, even if she does look slightly jacklegged. The spotted tiles lining the hallway pass beneath her feet like river stones covered in some brown primordial algae, and Violet shuffles across their facades, cautiously, deliberately, until she is tired enough to sit down. She chooses a chair in the picture window about twenty feet from her doorway, and relaxes her legs with a sigh. At this rate she will be dancing again by age one hundred, that is if she can still remember how to put on her shoes. Horseshoe Bay here she comes.

The windows at the Avondale are all rectangular pieces of smoked glass that look as if they belong in a cathedral, long and slender, lofty and dirt-specked, with surfaces like oiled puddles that are supposed to deflect the sun and keep out peeping toms. Violet can't imagine what sort of pervert would get his thrills by sneaking glimpses of the octogenarian residents in the throes of having their backsides swabbed, or the skin grazed off the bottoms of their feet by the visiting orthopedist and his slab of pumice; such a person would have to be truly sick, a psychology student perhaps, conducting research; either that or someone severely hard up for entertainment. Movies aren't cheap these days, almost ten dollars, and she supposes many people can't afford the price. She does appreciate the windows, however, because their one-way stratum gives her the opportunity to look out onto the

Avondale grounds and watch the surrounding landscape and the people it contains without being seen by anyone.

Today she is facing Grouse Mountain, where people in turtlenecks ski the well-iced peaks. She can also see the Lion's Gate bridge, swollen with cars, and the circular apex of the big 'Q' revolving on top of the Lonsdale Quay where the shipyard docks used to stand. She can see the yellow haze of downtown Vancouver clinging to the buildings like the sour ring of a chain-smoker. If she cranes her neck she can also make out the flat slate roof of the Lonsdale school, and down the hill several blocks, her house (although she has to imagine that part because she is not built of rubber bands). Inside this house Elsie is using *her* kitchen sink; she is washing *her* dishes using *her* dishcloths, and cooking her food using *her* stainless steel pots. She is probably even taking baths in *her* bathtub, because sooner or later everyone has to get clean.

Violet wonders what Elsie thinks of her interior decorating, something she was never very good at but which she attempted for the sake of the boys, because neighbours talk and she would not have them living in a pigsty. She wonders what her granddaughter will make of the basement, of the rubble matterhorn that she piled in the centre, around the furnace, to impede the burglars should they return with a crowbar and pry open the bars on the windows. She developed a number of clever strategies after the first break-in—when the police told her that the pattern was to strike twice and clean out the replacement items funded by house insurance—storing her gold watch from Clifford in the refrigerator crisper,

[393]

and individually freezing her earrings in ice cube trays like joke store party favours. After she put one in her drink, however, and had to hotfoot it to the emergency ward, she settled on the flour jar for the earrings and has stuck to it ever since.

The thought of living alone again makes Violet shiver. One advantage to the Avondale (she hates to admit) is the company, albeit too much of it, but enough so that she no longer has to huddle under the covers listening for the sounds of lock-picking and shattered glass and girded leather boots with the pointed, hackled toes that can puncture an abdomen with one kick. At the very least she is protected here, in this corral of muttering, gesticulating individuals with hairdos like silver shower caps and the smell of lavender talc mixed with milk of magnesia; she is safe. But safe from what? From the world outside? From herself? Sometimes she gets so fed up with the type of existence where the biggest, most anticipated event on everyone's minds is death, their own death, that she would rather take her chances with the outside world, with the switchblades, the brass knuckles, the arsenic, the meat mallets, the cleavers, the chains, the baseball bats, the bricks, the drive-by-shootings, living a little in the meantime. No matter how frightened she might become, these moments are hers; they are precious and she does not want to see them wasted. She has wasted so much already.

Of course she can't have everything she wants, she is beginning to see this; she is also beginning to see that what she wants isn't always good for her, not in the long run. In that case, all she can do is make the best of things, take one day at a time, enjoy the sunrise; and have a little faith. *Have faith* was something Lila used to say to Violet when she was feeling the harshness of the world. The obliqueness of the statement used to anger her, cause her face to go red, but now she thinks perhaps it is as simple as that. *Have faith*. Simple and not so simple.

This time, however, she may need more than faith. She may need action. She retrieves her steno pad from her pocket and pens herself a list. Things she will do as soon as she is able: *phone Tia, phone Elsie, invite Lawrence and Alexandra to the house for a holiday.* And when she has them all in one place: *bake a huckleberry pie for dinner.*

31

Tia's apartment is small but exquisite, a ground floor suite in Kitsilano with ivy growing up the outside walls. When she enters, Elsie can tell Tia reads *Architectural Digest*, either that or *House Beautiful*; the rooms are sparsely furnished with wiry Halogen lamps, bird-like in their curves and swoons; Japanese globes covered in opaque rice paper hang from the ceiling like luscious, phosphorescent fruit; grey woven mats cloak the hard-wood; a wall-to-wall stereo, jet black, and an impressive collection of CDs claim space beneath a far window. The entire apartment is painted mango orange, save the white enamel ceiling and fluted moldings that gleam in the obscurity like glow-in-the-dark bed sheets. Against this slate, reproductions of famous abstract works of art Elsie recognizes from Daniel's textbooks are hung in gilded frames. The effect is of a Zen monastery gone hip, or of the inside of a piece of cheese, warm, sensuous, and slightly high, covered in the geometric scribblings of artistic rodents.

Elsie takes off her shoes, clutching a six-pack of beer. She wanted to bring something to drink at the very least, and settled on a local micro-brewery after hedging for twenty minutes in the liquor store. She figured Daniel would approve her choice—the ale is darker than a double espresso.

For her outfit she chose something safe: a black velvet top with a sheer over-blouse, and a pair of jeans verging on snug. Ever since university, black has been her idea of a neutral colour, slyly chic with a diplomatic but ingratiating edge. Wearing black meant blending in like a shadow, like a carpenter ant in a pool of tar. As far as Elsie could tell, no one ever got admonished in fashion magazines for wearing too much black, unless, of course, they were attending a wedding. She does wish, however, that she had paid more attention to her hair. By the look of things, back-combing is in, and here she is looking like a festively shellacked walnut.

"Elsie," says Tia, sliding through the bodies. Already people are milling about, laughing, shouting, clutching glasses of various liquids to their chests. The apartment is filled to capacity, which is no more than twenty-five or so, Elsie surmises. Most of the guests are well dressed, suits, ties, one or two flamboyant neon skirts or a silver waistcoat; there is even a woman in knee-high elevator boots which Elsie thinks must be the ultimate in sacrificing comfort for fashion. They look like highly inflexible skyscrapers.

"You must meet some people," says Tia, grabbing hold of Elsie's wrist and hauling her through the din. "Jeff is over in the corner."

Elsie had expected a younger crowd considering Tia's

age, but as they weave their way among torsos she can see there is a healthy mix, even a few bald spots and grey hairs. That's me in a few years, Elsie thinks. The grey hairs, not the bald spots. God willing.

Tia makes a round of introductions—Jeff, Mark, Tony, Sylvia—and springs off again to pounce on another newcomer struggling to get in the door. Through shouted conversation Elsie meets Jeff's boss, a lawyer from downtown Vancouver; she also meets his sisters, Sylvia and Eunice, as well as some of their friends from university, a gourmet chef, a computer programmer, a freelance writer for the *Vancouver Sun*. She drinks her beer directly from the bottle, talking to strange women in tight skirts and men in argyle socks.

Along with the writer and the computer programmer, she stands against one of the mango walls in a group of five or six and participates in a conversation about the end of the west coast fishery. Although she knows less about the state of salmon in British Columbia than she does about socializing, she can see by her companions' morose expressions that things do not look good. There isn't much time, they say, shaking their heads. Just look at the creeks. Full of silt, not to mention all those nitrates.

Elsie finishes off her first beer and starts on a second, offering a bottle to the man next to her clothed urbanely in a hound's tooth dress shirt. The conversation shifts to lighter topics: a new restaurant, films. The man on Elsie's right tells a story about visiting Mexico and getting stung by an eel; when he tried to get help from the locals in broken Spanish—*Donde esta l'hopitale?*—one of the men unzipped his fly and urinated on his foot. "A surefire cure for the sting, apparently," says the man shrugging his shoulders. "But at the time I thought I had landed on the planet of the apes." Everyone laughs, including Elsie. She is surprisingly relaxed; surprisingly, because she doesn't know a soul and already she is feeling more or less comfortable, despite the decisions she will inevitably have to make regarding Violet, one way or another. It must be the apartment, she thinks; the colour of the walls. Don't they use colours like that to calm you down, in spas, in lunatic asylums? Colours to soothe the nerves. Or maybe it's the people, friendly, sincere. She can't remember the last time she felt at ease in a crowd of strangers.

Tia reappears with her make-up smudged and pushes a glass of wine into Elsie's free hand. "Here my dear. You seem to be having a good time."

Elsie nods. "Yes, I like your friends."

"Me too," says Tia. "They're fabulous, although I did just meet a few of them tonight. Colleagues of Jeff's. Very handsome. Perhaps I could fix you up with one of the more eligible ones. I seem to know how to pick them."

Elsie winces at the brashness of this statement; she could probably use the help, that is, if she were looking; but she is not. Never again. "No thanks," she tells Tia, feigning jocularity. "I have enough on my plate. Violet and all."

"Oh yes," says Tia. "How is she? I've been meaning to get over there for a visit."

"Good," says Elsie. "Very good." Then adds, in a flash of insight: "How are you at doing laundry?"

By midnight she finds herself seated on the couch with something resembling a margarita in her right hand.

Three other women lounge beside her, slapping their knees and shrieking. Two of them are Jeff's sisters. She had been navigating her way to the bathroom after filling up on spinach dip and slices of pumpernickel bread, only to be intercepted by Sylvia and Eunice who told her fervently that they were her own age and hadn't she better sit down and fraternize? She was being too much of a hermit. Elsie went with them willingly, relieved at having someone else take control of her situation. She was starting to feel a little drunk.

"Here's a question," one of them says. "What's the worst thing a man has ever said to you? I mean the absolute stupidest, most ridiculous worst thing."

"There are too many to choose from," says another.

"I've got one," says the woman who Elsie thinks might be Eunice. She deepens her voice: "I'll try to be faithful, but if I get drunk, I'm not responsible for what might happen."

"Oh that is wretched, just wretched," says a woman who Elsie realizes has an English accent. She is wearing a long red skirt with Scottish pleats and matching slingback shoes.

"I've got one too, and this from a man I hardly knew!" says Sylvia, waving her arms in the air. "I can't get to sleep unless I can put my hand on your breast."

The women explode with laughter, tilting their heads back like wolves at the moon. "Can you imagine? What a nut."

"What a clown."

"What about you Elsie," says the woman with the English accent. "You must have some good ones too. Tia tells us you are an experienced individual."

Elsie thinks back, the past blurred by the conspicu-
ously missing beer bottles. She hates to disappoint: "Of
course you can support me," she says, imitating Daniel's whine of reason. "It's too hard for a white male to
get a job these days."

"That's brilliant," says the English woman. "Really
brilliant. He should use that one on the federal government. Maybe they will give him full benefits. Oh Elsie,"
she stops and stares. "I'm sorry, are you all right?"

Elsie puts down her margarita and wipes the tears
from her eyes. Smooth, very smooth. Up until now the
evening had been perfect.

"Darling," says Sylvia, leaning over and placing a
warm hand on Elsie's knee. "It's O.K. We understand."

"It's not that bad," Elsie snivels, struggling to scrape
up her dignity. How can she explain? She feels like a
traitor. "I'm just not used to making fun of him like this.
You see, he's the only one I've ever had. It feels, well,
sacrilegious."

"Don't you worry," says Eunice smiling emphatically.
"We were just poking fun. We know we're terrible. But
so are they. We're all human. Flawed to the bone. If you
can't laugh at human foibles, then what good are they?"

"Yes. You can learn from them. Learn what to watch
for."

Elsie smiles and dabs at her eyes with her sleeve. Sylvia
hands her a handkerchief. "But I was with him for seven
years," she says. "I guess I just haven't figured out what
to do with myself."

"Seven years!" says Sylvia. "I was married for eight.
That was a laugh. High-school wedding! But I don't hate
my ex. He taught me how to stick up for myself, before

he buggered off that is. You'd be surprised at how being walked all over can toughen up the old skin!"

"Yes," chimes the one with the accent. "Very true."

"But don't you feel like you have wasted your time?" Elsie says, eyebrows raised. She is not used to such flippancy, especially not concerning relationships. "That you could have been doing other things?"

"Not at all," says Sylvia. "We definitely had good times, and then, well, things changed. Such is life. In the end he did me a favour, sneaking off like that."

"Good riddance and so on."

"But Daniel wasn't that bad," says Elsie, appalled. "Things just got a little stale."

"Ah my dear," says Eunice. "The question is not whether he was bad, but was he good? Was he the right one?"

Elsie looks at her crumpled handkerchief, then up, at the faces encircling her like promising white eggs. "I don't know," she says meekly, snivelling back fresh tears. "That's the part I don't know at all."

When some of the crowd has started to thin, Elsie, consoled and coddled and feeling better, gets up to examine the framed reproductions on the wall behind the hors d'oeuvres. She takes her glass, almost drained, and presses to it her cheek like a powder puff. The coolness of its surface is relieving.

The image that catches her eye is what Daniel would have called *purposefully naive*; either that or primitive. It is a shot of an oil painting done in numerous colours, blues, reds, a slice of black, with a foreboding shadow left of centre looming like a sasquatch. Elsie eyes the shadow, feeling its weight.

"It's a nice painting," says a voice. "Do you know it?"

Elsie turns to see a man: dark cropped hair, skin like the sapwood of a maple tree. His hands are placed casually in the pockets of his black jeans. He wears a pair of steel-rimmed glasses, a crisp, white shirt.

"I thought I did," she says. "But maybe I just recognize the artist. Something about it seems familiar." She takes a step back and watches him move, quietly, like a lion, towards the picture.

"That," the man says, pointing to the shadow in the centre. "Is a demon, a monster." His face is expressionless as he speaks, silently unfurling. "He is under a spell."

"How can you tell?" says Elsie. She is always skeptical when it comes to interpreting abstract art. She has sat through too many critiques in which Daniel convinced his classmates that a blank piece of masonite was actually the manifestation of world angst, using words like *emptiness* and *abyss* and moving his lips around in a beseeching circle.

"I can feel it," the man says, smiling.

This is too close to the dialogue in a B-movie for Elsie to keep a straight face, especially after innumerable glasses of alcohol. She laughs, covering her mouth, and the man joins in grinning knavishly from sweet lips. "I also wrote a paper on the painting once," he says. "So I can sound ridiculous along with everyone else."

"What is it called?" says Elsie, gesturing to the image. She is curious about this person. Her skin bristles slightly with attraction.

"Dance You Monster to My Soft Song," he says, letting out a deep breath. He regards her seriously, but with avid softness. "Do you like the title?"

"Yes," says Elsie, permitting herself to slouch against the wall. Something about his voice makes her comfortable; too comfortable. She wants to curl up in the crook of his neck. She is losing momentum. "What does it mean?"

"We all have our demons," he says, looking at her from charcoal eyes. "But perhaps not as big as this." His hand goes to the demon in the picture and taps gently.

"Or perhaps bigger," says Elsie, putting her glass on the floor. From somewhere inside her a memory stirs, a memory from her past, from her childhood or beyond, of demons and fear and a stifling cellar, but she is too tired to pay attention. She slides down the wall, easing her feet out from underneath her body, bringing her arms to her sides like heated molasses, and sinks gloriously to the ground. The motion sends prickles of thanks up the runway of her spine. The relief of giving in, of giving up; of forgetting, for one moment, all the things that being Elsie involves. The man sits down beside her, quietly crossing his legs. She puts her head on his shoulder, and falls asleep.

32

The night is cold around her. She is in a cab, pre-paid by Tia who may turn out to be an ally after all. Elsie huddles down in the back seat, shivering in her sandals. She should have brought warmer clothes, but then again, she didn't expect to be staying until four in the morning. She must have dozed off after drinking too much, because she found herself curled up on the floor with a cushion tucked under her head. In her pocket was a note printed in neat letters across the back of a paper napkin—*Sweet dreams for fighting demons*—probably from the man with the dark eyes. She has a vague memory of talking to him about a painting, but what was this about fighting demons? She hopes she didn't make a fool of herself by telling him her life story; for some reason it is always drunk women that end up limp, crying into their glasses about their parents or their boyfriends, dishing out the woes of their last twenty years as a human being to anyone who will listen. Men, it seems, steer clear of such uncouth demonstrations, concentrating instead on challenging each other to arm wrestling competitions or getting into fights. Perhaps they don't have as much to confess, thinks Elsie, or perhaps they just have shorter memories. Still, it could be worse. She could have thrown up in the toilet.

The blond head of the cab driver hovers in front of her like a sheep dog in need of a haircut. "Excuse me," says Elsie, leaning forward. "I'd like to get out now."

"You paid all the way to Thirteenth Street," he says, somewhat annoyed.

"I know. But I want to walk the rest of the way. Can you please stop?"

The driver pulls over to the curb and lets Elsie out, complaining that she has thrown off his schedule. He will have to drive by her house anyway because he already called in the route to his dispatcher.

"Go ahead," says Elsie, motioning him on. "I'll be fine."

She stretches her arms above her head, hoping to increase blood circulation to her outer extremities and warm up her limbs. The walk uphill to Violet's house should get her heart beating a little faster, not to mention clear the fog in her head.

We all have our demons.

Elsie moves quickly, guiding her feet over the cracks in the sidewalk. The night is still. No one else is around. There are only a few lights on in the houses or apartment complexes lining the street, although Elsie does recognize the icebox glow of several television sets flickering on and off in the blackness.

As she walks she realizes that she feels comfortable in the neighbourhood. Not only that, she has come to depend on the mountains, the sky; the restless, churning ocean. Each one helps her orientate herself in the city, gives her direction. *North to Grouse. South to the Inlet.* Living in North Vancouver is not so bad after all. She can get used to the flowers, the plants, the yucca and palms and all those other Mediterranean creations that overzealous gardeners put in their front yards thinking they are Californians. She can even get used to the rain.

Marian would have hated the rain. Perhaps that is why she and Clifford ended up in Brimstock, far from the unpredictable tantrums of coastal weather, although she also detested the mud. There was a lot of mud in Brimstock, in the spring and again in the fall; too much of it ended up on the soles of Elsie's boots, and then, inevitably, on her mother's clean floor. Marian did like the snow, however, which fell in abundance on Brimstock streets. It covered up the miry, dying grass, the cesspools of mud and sludge that children wallowed in like pigs in rubber boots; it made everything crisp and white and shiny, like a winter postcard, and when there was fresh snow around, Elsie detected the slightest improvement in her mother's temperament. Perhaps, she thinks in retrospect, we would have been a happier family if we lived at the North Pole.

When she arrives at Eighth Street she is panting; breath goes in and out of her like the sighing of a see-saw. On the corner, shrouded in the dense fingers of some kind of deciduous shrubbery, Elsie sees a building with a steeple and bell tower rising up the front and ending in a sharp, but modestly proportioned spire. From the centre of the tower a light is cast out into the night. The light is the colour of the sea that Elsie has seen on posters for Mexican holidays displayed in the windows of travel agents, the kind where women recline topless on beaches, and men in Speedos or sackcloth pedal-pushers the colour of mayonnaise frolic in the intertidal zone. Blue-green. Aquamarine. The colour is decidedly familiar.

As she moves closer Elsie realizes the building is a church. *St. Edmund's Catholic Church*, says a sign next to the main doors. She also realizes the light is coming from a stained-glass window that depicts the Ascension of the Virgin into heaven.

You've got to look your demons in the face.

The doors are not open, she didn't expect them to be. Things get stolen these days: chalices, crosses, incense burners. White tasselled tablecloths ironed to consummate smoothness. Not everyone is superstitious. She imagines a pair of brass candlesticks like the ones that stood on the altar at the Church of Our Lady fetch a good price on the black market, even if they are obtained by sinful means.

You will have to sit and think about your disobedience.

She looks up at the window. At Mary's serene face. "Mother," she says.

She doesn't know who she is talking to, there is nobody but herself for blocks, but at the same time she doesn't care. Speaking out loud to dead relatives is acceptable in the city. Everyone does it.

"Marian," she says. She is waiting for something to happen. A lightning bolt. The bursting into flames of the deciduous shrubbery. She wants something to happen, so she can understand why she feels this way: tired, worn out, ready to give in if only she knew what she had been fighting against all these years. Now she realizes what Daniel's friends meant when they said they were *on the verge,* only in her case she has been there indefinitely. As long as she can remember.

You can learn from your experience.

She doesn't know how to forgive, nobody taught her how.

She can't bring herself to get down on her knees, that would be too trite, too Hollywood. Besides, if she really wanted to pray, she would go to a field full of wild daisies, throw her arms in the air. She would sing at the top of her lungs, *Here we go gathering nuts in May,* because playing that song was the closest she ever came to feeling perfectly at ease. Loved. For a while anyway. She would do all those things if she wanted to pray, but she doesn't. Not yet.

Instead she approaches the window. "If you can hear me," she says, her voice a whisper. "I want you to know that I tried my hardest. All the time, I tried. But I never really was what you wanted, was I? I wasn't the right daughter for you." She pauses, looks at the sky. City lights block out the stars but she can make out a satellite, blinking on and off in its journey around the earth; a mechanical eye, winking at her from space. Is her mother up there with the satellites? Or down in the ground where they buried her? Neither, Elsie suspects, or both. Marian always did resist definition.

"Violet's right," she continues, her eyes watering. "We are just human, all of us." *And you were at a disadvantage from the beginning,* she adds mentally, not ready to say it out loud.

A car passes her on the cross street, inching slowly along the pavement. Elsie picks up a handful of dirt from

[409]

one of the flowerbeds and squishes it in her fist, forming ribbons of soil between her thumb and forefinger.
She walks over to the church steps and tosses it gently
on the concrete, listening as it patters to the ground. She
knows someone will have to sweep up the mess come
Sunday morning, but she doesn't think they will mind.
This is, after all, a sacrament of sorts.

"Goodbye Mother," she says, feeling ceremonial. If
she had ashes she would spread them; if she had a flower
and was anywhere near Brimstock she would stick it in
a pot and put it on Marian's grave, a richly coloured rose
with petals like velvet wallpaper and a centre buried too
far down to see; thorny and enchanted, curvaceous and
devastating, all these things, all at the same time. But
she doesn't. So she can't. This slice of earth is the best
she can do; and for now, for some reason, it's enough.

"You all right?" says a voice.

Elsie turns with a start. A man in a brown jacket and
knit scarf stands on the sidewalk removing his gloves.
The darkness is waning. She wonders how long she has
been standing here outside the church, talking to herself; to her mother. She doesn't know if she should answer him. He might be looking for money.

"I heard you praying just now," he continues. "If you
want I can unlock the door. I'm on the morning shift
today."

Elsie relaxes. He is legitimate, while she is talking to
dead people. She strains to make out his face. "Are you
the janitor?" she says.

"So to speak," says the man. "I take care of things.
Would you like to go in?"

The thought of going into the church sends a wave of anxiety to Elsie's heart. She hasn't been to confession in over ten years. "No," she says, backing up. "I was finished anyway."

"Fine," says the man, moving into the light, revealing a weathered face accented by thin white eyebrows. "It's a nice time of day isn't it? Early dawn. I like the silence." He fishes a ring of keys from his pocket and jiggles them in the lock.

"I wasn't praying," says Elsie in a sudden urge to come clean.

"Oh?" says the man. He looks at her questioningly, his eyebrows raised into courteous arcs, and Elsie thinks of Santa Claus, the shopping mall kind with pink cheeks and a perpetual smile, only more subdued.

"I was talking to my mother," she says. "She's dead." She wraps her mind around the word *dead*, burying Marian for the second time.

He pauses. "I see."

"Do you think I'm crazy?" says Elsie. She can't believe she is having this conversation, at dawn, with a stranger, in the middle of the city. For almost thirty years she has avoided talking to strangers, but here she is for the second time in one night, revealing personal information to a man she has just met. Incriminating information. She doesn't even know his name.

"No," says the man. "I'd say that makes you normal."

A noise comes of out Elsie's mouth: a laugh or a gasp. She feels the knot inside her slowly unravelling, and wishes she could tie it back up—less painful. There really are miracles, she thinks, if I can be normal coming from that family.

"I used to think it was my fault," she says. "When I was a kid. But now I don't think so. She was sick all along and I couldn't really do anything about it."

He turns to Elsie with a look of genuine concern.

"Why did you think that?"

"Because I was bad. Or I thought I was. I forgot to do things she wanted me to do. Important things."

"That's hardly cause for death," says the man opening the door. "I'd say you're innocent." He smiles and removes his scarf. "Are you sure you wouldn't like to come inside? I can make tea."

The scent of lemon-oiled floors and husky incense escapes from the building.

Beneath his scarf Elsie sees the lapels of a black blazer, a tooth-white collar jutting out from his neck. Suddenly she is uncomfortable. "No," she says, winded, shifting her weight. The man is a priest. She straightens her posture and checks herself for sobriety. "Thank you. It's late. I really should be going home." By home she means Violet's house; but home is still the right word.

"O.K.," he says. "But it was nice talking to you."

"Yes," says Elsie. "Thank you." She walks up Chesterfield to Ninth, drawing her coat close around her body. Her skin is on edge from the cold, from standing still too long in one place. When she crosses Tenth the realization hits, smacks her like a sack of lead: she just spoke to a priest. She just *confessed* to a priest and he didn't give her any penance. Not even one Hail Mary or an Our Father. Not even a Glory Be.

Maybe, she thinks for the first time in forever, she didn't need any.

When she gets in to Violet's house, the phone is ringing. She leans on the piano to unbuckle her shoes, then
answers, slightly out of breath. If this is a crank call she
will be the heavy breather.

"Elsie?" says the voice.

"Yes," says Elsie, wiping the perspiration from her
face. What time is it anyway? She fumbles with the clock
standing on her grandmother's television set. 6:00 a.m.
She feels profoundly awake.

"It's Daniel."

Elsie makes a noise as though someone were standing on her lungs in heavy boots. "Oh," she says. "Hi."

"Were you awake? I was up early, to watch the sun
rise. The sky was full of these incredible blues and pinks.
Metallic clouds. You know the kind."

Elsie nods, forgetting that Daniel can't see her actions—she feels exposed, scraped raw, of course he must
know this—and breathes deeply. Watching the sun rise was
not something they ever did together. How would she know
what metallic clouds look like? "It's 6:00 a.m. here Daniel.
It's still dark." She tries not to sound irritated.

"Oh, I guess I forgot about the time difference." His
voice is thin and quavery, which could be the result of
poor telephone lines or weak reception. Or a broken
heart. Or malnutrition. "I just thought I'd call and see
how you were doing."

"I'm glad you did," says Elsie, relenting a little. She
can afford to be this brief; he's the one that phoned. "I'm
doing O.K."

"Just O.K.?"

"Well, yes. There is a lot going on with my grandmother. It seems she is not as sick as I thought, not by

far. She's pretty spry in fact. She might even be coming home in a few months."

"Does that mean you'll be coming back?" says Daniel.

"No. That is, I don't know." Elsie pauses. "Why?"

Daniel clears his throat. "Because I miss you."

"You do?"

"Yes, I do."

What Elsie wants to say, what she should say, is that she misses Daniel too. There is a hole in her heart, a gash in her side; absolute evidence of missing him. It's bleeding, it's surging. It feels like hell. But for some reason she can't say it; for some reason, a reason that just occurred to her this instant, she isn't so sure that she does. She does miss someone, that much is certain, and there is indeed a hole; but the hole has been there in Daniel's presence, it has been there longer than she has been away. Well into her childhood. She suspects for the first time that she needs to work on patching up this hole, before she can let herself near anyone again. She suspects that the person that she has truly been missing is, in fact, herself.

"I'm glad you called," she says again, unconcerned about repeating herself. Who cares if she's loony? Being loony is better than being possessed. "Why don't you come out and visit me when you get the chance? We could see the sights. Walk the seawall."

"Elsie," says Daniel, hurt. "You know I can't afford it. It would take me months to save up for a trip like that."

"Well then," she says. "You might as well get started saving, because there are a lot of things we need to talk about, you know, as friends. And don't worry about how long you take. I'm going to be here for some time."

After she hangs up the phone, Elsie makes herself a cup of tea and sits on Violet's porch waiting for the sun to come up. Maybe Daniel's idea was not so loopy after all; she hasn't done this since she was a child. She pats the pocket of her blouse in search of a handkerchief to wipe the end of her nose, which has been running since she got out of the cab. She finds a Kleenex and two notes, the one from the dark-eyed man who Elsie will probably never see again (although you never know), and another from Jeff's sisters. *Call us!* the latter one says, surrounded by exclamation marks and happy faces, written in red pen like the messages between blood sisters. Elsie tucks the note into her pocket, smiling at the directness of the order. Call us. When the sun comes up and she has had her breakfast, she picks up the phone.

WOOD VIOLETS

33

Elsie packs the sandwiches into a recyclable canvas tote bag along with three apples, a container of carrot sticks chopped lengthwise and then in half, and a tin of homemade oatmeal cookies mixed in with the latest contributions from Mrs. Wang. She wasn't going to bring the apples—aren't they a little hard on the teeth?—but during the last visit to the Avondale she asked Violet what she would like to eat and apples were one of the things she named.

"Apples," she said definitively, drawing out the s, "And anything else that is firm. Everything here is mushy."

Hence the Macintoshes; and the carrot sticks. And the walnut-and-raisin-filled cookies that she baked last night from one of Violet's recipe books called *Secret Recipes from the North Shore*, with pictures of the suspension bridge and the Hotel Capilano ornamenting the pages in watery sepia.

She smiles at the memory of her grandmother's voice. Since she has been spending time at the Avondale, Elsie has noticed that Violet is a remarkably good-humoured woman; comical even. She wonders if she was always this way, or if her jokes are a recent development brought on by the long period of silence following her stroke. She doesn't remember her being particularly funny on any of her visits to Brimstock, but then again she was young and what she recalls is questionable: a woman covered in showy, holographic scarves tessellated with mirrors and ornamental filigrees, flashing episodes of her lurid past in front of Elsie and her family like the metal teeth of gypsies, or pitching them out into the open air where they were captured by the wind then projected, like wafer-thin slides, onto the backdrop of the sky. Her eyes were always glinting, her lips were always parted in self-deprecating folly. *What a bunch of kooks we were Elsie! Kooks!* she said eagerly, laughingly, winking at her from the jewels of her iris. In those days her presence was unnerving, to say the least.

Now things are different. Violet is getting better; she is getting well. She is even a pleasure to be around. According to Claire, Violet will be ready for a trial visit home in the next few weeks, a visit that will last three days and two nights and will establish Violet's capability to cope, as well as the additions that will be necessary to accommodate her in her somewhat lapsed condition. Elsie isn't sure what to expect, but she has already started to prepare: in the bathroom she fastened two chrome handrails to the walls surrounding the tub, using a square-headed screwdriver that she dug up from the basement; she had the sagging backyard steps replaced with stiff new ones, sloping gently upward to the landing behind the kitchen. She even thought about purchasing a chair shaped to fit the ageing spine, but decided against it when she saw the price. She wants to consult Violet first and see if it is something she will use.

On the way out the door she hears Tia honking her fashionable European-style horn with the padded leather centre that looks like the underside of a ladybug. Tia drives a red coupe, and today what there is of her is coated in hues of red to match, like the test strips of acrylic paint Daniel used to leave lying all over their suite. This includes her fingernails (shocking red), her lips (sultry scarlet), and her eyelids (autumnal mist). Elsie makes a queenly wave—unadulterated in her blue jeans and transparent lip balm—and climbs into the front seat with her canvas bag. She feels strangely serene despite the realization that she needs a new haircut.

The month is April. The day is uncharacteristically sunny, with a ledge of jet-stream clouds hovering in the distance, and the smell of the salt chuck and skinned cedar logs floating in on the breeze from somewhere near the waterfront. Spring flowers dominate outdoor planters. Primulas, cottoneasters, and zesty hyacinths spill forth from wet earth and cork the air with the musky scents of their soil beds, their bee balm, their heavenly epithets to the rain-soaked public that traverses the streets making reckless promises to the sun. *Please keep shining, oh please.* Violet waits in the lobby with her purse in her lap, her wheelchair brakes pushed into the 'ON' position by a worrisome nurse's aide covered in a rash of brown freckles. Her hair is loaded with tenacious curls set last night by her own hands. She wears white double-buckle sandals, a pair of thin summer pants, and her spring raincoat which can also masquerade as a wind-breaker when the need arises; and today the need will arise. Today she is going to the seashore.

When Tia phoned this morning she told her to dress casually, in something free-flowing and loose; she also told her to bring her wheelchair and a hat with a brim, because they might get caught in the sun without a place to sit down, depending on the crowds, this being the first nice day in several weeks. Violet did even better: she put a layer of extra-strength sunblock on her nose to ward off the kind of cancer that had Mrs. Troy wearing a band-age in the centre of her face. She also brought her cane as an alternative way of getting around. Now that she is capable of walking short distances she is eager to put it to use.

In front of the Avondale, several pin cherry trees in mid-flower are dropping their petals to the ground. A ring of pale pink litters the grass around their trunks and shifts with the wind, spackling the adjacent parking lot with delicate jots. Violet watches them from behind the glass, looking out at the blue sky, at the tentative, calligraphic clouds. She smiles. Somewhere in the woods, in Stanley Park around Lost Lagoon, or deeper, near Beaver Lake; somewhere amongst the fir trees at the foot of Grouse where the snaky, sawdust-laden trail known by hikers as the *Grouse Grind* curves its way up the mountain, wood violets unfurl in dusky shadows. Wood violets in soft yellow; wood violets in royal pur-ple, pressing up on the pithy debris of the forest floor, through needles and leaves and salal rot, into the sun and the sky and the risks of living, stretching their slen-der necks, their minuscule green wings, aiming to grow.

Violet is not sentimental, at least when people are watching, but she likes the thought that these plants are awakening at the same time that she might be going home. The idea comforts her: things aren't so awry after all, if there is still space for wood violets.

Another comforting thought that she just heard on the news: the Queen Mum will turn ninety-six this summer. Ninety-six! Even older than Violet, and traipsing around like a socialite. If she can make it, after the scandals, the world wars, the pregnancies, the mixed familial blood, well, there's got to be hope for the average person. Indeed there does.

Together they drive west along Marine Drive, past the strip malls and the strident Future Shop, past the Ginger Jar emporium of imported goods and the Capilano Mall with its interior totem poles. They turn into the parking lot at Ambleside, and Elsie hears shouts coming from the grassy hillocks where excited children race with their dogs in the dog-running zone. Today, Elsie thinks, they will have to avoid the dog-running zone. They happen to have a cat.

Bringing the cat was Elsie's idea. Every time she left the house the cat followed her to the corner and sat down, silently, like a statue. Sometimes he was still there when she got back, waiting patiently, smiling at her from his orange lips. Elsie thought Violet would appreciate seeing the cat after so many months, and she was right, but only partly. The cat also appreciated seeing Violet. He is sitting in her lap now, glued to her thighs since she got in the car. As she unpacks the lunch, it occurs to Elsie that she doesn't know the cat's name. She has gotten so used to referring to him as "the cat," or "kitty," that she hasn't even noticed the absence.

The ocean is the colour of sapphires, Violet thinks. She can't remember ever seeing it so blue, but she must have at one time or another; she spent so many days here during her childhood. The beach is crowded, but with a different sort of people than the ones that populate the place in summer, the bronze-bodied sun-worshippers that lay themselves out under the ozone, lubricated and buffed and ready to grill. Most of the ones here now are the athletic types, men out for a brisk stroll, or women jogging down the waterfront with headphones and sweat socks and matching breast-hugging spandex suits that look hotter than all hell as far as Violet is concerned, but she is not about to volunteer this opinion. If people nowadays want to gad about in florescent scuba gear glistering like the backs of killer whales, she doesn't mind. She might even go as far as to say that she is inspired by their presence. At least they are trying to remain active, Violet thinks. *I can relate to that.*

Elsie hands her an apple and a piece of cheese, part of which Violet feeds to the cat, then a lettuce-and-tomato sandwich on brown bread. The meal is followed by a cup of steaming hot tea served in Violet's bone china mugs with the wild forest berries on the sides, and a selection of cookies that look to Violet like clumps of muesli dipped in honey. Violet inhales deeply, her tea at chin level. How wonderful, the heat, the aroma, the lovely, familiar flavour and scent, like moist garden dirt or autumn leaves crinkled sumptuously under the nostrils! How she longs for a good cup of tea when she is at the Avondale, after that anemic cricket's piddle served tepid and tasting of dish detergent! *(I don't like Earl Grey,* she tells them over and over. *I'm sorry Mrs. Leggett, Earl Grey is all we have.)* How wonderful to have granddaughters who appreciate the finer points of tea-making, who get the measurements mostly right and who bring along real milk to boot. Perhaps Violet has passed on some of her genetics after all; the good parts, the successful small touches. Perhaps learning from one another isn't going out of style, as she was beginning to fear.

"It looks like the tide is going out," says Tia, collecting up the dishes.

"Yes," says Elsie. "It looks that way." She is still confused by the way the ocean shape-shifts every six hours. Some days it lurches toward the shore and buries everything in sight; other days it falls away from the rock and cobble and muddy sand and leaves the dregs of seaweed ropes and broken, water-softened pop bottles exposed to the air. She hasn't yet figured out why these things don't happen at the same time every day—on a schedule—the way she expected them to when she was land-locked and living in Ontario, but she knows the answer has something to do with the moon. The moon, and to a lesser extent, the sun; the same things that govern her own, internal cycle, although she hasn't figured out the connection there either. There are a lot of things she wants to learn about now that she is in a new place: things about herself, and her environment. She just doesn't see the need to rush, now that she has made a commitment to stay for a while.

Living in her grandmother's house, with her grandmother, will be a challenge; she has never promised herself to anything like this before, let alone to anyone. What if Violet is domineering when she gets on her home turf, or too much to handle? What if she refuses to take her pills, or has temper tantrums in the supermarket? Elsie can't imagine her doing any of these things—she is a calm woman, with plenty of decorum—but she runs the scenarios through her mind just to be on the safe side. The last thing she wants is to be caught off guard with no place to go.

If things work out she will be able to stay in the Chesterfield house indefinitely. Violet has made the house legally available to Elsie and other members of the Leggett family through a life estate clause written into her will. Upon her death a land conservancy will assume ownership of the property, but Elsie is first in line for rent-free tenancy. Providing members of the family continue to inhabit the building after Elsie moves on, the house will remain on Chesterfield Avenue. The day the Leggetts choose to die out, pass on, or shove off to another community, the house will come down and the land will be made into a park.

The idea is sufficient to irk developers. Several of them have upped their offers substantially since news of Elsie's arrival. "We could make you a rich woman," one of them said to Elsie over the telephone. "You're sitting on prime real estate."

"I may be sitting on it, but it isn't mine to sell," said Elsie in rebuff.

"Your grandmother then, talk some sense into her. Surely you can see the advantage, for yourself as well as her."

"My grandmother isn't interested in money," said Elsie.

"Then your grandmother's an old bat," said the developer.

"Perhaps," said Elsie. She had often heard her grandmother refer to herself as *an old bat*. "But she likes things the way they are, and I agree with her."

What Violet likes is the idea that she can leave a little land behind. Even if the whole north shore is covered in pavement, she said to Elsie, Chesterfield Avenue will have one green space. The cedar tree will also stay. She put that in the covenant.

Elsie is especially glad that Tia decided to help out. The three of them seem to get along very well; Violet was especially taken with Jeff, Tia's husband, when they came to visit on bingo night last week.

"Bring that man back," she told Tia slyly. "I like him. He's very refreshing."

"I like him too," said Tia, "which is a good thing."

When they were finished for the evening and walking Violet back to her room, she took Elsie aside and said semi-privately from closed lips, "What about you? Where's yours?" Her voice was thin and respectfully quiet.

"Well," said Elsie grimacing apologetically. Where should she begin? Daniel had called that afternoon. He had been calling regularly, updating Elsie on his progress as the new director of Elgin House, a local historical museum. He liked to tell her about some of their old acquaintances who had moved to Toronto to sell furniture or deliver documents on their bicycles, to keep her in touch with the east; but he did not press her to come back. He was starting, Elsie thought, to respect her need for leaving. She appreciated this. "I don't have one," she said at last. "Or rather, I did, but he's in Ontario, working, saving. Getting himself together, like me. We—that is—he and I, have some growing up to do."

"Well," said Violet patting her on the shoulder. "Don't grow up too much. I already need a ladder to whisper in your ear."

No one seems to be walking along the shoreline. Not immediately next to the waves. They stick to the cement and the lawns where there is less chance of getting something viscous and unidentifiable wedged in the treads of their shoes, a slimy blade of seaweed, or the crushed, gelatinous body of a sea cucumber. Lengths of kelp whips looking like the spilled innards of some outrageous mammal, the wet-rot smell seeping from their leaves. Still, there are always the dogs—so many dogs!—and what inevitably must come out of them. Violet prefers the seashore to the cement. She wants to go down there now, and wonders if her wheels will make it as far as the jetty.

"Let's go to the shore," she says encouragingly, her voice full of what she hopes is gusto. Tia and Elsie look at each other. "Right down to the water," she adds. For some reason she has a sudden urge: she wants them to come with her.

"O.K.," says Elsie reluctantly, moving forward. Violet knows they are humouring her, but who cares?

They cross the grass to the concrete sidewalk, then follow it to the beach. When they get to the sand Violet's wheels seize up; she pushes forward with Tia's help, but they seize up again.

"Looks like we can't go any farther," says Tia. "We can stay here or turn back."

Violet reaches forward and undoes the laces on her shoes. She fumbles with the heels—why didn't she bring a shoe horn?—and tries to peel them from her ankles. No luck. She could try to pry them off with her cane, the blunt, rubber-covered end, but unfortunately she is not that coordinated. Shoes are tough. What she needs is someone's help.

"You can't do that Violet," says Elsie. "You can't take off your shoes. You might catch a cold. Or a disease. Do you know how many things wash up on this beach?"

Violet looks up at her, her lips wet from struggling, then lets her hand fall to her side in a gesture of defeat. Elsie realizes that she sounds like her mother. Paranoid. Hard-edged. She also sees the need in Violet's eyes, the raw need she used to see in her father's. And her mother's, come to think of it. Such a small thing, why not let her have it? "O.K.," she says, clenching her teeth and pivoting in front of Violet's wheelchair. "We can do it."

"Do what?" says Tia.

"Take off our shoes. Our socks. Wade in the water."

"In the water!" says Tia. "But it's April, Elsie, it will be frigid. I'm wearing stockings."

"Leave them on the sand," says Elsie. "We'll need your help."

She removes Violet's shoes and socks, because this is what she wants, then her own. What a difference in feet, but Violet's are a lot warmer, despite the cracks.

It will be cold, Violet thinks, but she is too revved up to notice. When was the last time she went in the ocean?

She can't remember. Far too long ago. Together they tee-
ter toward the waves, Tia on one arm, Elsie on the other,
and Violet balanced in between like a toddler, trying to
carry her own weight but thankful for the girls just the
same. The cat stays behind to guard the wheelchair.

"It's freezing," Tia shrieks.

"Yes," says Violet. What is she, nuts? But what a feeling! Invigorating as a Swedish massage. Her skin prickles, her eyes fill up with happiness. That old salty soup,
still constant, still available. Some of it gets in her eyes.
She picks up a surf-softened morsel of driftwood and
pokes at one of the piles of japweed lolling in the
waves, stirring up a frenzy of sand fleas, uncovering
the backbone of a salmon and its pin-sharp spine.
Around her feet are ribbons of sea lettuce, the purple
opalescence of kelp.

We are crazy! Elsie thinks, but she is laughing, running her fingers through the water. She could not have
done this last year, not without feeling ridiculous. She
breaks free from Violet, just for a minute, and splashes
both Violet and her cousin. How rotten of her, and also
how glorious! No harm done. They get her back, of
course, and soon they are three dripping women, their
hair mussed, their faces wet and salty, joined at the elbows like Siamese triplets. Elsie feels the squeeze of Violet's arm around her own; it is a squeeze of trust, of faith,
and Elsie thinks for the first time in her life, that she may
be able to live up to it; that she may, in fact, *deserve* it.

"Look," says Tia, pointing back at the beach.

Violet turns her head toward the wheelchair where
the cat is standing on his hind legs. His paws hang loosely
down in front so that he looks slightly marsupial. A

redheaded kangaroo. Such a show-off! Violet taught him that trick herself.

"I don't think he wants you out of his sight Violet," says Elsie. "He's watching you like a hawk."

"He looks like bear," says Tia. "A big fat bear. What's his name anyway?"

"Yes, what is his name?" says Elsie, looking at Violet. "I've been meaning to ask."

Violet smiles, then opens her mouth to speak.

About The Author

Shannon Cowan grew up in Hockley Valley, Ontario and moved to British Columbia in 1991. She returned to Ontario to study Visual Arts at the University of Guelph, and spent summers with her family on Vancouver Island. In 1998 and 1999 she was awarded delegation to the BC Festival of the Arts "Otherwords" literary component in Prince George and Victoria. She attended the Banff Centre for the Arts Fall Writing Studio in 1998. She won first prize in the Anne Horsefield Memorial Contest, 1997, and third prize in the *Books in Canada* Student Writing Competition in 1995. Her work is published in *Contemporary Verse 2* and in *The Harpweaver*. *Leaving Winter* is her first novel. Shannon Cowan lives in Errington B.C., on Vancouver Island.